bookvault
Publishing

The Fury of a Vampire Witch (Books 4-6)

Copyright © (Theophilus Monroe 2023)
All Rights Reserved

No part of this book may be reproduced in any form by photocopying or any electronic or mechanical means including information storage or retrieval systems, without permission in writing from both the copyright owner and publisher of the book.

ISBN: 9781804674857
Perfect Bound

First published in 2023 by bookvault Publishing, Peterborough, United Kingdom

An Environmentally friendly book printed and bound in England by bookvault, powered by printondemand-worldwide

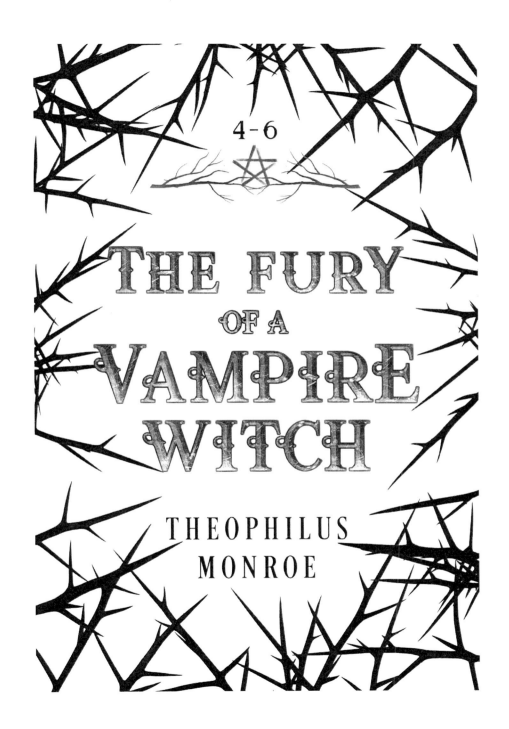

4-6

THE FURY
OF A
VAMPIRE
WITCH

THEOPHILUS
MONROE

THE FURY OF A VAMPIRE WITCH
BOOK 4

BLOODY BASTARDS

THEOPHILUS MONROE

Chapter 1

THE PORTAL SNAPPED SHUT behind us as we stepped into chaos. Screams and the copper tang of blood saturated the air of the Providence Place Mall. I scanned the marble floors now strewn with bodies and blood.

"Talk to me, Mel," I muttered, checking my Glock. Fully loaded with iron rounds. Mel was back at headquarters, hacked into the mall's security feeds. She served as our eyes. Our best chance at getting ahead of Cal's Unseelie gang.

"Redcaps on the second floor tearing through Abercrombie. More Redcaps with Cal are gathering hostages near the food court." Mel's voice was tinny in my earpiece.

"Let's move," I said. Ladinas and I took point while Muggs and Antoine fanned out, weapons drawn. Alice stalked ahead, her face an emotionless mask.

We stalked through the empty halls, following the screams and scent of blood. At the top of the escalator, we found them.

Five Redcaps in their stolen meatsuits, claws extended and hats soaked crimson. One held a woman by the hair, ready to open her throat.

My team opened fire, iron tearing through the Redcaps with wet thuds. The creatures shrieked, clawing at their wounds as their stolen bodies failed them.

Iron weakened the Redcaps, exorcising them from their human hosts, but didn't kill them. It didn't save their hosts, either. When the Redcaps fled their hosts, they materialized as Unseelie goblins. They didn't "eat" in the conventional way. They derived their sustenance from the blood soaked into their caps. But they needed human hosts to "eat." That didn't mean the exorcized goblins weren't a threat. They'd find more humans, effectively killing the people they possessed, and resume their murders in short order if we didn't burn their hats. That was the only way to kill the little bastards.

I put a round through the one holding the woman. His host collapsed, but the goblin bastard tore into the woman with his claws and claimed her body as his next meatsuit before we could save her. It was a gruesome sight—the way the goblins took their hosts. More Hannibal Lecter in flesh than traditional demon-style possession.

I shot at her—but my gun didn't fire. Before I could load another magazine of iron bullets, the bastard slipped away.

"Fall back!" I yelled, reloading. We retreated down the escalator, the remaining Redcaps in pursuit. At the bottom, Ladinas tossed a grenade filled with iron shavings.

The blast ripped through them, leaving empty husks and scrambling goblins behind. I aimed my wand. "*Incendia*!"

I was a crack-shot with my wand. The flames erupted on the goblin's head, consuming his cap. The goblin's emaciated body withered into something like a charred fifty-pound raisin. One down. Probably dozens to go. There was no way to deal with these fuckers without the loss of human life. The best we could do was take them out whenever we got a chance. We put a dent in their numbers, but it wouldn't stop them.

Cal Rhodes—the gangster who formerly served the Unseelie Queen, Malvessa—was the new leader of what used to be the Unseelie Court. He wasn't a Redcap. He was now possessed by an Unseelie faerie named Gan Ceanach. After I sent Malvessa back to the faerie realm, and took out the trickster who initially claimed her authority, Gan Ceanach stepped up and took charge of the Redcaps and several other Unseelie species who remained on earth.

Unlike other hosts taken by faeries, Cal remained at the helm. He did Gan's bidding, but it was still Cal, even if the faerie was pulling his strings.

Cal didn't feed on blood. He fed on souls. Gan was an incubus who kept a harem of human women, gradually draining their energy until they died. He had a seductive allure that made him irresistible to females. Thankfully, his powers didn't work on vampires.

Like the Redcaps, we were pretty sure if we shot up Cal with iron, Gan Ceanach would survive but remain vulnerable without a second host. He didn't have a hat I could burn to do him in, though. The only way to kill an incubus, according to what we'd learned from Muggs and our uncourted faerie ally, Willie, was through forced celibacy. Isolate him from human females until he starved to death.

Easier said than done.

We continued toward the food court, weapons ready. The skylights let shafts of sunlight slice through the mall's dim interior. Our kevlar suits protected us, mostly, but with our goggles off—the damned things fogged up too much that fighting with them on was impractical—we had to avoid the light as much as possible. I hated fighting at a disadvantage, but Cal and his Redcap gang always attacked during the day. He knew it gave them the upper hand.

I signaled for my team to fan out as we approached the food court entrance. The scent of blood hung heavy in the air. Inside, overturned tables and smashed kiosks revealed signs of the earlier carnage. Bodies lay strewn about, throats slashed or heads bashed in. The Redcaps' handiwork.

A flicker of movement caught my eye. A Redcap darted behind the Panda Express counter. I fired two shots in his direction. A howl told me I'd hit my mark.

"Got one!" I said into the comm. "In pursuit to burn his hat."

"I see two more over by the Orange Julius," Ladinas responded. His gun barked twice. "Make that one more."

Ladinas carried a small blow torch he could use on their hats if he could catch them. My magic was still the best way to put down the Redcaps. I fired *Incendia* at the goblin I'd shot before. It wasn't remotely satisfying—mostly because I couldn't save his former host. At least I'd taken out another bastard and saved the lives of anyone he'd claim or kill in the future.

We were handling the Redcaps one-by-one, but there was still no sign of Cal. Where was he?

A deep laugh echoed from another floor, overlooking the food court. All we could see was a crowd of scantily dressed women—Cal was gathering women for his harem, a temporary human shield.

"That's him. I know it is," Alice said. Before I could stop her, she took off running.

"Alice, wait!" I shouted, but she ignored me. Ever since Ladinas told her he'd chosen to be with me, she'd been a bit of a loose cannon. She said it didn't bother her, that she didn't care, but I knew better. I could see it in her eyes. This wasn't the first time she'd ignored my orders.

Ladinas glanced at me, concerned. "Want me to go after her?"

I shook my head. "No, stick to the plan. We need to clean up here, then we'll get Alice. Watch my six."

He nodded, lips pressed in a grim line. I didn't like it either, but we had no choice. I just hoped Alice could handle herself until we got there.

I took aim at another Redcap, but before I could pull the trigger, Mel's panicked voice sounded in my ear. "Police! They're gathering outside. Full SWAT. Dozens of them!"

I swore under my breath. The last thing we needed was human law enforcement complicating matters—but it was inevitable. They showed up everywhere the Redcap gang attacked. The only way we made any progress at all was by beating the human authorities to the scene via Muggs' portals and taking down as many as we could before they showed. We had maybe a minute before they stormed the building.

The cops didn't stand a chance against the Redcaps. They didn't know how to kill them. Their rounds weren't iron. They didn't know about burning their hats. But the Redcaps never attacked them—mostly because they knew the cops gave them an easy escape, complicating my team's pursuit.

"New plan, let's move!" I barked. "Alice, I know you can hear me. We have to get out of here!"

She didn't respond. I'd known Alice as long as I'd been a vampire. Our history was complicated—but she'd never been reckless. Not like this.

"Damn it!" I shouted. Alice was either ignoring me or had removed her earpiece. Either way, we were going to have words when we got back to HQ. "I don't know if you can hear me, Alice, but we're coming for you. We won't leave without you."

Again, no response. Usually, once Mel warned us that the cops were en route, Muggs portaled us back to HQ.

We took off running, heading up to where Alice ran in pursuit of Cal, two floors above. My mind raced as I tried to figure a way out of this mess. But a SWAT team, armed up and guns drawn, intercepted us.

"Freeze!" one shouted. "Hands in the air!"

Slowly, we all raised our hands. I caught Ladinas's eye and gave a slight shake of my head. We couldn't afford a confrontation here. But we couldn't leave, either. Not with Alice still missing.

"Officers, I know how this looks, but we're not the bad guys here," I said evenly. "If you give me a chance to explain— "

"Shut up!" the cop snapped. "Drop your weapons on the ground!"

I glanced at Muggs and clicked my tongue. He couldn't see me. All he could see was magic through his spirit gaze. He heard me, though. A signal to get us the hell out of there as soon as he had an opportunity. The problem was that casting a spell in front of the cops, especially something so flash as one of his portals, would probably create as many problems for us as it solved.

I dropped my gun and kicked it across the floor. Ladinas and Antoine did the same. Only Muggs remained unarmed. My wand was tucked in a sleeve on my thigh.

"Keep your hands where I can see them! On the ground! Now!"

"Okay, okay, just don't shoot," I said. I kneeled down, signaling for the others to do the same.

I glanced around the mall, looking for any sign of Alice while also trying to figure out how we were going to get out of this mess. The cops were closing in while customers screamed and ran for the exits. I caught a flash of red out of the corner of my eye—a decorative poinsettia near the railing on the second level was moving unnaturally.

"On your stomachs! Hands behind your heads!" the cop shouted.

I complied, pressing my cheek against the cold tile floor. The poinsettia stretched and reached over the railing, extending down toward us like a vine. Muggs' doing, no doubt.

Just then, two more cops came around the corner, guns drawn.

"Where's the fifth?" one asked.

"No sign of her yet," the first cop replied.

So they knew about Alice. Damn it, we were running out of time. I tensed, ready to grab my wand and start throwing spells if it came to that.

A long, thorny tendril curled down, almost touching the floor in front of me. I looked at Muggs and he gave a slight nod.

"Now!" I yelled.

I grabbed the vine as Ladinas and Antoine leapt up. Muggs' eyes glowed green and the giant poinsettia surged towards us, wrapping us in a cocoon of leaves and whisking us upwards through a shimmering portal just as the cops opened fire.

We tumbled out the other side onto the cold stone floor of the Underground. I slammed my fist down in frustration.

"Dammit! We left Alice!"

I paced back and forth, fuming. Ladinas watched me carefully.

"We had no choice," he said gently. "The police were closing in. We'd all be in custody if we stayed."

"Since when do we run from the cops?" I snapped. "It's not like they could take us."

Ladinas frowned. "Mercy..."

"Forget it," I said, waving him off. I wasn't in the mood for a lecture. I knew why we weren't engaging the police. They weren't the enemy—even if they thought we were.

Alice was out there alone, chasing that psychotic faerie, Cal.

I should never have brought her on this mission. She'd been too reckless lately, too quick to ignore orders. Ever since Ladinas chose me over her, there'd been a coldness between us. I didn't fully trust her anymore.

Ladinas moved closer, lowering his voice. "You know how she feels about me. About us. She's hurting."

I whirled on him. "So you're taking her side now?"

He held up his hands defensively. "I didn't say that. But we need to—"

A sudden noise at the entrance cut him off. We turned to see Alice stumble through, clutching her side, her leather jacket ripped and soaked with blood.

"What happened?" Ladinas asked, rushing over to help her.

She waved him off angrily. "I'm fine."

I crossed my arms. "You directly disobeyed orders. Again."

Alice glared at me. "While you were busy running away, I was doing our job. Tracking Cal."

"Did you eliminate him at least?" I asked coldly.

She looked away. "No. But I know where he's keeping his new harem. We can hit him there, finish this."

I shook my head in disgust. "We're done here. You're off this mission."

"The hell I am!" Alice shouted, stepping towards me. "I'm following this lead now, with or without you."

Ladinas moved between us, holding up his hands. "Enough! We're on the same side here." He looked at me pleadingly. "She risked her life for this information. We should use it."

I held his gaze for a moment, then sighed. As much as I hated to admit it, he had a point. And right now, we needed unity, not more divisions within our ranks.

"Fine," I said through gritted teeth. "Patch yourself up, Alice. Everyone else, reload your weapons. We leave in ten."

Chapter 2

Our new sunlight-resistant suits were supposed to give us an edge, let us take the fight to the enemy during the day. Instead, they just let us run ourselves into the ground without a moment's rest. Before, we'd been forced to stand down when the sun rose, to reload, feed, and recover before the next round. Now it was just an endless loop of hunting Cal's gang, tracking Ramon and his family, or trying to interfere with one of Oberon's latest abductions—his Seelie faeries were still off the grid, we didn't know where they were, but they were taking human slaves. For what purpose? Didn't know. Willie was busy trying to figure that out. He spent most of his time buzzing around the city and the forests trying to gather information, but even with his advantages as a faerie, now "uncourted," we hadn't had a good lead on Oberon in weeks.

My team shuffled out into the warehouse where our SUVs were parked, some of them bleary-eyed and bruised beneath their goggles and suits. Muggs leaned heavily on his staff, for once looking his age. I wasn't sure exactly how old he was—and he didn't remember, either. He'd crossed through so many dimensions, skipped through time so many times, that he'd lost track of his birthdays.

Muggs wasn't *technically* immortal before I turned him into a vampire. By his appearance, though, he wasn't a day younger than eighty. Younger than me, technically, but that didn't make me wiser.

Alice's eyes were wide with manic energy. This mission was her idea. She'd followed Cal and his gang back to their current base. Given how elusive they were, as much as I hated to justify her actions on our last mission, the information she brought back was actionable. I didn't know how long that would be the case.

Alice ran her fingers across the hilt of her katana, sheathed at her waist. She was good with a blade, not a great shot with anything ranged, especially firearms. When it came to close combat, though, she was vicious. Her usual blades were made of refined steel, but the ones she carried now to face off against the Unseelie were forged of pure iron.

We'd been dealing with faeries for a few months now since I'd dispatched both Malvessa and Reynard, courtesy of Oblivion. Oblivion was the dragon-gatekeeper spirit whose blade I took, whose spirit now lingered somewhere within me. Subdued, quiet... too quiet. I could speak his name, "Oblivion," and I'd feel a stir, but little more. He'd come to my aid when the time was right, when all was ready. Until then, he was little more than an insurance policy, a powerful and ancient being who'd hitched a ride in me. But lately, he'd been more like a stowaway than a first-class passenger. I barely noticed he was there.

"The factory is just off the shipyard. It looks like it's been abandoned for years, but it's got good sightlines and multiple exits. Mel's got eyes on it now via satellite. The imagery is a few months old, but it gives us a solid lay of the land."

"Any barriers to entry?" I asked. "It'll be heavily guarded."

Alice nodded. "There's a chain-link fence with some barbed wire around the perimeter. Main entrances are padlocked, but it looks like they jimmied open a side door facing the water. That's how Cal's gang is going in and out. By the looks of it, they haven't been there for long, and if our experience means anything, we can't count on them staying there for much longer, either. If we wait until sunset, we might be too late."

I nodded, picturing the layout. "How many hostiles are we looking at?"

"At least a dozen Redcaps patrolling the outside. Windows are blacked out, so there's no telling how many faeries or humans are inside."

"And Cal?" I asked.

Alice's lip curled. "Oh, he's in there. I caught a glimpse of his ugly mug through a window on the second floor. I saw little more. That's when one of those damned Redcaps snuck up behind me and caught me in the ribs. I'm betting he has several women captive inside, all seduced by his power. If we're going to take him down, we'll have to be careful about collateral damage.."

My gut twisted. The women they'd taken, the ones still alive, were in that building. We had to get them out fast, before Cal and the incubus who possessed him drained their spirits. But a direct assault through the rear doors they were using would be suicide. We'd have to find another way in. Busting a lock was easy for a vampire. Grab and twist. Usually did the job. But if there were patrols outside, we'd need a distraction. Muggs could get us past the doors without bothering with the locks, but teleporting us into a building that we weren't familiar with came with risks. There was no telling what we'd have to face the moment our boots hit the floor.

Our convoy parked on the streets a few blocks away from the old factory. We didn't park together. Too many identical black SUVs in a row looked suspicious. Not to mention, after we'd had a run in with law enforcement already, we couldn't risk them identifying us in the neighborhood. I wasn't totally sure the police knew what vehicles we drove, or even knew our names, but we couldn't be too careful. This was an opportunity to take a fight to the Unseelie without interference from the local authorities. We needed to make the best of it.

I brought my hellhound, Goliath, along. If we encountered any Baobhan Sith, he could make a quick meal of them. They were like faerie vampires. Technically, they were our evolutionary ancestors. A part of what contributed to what we are. I only knew a little about them. My sire, Nico, told me a story about one he'd once captured and imprisoned in a tomb in the old country. They didn't consume blood through fangs, but through their claws. Any man they fed upon died in an instant. Every woman they attacked became one of them—bound to her creator like a vampire progeny was to her sire.

With an incubus who could attract human females, and a horde of Baobhan Sith who could turn them, it was a wonder they hadn't overrun us already. We didn't know how many Baobhan Sith there were, or why they hadn't multiplied faster, but it didn't take a genius to figure out Cal's long-term plan. Be fruitful and multiply. Subdue the earth.

If we took out a Redcap, Cal couldn't replace him. Their numbers were finite. The Baobhan Sith, though, could spread faster than a coronavirus. So long as a single one remained, it wouldn't take much time at all before the city was swarming with them. All they had to do was send a few out to different places around the world, probably big cities, and they'd grow their numbers until they took over everything.

There was a good chance we were already too late. If Cal was smart—and if he wasn't, the incubus within him was—he'd send out the Baobhan Sith discreetly, seed every major city in the world with at least one of them, and order them to reproduce all at once.

We didn't know for sure if that was his plan—but if I were in his situation, if I had the resources he did, and had aspirations on world domination, that's what I'd do.

The biggest advantage we had against them was Goliath. If the hellhound ate one, the connection I had to the hellbeast made me stronger. It didn't last long, but it gave me enough of a surge that it made me nearly unstoppable for a good ten or fifteen minutes. After that, I'd crash and have a case of the vampire munchies.

Any time we were facing off with Unseelie faeries and thought we might encounter a Baobhan Sith, or if we were fighting other vampires, I brought Goliath along. Cal was clever, though. He only brought his Redcaps out as protection when he was hunting prospective women.

I grabbed Muggs by the arm. "Let's do some recon. I want you to get as close as you can without being seen. Listen in, tell me what you hear."

"Thankfully, I can see the magic in all those faeries in spirit gaze. I'll steer clear of their line of sight. Keep in mind, though, the women in Cal's thrall will do just about anything he asks. He could have a few on the lookout. Since they don't have any magic, I won't be able to see them."

"Stay behind cover. Don't get any closer than necessary to pick up what you can hear from inside. Just a rough idea of what we're dealing with in there will work."

Muggs crept off into the shadows while the rest of us took cover behind stacks of rusted shipping containers just outside the old factory's fences. The faint scent of blood hung in the air. Probably from the Redcaps. My fangs throbbed, but I swallowed back the hunger. Squeezing the blood from a Redcap would be a little like stealing the food off of a stranger's plate at a restaurant. Not just rude, but a little gross.

Several tense minutes passed before Muggs returned. "It's bad in there," he whispered. "Women crying, some barely conscious. They're both in agony but also begging for Cal's attention."

My stomach turned. "That's horrifying. Pick up anything about what we have to get past to reach them?"

Muggs tugged at his beard. "From the sound of it, there are at least twenty faeries inside, but I have no idea what they are."

I clenched my fists, fury rising. If we were on an open battlefield, we'd be evenly matched with twenty. That depended, of course, on what sort of fae they were. Redcaps were difficult—but not impossible to eliminate. The Baobhan Sith were consumable—for Goliath—but for us to take them down required iron delivered directly to the heart, a lot like how wooden stakes handled vampires. We didn't know, though, how many other species of faerie escaped from the Unseelie forest and were following Cal's lead. The bastard had been playing everything close to the chest. That meant we weren't sure exactly how to kill whatever we might encounter.

I took a deep breath, forcing calm. Rushing in would only make the situation worse.

"We need to draw them out and figure out exactly what we're dealing with," I said. "Create a distraction."

Alice's eyes flashed with impatience. "While they continue to torture and kill those women? We don't have time for games, Mercy."

"I know." I put a hand on her arm. "But if we charge straight in, we'll be overrun. We have to be smart about this."

She glared at me, jaw tight. Alice had always been fiercely protective of humans. It was one of the things I admired most about her.

"The rest of the Underground will provide cover fire if necessary," Antoine said softly. "Can Muggs do something druid-like to distract them, draw them out, so you can hit the front doors?"

"I have a few ideas," Muggs smirked as a green glow appeared at the end of his staff. "This will take most of my energy. While I'm channeling my power, I won't be able to make portals."

I nodded. "If you can draw out the guards, we might not need portals. We'll bust in there and save as many of the hostages as we can grab. Once we're out, drop your other spell and send them to the warehouse at HQ. If they're free of Cal's influence, they might have valuable information we can use."

Chapter 3

MUGGS GAVE ME A nod, his eyes beginning to glow green as he called on his druid magic and it coursed up and down his staff. Alice's hand rested on the hilt of her katana, ready to draw at a moment's notice. Ladinas had his crossbow loaded and ready, his jaw clenched.

With a loud creak, the trees surrounding the old abandoned factory began to move, their branches reaching toward the guards like gnarled hands grasping for prey. The shouts of surprise were music to my ears.

But Muggs wasn't done. With a wide swing of his staff, the cracked pavement around the facility rippled and grass exploded through, towering over us.

"Go, go!" Muggs ordered. "The Redcaps are distracted and the grass will provide cover. I can't hold this forever, so hurry!"

We burst from cover, sprinting toward the chain-link fence. Alice hacked at the fence with her katana, providing enough of an opening that we managed to squeeze through. Goliath followed behind, but the opening wasn't large enough. He almost pulled the whole fence down as he forced himself through. He got through—but only just.

"Keep your sights on the perimeter," I ordered Antoine via comms. "Take out any Unseelie bastards who try to escape."

"Ten-four," Antoine replied, confirming he understood the order.

We raced toward the factory entrance, the tall grasses grazing each side of my face. I twisted the lock and yanked. It wasn't going to break so easily. I was strong, but Masterlock was a bitch. I aimed my wand at the lock. "*Incendia.*"

The flames blasted the lock, causing the metal to glow red. Then, with a swift kick of my boot, the lock broke. Another kick, and the doors swung open.

We were in.

The interior of the factory was shrouded in an ominous mist that clung to us as we crept forward.

"What the hell?" Ladinas asked. "Some kind of fog machine?"

I shook my head. "There's magic in this shit. I can feel it."

"We *are* dealing with faeries," Alice said. "It reminds me of the mist in the air that Willie cast around the forest before."

"This isn't the same stuff." I narrowed my eyes. "It's darker. I'm not even sure it's faerie. It feels... different..."

"Are you telling me that Cal is working with something else? Someone who can cast magic?"

"Some kind of witch," I said. "I'm not saying this isn't faerie magic. It feels infernal though."

"Hell magic?" Alice rolled her eyes. "Well, isn't that fantastic? How can you tell?"

I glanced at Goliath. His one eye, the one coursing with hellfire, was blazing brighter than his other eye, the one that radiated the druidic magic that Muggs used on him to alter his essence before. "Just look at how Goliath is reacting to it." I scratched the hound behind his ears. "Can you see through this stuff, boy?"

Goliath growled a little and bounded ahead, leading the way. He was a seeing eye hellbeast.

I could barely make out the hulking shapes of machinery through the gloom. But Goliath charged ahead and we followed his tail.

Ladinas moved with cat-like grace at my side, crossbow aimed steadily into the shadows. Alice was as tense as a coiled spring, her katana unsheathed and ready. I held my Glock in one hand, my wand in the other. Between the three of us, we were ready for just about anything. Anything we knew about, at least.

We inched forward, the mist swirling around us. I blinked rapidly, trying to clear my vision. But the fog was unnatural, seeming to cling to my skin and hair.

Goliath turned around, his fangs bared, and snarled. I whipped around, following his gaze just in time to see a gnarled body, claws outstretched, charging toward me.

I fired an iron round at the Redcap. It screeched as it fell to the ground. I aimed my wand at its cap. "*Incendia.*"

The fire engulfed it, the stench of burned blood filling the air.

More shrieks echoed from the shadows as two more Redcaps rushed us. Ladinas' crossbow twanged, the iron bolt punching clean through one Redcap's forehead. It dropped like a stone.

Alice was a blur of deadly grace, her katana slicing in a silver arc. The last Redcap's head toppled from its shoulders.

I quickly ignited their blood-soaked caps. We couldn't risk the damn things reanimating.

"More will come." Ladinas reloaded his crossbow.

"Then let's get moving," I replied. "We need to find the hostages."

Ladinas gestured to a door barely visible through the mist. We hurried over, senses alert for more attackers. But we seemed alone again, for now.

Ladinas tried the door, finding it unlocked. The heavy metal door creaked open, revealing a staircase leading up into darkness. We exchanged tense glances, then started up the steps.

We ascended cautiously, our footsteps echoing in the narrow stairwell.

At the top was another door. I grabbed the handle, my wand ready in my opposite hand, and my gun tucked into my holster. I could grab it and shoot in a second. I took a deep breath, bracing myself for whatever we'd encounter on the opposite side, then threw it open.

The scene that greeted us was like something out of a nightmare.

Dozens of women lay strewn about the large room, some ghostly pale and still, while others writhed and moaned faintly. The metallic scent of blood hung thick in the air.

On the far side of the room, Cal stood with a vicious grin, his eyes burning crimson. At his side was a woman with dark greasy hair that fell to her ankles. Her skin was smooth, but on each hand she had long blood-soaked claws—a Baobhan Sith.

"Goliath, take her!" I shouted.

With a roar, Goliath bounded toward the Baobhan Sith, three-hundred pounds of muscle and fury.

But as he pounced, several of the pale "corpses" suddenly sprang up, their fingers extending into gnarled claws. Their eyes were hollow, feral, their mouths open in silent snarls, revealing jagged fangs.

Not corpses. Newly turned Baobhan Sith.

One leapt onto Goliath's back, claws raking viciously. He howled in pain, then craned his head back, seizing its arm in his powerful jaws. With a violent shake of his head, he ripped it off in a spray of dark blood.

My veins burned as his strength flowed into me through our bond.

With my enhanced strength and speed, I charged the original Baobhan Sith at Cal's side. She bared her fangs and claws, ready to fight.

Out of the corner of my eye, I saw Ladinas take aim with his crossbow, but a writhing, newly turned Baobhan Sith blocked his shot. Cursing, he quickly reloaded and fired a bolt straight into its heart. It fell back with a gurgling shriek.

Alice darted through the chaos, her katana flashing as she sliced through two more of the clawed bitches in her pursuit of Cal. Nothing would stop her from getting to him.

The Baobhan Sith leader slashed at me with her razor claws. I dodged just in time, the tips grazing my kevlar jacket.

"You'll have to do better than that," I taunted.

With a feral hiss, she attacked again, her movements almost too quick to follow. But the power flowing from Goliath guided my reflexes. I sidestepped her swipe, then smashed my elbow into her face. She staggered back with a scream of pain.

I whipped out my wand and leveled it at her chest. "*Incendia*!" Flames erupted from the tip, scorching her torso.

But instead of burning her, the fire seemed to bend around an invisible barrier. My eyes widened in shock. This was no ordinary Baobhan Sith—she was a witch, too!

Shit.

Her lips curled into a cruel smile, revealing fangs dripping with venom. I didn't know what her bite could do—and I wasn't in a hurry to find out. She reached into the folds of her dress and pulled out a large crystal orb that glowed with an eerie inner light.

I tensed, ready to dodge whatever magic she was about to hurl my way. But she turned and hurled the orb toward Cal and Alice.

It struck Cal directly in the chest just as Alice's katana sliced toward his neck. He seized Alice's hair in one clawed hand, stopping her blade inches from his flesh.

With his other hand, he grabbed Ladinas who had been rushing to Alice's aid. The orb flared brighter, enveloping all three of them in a pulsating glow.

"No!" I screamed, but I was too late. There was a flash of light, and Cal, Alice, and Ladinas all vanished.

The Baobhan Sith cackled, her voice like fingernails on a chalkboard. "You'll never find them now."

I bared my fangs with a growl. She would pay for taking my people. But then the bitch revealed a second orb and dropped it at her feet. She disappeared, as Cal did with Alice and Ladinas before.

"Fuck!" I screamed. A clawed hand tore at my kevlar vest from behind. I spun around to see three remaining Baobhan Sith, their teeth dripping with the same venom as their master. I kicked the one who clawed me in the chest, forcing her to stumble back.

Goliath snarled at my side, ready to rip them apart. I cracked my knuckles and rolled my neck, my rage rising. "Let's dance, bitches."

With inhuman speed, I launched myself at the nearest Baobhan Sith. My fists pummeled her face relentlessly as Goliath tore into another one's throat. Black blood sprayed across the concrete floor.

The third leapt onto my back, her claws raking my shoulders. I reached back and grabbed her by the hair, flipping her over my shoulder and slamming her into the ground. Her skull cracked against the concrete with a sickening thud.

I stomped down hard, crushing her windpipe under my boot. Two down, one to go. The final Baobhan Sith scrambled back from me in terror.

"Please, don't!" she begged.

"Mercy's fresh out of mercy today," I snarled. With a flick of my wrist, I drew my wand and uttered a single word: "*Incendia!*"

Flames erupted from the tip of my wand, engulfing the Baobhan Sith. Her screams echoed through the empty factory as she burned. The stench of charred flesh permeated the air.

When the last of the flames died down, only ash remained. I took a deep breath, regaining my composure. Then I heard Antoine's voice in my earpiece.

"Mercy, we're being overrun out here! We need to retreat!"

I fired a couple of iron rounds into the mangled bodies of the other Baobhan Sith I'd dropped before—just for good measure. There was no telling what they could come back from. Burn them up, or iron to the chest. That worked for sure.

I was about to hurry to the exit when I felt a hand grab my leg. "Please, help!"

It was one of the hostages, her skin graying as if Cal had sucked half her life-force out of her. I couldn't just leave her behind. Then, I noticed two more women in a similar condition.

"Damn it," I muttered. Trying to get out of here with three women who could barely move would not be easy.

I reached down and touched the first woman's hand. She was icy cold. "I'll get you out of here, but I'll need a little help."

"Don't go!" the woman pleaded.

I brushed a stray auburn curl out of her face. "I'll be back. Promise."

I hurried toward the exit, Goliath at my heels. "Fall back to the SUVs!" I barked into the comms. "Get the hell out of here!"

Once outside, I saw dozens of Redcaps swarming my people. I drew my Glock and fired iron rounds into the advancing horde.

"Muggs!" I called out. "I'm going to need a fancy portal or two. Stat!"

A moment later, he appeared at my side in a swirl of leaves.

I tilted my head. "Neat trick. You can explain that one later. There are three women inside, still alive. We need to get them out of here."

With a twirl of his staff, Muggs teleported us back into the room where the women waited. I heaved them together into one spot and Muggs spun his staff a second time, dropping us a few blocks away next to the SUVs. My people were battered and bloodied, but still fighting with everything they had against the relentless Redcaps, who were now charging toward us down the street.

I looked around. "Where the hell is Goliath?"

"I think he went after another one of those Baobhan Sith," Muggs said. "Don't worry about him. He can take care of himself. You know how he is, he always comes home again."

I still didn't like the idea of leaving my hellhound behind. But there wasn't anything I could do. Shots rang out from Antoine and the rest of our vampire soldiers, dropping Redcaps one-by-one as they charged our position. Without burning their caps, they'd revive, but we didn't have time for that. There were just too damn many.

I opened the back hatch of the nearest vehicle and helped the women inside. They were so weak they could barely move, much less stand. I didn't know if they'd even recover. I'd never dealt with someone drained by an incubus before. But I had to try. At the very least, maybe they'd know more about what Cal and that damned Baobhan Sith were up to, or where they'd taken Ladinas and Alice.

I looked back one last time for Goliath. Where the hell did he go? Muggs was right. I'd have to trust he'd handle himself and make his way back to me later. With our connection, he'd always find me. Eventually.

I jumped into the driver's side and Muggs hopped in to ride shotgun. As I started the ignition, several Redcaps slammed into the vehicle, cracking our rear window. No time to screw around. Tires squealed as I slammed the gas, peeling out onto the street.

"They took Alice and Ladinas," I said through gritted teeth. "That Baobhan Sith bitch snatched them up somehow. She had these strange orbs that released some kind of teleportation spell. We need to figure out where she took them."

Muggs nodded grimly. "I felt her magic when she used it. I've only dealt with that kind of power once before. There's only one witch, if you can call her that, who harnesses power like that."

"Infernal magic?" I asked.

"Of a sort," Muggs said. "When we fought Reynard, and the Order's Seraphim, we dealt with the combination of celestial power and faerie magic. This is just the opposite. Infernal magic mingled with faerie."

I glanced at him. "Spit it out, Muggs. Who was that witch?"

"Morgana," he replied. "Sometimes known as Morgana of the Fae."

I raised an eyebrow. "Seriously? From the King Arthur legends?"

Muggs nodded. "After Arthur died, Nimue, the Lady of the Lake, reclaimed Excalibur. The twin-blade to your Oblivion. Also, we must surmise, a blade that contained the spirit of a gatekeeper dragon. There are stories that Nimue used the blade on Morgana, sending her back to where she belonged."

I sighed. "When the faerie realm was open at the convergence, she must've skipped town with the rest of the Unseelie."

Muggs tugged at his beard. "Morgana is an ancient witch of great power. She can fold space back upon itself. My portals work differently. What you see when I cast my portals, the vortex of energy, pierces through the fabric of space and connects it to a fold in space elsewhere. She doesn't just teleport between places. She folds space itself to bring locations together. She must've bent space, brought another place to where you were, and then unfolded it, ripping Ladinas and Alice away."

I tightened my grip on the wheel. "Along with Cal. They went together. She used a second orb to escape herself."

"They could be anywhere. The fabric of space, like the fabric of time, has natural ripples that are in constant flux. Her magic forces something like a tidal wave through the fabric of space. It can be *catastrophic*. If her magic is interrupted, the two sides of the fabric can get caught up together, altering this plane in startling ways."

"What do you mean?" I asked. "This is a lot to get my mind around."

Muggs twirled his beard around his finger. "Say she folded London over Providence, just for example. We might find Windsor Castle suddenly standing in the middle of Federal Hill. But that's not the worst of it."

I took a deep breath. "Keep talking."

"Sometimes, the intersection of two folds can create a fissure in space, a torn piece of space that's no longer connected to this plane. It forms something like a pocket dimension, a prison of a sort, that only she can access."

I narrowed my eyes. "Are you telling me that Ladinas and Alice might not even be in this world at all anymore?"

Muggs took a deep breath. "It is possible."

"Can your portals connect us to those pocket dimensions? Rather than teleporting us to another ripple in the fold of space, send us to wherever she took Ladinas and Alice?"

"Theoretically, sure," Muggs folded his hands over his lap. "But I've done nothing like that before. To do it, I'd need to know exactly where in the void, the space outside of space itself, the pocket dimension exists. Trying to find something in the void, a place where there is no space, would be damn near impossible."

I glanced at Muggs again. "We'll figure it out. Let's hope you're wrong about that. They could be on earth, somewhere, right?"

Muggs furrowed his brow in thought. "They could be anywhere. The good news is that Morgana's power requires massive amounts of energy. Those orbs she carries, that's how she collects her power."

"Collects it how?" I asked.

"From human spirits," Muggs said. "I suppose that's why she's working with the incubus. He can extract the power she needs from human spirits, and she can build the army of Baobhan Sith he requires."

I tilted my head. "I thought her magic was infernal and faerie."

"It is," Muggs said. "But she uses the power of spirits to wield it. It's how she controls her magic, how she bends it to her will. Without human spirits, siphoned into her orbs, her magic is unwieldy."

"We don't know how much magic she still has. Those orbs. It was like she pulled them out of thin air."

Muggs nodded. "But at some point, she'll require more. Even if she sent Ladinas, Alice, and Cal to a pocket dimension, she'll need more magic to retrieve them. She can't do that without Cal."

"Which means she must've sent them somewhere on earth?"

Muggs shook his head. "Not necessarily. It just means she still has enough magic that if she sent them to a pocket dimension, she'll need to go back there to retrieve him. Unless there's another incubus somewhere willing to lend her more power."

I pressed my lips together. "We need to find Willie. He might know more about whether there are other incubi out there she might go after."

Muggs cleared his throat. "I don't think Willie will have the answer to that. He was a Seelie faerie before he declared himself uncourted. There's no reason to suspect he had a full catalog of knowledge about the population of the Unseelie forest. I hate to suggest it, but..."

"We need Oberon's help." I shook my head. "Let's hope Willie shows up eventually and knows where we can find him."

Chapter 4

THE ROAR OF THE garage doors to the warehouse that concealed our entrance to the underground ended with a thud. Then, a few moments of silence before I climbed out of the SUV. Muggs stepped out after me.

"Bring these women to the most comfortable quarters we have. There are a few open rooms in the blood maid wing. I want to give them a little time to rest and hopefully recover before inundating them with questions."

I opened the rear-hatch to our SUV and Muggs dropped a portal over the ladies. They were still weak. They needed food and water—and we had plenty available for the blood maids we could offer.

I tapped on comms. "Mel, I'll be in shortly. Check in with Clement, would you? See if he and the orphans have a little time to spare to help get these ladies situated."

"Got it," Mel replied. "See you inside shortly?"

"Meet me in the throne room once everyone's situated."

The rest of the team exited their vehicles. They'd all heard it go down on comms—Ladinas and Alice, gone. Snatched by that Unseelie witch Morgana before we could stop her.

Everyone looked at me, their faces etched with worry and fear. "Get changed and meet in the throne room in fifteen minutes," I barked. No time to waste on comfort or sympathy. Action was needed now.

We had a secure armory in the warehouse, separate from the rest of the underground. It was where we suited up before a mission. The rest of the team went in to change. I headed straight into the elevator and made my way to the throne room, my sunlight-resistant suit squeaking with each step. Didn't even bother to change—I wasn't planning to stay long. While the ladies we brought back recovered, I needed to get back out there. I didn't know exactly how I'd find Willie, but I needed to try.

I had a few moments alone in the throne room before Mel returned. I sprawled out across one of our couches and rubbed my face. Those damn goggles we had to wear when we were out in the sun not only had issues with fogging up, but they left my skin a little clammy. When Mel stepped through the doors, her eyes were glued to her tablet. It was a wonder she didn't trip over anything as she made her way toward me. I lowered my feet to the ground to make room for her beside me.

"Everyone situated?" I asked.

Mel nodded. "Clement and Muggs are making the ladies feel at home. Best they can, anyway. They look awful. Are you sure they don't require medical attention?"

I shook my head. "An incubus partially drained their essence. I don't think there's anything conventional medicine can do to help. Hopefully, they'll recover in time. I really don't know if a human spirit regenerates, though."

Mel cleared her throat. "What if they don't get better?"

I sighed. "I don't know. My mind is too occupied trying to figure out a way to get Ladinas and Alice back. We'll cross that bridge if we get there. Any ideas?"

"The comms have GPS trackers," Mel sputtered, still tapping away on her tablet as she kicked her feet up on the coffee table. "I should be able to find them. But there's nothing. It's like they just disappeared!"

She glanced up at me, eyes wide. "At first I thought it was just a delay, but it's been too long. Either Cal destroyed their earpieces or the batteries died."

"Not necessarily," I said. "Did you pick up any of my conversation with Muggs on the drive back?"

Mel nodded. "You really think they might be in some kind of pocket dimension? That would explain the GPS conundrum."

"It's possible. I'm hoping that's not the case, but you know how it goes. Hope for the best, prepare for the worst."

"What do you think a pocket dimension is like? It can't be pleasant."

I shook my head. "Maybe a small slice of the real world. I doubt they have a lot of room to move around. I can't imagine what they're going through if they're trapped there with Cal."

Mel forced a nervous laugh. "It's a small world, after all. For them, anyway."

I cleared my throat. It was a lame joke, but that's how we rolled. Sometimes the only way to deal with the gravity of a situation like this without losing our heads was to force a little humor. "We need to find Morgana. If she's still in our world, she'll need another incubus to recharge. So far as we know, the Unseelie who escaped through the convergence are still in the area. She can't have gone far."

Mel nodded. "Any other incubi you know of?"

I shook my head. "We'll squeeze Willie first. If he's no help, we go to Oberon. Provided we can find either of them."

The clatter of footsteps sounded behind me. Antoine and more of our vampire soldiers filed into the room, their faces etched with worry and fear, just like the others. Time to take charge before mass panic set in.

I took my seat on the throne and met their eyes one by one. "It's true about Ladinas and Alice. But I've got a plan to find them. Just be ready."

Several of the older vamps bristled, wanting to rush out right away to search for Ladinas. Most of the vampires in the Underground had followed Ladinas long before I joined them in Rhode Island. They were allies, vampires he trusted back in Romania. I understood their loyalty, but we needed to be smart.

"With the cops after us, we stick to the shadows at night without those suits they recognize," I said firmly. "My goal the rest of the day is to gather whatever intel I can find. Hopefully, the women we saved will be in better shape when they've had some time to recover to share what they know. One way or another, we'll bring them home."

The vamps murmured but didn't argue. My leadership was being tested here tonight. I'd be damned if I let Ladinas and Alice down.

"Feed if you need to," I said. "I need everyone at full strength come nightfall."

With several nods, Antoine and the rest of the soldiers filtered out of the throne room. I glanced at Mel. "Keep trying those GPS signals. Let me know if you come up with anything. I'm going to check on Muggs and the ladies we saved."

I hurried out of the throne room and into the sewers. The blood maids had quarters a few tunnels removed from the main section of our headquarters. It was for their safety and ours. We had a few younglings who might not be able to resist with humans living just down the hall. We also needed to be careful. While I had no reason to suspect any of the blood maids would betray us, if there was a way for our enemies to get inside and infiltrate our ranks, using a potential blood maid to do it would be a clever way to gain access to our facilities. So far, we'd never had a problem with it, but the security of our subterranean compound was top priority.

I found Muggs and Clement mid-conversation outside a few of the rooms where they'd taken the ladies. "How are they holding up?"

Clement took a deep breath. "Not well. I sent Isaac to gather some food. Hopefully, that will help."

Isaac was one of the vampire orphans who stayed with Clement in the orphanage wing of the Underground. He'd had a tough time of it. Anyone who was turned at a young age was bound to have challenges. The younglings in the orphanage also lacked involved sires. Most of their sires were staked and gone. Some of them, just absent. You'd think given the connection a vampire feels to his progeny, they'd stick around, but you'd think the same of humans as well. Orphans were as much a reality in the vampire world as the human one.

"Muggs, is there anything you can do to help? Any druidic spells that might help their spirits recover from the incubus?"

Muggs hesitated, scratching his chin. "It's possible. I might be able to channel some energy into them to help boost their spirits. But it won't be a permanent fix. They'll need time to recover fully."

"Anything helps," I said. "We need them functional if we're going to get any information out of them. And we need to know what we're dealing with."

Muggs nodded and followed me into one of the rooms where a woman we'd saved was resting. She was still pale, her eyes sunken in. I introduced Muggs as a "specialist." Trying to explain druidry, or any of the realities of the supernatural world to her, would not help. I imagined she was already more than a little confused by what had gone down with Cal and everything she'd witnessed while under his thrall. I explained Muggs was going to do his best to help her recover. She groaned a little and looked at Muggs with a mix of fear and hope.

"What's your name?" I asked. "Mine's Mercy. This is Muggs."

"Megan," she said weakly. "Thank you for saving me."

"It's what we do," I said with a reassuring smile. "Muggs, do your thing."

Muggs nodded and closed his eyes, his hands hovering over Megan's chest. I watched as a faint green glow emanated from his palms. I could feel the energy in the room shift, as if the very air was charged with something potent. I watched Megan's expression change from anguish to something less pained and more... content.

"Thank you," she murmured, her eyes drooping. "I feel... better."

Muggs nodded and stepped back, wiping his forehead with the back of his hand. "That'll do it for now. She'll be able to rest easier."

I nodded, satisfied. "Good work. Go do the same for the others. I'm going to sit here with Megan for a minute."

Muggs nodded and left the room, tapping his staff along the floor to find his way.

I took a seat on the edge of the bed, watching Megan's breathing even out. She looked younger than I'd first thought. Her skin was smooth, unmarred by wrinkles or blemishes. But the trauma she'd experienced had aged her in ways I couldn't imagine. I couldn't help but wonder what kind of life she'd led before Cal had taken her. Was she a mother? A student? Did she work at a job she loved?

"Megan, can you tell me what happened?" I asked gently. "Anything you can remember."

She shifted a little, her eyes still closed. "It was so dark... I don't remember much. Just... his voice. And the way it made me feel. Like everything was going to be okay. Like... I didn't have to worry about anything."

I frowned. I didn't have a lot of experience dealing with creatures like incubi or succubi that fed on human spirits, but it made sense given the little knowledge I had.

"I'm sorry you had to go through that," I said softly. "But we're here to help you now. Do you remember anything else? Anything that could help us find the others who were taken with you?"

Megan shook her head, her eyes still closed. "No, I'm sorry. It's all just a blur."

I sighed and stood up. "That's okay. You rest now. We'll take care of you."

Megan cleared her throat. "What is this place? Is it a hospital? My husband, he must be worried..."

I hesitated for a moment, unsure how to answer her question. I couldn't just tell her that we were a clandestine organization of vampires. I didn't want to scare her any more than she already was.

"It's a safe place," I said finally. "You're among friends here. We'll make sure you're taken care of, and when you're ready, we'll help you get back to your husband."

Megan nodded, seeming to accept my answer for now. "Thank you."

I smiled at her and patted her hand. "Get some rest. We'll bring you food and water shortly. I'll check in on you soon."

As I left the room, I couldn't help but feel a pang of sadness for Megan and the other women we'd saved. They were innocent victims, caught up in a supernatural shitshow they'd never imagined apart from a few shows they might have watched on the CW.

But that was the reality of our world. A reality that most humans were blissfully unaware of. It was up to us to protect them. Most would think protecting them *from* vampires was most important and under most circumstances in the past that was true. Not all of our kind were so committed to protecting humans. Now, though, the threats that faced humanity made a few rogue bloodsuckers looking for a meal seem like child's play. We were creatures of the night. The original monsters of classic horror flicks. But we were also humanity's best hope.

Chapter 5

I STALKED BACK INTO the throne room. Megan was a dead-end information wise. I didn't expect the other ladies we'd saved could offer anything more. That didn't mean it was a loss. We'd saved their lives. At least, I was pretty sure we did. Muggs' magic helped them considerably, but the human spirit is fragile. There was no telling how deep the incubus's damage went. If there were other incubi who'd escaped through the convergence, though, tracking them down couldn't be that difficult. Follow the bodies.

"Still no luck tracking Ladinas or Alice," Mel said as soon as I stepped back into the throne room. "I'm thinking this whole pocket dimension nightmare scenario might have something to it."

"I'm not saying don't keep checking." I hurried over to Mel and sat beside her. "The women are doing better thanks to Muggs, but I had a thought. We know Morgana needs an incubus, whether she intends to pull Cal out of the pocket dimension or not. If there is an incubus in the area, there will also be a lot of missing persons. It's been months now since the Unseelie poured into our world. That means there should be some data in the police databases we can track."

Mel tilted her head. "Not bad thinking. I'll do a little digging. It might not be that easy, though."

I shrugged. "Why not?"

"Well, a lot of people go missing. Technically, an incubus could feed on anyone, right?"

I bit my lip. "So far as I know. I think I see where this is going. Just because Cal had a taste for women in early adulthood doesn't mean that every incubus shares his... feeding preferences."

Mel nodded. "Exactly."

Muggs stepped into the room and cleared his throat. "But an incubus's power only works on females. Just like how the Baobhan Sith's power only turns women, but kills men."

"No such thing as a gay incubus?" Mel asked.

Muggs tilted his head. "I didn't say that. Reproduction and eating are two different things."

Mel smirked. "Most of the time. I mean, whipped cream, chocolate sauce... mixing food and fornication can be fun."

I rolled my eyes. "Point taken. Both of you. Still, Mel. Try to find any clusters of missing persons. I doubt any bodies have turned up. These incubi are probably used to cleaning up after themselves."

Mel nodded. "Don't clean your plate. No dessert."

Muggs laughed a little harder than he should have. "Keep in mind, these incubi, if they are wandering around Providence, haven't fed on humans for centuries. They might not be so practiced in covering their tracks. There might be a few bodies. I'd expect if there are, the coroner will declare the cause of death undetermined."

Mel tapped on her tablet a few times. "All things I should be able to find out if I can get into their records. I've been following some of Demeter's protocols, and learning what I can from YouTube about hacking law enforcement databases, but it's still a work in progress. The feeds we were getting when Demeter was around aren't updating anymore. I'm guessing some IT nerd at the precinct closed a few security loopholes in their system."

I tilted my head. "You can learn how to hack on YouTube?"

Mel shrugged. "What *can't* you learn on YouTube?"

"In the meantime," Muggs added, "I've got an idea to get Willie's attention. But it might stir up some other nasties in the area, too."

I arched an eyebrow. "Do tell."

Muggs held out his hand and a subtle golden glow formed in his palm. "The Seraphim's energy that hit me before was both celestial and faerie. I'm hoping I can release it like a beacon. Since faeries can sense their magic when it's used, hopefully it will get their attention."

I bit my lip. "That sounds risky. I don't suppose faeries have their own magical phone numbers. How do you know Willie is the one who will respond?"

"The trick is releasing it in a way that Willie recognizes it's us and comes running," he said. "Or flying. His itty bitty legs don't carry him too fast."

I chewed my lip, considering. It wasn't a terrible plan. But the risk of luring the wrong faerie was high. Still, we were desperate. Who knew what hell Ladinas and Alice were enduring, or how much time was passing there?

I nodded slowly. "We'll go to the forest near the convergence. Willie has been protecting that place since he came to earth. If he senses a disturbance there, it should get his attention. But it's just as likely to get Oberon's attention. If the Seelie King thinks someone is trying to open the convergence, he won't ignore it. He wants nothing more than to go home and claim the entire faerie realm for the Seelie."

"If Oberon shows, maybe we should try sending him back," Mel suggested, not looking up from her screen. "Call Oblivion, get him to reopen the convergence. At least that's one less faerie court to deal with. Oberon's enslaving humans—he needs to go."

I shook my head. "Oblivion's not answering. The dragon's been radio silent ever since we sealed the convergence and got rid of Reynard. Oblivion said he wouldn't reopen the portal until the faeries put aside their petty squabbles and unify."

Mel scoffed. "Unify? They've been at war for centuries. What makes Oblivion think that'll change now?"

"I don't know," I admitted. "But he wanted me to broker some kind of peace between the courts. If we sent Oberon back now, he'd just go after Malvessa. Without her fellow Unseelie faeries at her side, she wouldn't stand a chance."

Mel threw up her hands in frustration. "Who cares? Let Oberon wipe out Malvessa. One less psycho faerie bitch to worry about."

I gave her a pointed look. "You know it's not that simple. Oblivion wants balance restored, not more bloodshed. If Oberon killed Malvessa, it would only escalate the conflict between the two sides. Not to mention, there's no way to broker a faerie peace if there's not a queen on the Unseelie side to represent the rest."

She sighed. "Yeah, yeah, I get it. It was just a thought."

I put a hand on her shoulder. "I know. But right now, finding the others has to be our priority. Keep monitoring for their GPS signals. See what you can find out about missing women in the region."

Mel nodded, her expression serious. "I'm on it. Be careful out there."

I gave her arm a grateful squeeze. With our plan in motion, all we could do was hope our efforts or hers would give us an actionable lead to save Ladinas and Alice. In truth, I didn't give two shits about faerie peace. So long as they kept their little conflict confined to the faerie realm. But Oblivion was insistent. He knew a lot more about the implications of the Seelie/Unseelie divide than I did and, while I barely knew the dragon-gatekeeper, I trusted his wisdom. I had to see this through. One way or another. But faerie politics would have to wait. Saving my friends came first.

Muggs twirled his gnarled staff overhead, summoning his magic. A swirling portal of emerald light materialized before us.

"Ready when you are," he said with a small bow.

I stepped into the portal, the cool tingle of magic washing over my skin. When the light faded, we stood amidst the shadowed trees of the forest where the convergence lay. It was still cold and dark—sealed tighter than it had been since before the convergences around the world broke open. Having a dragon-gatekeeper at my disposal was handy. I could only hope, eventually, Oblivion might close the rest of the convergences scattered around the world. Until that happened, there was no telling how many new threats might emerge. All I knew was the hell that we'd had to deal with on account of the convergence near Exeter. My friends back in New Orleans were just as busy dealing with theirs. There were supposed to be guardians appointed in advance by Merlin, the last and original human gatekeeper, to protect the earth in the post-gatekeeper era. I could only hope whoever those guardians were, they were doing their jobs.

I was doing my best protecting the world from this convergence—and I'd dealt with more than one world-ending threat in less than a year. I cast those worries aside. For now, we had to deal with the crisis at hand.

My senses were on high alert as I scanned our surroundings. The birds had gone silent, the very air heavy with anticipation. This place teemed with ancient power—some of it lingering from the make-shift faerie forest Willie planted to protect the convergence.

"How does this work?" I asked. "Are you sure you can isolate the faerie magic within you?"

Muggs nodded. "I think so. I've been meditating, focusing my spirit. There's one catch, though."

"What's that?" I asked.

"That magic might be all that's keeping me safe from the sunlight. Once I release this magic, I might have to get out of here. My vampiric susceptibility to the sun might return."

I took a deep breath. "Are you sure this is worth it? We can find another way. Being able to walk in the sun is a unique advantage. Alice is the only other one of us who can do that, and she's gone. You'll have to wear these damn suits like the rest of us if you lose that power."

Muggs nodded. "If there's a chance this can bring our friends home, it's a small sacrifice."

Muggs slammed his staff into the earth. Golden faerie magic erupted in a blinding column, arcing high into the overcast sky. The light seared through the treetops like a beacon.

The canopy and the cloud cover offered some protection, but even so, Muggs' skin simmered the second he released his magic.

"You need to get out of here," I ordered. "I'll take it from here."

Muggs shook his head. "Not until we know who's coming. My magic can help me to a point. I can endure the sun longer than most. I'm not leaving. You might need a quick escape."

I squeezed Muggs' arm to communicate my gratitude. I'd severely underestimated how much help the old druid would be when I first made him a vampire. He'd exceeded all expectations several times over. That he gave up his ability to walk in the sun, and now was willing to endure the pain as long as he could to ensure my safety, spoke to his character. To think, when I first met the bastard, I thought he was an enemy.

I turned my attention back to the clearing, waiting for any sign of movement. The trees and underbrush rustled as creatures fled the disturbance.

A flash of light appeared about twenty yards away. I tensed, ready to strike. But as my eyes adjusted, I made out two familiar figures.

Ramon stood poised for battle, glaring in my direction. At his side was a gangly teenage boy with a mop of unruly dark hair. His features were distinctly Ramon's, but his build was lankier, his face younger. Still, I recognized him. I'd met him when Oblivion sent me five years into the future.

"Adam?" I gasped.

The boy offered a shy smile. "Hey, Aunt Mercy."

I rushed forward and pulled them both into an embrace. Adam had grown exponentially since I'd last seen him as an infant. As a faerie-human-vampire tribrid, he matured a lot faster than normal folk. Physically, at least.

"So I guess you're not planning to kill us?" Ramon asked.

"Why the hell would I do that? Not to mention. *Aunt* Mercy?"

Ramon chuckled and shrugged. "We've shown the boy pictures. That's what we called you."

"Named after my sister, right?" Adam asked.

"Other way around," Ramon clarified. "Mercy is like your mother. Technically, she saved your mother. Made her what she is. And a part of what you are. She played a role, anyway."

"What happened to you two?" I demanded, holding Ramon by the shoulders.

Ramon glanced away, shamefaced. "It's complicated. But we had to leave. You don't understand. After Clarissa and Adam drained that poor woman, we were worried about what you and Ladinas might do to Adam. We left to protect our son."

I shook my head in disbelief. "You should have come to me. Damn it, Ramon, do you have any idea what we've been through? To think I'd ever hurt Adam? I thought you knew me better than that!"

Ramon furrowed his brow. "Language, Mercy. A child is present."

I glared at Ramon. "Fine. *Darn* it, Ramon? What the fuck were you thinking?"

Ramon stifled a chuckle. "I know, and I'm sorry. But Adam was already so powerful, even as a baby, and then when he... when he drank from that human—"

"It doesn't matter now," I said firmly. "It was a mistake. He didn't know what he could do. It was our fault for leaving you three unsupervised. It was too much for me to ask you to stop your wife and son from feeding. Trust me, handling a youngling as their sire can be challenging enough."

"She speaks the truth," Muggs chuckled, steam still rising from his skin as his green magic flowed from his staff, slowing down the assault of the sunlight that pierced the canopy above us. "It took me a while to get my cravings under control. Without Mercy's sire bond, I would have devoured half the city."

Ramon nodded, resolve hardening his features. "Tell me what you need. I sensed the magic here and came immediately, but others won't be far behind."

I raised an eyebrow. "How did you get here so quickly?"

Ramon wrapped his arm around his son. "You'd be surprised what this boy can do. There's a lot he has to learn, and we're still sorting it out."

"Any chance he can fold space over itself?" I asked.

Ramon tilted his head. "I'm not sure what you mean."

"We're dealing with an Unseelie faerie witch. Morgana. Before you ask, yes, she's the same one from the stories. She used some kind of power to send away Alice and Ladinas, along with an incubus we were trying to kill."

Ramon shook his head. "I don't know. Adam can teleport us, but only where he feels magic. That's how he brought us here."

Muggs shook his head. "Even if Adam can do it, it won't matter. Morgana is the only one who knows how to access the pocket dimension. She created it. She alone knows exactly how to fold the fabric of space back upon itself to reintegrate the pocket dimension with our world."

Ramon pinched his chin. "What were you two trying to do out here, anyway?"

"Trying to get Willie's attention," I said. "He's been tracking Oberon, gathering intel. Haven't seen him for weeks. We were hoping he might know about how to find an incubus, since we think Morgana is looking for one. If he couldn't, at the very least, we thought he could tell us where to find Oberon."

Ramon sighed. "Well, that will be a problem. Oberon captured Willie three days ago."

My eyes widened. "What? How do you even—"

"Like I said," Ramon added. "My boy can take us wherever we sense magic. When Oberon took Willie, the little bugger released some pretty powerful faerie juice. We showed up just in time to see the little guy in chains."

"Can you take us to him?" I asked.

Ramon shook his head. "Like I said, Adam can only create portals to a place where magic is flowing strong and unfettered. Not just any magic will do."

"But you know *where* Oberon is?" Muggs asked, wincing as his magic struggled to keep up with the sun's assault.

"Of course!" Ramon nodded. "I can tell you where to go."

I nodded. My goggles were fogging up so badly I could barely see. "Muggs, you've had enough. Take us back to the Underground. We'll plan an assault on Oberon at nightfall."

Ramon grabbed Adam's hand and took a step back. "I don't know..."

"You aren't a prisoner," I said. "But we still need your help to find him. After that, if you need to get back to Clarissa, I understand."

Chapter 6

THE GAUDY GOLD TRIM glittering around my throne room was more Ladinas' style than mine. It was a stark contrast to the mucky sewers that surrounded our subterranean lair. Adam was taken by all the shiny. Mel kept the tribrid tyke distracted best she could as the "adults" got down to business.

"So where's Oberon hiding?" I asked Ramon. "We have had no luck tracking him down."

"Somewhere off the Appalachian Trail," Ramon said. "Far from any roads. We won't reach him by car."

"If you have an exact location," Muggs grunted, "I can port us there directly."

I nodded, already turning scenarios over in my mind. Oberon had leverage with Wee Willie as his prisoner. We needed that intel on incubi in the area, and to get Willie back safe. I'd have to play this carefully, or that puffed-up pixie would end up holding all the cards.

Mel walked over, tablet in hand. Adam scampered after her, his eyes wide and curious.

"I've got a topo map up," Mel said. "Ramon, can you pinpoint Oberon's location?"

Ramon leaned in, scanning the map. "Hard to say. Adam teleported us in there. We had to find our way home on foot. It's harder to identify his location from above."

"Any landmarks you recognized?" I asked.

Ramon pinched his chin, wracking his brain. After a moment, he tapped the screen.

"I'm not sure exactly, but this will get us close. If I go with you, I should be able to sense their presence and take us the rest of the way." Ramon shook his head. "Once we get close, it will be obvious. Oberon has made a few changes to the forests there. Sort of like the way Willie did near the convergence outside Exeter."

I shook my head. "If that's the case, there's no way to sneak up on Oberon. He'll know we're coming well before we get to his court."

"That's only a problem if you hoped to sneak in to rescue Willie," Ramon said. "From what you've told me, you don't know for sure that Willie has the information you need. You may still need Oberon's help. It's best if you approach him in good faith."

I sighed. Ramon was right. I didn't like the idea of paying homage to the Seelie king, but we had to get Willie back. And we desperately needed whatever intel Oberon had on incubi in the area. If he knew anything about what Morgana was planning, this was going to require diplomacy. Usually, in situations like that, I'd let Ladinas take point. He had more patience than me. Especially when dealing with pretentious holier-than-thou types.

"I want to help!" Adam piped up eagerly.

I hesitated. The kid was powerful, but unpredictable. And Oberon was cunning—one wrong move could put us all in danger.

"I don't know if that's wise," I said slowly. "You're just a kid, Adam."

Adam's face fell. Before he could protest, I squeezed his shoulder gently.

"We need you here to keep an eye on things." It was a white lie, but it seemed to mollify him. I'd used the same strategy with Mel before. Make her feel useful, like keeping her out of harm's way was less about distrusting her abilities, and more about needing someone I could trust to handle other important tasks. We didn't know much about Adam's power and given the fact that he only appeared to be a teenager, and was emotionally even younger than that, bringing him on a sensitive negotiation with a crafty faerie king wasn't a good idea. Especially since Oberon might know a lot more about what Adam was capable of than we did. I didn't want to give Oberon any leverage.

"Yeah, we can hang out here and keep tabs on everything," Mel said brightly. "And Clement's way better with the younglings than I am. I'll introduce Adam to some orphans. Maybe he can make a few friends. We'll be alright."

"Just stay out of trouble while we're gone," I chuckled. "No throwing any wild parties or starting any wars. Got it?"

Mel took a deep breath, laughing as she exhaled. "No wars? C'mon, Mercy. You're no fun."

I turned my attention back to Ramon. "So you really think Oberon will just hand over Willie and spill the beans about Morgana's incubus if we ask nicely? He's been deceptive at every turn. He's nearly as bad as that fox, Reynard."

Ramon shrugged. "I wouldn't say he'll just hand them over. You must have something he desires."

I shook my head. "I can't give him Oblivion. The dragon-spirit is within me and won't leave. He won't even answer my call."

"Then perhaps you'll need to make a show of strength. Prove your worthiness to the king."

"How do you suggest we show our strength?" I asked. "Threaten to stomp on his faerie circles and piss in his magic mushrooms?"

Ramon laughed under his breath. "Nothing so uncouth. Oberon granted me safe passage before, when I was at my lowest. As a vampire, something of the Unseelie still lingered within me. But as I grew, and the power within me evolved, he saw something different. I'm not entirely sure what it was. But he brought me into his fold without question."

I narrowed my eyes. There was a lot Ramon didn't know—even about himself. Baron Samedi made him a vampire. He wasn't turned like others. Apart from my sire, who was the first, Ramon was the only one that the Baron created that way. I had to wonder, though, if Ramon wasn't made a vampire differently. If something else accounted for his unpredictability through the years. If it was that something else that awakened when he encountered the power of faerie magic and evolved.

But all Ramon knew was that he'd spent his last night as a human, drunk. That he'd wandered into the woods and returned changed. Nico never told him—or anyone else until he revealed it to me postmortem—about his true origins. I suspected, now, that Oberon knew more. Oberon never accepted vampires in his domain. Not until Willie brought Ramon to him, nearly dead, mid-metamorphosis.

"Alright," I said finally. "We'll try it your way. But if this goes south, I reserve the right to say 'I told you so' while blasting the smug bastard through the nearest tree."

Ramon smiled slightly. "I would expect nothing less."

I nodded, feeling a spark of something almost like camaraderie. Ramon and I had a messy history, but if we were going to move forward, we had to work together. And maybe, just maybe, we could pull this off after all.

"Let's go pay the Seelie Court a visit," I said. "Time to get our friend back."

Ramon raised his hand. "Not so fast. We must also consider what to do with Clarissa. We cannot leave to go after Oberon until nightfall. At least we shouldn't. Even if you wore those suits and chanced it, there's no guarantee we'd get back in time. The only thing keeping Clarissa inside at the moment is the daylight."

I nodded. "It's just as well. She is my progeny, Ramon. I can command her not to feed, to stay inside until you return. You just have to tell me where you've been holing up so Muggs can take me there."

Chapter 7

THE STENCH OF FRESH blood hit me like a punch in the face as Muggs' portal spit us out in the dingy hallway. Ramon's so-called "safe house" was a shit-hole—peeling wallpaper, exposed wiring, floors sticky with god knows what. But the blood was fresh. It felt like he'd just teleported us into an all-you-can eat vampire buffet. Or, perhaps, into a crime scene. Six of one, half a dozen of the other.

My stomach growled in response to the sweet fragrance as I scanned for threats, but the hall was empty.

Muggs shuffled behind us, sniffing loudly. "Smells like O-negative. Yummy."

Ramon pushed past me and through the front door to what must've been his apartment. "Nico! Mercy!"

He wasn't calling out to me or my sire. He was calling out to his human children.

"What the fuck, Ramon? You left your human kids with your youngling wife? Are you mental?"

Ramon didn't respond. He was in too much a panic to protest. You'd think, though, given Ramon's history trying to resist his cravings, he'd know better. There was no point chastising him further.

I followed Ramon into the apartment, scanning the dark room. The windows were boarded up light tight. The tang of blood was overpowering.

My eyes fell on Clarissa, curled in the corner. Her pale skin seemed to glow in the dim light. Dark rivulets of blood trailed down her chin and neck, staining the collar of her dress. Her crimson eyes were wide and feral.

At her feet lay a body. Male, twenties maybe, dressed in a pizza delivery uniform. His throat had been ripped out. I didn't need to check for a pulse to know he was dead. Looked like Clarissa had ordered lunch.

As grim as the scene was, I was relieved. She hadn't killed her own children, at least. Not that murder was ever justified, or I didn't feel bad for the young man who'd deserved a tip, rather than an evisceration. But everything was relative. Most of us had a body or two in our past. That poor boy would haunt her forever—if she ever managed to overcome her bloodlust.

"What the hell happened?" Ramon demanded, though it was pretty damn obvious.

Clarissa licked the blood from her lips slowly. "I got hungry," she purred.

Ramon's two kids huddled behind him, staring at their mother in horror. Guess this was their first glimpse at the monster within.

I met Clarissa's gaze and held it, letting her see the force of my will. "I've seen enough, little girl. You're coming with me."

She hissed, baring her fangs. "You're not my mother."

"No," I said coldly. "But I am your sire. And you're damned lucky I haven't already staked your ass for this bullshit."

Clarissa giggled uncontrollably. "You stake *asses*? What kind of vampire pervert are you?"

I rolled my eyes. So far, with my progenies, I'd been lucky. Mel was grateful I'd turned her and eager to tame her cravings. Muggs was a little more wily, but we had the advantage of being able to lock him away in a cell in the Underground while we controlled his feeds until he got his shit together.

Ramon tried to soothe his terrified kids while I focused on leashing the beast within Clarissa. This wasn't going to be pretty.

I crouched down to examine the pizza boy more closely. Yep, definitely dead. His neck was torn open, blood still oozing. It was like Clarissa bit him a dozen times, kept missing the artery, and ripped him apart instead. I sighed and stood back up.

"You killed a pizza delivery guy? Seriously?"

Clarissa shrugged, licking her fingers. "I was hungry. And the kids needed to eat too."

Ramon's children were huddled together, pale and trembling. They hadn't touched the pizza. Guess seeing your mom rip out a guy's throat kind of ruins your appetite.

"Time to stop playing house," I told Clarissa bluntly. "You're coming back to the Underground with me before you get us all exposed."

Clarissa's eyes flashed with anger. She spat right in my face. "Fuck you. You don't control me."

I slowly wiped the spit from my cheek, swallowing back a rising tide of rage. She was testing my patience in dangerous ways. I had staked younglings for far less insolence than this.

"As your sire, I do control you," I said evenly. I could have forced her with a command. All I had to do was speak it firmly, meeting her eyes with mine. It was a last resort. I'd learned in my experience with Mel and Muggs that using compulsion with a youngling was like giving children a time-out. It had to be used strategically, and sparingly. It was better if Clarissa came willingly. Not to mention, as grim as the situation was, that she hadn't bitten her own children was a good sign. She had enough control to resist the urge. That meant she wasn't a natural-born ripper. She had potential. "We can do this the easy way, or the hard way. It's your choice. But you're coming with me regardless."

Clarissa ignored me and turned back to the dead pizza boy, lapping up the blood from his cheeks like a rabid animal.

Ramon tried to soothe his kids, then said to me, "Get her out of here. I'll take the kids to a sitter and meet you back at the Underground by nightfall."

I grabbed Clarissa's arm in an iron grip. "Last chance. Come with me willingly, or I'll stake you with a chair leg and bring you back when you've had a little time in hell to consider what you've done."

She wisely chose not to fight me. I wasn't actually going to stake her—sending a youngling to hell could only make them worse. But she didn't know that.

Clarissa snarled but allowed me to drag her outside. Muggs was waiting, twirling his oak staff.

"Time to go home, little sis," he said, moving in for a hug.

Clarissa recoiled, wrinkling her nose. "Don't touch me, creeper. You smell like cheese."

Muggs just chuckled. "Cheese? Delicious. Who doesn't like cheese?"

I gagged. "Let's just get back already." I'd grown used to Muggs' natural odor. Hanging around him a lot was sort of like living in the sewers. The smell gets to you at first, but after a while, you barely notice it. She was right, though. Muggs did smell of fromage.

Muggs swung his staff in an arc and a shimmering portal opened up. "Ladies first," he said with a dramatic bow. Clarissa looked back once more at the dark apartment where she'd played house. For a second, I thought she was going to make a run for it. I grabbed her and pushed her into the swirling portal and jumped in just behind.

Clarissa tumbled onto the floor of my throne room. I landed on my feet. I extended a hand to help her up. She didn't take it.

"Welcome home," I said wryly.

Clarissa didn't even stand up. She folded her legs under her. "This isn't my home. I want to go back!"

I rounded on her, eyes flashing. "You killed a man tonight. That apartment, that life—it's over. As over as that poor boy's life you ended because you ran away and didn't let me help you from the start." I grabbed her chin, forcing her to meet my gaze. "It's time you learned what it really means to be a vampire. We are *not* monsters."

She trembled, but didn't look away. Behind me, I heard Muggs step through the portal just before it snapped shut.

"Take her to the dormitory," I told him. "Help her get cleaned up. I need to speak with Adam."

Muggs inclined his head. "Of course. This way, little sis."

Clarissa cast a venomous look at me. "Adam? He's here. I want to see him!"

I shook my head. "You don't want him to see *you*. Not like this."

"Bring my boy to me! You can't keep a mother from her children, you bitch!"

I took a deep breath. Clarissa was going to be a challenge—as if I didn't have enough on my plate already to worry about. The girl was wild, untamed, and dangerous. But she was *my* blood, *my* responsibility.

I straightened my dress and headed out of the throne room toward the orphanage. I needed to see how Adam was settling in and, probably, prepare him for what he was going to have to face. No, not with Oberon and all of that, but regarding his mother. Not to mention, I was his grand-sire. Or, perhaps, just his sire. I wasn't sure how that worked since I'd bitten his mother while she was pregnant with him. So far as I knew, this was uncharted territory.

Chapter 8

My eyes swept over the dimly lit rec-room in our orphanage. Over the last several months, since we welcomed Clement and the orphans to the Underground, we'd made some serious renovations. Between Ladinas and me, we had plenty of funds to do it. The trick, of course, being who we'd get to do the work. Hiring human contractors to work in an underground lair of vampires comes with hazard pay. Not to mention, it risks exposing our existence.

We all rose to the occasion and did most of the work ourselves. Antoine had a construction background dating back to his human days. Granted, his building experience was more Victorian than modern chic, but he was addicted to HGTV. He'd picked up a few tips from the Property Brothers. Maybe, some day, he could get his own show. Remodeling lairs for vampires who needed an upgrade. Just imagine the surprise reveal at the end.

The orphanage design was what Antoine called an "open concept." The couches were both stylish and comfortable. The television set was a major focal point in the rec-room. Adam was on the largest couch, eyes glued to the TV screen, thumbs working furiously on a video game controller. Isaac and a few other vampire kids were crowded around him, equally enthralled by the hyper-realistic violence unfolding on the screen.

Blood sprayed across the sixty-four inch screen as Adam's character tore into Isaac's with a chainsaw. The kids oohed and aahed, practically salivating. I wrinkled my nose. It was like dangling a juicy steak in front of a pack of hungry dogs.

Shaking my head, I made my way over to Clement, who was leaning against the far wall, watching the gruesome gaming session.

"Isn't this a bit much for them?" I asked, gesturing to the screen where Adam was now using a vampire to rip out his opponent's throat. "Gotta be torture having that virtual bloodfest waved in front of their noses."

Clement shrugged. "It's oddly therapeutic. Gives them a safe way to indulge those bloody cravings without actually sinking their fangs into anyone." He nodded at Adam. "See the laser focus? He's getting the hunt out of his system."

I watched Adam decapitate a werewolf, flecks of crimson coating the screen. His shoulders were relaxed, movements fluid and controlled. Huh. Maybe Clement was onto something.

I chuckled. "Who'd have thought violent video games could be the salvation of the next generation of vampires?"

I leaned in close to Clement, keeping my voice low so Adam wouldn't overhear.

"Speaking of the next generation... I've got a bit of a problem fledgling on my hands. Clarissa, Adam's mom?" I rolled my eyes. "Total wildcard. She killed a pizza delivery guy last night. Just ripped his throat open right in front of her children. Her human children."

Clement raised an eyebrow. "Messy."

"Right? She's out of control. I had to drag her down here to keep her from exposing us all. But I'm worried about her being around the others." I nodded toward Adam again. "Especially her own son. She's too unstable, too volatile. I'm not sure she'd be a good influence."

Clement crossed his arms, frowning. "Hmm. That is concerning. New vampires can be unpredictable as they adjust to their enhanced abilities and cravings."

I stared at Clement blankly. He was mansplaining the obvious. "Yeah. I know that. This is next-level, though. The only thing that gives me any hope at all is that she didn't bite her own kids. She had enough control to resist that."

"Rumor has it you bit your own brother after you were turned..." Clement's eyes darted back and forth, unsure if he'd overstepped.

I shrugged. "I guess you're right. But then again, my feelings toward Edwin, my human brother, were complicated. I envied the privileged treatment my father gave him."

Clement pinched his chin. "Vampirism enhanced your feelings toward him. It made your brother vulnerable. For a mother like Clarissa, her love for her children could be even stronger, more instinctual, than it was when she was human. Everything is heightened for a youngling. While that usually involves some unnecessary bloodshed, since most every human has a suppressed darkness that their vampirism awakens, there are also some virtues that humans possess that vampirism can likewise enhance."

I sighed. "Like mothering..."

"Indeed," Clement said. "Or an innate curiosity, a keen desire for justice, to become someone who matters. Have you ever considered, perhaps, how your experience as a human might have set the stage for the leader you've become today?"

I rubbed my brow. "I don't know, Clement. If I wanted psychoanalysis, I'd check in at the Vilokan Asylum for the Magically and Mentally Deranged. Been there, done that. Right now, Clarissa is my concern. As is Adam. Not to mention saving Ladinas and Alice."

He put a hand on my shoulder. "You're overwhelmed. You were right to bring her here. Perhaps I can provide some guidance, help her find balance. But as her sire, the bond you two share is critical. I can help babysit your younglings for now, but the time will come when they'll need their sire."

"You're probably right," I admitted. "I turned Clarissa, so I'm responsible for helping her, even if it's inconvenient timing. And Adam..." I trailed off, watching the boy laughing with the others across the room.

"I'm not sure I'm technically his sire," I continued. "He was in utero when I turned Clarissa. I don't know if he became a vampire directly from my bite, or if he inherited it through Clarissa. That might make her his sire. And there's the faerie blood too." I shook my head. "As powerful as that boy can become, I'm even more worried that if Clarissa holds influence over his vampirism as both a mother and a sire, that she might not be the best influence right now. But he is family, in a way. And he seems to have a good heart, despite everything."

Clement smiled. "That's his humanity shining through. Unlike most vampires, due to the way he was made, he retains a human soul. Every vampire, if they live long enough, gets a feel for humanity again. Or some version of it. He has an advantage most of us never did. His potential, not just because of his power granted by his faerie nature, but because of his humanity, knows no limits."

I chuckled dryly. "Our humanity is just an illusion, though, isn't it? A neat trick at most, the result of feeding off human souls. Ironic, I suppose, that by doing something so abominable from a human perspective, we eventually feel more human. Takes a while, though. It gets worse before it gets better."

Clement smirked. "You are what you eat, you know."

I rolled my eyes. "Hilarious. Let me guess. You'll be here all week."

"Not a joke," Clement said gently. "It's how it works. Maybe it is an illusion, but does it matter? The impact is real. Your compassion, your leadership—these came from somewhere, Mercy."

I sighed, glancing over at Adam playing video games with the other orphans. He seemed so normal, just a kid enjoying time with his friends. Hard to believe the immense power contained in that small frame.

"There was a time that I might have done the same thing Clarissa did. Without Nico, there's no telling the monster I might have become. I'm no saint, but these days I at least try to do more good than harm."

Clement nodded. "Exactly. Does it matter if it's real humanity or not? If it walks like humanity, squawks like humanity... chances are... "

"That I'm a duck?" I chuckled. "Kidding. I know what you're saying."

"The same will happen for Clarissa, given enough time and guidance."

"Assuming we can keep them both alive that long," I said darkly. "Clarissa is reckless. And Adam... who knows what he's truly capable of? I hope I can provide guidance, as needed. But I have so much on my plate already."

Clement patted my shoulder reassuringly. "You'll manage. A good mother always does. Keep in mind, though, that humanity comes with its own potential for darkness. The history of this world proves as much. He needs a good role model. A mother, or maybe grandmother, like you."

I winced. Thinking of myself as a grandmother, or grandsire, made me feel old. "Motherhood was never part of my plan. Ladinas has emphasized the need to become a strong queen. I'm not so sure that's compatible with mothering."

Clement raised an eyebrow. "And what makes for a good queen, if not a strong mothering instinct to protect her people?"

I had no argument against that logic. With a rueful smile, I said, "Maybe you're right. What made you so wise? Maybe you deserve a bigger role here in the Underground."

Clement smiled. "I'm doing what I love. As you know, Mercy, I have little taste for battle. I'm not saying there's not a place for standing up to fight. You do that well. But I saw enough of that during the American Revolution. Enough to know I'm not suited for it. This is my calling. You have yours, I have mine."

"Right now, I need to play the role of a diplomat. Not my greatest strength, but I have to try. That's the only way I'm going to convince Oberon to tell me how we might save Ladinas and Alice."

Clement's eyes softened with understanding. "No one expects you to be perfect, Mercy. As a mother and a queen, you're also an advocate for your people. You'll find the words and wisdom. Do your best. It will be more than enough."

I sighed, the weight of responsibility pressing heavily on my shoulders. "Everyone is depending on me—the vampires here, Ladinas, Alice..." My voice trailed off.

Clement gripped my shoulder firmly. "You can do this. I know it's difficult, but you're stronger than you realize. That's why the vampires here follow your lead. It's not because you're Niccolo's favored progeny. That might have given you the opportunity to lead, but it's what you've done since that has earned their loyalty. I have no doubt you'll succeed."

I blinked back bloody tears, touched by his faith in me. With a deep breath, I straightened my spine. I would save them all, even if it killed me. Again.

"Wish me luck," I said.

Clement smiled. "You won't need it. But you'll have my prayers, regardless."

I stifled a laugh. "You sound like Alice. Not sure how much good those will do. But I appreciate it."

I strode out of the orphanage, my boots clicking sharply on the stone floor.

The role of queen had fallen to me, whether or not I felt ready for it. There was no one else now. Ladinas was a safety-net before. As a prince, dating back to his human days, he knew what it took to be an effective ruler. Now he was gone. However inadequate I felt, I needed to step up.

Chapter 9

THE BLUE LIGHT FROM Mel's tablet cast a glow on her face in the otherwise dim throne room. She hunched over the screen, brows knitted, scrolling and tapping while I sat back in my chair and watched. The firewalls protecting the police databases were giving her hell, but she was determined to break through and get what we needed—any info on potential incubi victims reported missing recently in the area.

"Dammit," she muttered. "This precinct has their data on total lockdown."

"Any luck finding a pattern with the public stuff at least?" I asked.

She shook her head. "There's not much here that screams 'incubus attack.' And we can't even be sure if any missing women who might be due to an incubus were taken by Cal or someone else."

I sighed, the sound echoing in the empty chamber. We were grasping at straws and coming up empty. But we had to keep trying. If Oberon proved a dead end, Mel was the last chance we had to try and figure out where Morgana might be. Not to mention, an incubus running loose and snacking on locals was bad news for everyone.

Mel's tablet let out a shrill beep and her eyes went wide. "We've got movement in the sewers. East tunnel." She tapped the screen and a grainy security feed popped up, showing a lone figure slogging through the muck. Even with the poor quality, I recognized the set of those shoulders, the determined stride.

"Well well, look who finally decided to show up." I leaned in to get a better look at Ramon on the screen. "Should I let him wander around down there for a while? Might be good for him."

Mel laughed. "As tempting as that is, we're on the clock here. The sun will set soon. Unless you want to go out to meet Oberon in kevlar, we can't waste time screwing with Ramon."

"Alright, fun's over." I stood, smirking. "Go get everything prepped. We'll need comms and weapons, iron bullets, just in case this thing with Oberon goes sideways."

Mel powered down her tablet and headed for the armory while I went to grab Muggs.

I found Muggs lounging in his private quarters, his eyes closed and legs crossed in meditation.

"Time to go to work, big guy," I said, tapping my nails on his brushed-metal doorframe.

Muggs carefully stood. He was tall and lanky, vaguely resembling a tree—fitting for a druid. Even his beard had a few green highlights in the gray. I didn't know if it was a buildup of mildew, or a few stains left behind from the magic he wielded.

"Ready to depart?" His voice gurgled with phlegm. "I've been focusing my mind, preparing for what we might face. Druids and faeries have a long history of cooperation. Perhaps, if we play this right, I'll be able to appeal to the king's better sensibilities."

I nodded. "Good thinking. Given my temperament, and Ramon's, we need someone with diplomatic tact. First, though, Ramon is trying to get back. I think he's lost in the sewers."

Muggs chuckled. "You'd think he'd know his way by now. Never mind that. I'll hear his footsteps as soon as I get into the tunnels. I'll grab him straight away."

I nodded. "Bring him straight to the armory. We need to arm up and head out. No time to spare."

I left Muggs as he disappeared in a portal and headed for the armory. Mel already had an array of weapons and equipment laid out on the central table.

"Is the armor necessary?" I eyed the tactical vest dubiously. "We're dealing with faeries, not trigger-happy gangbangers."

"Faeries that know how to kill vampires." Mel held up the vest, her expression stern. "Can't be too careful with Oberon. Now suit up."

I reluctantly donned the vest and strapped on my holsters. Mel handed me several magazines loaded with iron rounds. She placed a freshly-charged ear-piece in my hand.

I nodded, sliding the comm into place. Time to go confront the Seelie King. This would either be a short conversation, or a very long night.

I felt the familiar pull of magic as Muggs' portal opened behind me. He stepped through, a disgruntled Ramon in tow.

Ramon brushed sewer muck from his designer jeans, cursing under his breath. He eyed the weapons on the table disdainfully.

"I don't need any of that, ma chérie. I'm going as a faerie emissary, not your bodyguard."

Mel pursed her lips, but stayed silent as she checked our gear one last time. I raised an eyebrow at Ramon.

"Just trying to keep you alive. Get your kids situated?"

Ramon nodded. "They're with their grandmother. An awkward situation. They haven't seen Clarissa since, well, you know... and they still think I walked out on the family for several months. But the children are in good hands. How are Clarissa and Adam?"

I scratched my head. "Adam is great. Not so sure yet about Clarissa. But she's in a secure facility, for now. Clement is going to keep an eye on them for us."

He sighed. "Merci, ma chérie. Let's just get this over with. Oberon has never wronged me. He saved me once. Coming in there armed wouldn't befit our history."

Muggs lifted his staff. The air spun violently as he summoned a portal. Jade energy swirled before us, ready to transport us as close as we could get to Oberon's new domain.

I took a deep breath, steadying my nerves. Diplomacy with Oberon was a long shot. But if anyone could pull it off, Ramon's relationship with Oberon and Muggs' druid connection offered us a better shot than if I attempted a parlay alone.

We stepped into the portal, letting the magic whisk us away. An instant later, the cool night air of the forest greeted us. The Appalachian foothills rose in the distance.

Muggs held onto my arm. Without any magic on the trail, his spirit gaze didn't afford him any sight. We followed Ramon down a winding path through the thick trees, the moonlight barely filtering down to light our way. Strange chittering sounds echoed around us and glowing eyes peered from the underbrush. This was no ordinary forest.

"We're close," Ramon murmured. "Can you feel it?"

The hairs on my neck prickled. A shimmering haze lay ahead, marking the boundary between Earth and Oberon's domain. I tensed, ready to draw my gun at the first sign of trouble. But Ramon lifted a hand.

"Wait here. I need to go first, alone."

Before I could protest, he stepped into the haze, vanishing from sight. The forest seemed to hold its breath, waiting.

Long moments passed. I shifted uneasily, glancing at Muggs. He stood calmly, eyes closed as if meditating.

Finally, the haze rippled. Ramon emerged, face grim.

"Oberon will see us. But you must approach unarmed and unclothed."

I stared at Ramon blankly. "Why? So that pervy king can gawk at me? No thank you."

Ramon was already kicking off his pants. "The rule applies to all of us. It's a matter of security, nothing more. He does not trust our intentions."

"I'm not leaving my wand in the forest," I protested. "You know how valuable this thing is?"

"It will be fine," Muggs said. "I can conceal our wares."

I shook my head as Ramon and Muggs stripped down to nothing. It didn't matter to Muggs. He was blind. He didn't have to watch Ramon's bubble-butt bounce up and down as we followed him into the haze.

I reluctantly peeled off my leather pants, vest, and top. I set my glock and wand on top of my clothes.

"How are you going to protect our shit?" I asked Muggs.

Muggs grinned. "Watch and learn."

With a wave of his staff, a thousand roots and vines shot out from the ground. They weaved together into a protective shell over our things. Muggs shrank his staff to the size of a pencil and dropped it between the vines.

"Let's go," Ramon said, already striding forward. "We don't want to keep Oberon waiting."

I took a deep breath and followed, trying not to think about the fact that I was walking into the Seelie King's domain completely naked. The chittering of insects and the rustling of leaves grew louder as we walked deeper into the forest.

Something tickled my thigh and I slapped at it. "Damn bugs. I swear, Ramon, if I get any ticks."

Ramon raised an eyebrow. "I'll check you over when we're done. For old time's sake."

"You're not checking me for ticks, Ramon. You're a married faerie. That's inappropriate."

Ramon chuckled. I wasn't sure if ticks bit vampires, anyway. Maybe they did. Bloodsuckers attract bloodsuckers. I was eager to get this over with as soon as possible. Once I thought I felt one bug on my body, suddenly, I was struck by the sensation of bugs crawling everywhere. My mind playing tricks on me, most likely, but it was annoying as hell. So much so that I almost failed to appreciate the beauty of the forest that we'd stepped into.

There were several trees still native to Appalachia, but among them were lanky oaks with multicolored foliage, giant mushrooms like the ones in Willie's forest near Exeter, and hundreds of glowing wisps darting around in the distance.

As we walked further into the forest, the glow of the wisps grew brighter and more numerous. They swirled around us, darting in and out of trees, almost like they were leading us somewhere. I couldn't help but feel a sense of wonder at the magic of it all, even amidst the tension of our mission.

Suddenly, the wisps turned as one and shot off in a single direction. We followed their lead, and soon enough, we saw a clearing up ahead.

"We're here," Ramon said as he approached the tree. "Simply touch the trunk."

Muggs giggled a little. He was clearly fascinated by all of this. Practically ecstatic he extended his hand. I grabbed it, stopping him before he touched it.

"What's going to happen when we touch the trunk?"

"It will take us into Oberon's throne room," Ramon said. "Faeries have expansive domains within the trees. Doesn't look like much from the outside, but it's much more vast within."

"I can't wait!" Muggs blurted out.

I raised an eyebrow. "Got a little wood, for wood, buddy?"

Muggs tilted his head. "I don't know what you mean."

I smirked. He wouldn't. "Never mind. Let's just get this over with."

Ramon and Muggs touched the trunk and disappeared. I took a deep breath and followed their lead, placing my hand on the rough bark.

The world twisted and warped around me, and suddenly, I was standing in the throne room of Oberon, King of the Seelie Court. The room was massive, with towering walls made of living wood and a ceiling that seemed to stretch up into the sky. The air was thick with the scent of flowers and I could hear the sound of a nearby waterfall.

Oberon sat on his throne at the end of the room, watching us with piercing green eyes. He was tall and lean, with long hair tied back in a braid and a regal bearing. He wore a crown of leaves and flowers on his head and a cloak made of shimmering silk.

"Greetings, Ramon," he said, his voice smooth as honey. "It's been a season since we last met."

Ramon bowed deeply. "Your Majesty, it is an honor to see you again."

Oberon stood from his throne and approached me. He was a lot taller in his tree-palace than he was when I met him in the real world. Just like a man. Given the chance to make himself bigger, he couldn't pass the chance.

"And the vampires." Oberon looked down at me. "I do not typically tolerate your kind in my realm."

I pointed at my face. "Eyes up here, buddy. Might I remind you that this isn't your realm. Your fancy tree house aside, you're in our world now."

Muggs cleared his throat and extended his arms stepping in front of me. I huffed a little but didn't resist. I knew I wasn't striking the right tone with the king. Perhaps he'd do better.

"As a druid, I must say, your Highness, I'm quite impressed by your power here. The harmony with nature is enviable, even for the likes of me."

"A druid and a vampire," Oberon narrowed his eyes. "A unique combination."

Muggs bowed deeply. "No other kind like me, your Highness."

"Indeed," Oberon said, his gaze shifting back to me. "But what brings you here, vampire? It must be important for you to have entered my domain so carelessly."

I straightened up. "We need your help. But first, I'm told that you hold a friend of mine captive. Wee Willie Winker."

"Indeed, I do," Oberon said. "He renounced his fealty to me. Declared himself uncourted. Such an absurdity. When I caught him spying on my activities, I simply decided to teach the boy a lesson."

I took a deep breath. "I could use his help. Yours, as well. It concerns the matter of an Unseelie Baobhan Sith known as Morgana."

"And an incubus," Muggs added. "Gan Ceanach, who now possesses a human known as Cal Rhodes. The two have partnered together, Gan Ceanach granting her strength through the spirits he harnesses, and her creating an army of Baobhan Sith to serve his purpose. However, there's been an incident."

"We believe Morgana has sent Gan Ceanach along with two very important friends of mine into a pocket dimension."

Oberon paced around us, his brow furrowed. "What you say is certainly concerning, but if it's true, I fear there's very little I can do to help your friends. Even if I was inclined to help, which I'm not."

Ramon cleared his throat. "Might I beg your pardon, Your Highness. You understand that if the incubus and Morgana work together they could soon overrun this world with their offspring."

Oberon heard Ramon but kept his focus on me. "But you, vampire, wield Oblivion, do you not?"

"His spirit is within me," I said. "But he won't answer. He won't do anything until both courts of faerie set aside their differences and unite."

Oberon clutched his gut and laughed. "It shall never be! I'd sooner die!"

I gritted my teeth, frustration building within me. "Then perhaps you're content to let Morgana and Gan Ceanach run rampant and destroy everything in their path. How long do you suppose it will be until they discover your location? You might be powerful, but your numbers are finite. They are growing an army all the time."

Oberon shrugged. "If the incubus is trapped in a pocket dimension, as you say, then perhaps Morgana lacks the strength to reach him. If she does not have access to the incubus, she will not have power to fuel her magic."

"But she could still reproduce," Muggs said. "She's a threat with or without Gan Ceanach."

"What if she finds another incubus?" I asked, hoping to squeeze an answer out of Oberon about the existence of other incubi without him knowing that's the information we were seeking.

Oberon took a deep breath. "You are not wrong. There is another she might seek. If Morgana were to ally with him, or if she were to find the power to bring Gan Ceanach back, she could do great destruction to our court."

"So you'll help us?" I asked.

"And will you free my friend?" Ramon asked. "I promise, your Highness, to keep Willie in check. He will not be a nuisance any further to your court."

Oberon raised an eyebrow at Ramon's request, considering it for a moment. "Very well," he said finally. "I will release Wee Willie Winker into your custody, vampire. But know this: if he causes any trouble in my court again, I will not be so forgiving."

I nodded, relieved that we were making progress. "Thank you, Your Highness."

"As for Morgana and Gan Ceanach," Oberon continued, "I will send my best trackers to search for them. If they are indeed in a pocket dimension, we will find them."

"And Oblivion?" I pressed. "Will you help me unite the faerie courts and awaken his power?"

Oberon hesitated for a moment, then spoke. "I will consider it," he said finally. "But know this, vampire: the courts of faerie have been at odds for centuries. Even if I were willing to set aside our differences, I cannot say that the Unseelie would be so willing."

"Yet even so," I said. "They lack a queen. I already sent Malvessa back to the faerie realm. She lingers there with nothing but clurichauns at her behest."

Oberon narrowed his eyes. "What you say is true. She is too weak, however, to break through the barriers that protect my native domain without her full court."

"So that's it? If you find Morgana, or the location of the pocket dimension, you'll let us know?"

Oberon laughed. "I didn't say that, now, did I? I told you I would send trackers to secure the information you seek. If you truly wish me to hand over said information, I'll require something in return."

"I already told you, Oblivion won't open the portal to your realm until you're ready to mend fences with the Unseelie."

"Perhaps not," Oberon said. "But there's more than one way to enter the otherworlds, isn't there, druid?"

Muggs nodded. "This is true."

I shook my head. "I gave my vow to Oblivion. I can't let you go back, not even through a back door."

Oberon raised an eyebrow. "You're bold, vampire. I can appreciate that. What I require, however, is livestock."

I narrowed my eyes. "Bovine livestock?"

"Human," Oberon smirked. "Surely for one such as you, who feeds upon the species, such a request will not pose any moral quandaries. One human, of good spirit, for one piece of information. The more you bring me, the more information I'll provide."

"What the hell do you need humans for?" I asked. "I know you're taking them as slaves. For the sake of a good faith negotiation, I haven't mentioned it until now. But you have to realize that humans aren't as weak as you imagine. They will seek their missing and fight back in time."

Oberon's smirk turned into a scowl. "I do not take them as slaves," he spat. "I take them for food, just as you. Their spirits can invigorate my magic just as it does for Morgana, whom you seek."

"You *eat* them?" I asked.

"I do not," Oberon said. "I feed on them sparingly, less so than the incubus you seek. I take only a little spirit until they recover. In the meantime, they serve my court well and live in luxury. Not unlike the humans you keep in your lair, I'm told, Mercy Brown."

I grunted. "That's different. Our blood maids come willingly. We give them life, we don't take it."

"You take their blood," Oberon said. "That you might satisfy your craving for souls."

I snorted. "Still, it's not the same. My warning still applies. If you continue to seize humans without their consent, they will fight back. They'll burn these forests to the ground if it comes to that."

"I am well aware of the humans' capability for violence. That is why I only take those who will not be missed. The homeless, the drunks, the addicts. They are considered a burden to society, and so I give them a purpose. A purpose that is mutually beneficial to both us and them."

I shook my head, disgusted. "I can't condone that. I won't trade human lives for information."

"Then I'm afraid we have nothing more to discuss," Oberon said, turning his back to us. "You may have Wee Willie Winker, but do not expect any more favors from me."

As he walked away, Ramon grabbed my arm. "We can't leave empty handed. We need his information. Otherwise, Ladinas and Alice are gone forever."

I narrowed my eyes. "I think I'll take my chances with Willie."

Chapter 10

THE CHILL OF THE forest air raised goosebumps on my bare skin as I hurried to pull my clothes back on. Around me, Ramon and Muggs did the same while Willie let out a low whistle.

"Well, well, quite a show back there!" He waggled his eyebrows. "I gotta say Mercy, even after all these years you still look—"

"Save it." I cut him off, my face burning as I wrestled with my jeans. Relief flooded through me as I finally got dressed. Being naked in front of Oberon and his lackeys was humiliating enough.

Willie just laughed, seemingly unfazed. But something about it seemed off. Strained. He gazed around the forest as if just seeing it for the first time.

"Wait..." He frowned. "How did we get here? Weren't we just..." He trailed off, confusion clouding his features.

I shared a look with Ramon. Willie didn't remember being released from Oberon's prison.

Unease twisted my gut. Something wasn't right.

I steadied myself and turned to Willie. "What's the last thing you remember?"

His face scrunched up. "I was in the old speakeasy, just got done playing a set. You and Ramon were there..." He gestured between us. "But then it's just blanks."

I gritted my teeth. "His mind is jumbled."

"Oberon." Ramon shook his head. "He can do that. Seen it happen. That's how the faeries punish their prisoners. They wipe their minds. Not a clean slate, just anything surrounding the offense, a few months before just for safe measure. He can't leave the mind totally blank, so he fills it with nonsense instead."

"Oberon wiped Willie's memory?" A cold fury burned through me at this violation. Was it really a punishment, or had Willie discovered something that Oberon didn't want me to know? Why else would Oberon take Willie as a prisoner? I'd assumed it was because Willie located Oberon, and the Seelie King didn't want his location found out. Now that we'd found him anyway, it made sense that Oberon released him. But I had to wonder if there was more to it than that.

"A prisoner?" Willie's wings stopped fluttering and he plopped down on the ground. "I don't remember that at all!"

"And a speakeasy?" I crossed my arms. "I haven't been to one of those in a hundred years. Not since prohibition. Where would Oberon get such a memory to shove into your head, Willie?"

Willie did a little spin. "I think I know! There was a time, you see, I had a friend by the name of Ramblin' Bob?"

I raised an eyebrow. "Ramblin' Bob?"

Willie nodded. "He used to steal, gamble and rob!"

I bit my lip. He couldn't get that one past me. I was too old to not know it. "Let me guess. You found out last Monday that Bob got locked up on Sunday?"

Willie waved his hand through the air and, with his wings fluttering behind his back, started to sing. "He's in the jailhouse now! He's in the jailhouse now!"

Ramon pinched his chin. "That song was from the same era as the speakeasies."

I nodded. "The nineteen twenties. For some reason, Oberon filled Willie's head with prohibition-era memories. But where the hell did he get those memories from?"

Muggs crossed his arms. "Human spirits. All I can figure is that the magic Oberon used to wipe Willie's mind was siphoned from someone very old. Perhaps if he were still in the faerie realm, he could use his natural power to replace someone's memory with whatever he wanted. Here, his resources are limited."

I tried to wrack my mind. All this was really taking me back. The song, by Jimmie Rodgers, dated back to the late twenties. Prohibition ended in thirty-three. Anyone who'd attended a speakeasy in those days must've been at least eighteen. That would put whatever human whose spirit Oberon stole to power his mind-wiping magic somewhere around a hundred-and-twenty years old. "That can't be right, Muggs. These references are too dated. There aren't many humans alive, if any, who'd have those memories intact."

Ramon took a deep breath. "Well, what kind of person *can* live that long, Mercy?"

I shrugged. "Vampires, maybe?"

Ramon nodded. "What if Oberon isn't just claiming human slaves, but vampires as well? Think about it. Vampires have faerie origins. There's already magic written into our essence. Well, your essence. I keep forgetting I'm not a vampire anymore, but you get the idea."

"Brilliant," Muggs piped up. "A vampire's spirit also replenishes with blood. Human spirits don't recover so easily. We've learned that with the ladies we recovered. The best I could do was patch them up and hope for the best. If Oberon got his hand on vampires, he could theoretically siphon them forever. They'd be like rechargeable magic batteries."

I narrowed my eyes. "So long as he kept them fed with human blood. That's why he needs humans."

"It's a possibility," Ramon added. "But we do not know for sure. It would not be wise to accuse the Seelie King of such things without proof."

I turned to Willie, who was now flying upside down and singing a song I hadn't heard in ages about a guy who apparently had the cutest little dinghy in the Navy. If I wasn't as old as I was, I wouldn't know the song was about a boat.

I had to hope Oberon's mind-altering patch job wasn't perfect. If there was anything Willie remembered at all about what Oberon was doing, what he'd found out, I had to jog his memory.

I took a few steps toward Willie, gently taking his hand to get his attention. His eyes lit up when they met mine.

"Mercy! Fancy seeing you here. Did you come to hear my new shanty?"

I smiled softly. "Maybe another time, Willie. I need your help with something important."

His brow furrowed. "Of course, anything for my favorite vampire queen."

"Do you remember where you just were? You were being held by Oberon."

He nodded eagerly. "Oh yes, it was quite the party! Lots of music and dancing!"

My heart sank. If he thought it was a party, Oberon's magic must have wiped his memory completely clean.

"What's the last thing you remember before that, Willie?"

He tapped his chin. "Hmm, let me think. Oh! We were tracking down that nasty incubus. Did we ever find the scoundrel?"

I shook my head. "When you were gone, we located him, but I need your help to find someone else now. An evil faerie named Morgana. Do you know any way we could locate her?"

Willie's wings drooped. "Oh dear! Morgana! I've heard of her, never met her. A terrifying creature. But don't you fret! I'll ask around the court, see if anyone knows anything."

I sighed. At least Willie remembered a few things about what we were up to before he went searching for Oberon. He still had knowledge about the faeries that might come in handy. What the Seelie King erased had to do with whatever he'd found out since he found Oberon in the forest.

"Thanks Willie," I said. "But you shouldn't go back. Oberon isn't in a welcoming mood."

"Pish posh!" Willie exclaimed. "But whatever you say, Mercy poo!"

I sighed. Why couldn't he have at least forgotten that he liked to add poo to the end of my name? Some people say their name is mud. I didn't much like having mine turned to shit.

"Here's a thought," Muggs interjected. "I know this doesn't help us get any closer to Ladinas and Alice, but if we probe Willie a little more and get him to share more of the memories from whatever vampire, or whoever's memories were infused in place of the ones Oberon wiped, we might get a clue who Oberon is holding captive."

"Nice thinking." I patted Muggs on the back. "But we're too close to Oberon's forest to continue discussing these matters. Someone could overhear us. We need to get back to the Underground."

"I concur," Ramon added. "We mustn't allow Oberon to know we're on to him."

I nodded at Muggs. "Let's get out of here."

Muggs raised his staff and spun it like a baton. A swirling vortex of emerald energy formed overhead. He expanded it until it was large enough for us to step through.

"All aboard the Muggs Express!" he said with a grin.

I took Willie's hand and led him into the portal, with Ramon following close behind. There was a brief feeling of weightlessness and disorientation as we passed through, and then our feet hit solid ground again. Except for Willie, whose wings were already fluttering in a blur behind him as he circled the throne room.

I snapped at Willie. "Get over here. We need to talk."

Willie crashed into my couch. "What you wanna talk about? Moonshine. Have any, by chance?"

I cleared my throat. "Moonshine. That's good. Tell me more about any memories that aren't yours."

Willie furrowed his brow, concentrating. "Memories that aren't mine? You guys are so silly."

I met Willie's eyes. "If Oberon has vampire prisoners, we need to find them. And free them if we can."

Muggs took a deep breath. "Try being less direct. Ask him more about what we're after. About Morgana, perhaps, or the incubi who might be in the area."

I bit my tongue, trying to rein in my impatience. Muggs was right—I needed to take this slowly with Willie.

"Let's talk about Morgana," I said. "That Baobhan Sith witch we mentioned before. You never met her, but do you know a way to track her down?"

Willie shrugged. "Short of flying all around the world and hoping I catch a whiff of her magic, I don't know."

I nodded. "What about incubi? Any of those working for the Unseelie Court that you know of?"

"Other than the one you said you already found?" Willie asked.

"Right. Are there any others?"

Willie nodded. "There's a few of them loyal to the Unseelie, but they ain't too picky about who they work for. Not as long as they get to feed."

My skin crawled at the thought. "So, how would we go about tracking one down if we needed to?"

Willie considered for a moment. "Well, hard to say. It's been ages since they dwelled on the earth. But back in the day, they frequented orgies. Anywhere there's an abundance of... sexual energy for them to feed on. They can feed on anyone, but they prefer their meals to be seasoned, marinated in the kind of energy they prefer."

I rolled my eyes. "A local strip joint, perhaps?"

"Tried looking there before," Willie said. "When we were searching for the other incubus. We turned up empty-handed."

Ramon stepped forward, clearing his throat. "I don't mean to interrupt, but now that we're back, could I see my wife and son?"

"You're worried about them, aren't you?" I said gently.

Ramon met my gaze. "I know they're safe here. But being apart from Clarissa and Adam...it doesn't feel right. I should be with my family. But if you need help questioning Willie."

"I'll keep chatting with him," Muggs said. "I don't think we're going to get anything out of him this way. But he gave us some ideas. We can try the strip clubs and see what we find."

I nodded. "Try to get him talking more about his replaced memories. My gut tells me that if Oberon is holding a vampire, or several vampires, that it's all connected."

"Can I see my family now?" Ramon asked again.

"Ramon, you saw how unstable Clarissa was earlier." I hesitated. "I don't know if she can control herself around Adam yet. It might be better if—"

"If she's left in isolation?" Ramon cut in angrily. "She's my wife, Mercy! Let me try talking to her. She never acted so reckless when Adam and I were with her before."

I nodded. "Of course. Let's go check on them."

We stopped by the blood maid quarters first. Clarissa needed blood. I also didn't want to risk a maid's life. So, I drew some fresh blood from one of the maids, which he offered without protest, and took the blood bag with us.

When we arrived, Clarissa was hunched in the corner, rocking back and forth. Her eyes were wild, fangs bared.

"Easy now," I breathed. "We brought you something fresh."

I offered her a blood bag. She snarled, slapping it away. The bag burst open, spraying the walls with red.

"Clarissa, please," Ramon begged. "You have to try."

With a guttural cry, she launched herself at him. He caught her wrists, holding her at bay.

"Get... Adam..." she choked out.

Ramon looked at me pleadingly. I pursed my lips. Bringing in Adam now seemed unwise. I wasn't sure how he'd react to seeing his mother like this, but if it helped Clarissa...

"Alright," I said. "I'll get him."

Chapter 11

THE BEAST WITHIN CLARISSA receded the moment I led Adam into the room. Her eyes, once feral and ravenous, softened at the sight of her son.

"There's my boy," she crooned, extending her arms toward him. Adam rushed into her embrace. Over his shoulder, Clarissa's gaze met mine, lucid once more.

"Thank you, Mercy."

I nodded, then turned to Ramon. "I'll grab another blood bag. She made a mess of the first one."

Ramon nodded, and I took off out the door.

Clarissa didn't react to my departure. She was focused on her son. Their connection intrigued me. There was something about being together that assuaged Clarissa's rage. I didn't understand it, but there must've been something between the bond between mother and son that affected her temperament. Since no vampire had ever given birth to a vampire child before, all I could do was hypothesize that they were linked profoundly, connected more deeply than even a progeny to her sire.

I secured another donation from one of our maids and brought it back to the room. I handed Clarissa the bag. She released her grip on Adam, and the boy took a few steps back. Clarissa tore open the spout and took a sip.

"Mom, what happened to you?" Adam asked, his voice edged with concern. "They said you lost control..."

Clarissa lowered the blood bag, her face creasing with remorse. "Oh Adam, I'm so sorry. I don't know what came over me. After you and your father left the apartment, it was like I lost control. It was like some monster inside of me was pulling all the strings."

She placed the half-finished blood bag on the table beside her and reached for her son's hands.

"Everything after that is a blur. Your brother and sister. Oh my god, Ramon... are they..."

"They're fine," Ramon intoned. "Confused and scared, but they're with their grandmother."

Clarissa shook her head. "I don't know what happened. All I can remember are flashes, interrupted by an overwhelming feeling of rage." Her voice broke. "I killed that man, didn't I?"

Adam squeezed his mother's hands. "It's okay, Mom. I'm here now."

I cleared my throat. "It could be some kind of separation anxiety," I suggested. "You two clearly share a profound bond. Being apart may have triggered something primal in you, Clarissa."

Ramon furrowed his brow as he considered my theory.

Clarissa trembled, blood-tinged tears pooling in her eyes. "I'm so sorry, Adam. I never meant to hurt anyone. I just... I just missed you so much."

She pulled her son into her arms again. He held her tight as she wept, whispering words of comfort. Watching them, I felt a pang in my barely beating heart. Their bond was something rare and beautiful, even if it came with a dark side.

I shifted uncomfortably as Clarissa continued to sob into Adam's shoulder.

After a few more awkward moments, Adam tensed. His eyes flashed with an otherworldly golden glow, and he pulled back from his mother's embrace.

"What is it?" Ramon asked, his voice sharp with concern.

"I sense something," Adam murmured. "A disturbance. It's faerie magic, but it feels... wrong. Dark."

I straightened, immediately on alert. "Where's it coming from? Can you pinpoint it?"

Adam closed his eyes, brow furrowed in concentration. "It's close. Somewhere in the city." His eyes snapped open, pulsing with frenetic energy. "It's not just one faerie. I don't like how it feels. Not angry, but it's really nasty."

Ramon and I exchanged a worried glance. Unseelie faeries. Probably Redcaps.

"Any idea what they're up to?" I pressed.

Adam shook his head. "I don't get pictures. Just feelings. These are evil faeries. I know it."

I sighed, hating what I had to do next. "Adam, I know your mother needs you right now. But we have to check this out. Can you take me there?"

Ramon's expression darkened. "Absolutely not. My son is not getting dragged into danger."

I held up a placating hand. "I'm not suggesting he fight. But if he can lead us to the source, we can handle it." I turned to Adam. "You might not have to go along. Any chance you could give me a location I can pass to Muggs?"

Adam frowned. "It's not like that. It's like the energy is tugging at me. I just have to give into it and it will take me there. But I can't tell where it's coming from. Only that it's close."

Before Ramon could protest further, Clarissa spoke up. "Let him go."

We both stared at her in surprise. She gave a sad little smile.

"Duty calls, right? I'll be okay." She squeezed Adam's hand, love and resignation mingling in her eyes. "Just come back to me."

Adam hugged her fiercely. "I will, Mom."

Ramon still looked uncertain, but kept silent. If Mom gave her blessing, how couldn't he?

I squared my shoulders, psyching myself up. "All right, let's do this."

Adam turned to me, resolve etched on his boyish face. He offered his hand.

I took it, bracing myself. Traveling via Adam's magic was always a hell of a ride.

Ramon stepped forward, jaw set stubbornly. "I'm coming too. Someone has to look after our boy."

I started to argue, but Clarissa cut in again. "Let him. Please. Don't worry about me. I will manage."

Her quiet authority brooked no debate. Ramon took Adam's opposite hand.

Adam's eyes blazed, and Clarissa's room folded away. My vision blurred, images of the ground above ripping away, the city in front of us bending and warping in front of me until we appeared on a dingy downtown street. Screams and crashes echoed from a nearby building.

Showtime.

We charged toward the building, a seedy-looking bar with a flickering neon sign that read "The Tipsy Faun." I could make out shadowy forms moving violently inside; hear the shrieks of terror.

We burst through the doors, taking in the scene. The place was trashed—broken glass, overturned tables and chairs. Several people cowered along the walls, sobbing and pleading.

In the center of the chaos were the Redcaps. Five of them, chuckling and whooping as they slashed their claws through the air. Blood sprayed, splattering their hats and faces. One Redcap held a man a few feet off the ground by his throat, claws piercing his neck.

Rage boiled through me. I raised my wand. "*Enerva!*"

A blast of magic slammed into the Redcap holding the man aloft. He froze, then toppled over, releasing his victim.

The other Redcaps spun, beady eyes fixing on us. Bloody claws extended.

"More fun!" one crowed. "Come play, lovelies!"

They moved in a blur, ricocheting around the room. I shot a few more spells, but I missed the fast-moving targets.

Ramon was at my side, teeth bared, poised to attack. But he held back, pulling Adam away from the fray.

One Redcap dove over a table and landed just inches in front of me, fetid breath washing over my face. I brought my knee up hard, catching him in the groin. He squealed and staggered. I jammed my wand into his gut. "*Enerva!*"

Two down. Three remained. The others would recover eventually. I still had my Glock, but my better demons told me it was best to keep at least one survivor. If Oberon would not help, maybe one of these bloody bastards could tell me where to find an incubus, or Morgana.

Adam stepped forward, eyes flashing. He approached the nearest Redcap with purposeful strides.

The Redcap turned, still grinning madly despite the situation. "Pretty boy wants to play?"

Adam's hand shot out, grabbing the faerie's shoulder. The Redcap's eyes went wide, a smile frozen in place. His skin paled as Adam's grip tightened.

The Redcap's mouth opened in a silent scream. His body convulsed, then went limp. Adam released him and he crumpled to the ground like a rag doll.

I stared in shock. What did he just do?

Ramon looked equally startled. "Adam?"

Adam didn't respond. He was focused, moving from one fallen Redcap to the next, placing a hand on each. Their chests heaved once, then stilled.

He was draining the life from them. I'd seen many things, but this was new.

When he finished, Adam turned to me, eyes still glowing faintly.

"We should go," he said evenly. "Before more come."

A whimper drew my attention. The bartender peered over the bar, face white.

I approached him slowly. "It's alright," I soothed. "This will all seem like a bad dream."

I placed my palm on his forehead, whispering a memory charm. It was a simple spell, one I sometimes used to make my meals forget our encounter. His eyes glazed over.

Sirens wailed outside. We needed to disappear fast.

I didn't have my comms. I had to use my phone. I quickly dialed up Mel. "We need an exit now. Grab Muggs and send him to The Tipsy Faun. It's a bar in midtown. Things got messy."

"On it," came the reply. "He's here with me. I'll look it up. Hang tight."

I pocketed my phone. Moments later, a portal swirled open nearby. Muggs stepped through, bushy brows rising at the scene.

"What in blazes happened here?"

Before I could explain, the bar doors burst open. Cops streamed in, guns aimed at us.

"Hands up!"

Adam lifted a hand, tilting his head curiously. "Why are you so upset?" His voice was smooth and compelling.

The officers blinked, looking confused. Their aggressive stances relaxed.

"Just a minor misunderstanding," Adam continued. "All is well here."

The police nodded slowly. "All is well," one repeated. Without another word, they turned and left.

I stared at Adam. "How did you do that?"

He shrugged, unfazed. "I don't know. It just felt like the right thing to do."

Muggs cleared his throat loudly. "As riveting as this is, shall we?" He gestured to the portal.

I sighed. "Back to the madhouse it is."

We stepped through, leaving the ruined bar behind. I had a feeling this was just the beginning of the chaos to come.

We emerged into the throne room, Muggs sealing the portal behind us.

Ramon immediately went to Adam. "Are you alright, son?"

Adam nodded. "I'm fine. Just a little tired."

I watched them, seeing genuine concern in Ramon's eyes. He seemed like a different person around his boy.

Mel rushed over. "What happened? I didn't even know you left."

"All taken care of," I said smoothly. Too smoothly. Mel knew me too well. "We didn't have time to gather the team. Adam felt something. People's lives were at stake, so we left."

"Without iron?" Mel asked. "What were you thinking?"

I shook my head. "I still had my gun. Didn't kill them, though. I wanted to take one hostage, but when the cops showed, priorities shifted to getting the fuck out of there."

Muggs sighed. "I can go back and grab one of them. Used your immobilization spell?"

I nodded. "He should be out for a while. There are two of them. Adam drained the other three."

Mel frowned. "Drained?"

I glanced at Adam, who was looking away, lost in thought. "He has a new ability. He can drain the life force from others."

Mel's eyes widened. "Like an incubus?"

I tilted my head. "Sort of. It had a similar effect on them, but he drained faeries, not humans."

Ramon stepped forward. "I don't like this one bit. If he can do that, what's to say Morgana couldn't use him the way she did Cal?"

I nodded in agreement. "We need to be careful. Keep a close eye on Adam. Until we know more, he stays here where he's safe and we can keep an eye on him."

Adam looked up at us, his expression unreadable. "I won't let anyone use me. I don't know who Morgana is, but if she tries to hurt any of you, I'll do to her what I did to the others. Easy peasy."

I raised an eyebrow, both impressed and troubled by his newfound confidence. "Easy peasy, huh? Morgana isn't like those Redcaps. She's powerful. Even more dangerous."

Adam shrugged. "I'm not afraid of her."

Ramon placed a hand on Adam's shoulder. "You should be, son. Morgana is not to be trifled with. She's been around for centuries, and she's one of the most powerful witches in existence."

Adam frowned. "Then why don't we just take her out?"

I shook my head. "It's not that simple. Morgana has an army of loyal followers, and she's protected by powerful magic. Taking her out will require careful planning and a lot of firepower."

Mel nodded. "And we don't even know where she is."

I scratched my head. "Rescuing Ladinas and Alice remains our primary focus. We need to deal with Morgana, and we might need to do that in order to save them. But we cannot kill her. If we do, we could lose them forever."

My words hung in the air for a few moments. Then I turned around and surveyed the room. "Where the hell is Willie?"

No one had noticed until now that Willie was missing. We searched the room, but he was nowhere to be found.

"He was here just a minute ago," Mel said, worry etched on her face. "Where could he have gone?"

Chapter 12

Frantic, I directed the team to fan out and search the entire Underground for Willie. Mel tapped at her tablet, pulling up the security feeds to scan for any sign of him. "That little bugger flies so damn fast he's just a blur on the screen."

"Let's move, people!" My voice echoed through the stone tunnels.

Just as everyone was about to head in their separate directions to search for Willie, Muggs' heavy footsteps halted. He raised his hands in the air. "Everyone, quiet!"

I took a few careful steps toward Muggs. I didn't want my footsteps to drown out the sound of whatever he heard. "What is it, Muggs?"

"I'm not sure," Muggs said. "This way."

Using his staff as a guide, Muggs continued down the labyrinthine halls toward the dormitories. As we got closer, I heard it, too. A faint off key melody drifted from somewhere ahead. "Is that... singing?"

"If you'd call *that* singing." Muggs' brow furrowed. "It sounds like Willie. But what's he singing? Some church song?"

"An old hymn, by the sound of it." I quickened my pace, following the eerie chorus. The hairs on my neck prickled as we traced it to Alice's quarters.

We reached Alice's door, and the singing grew louder. I recognized the melody now. "How Great Thou Art," I murmured. Definitely not a speakeasy tune like those he sang before.

I exchanged an uneasy glance with Muggs. "I don't know how Willie knows that song. Could this be more tampered memories from Oberon?"

Muggs grunted. "Only one way to find out."

I burst through the door, the team close behind me. There, hovering above Alice's bed, was Willie. He wore one of Alice's bras over his shirt, along with a floral dress. As he spun lazily in the air, belting out the hymn, I cleared my throat.

"Ahem! What in damnation are you doing, Willie?"

He halted his spinning and plopped onto the mattress. "What do you mean? This is my room, right?"

I blinked, taken aback. "No, this is definitely Alice's room. Not yours."

Willie frowned, looking around in confusion. Considering the hymn and the fact he thought this was his room, a suspicion nagged at me. "Willie...do you think you're Alice?"

"Well, of course I'm Alice!" He huffed as if it were obvious. "Devout servant of God, slayer of vampires and witches, dedicated to the cause of the Order of the Morning Dawn..."

Willie's rant cut off abruptly as his eyes focused on me. They narrowed, and his face twisted in revulsion.

"Vampires!" he shrieked, pointing an accusing finger. "Foul demons of the night!"

Before I could react, he launched himself at me, fingers curled into claws. I stumbled back, barely avoiding his grasp. If he thought he was Alice, it was the *old* Alice. The same bitch who'd spent the better part of a century trying to put a stake in my heart.

"Willie, stop!" I shouted, but his frenzied attack continued. He swiped and grabbed at us, consumed by pure hatred.

Muggs tried to restrain him, but Willie smashed a lamp across his head. As Muggs reeled back, Willie whirled toward Ramon.

Just before Willie's hands closed around Ramon's throat, Adam stepped in. He seized Willie's wrists, and a visible ripple of calm seemed to flow from his touch into Willie's body.

Willie froze, blinking rapidly. "Why am I in Alice's room?" He looked utterly bewildered.

I let out a shaky breath. Oberon's mental manipulations ran deeper than I'd realized. We'd have to unravel this twisted web of memories, and soon, before it broke Willie's mind completely.

Willie shook his head, rubbing his temples with his fingers. "I don't understand. Why do I have these memories? They're not mine."

THE FURY OF A VAMPIRE WITCH: BOOKS 4-6

He looked at me, his eyes pleading for an explanation. Somehow, Adam's touch gave him a moment of clarity.

I chose my words carefully. "When Oberon had you captive, he tampered with your mind. It seems some of Alice's memories are filling the void he erased."

"But why?" Willie asked. "They're not just one memory. There are bits and pieces. Some feel decades old. Others more recent. Like I—I mean, Alice bought this bra just last week. It's my favorite. Her favorite, I mean. And I knew this was her room. I thought it was mine!"

He started fluttering around the room, growing more agitated.

"I remember hunting vampires with a crossbow and celestial crucifix, stalking them at an illicit bar in the twenties. But I also remember being under Mercy's command, serving loyally in the Underground."

I took a deep breath. It was making sense now. The memories from the speakeasy must've come from one of Alice's old hunts. A place like that would have been prime feeding ground for vampires in the prohibition era.

He gripped his hair in frustration. "None of them feel like my memories, but they're in my head!"

I clenched my fists as the implications of it all dawned on me, a hot flare of anger burning in my chest.

Oberon knew.

He knew where Alice was all this time. Ladinas, too.

Muggs spoke up, voicing my own dreaded thought. "If Oberon has Alice and Ladinas, he's probably got Cal as well."

Ramon looked between us, brow furrowed. "Why would Morgana deliver them to Oberon? Could she have made some kind of mistake?" He shook his head in disbelief. "I can't fathom why a Baobhan Sith would hand over an incubus and two vampires to the Seelie King."

I took a deep breath before answering. "It's because the Unseelie aren't rulerless anymore. They've joined forces with Oberon."

Willie's mouth fell open in shock. Ramon looked similarly stunned.

"But the Seelie and Unseelie courts have been at war for centuries!" Ramon exclaimed.

I nodded grimly. "Exactly. This alliance is unprecedented. And clearly dangerous. With Malvessa gone, we'd assumed the Unseelie were disorganized, looking to Cal for leadership. It appears we were wrong. Cal was following Oberon's orders."

79

Ramon crossed his arms as his wings flinched beneath his trench coat.

I turned to Willie. "You must have figured it out during your captivity. That's why Oberon wiped your mind—to erase any clues about his new alliance."

Willie sank into a chair, shaking his head in disbelief. "That last thing I remember is finding the forest. I went in, intending to confront Oberon. I knew it was a risk, but... they must've caught me. Wiping a prisoner's memories is standard punishment."

"Like a reset button," Mel chimed in. "Take away the memory of an indiscretion, condition the mind to behave in the future. It's brilliant, really."

"In the faerie realm," Willie explained, "a prisoner's memories are replaced with a blank slate. But there, Oberon relied on the magic of the forest. Here, he must've used magic he siphoned from Alice."

"You must've found the forest recently," I added. "We'd lost track of you before Alice, Ladinas, and I confronted Cal and Morgana."

Willie huffed. "I screwed up. I never should have gone into that forest without reporting in. I wanted to come back and impress you, Mercy. I wanted to tell you everything Oberon was doing. Instead, well, I got myself caught. I'm such a dummy pants!"

I shook my head. "You don't need to impress me, Willie. I know your value. Don't beat yourself up over it. What's done is done."

Ramon spoke up hesitantly. "If they've truly joined forces, Oberon might not realize Willie has traces of Alice's memories. Otherwise he never would've let Willie leave."

"You're right," I said. "He wouldn't want Willie revealing anything that could expose his alliance with Morgana and the Unseelie."

My fists clenched again as the implications sank in. Oberon and Morgana together, with Ladinas, Alice and Cal under their control. This changed everything.

"If they're working together, it means Oberon isn't just abducting humans for their life force," I said. "He's using them to feed Ladinas and Alice...so Morgana can siphon their power."

Muggs' eyes widened. "Of course! The Seelie have trouble reproducing on Earth. Oberon must have recruited Morgana to create an army of Baobhan Sith."

"And he's giving Morgana stolen life force in exchange. But why does he need an army of Baobhan Sith?"

The others exchanged uneasy glances. No one wanted to voice the obvious.

An army like that, controlled by Oberon and Morgana... their ambitions could be limitless. They'd be unstoppable. They could wipe out any who stood in their way. Every woman attacked by a Baobhan Sith, would join their ranks. Every man they attacked would die.

"This isn't all bad news," Mel said. "It means we know where to find Alice and Ladinas."

I turned to Mel with a forced smile. Leave it to her to see the positive in a tempestuous shit storm. "You're right. This means Ladinas and Alice aren't trapped in some remote pocket dimension."

Willie shook his head, brow furrowed. "Not necessarily. Faerie prisons aren't constructed of iron bars and walls. There's magic in the faerie realm that Oberon can use to create prison dimensions. Oberon might be using Morgana to do the same. She can use the magic she draws from human spirits to do what Oberon used to do with the power of the forest."

I considered this. It complicated things, but not beyond hope. "Even if that's true, we can still save them. We'll just have to force Morgana to open the portal."

Ramon gave a grim smile. "Easier said than done."

The others nodded, resolve in their eyes. We'd find a way. Come hell or high water, we weren't leaving our friends in faerie prison to be used as batteries to power Morgana and build an army.

"It won't be easy, even getting to them," Willie said. "Storming Oberon's court is dangerous enough. I thought I could sneak in before, but was wrong. If Morgana is with him there..."

He trailed off. We all knew the risks. But we'd brave them for Ladinas and Alice.

I straightened, determination steeling my spine. "It doesn't matter. We'll do whatever it takes. Oberon and Morgana have no idea who they're dealing with. We're going to make them regret the day they crossed us."

Adam took a step forward. "I think I can help."

"Son, it's too dangerous—"

Adam turned toward Ramon and placed a hand on his father's shoulder. "Trust me, Dad. I can do this."

"You don't even know all that you can do!" Ramon insisted. "I won't allow it. Not until we know exactly what your powers are and how you can use them."

"Your father is right, Adam." I took the boy's hand in mine. "I admire your bravery, but you're younger than you look, and you look like you couldn't be over sixteen. You were lucky with those Redcaps. We can't risk your life hoping that your gut tells you what to do when confronting faeries as powerful as Oberon and Morgana."

Adam pulled his hand out of mine. He approached Willie. "Then teach me."

"Teach you?" Willie asked. "Teach you what? I don't know what you can do, either."

I shook my head. Willie wasn't himself. Even if he was, I didn't know if he was prepared to help a being like Adam master his power. There'd never been anyone *like* him before. "We'll all help," I said. "I don't know how we'll do it, but between Muggs and myself, not to mention Ramon and his own faerie power, we'll help you learn what you can do."

"Mercy..." Ramon's voice was shaking. "This is my son, my baby."

"I'm more than that, Dad," Adam insisted. "I *want* to do this!"

"I saw what Adam was capable of in the future," I added. "He was practically unstoppable. Malvessa knew what he could do and manipulated him like a puppet."

"We could return to the faerie realm," Muggs added. "Perhaps we could convince Malvessa to help. We'd need leverage."

"How would we even get there?" Ramon asked. "I know there are ways to access the otherworld, but it's not easy. Not without risking opening the convergence again."

"There is a way," I said. "Oblivion, I could really use your help right now."

A warmth spread through my chest. *I will honor this path. True unity between the faeries will require Malvessa's cooperation.*

As the dragon-gatekeeper's voice echoed in my mind, I didn't even notice that my entire body was enveloped in a golden aura. Not until Mel pointed it out.

"Mercy, is he talking to you?"

I nodded. "He is. This is the path we must take. Malvessa knows how we can help Adam grow into his power. The only way we're going to save Ladinas and Alice and stop Oberon and Morgana is with her help."

Chapter 13

THIS WASN'T THE FIRST time I'd planned a trip into the faerie realm, but the stakes felt higher than ever before.

"I don't like this, Mercy," Ramon said, his dark eyes clouded as he watched Adam discuss with Willie the nature of his power, everything he'd experienced so far, and how thrilled he was to learn how to master it further. "Leaving Clarissa alone, even for a moment..."

"I know," I sighed, meeting Ramon's gaze. "But we have no choice. We need Malvessa's help to defeat Oberon once and for all."

Ramon frowned, his brows knitting together. "And what if time moves differently there? Years could pass on earth while we're gone."

Damn. He had a point. I chewed my bottom lip, considering. We'd used an iron chain to hold the portal open last time, but that might not work again. Still, I had to try to reassure him.

"Mel and Clement will be here to watch over Clarissa," I said gently. "We'll take every precaution to get in and out quickly. I'll ask Antoine to hold the portal open for us."

Before Ramon could respond, a familiar pulse of energy rippled through me. Oblivion's presence stirred within my mind.

There's no need for that, Oblivion said, his voice echoing only in my thoughts. *I can return you to earth only moments after you leave, once your task is complete. No time will be lost.*

I blinked, processing this new information. I turned back to Ramon.

"Oblivion says he can bring us back seconds after we leave," I explained. "Even if it takes years there."

Ramon's expression remained troubled. "I don't know if I like the idea of Adam being away from his mother for so long," he said. "And what if Malvessa tries to manipulate him against us, like you said she could in the future?"

I shook my head firmly. "That won't happen this time. We have leverage over her now."

Ramon still looked uncertain. "How much leverage could we possibly have over her? Malvessa stands unchallenged in the Unseelie Forest. There's no one so dangerous as someone with nothing to lose."

I took a deep breath, choosing my next words carefully.

"Malvessa may seem to have nothing left to lose, but that's not entirely true," I said. "With Oberon controlling the Unseelie on earth, her position in the faerie realm is more precarious than she knows."

Ramon raised an eyebrow, waiting for me to continue.

"Right now, Malvessa is alone in the Unseelie Forest, stripped of her court and her power. But if Oberon gains enough strength, he could potentially return and bring all of the Unseelie fae back with him. They would return as his subjects, not hers."

I met Ramon's gaze steadily. "Malvessa won't want that. She'll help us if only because she'll want to stop Oberon before he gets too strong. Whatever her past manipulations, helping us is in her own best interests."

Ramon considered this, his expression thoughtful. After a long moment, he sighed.

"I suppose you're right," he admitted. "As a father, though, I don't like the idea of such an insidious creature holding sway over my son. And as a husband, I am concerned for Clarissa. But if we truly return mere moments after leaving..." He trailed off, looking back up at me.

"Then she should be fine," I finished gently. "We'll get this done quickly, Ramon. Clement will take care of Clarissa in our absence. If all goes according to plan, she won't even know we were gone."

Ramon stared at the wall, lost in his thoughts. Eventually, he released a drawn-out sigh. "As long as I've know you, Mercy, you've never failed me. But this time, I have a family to think about."

I nodded. "I understand. This isn't without its risks, but think about what will happen if we don't succeed. Losing Ladinas and Alice will be one thing. But if

Oberon succeeds, if he and Morgana raise an army... is that the kind of world you want for your family?"

Ramon forced a smile. "I'm trusting you, Mercy. But if things don't go well with Malvessa, promise me you'll get Adam out of there and back to his mother."

"You'll be with me, Ramon. Give me the word, and if things are getting out of hand, we'll leave. I won't let her hurt Adam."

Willie flew over, Adam shuffling up behind him. "One thing to consider, Mercy. Using Oblivion's power to open the convergence, even for a few seconds...it could draw Oberon's attention."

I paused, considering his words. He had a point. Oberon would probably sense it the moment Oblivion opened the portal.

"You're right," I said finally. "As soon as we return, Oberon may make a move against us." I met Willie's eyes resolutely. "We'll need the entire Underground on guard at the convergence. The moment we get back, we'll need to be ready to fight him off."

Willie nodded slowly. "Long as we really do zip right back here, we should come home with the kid in full command of his powers. That'll give us a fighting chance."

Before we could leave, we needed to prepare the team. I needed Mel and Clement to stay on guard at the Underground. Antoine and the rest needed to prepare. I called Antoine into the throne room via our intercoms.

"Get everyone ready for a fight with the faeries," I said when he entered. "We're moving out soon. Load the SUVs with iron rounds, knives, swords, everything we've got."

Antoine raised an eyebrow. "What's the play?"

"We're opening a portal to the faerie dimension. But the moment we return, Oberon may bring the battle to us."

Antoine nodded. "No problem. We'll be ready to roll out within the hour."

As Antoine left, I hurried to the orphanage while Ramon and Adam stopped in to check on Clarissa. Ramon said he wouldn't tell her exactly what we were up to. The last thing Clarissa needed was something to worry about. But they wanted a chance to say their goodbyes. For Ramon and Adam, there was no telling how long it would be before we got back. Even if, for Clarissa, we'd only be gone a few hours at most.

I found Clement supervising the orphans per usual. I briefed him on the plan. "I need you to keep an eye on Clarissa while we're gone. Make sure she's fed, if necessary."

He frowned but nodded. "Of course. But...how long will you be gone exactly?"

"No time at all, for you. But it could be days, months, or even years for us. There's no way to know. Just... keep her safe."

Before I knew what happened, Clement hugged me. I wasn't a hugger. I awkwardly patted him on the back. "I'll take care of her. Be careful, Mercy."

I grinned. "Careful? Please. Careful is my middle name."

Clement deadpanned. "No it isn't."

I chuckled. "You're right. But in this case, we'll have Adam with us. We're going to be in for one hell of a fight when we get back. We can't afford any losses in the Unseelie Forest. So, yes. Despite the protests of my lesser demons, I will exercise an abundance of caution."

After I left the orphanage, I met Ramon and Adam at the elevators. Antoine, Muggs, Willie, and the rest were already in the warehouse, ready to depart.

"How was Clarissa?" I asked.

"Relieved when we walked in," Ramon said. "Distressed when we left. I hated not being able to tell her the truth about what we're doing."

I nodded understandingly. "It's for the best. The last thing she needs is anything to make her more anxious than she already is."

We met up with the rest of the team and took the SUVs out to the forest, parking just shy of the wide clearing surrounding the convergence. My legion fanned out, encircling the shimmering portal, weapons raised. The air hummed with energy.

I stood at the convergence and whispered, "Oblivion. It's time."

A pulse of green light appeared before me, coalescing into the form of a beautiful blond man in shimmering scale armor. He strode forward and placed a hand against the portal.

With a great rush of wind, the convergence opened in a swirl of golden energy. Oblivion turned to me and placed a hand on my chest. "It is done. Call me again when you're ready to return. Do not evoke my name before that lest Malvessa make an attempt to extract my essence from you."

"She can do that?" I raised an eyebrow.

"Remember," Oblivion toned. "She and Oberon once conspired to bind me to a blade. I do not know if she has the power to do so again without the cooperation of Oberon, but we'll be in her domain. There's no telling how much power she might extract from the forest."

"Got it. I won't call you until the mission is done."

With a nod, Oblivion dissolved back into vapor and returned to me. The warmth of his presence swelled within my chest for a moment, then faded.

I turned back to Antoine. "See you guys in a few seconds. Remember, be ready for a fight."

Antoine smirked. "I'm always ready for a fight."

Chapter 14

THE WISPS DANCED IN the trees, casting eerie shadows across our path. I shivered, the darkness heavier than I remembered. Too quiet. Even the constant drizzle couldn't mask the unnatural silence.

"Are we there yet?" Adam asked.

I chuckled. It was easy to forget that he was so young given his strength and usual calm demeanor.

"Not yet," Ramon said. "We aren't exactly sure when we'll arrive. We don't know where Malvessa is."

Thirty seconds later.

"Are we there yet?"

I snickered as Ramon explained again that it would take as long as it takes. We weren't heading for a destination; we were seeking the faerie queen.

I was a little surprised Malvessa didn't show up the moment we set foot in her domain. I expected she'd confront us straight away. Why hadn't she? I knew it wouldn't be a happy reunion.

Muggs tilted his head, listening. "Something's coming."

I heard nothing at all, but I readied my wand anyway. We weren't there to fight, but Malvessa didn't know that. We needed to be ready to defend ourselves.

Something fell from the trees and covered all of us. "What the hell?"

Ramon grunted as he thrashed against ropes. "It's a goddamn net!"

Muggs stood in the middle of us, laughing, the net resting over his head. He was the tallest of the bunch. Meanwhile, Willie fluttered about, darting from one side of the net to the next, trying to find a way out.

"Who's out there!" I shouted. "This damn thing won't hold us forever."

I grabbed the ropes and pulled. I thought I'd tear through it, but the ropes cinched tighter. I thrashed against the net as high-pitched cackles erupted around us. Fork-wielding clurichauns poured from the trees, their shrieks piercing my ears. I'd met a band of clurichauns before. They were annoying, but mostly harmless.

"Well, well, what have we here?" one slurred, prodding me with his dulled fork. I bared my fangs with a hiss. The idiot just grinned wider.

"Happy catch! Happy catch!" they chanted, stumbling around us. The stench of faerie whiskey burned my nose.

Ramon clutched Adam close as the clurichauns circled us, singing and dancing. Anger simmered in my veins. We didn't have time for this drunken idiocy.

"Enough!" I shouted, silencing their inane song. "Let us pass or you'll regret it."

The clurichauns blinked at me, mouths agape. One with wild red hair and a forked beard stepped forward.

"Mercy?" He tugged at his beard. "Never thought I'd see you back here."

I tilted my head. "McRory?"

"Indeed! Are you a fool? You barely got out of here alive the last time!"

"I need to see Malvessa," I said. "It's urgent."

McRory's bushy brows rose. "Come to finish the job, have you? Sending her away wasn't enough?"

I clenched my jaw. He didn't understand.

"There are bigger things at stake now," I said. "It concerns the faeries still on earth. Not only Oberon, but her former court as well."

McRory peered through the net, studying my companions. "Wee Willie Winker? Is that you? And Ramon, the vampire-turned faerie?"

Willie charged at the net, but it held him back. "Let us out, McRory!"

I tilted my head. "You know each other?"

"We've met," Willie said. "We fought a few times during the faerie wars."

McRory waved his hand through the air. "Ah, yes. Those were the days! I almost forgot how much fun our skirmishes used to be."

"How do you know me?" Ramon asked. "I don't believe we've met."

McRory shrugged. "We've never been formally introduced. But I saw you back when you met with Malvessa and Oberon to negotiate control over the portal. Clever work, then! Been a long time."

Ramon nodded. "Doesn't seem so long ago to me."

I cleared my throat. "It doesn't matter how you know each other. We're here for a reason. We need to speak to Malvessa."

"Good luck with that," McRory muttered. "We haven't seen her in ages."

My chest tightened. "What do you mean?"

McRory shook his head sadly. "Without her court, her power faded. She cannot draw more power from the forest without the aid of her Baobhan Sith."

"Where was she last seen?" I asked. "Can you take us there?"

McRory scratched his beard again, considering. I could almost see the whiskey-soaked gears turning in his brain.

"Aye, I could take you to her palace," he finally said. "I suspect she languishes within. Though can't say for sure. None of us dare approach the queen unless summoned."

"But you can take us there?" I asked.

"I could," McRory said. "But I have a better idea."

I tilted my head. "Oh?"

"We drink! We sing! We dance! You'll soon forget about your problems, you'll see!"

I sighed, knowing McRory's love for revelry often overshadowed more pressing matters.

"That's a kind offer," I said. "But I'm afraid we must decline. Perhaps another time."

McRory's face fell into an exaggerated pout. "You're no fun at all!"

"Sorry," I said flatly. "Now, about Malvessa..."

McRory held up his hands. "Fine, fine. I'll take you to her palace. Later. When we're done."

"Done what? Drinking?" I raised an eyebrow.

"Of course! And the drinking never ends! Hee hee hee!"

I cleared my throat. "If I have one drink with you, will you take us to the queen?"

"One drink?" McRory blew a raspberry. "You can't have just one! Once you start, you can't stop! At least I can't!"

Ramon sighed. "Been there, buddy. You might need a twelve-step meeting."

"Twelve stumbles!" McRory cackled. "I haven't taken a proper step since... well... since ever!"

I tugged at the ropes. "Can you at least take this net off of us?"

"Oh! I almost forgot!" McRory snapped his fingers and several of his companions raced over and pulled the net back over our heads.

He snapped his fingers again and his clurichaun companions began passing out carved wooden cups brimming with amber liquid. The scent hit my nose—earthy, pungent, with hints of honey and oak. Definitely faerie whiskey.

Adam's eyes went wide as a cup was placed in his small hands. "Can I try it, Dad?"

Ramon swiftly plucked the cup away. "Absolutely not."

"But Daaad!" Adam protested, stomping his foot.

"You're far too young for faerie whiskey," Ramon admonished. "This is not juice or milk."

"The boy's got spirit!" McRory chuckled. "Let him live a little."

I shot McRory a sharp look. "He's just a kid." I turned to Adam. "It tastes nasty anyway. You'd hate it."

Adam scowled, but seemed to accept my words. Ramon nodded gratefully at me.

I faced McRory again. "Now, the palace?"

McRory's perpetual grin faded. He pulled the end of his beard and looked away.

"The queen... she hasn't been herself for some time now."

I felt a knot form in my stomach. "What do you mean?"

McRory met my gaze, his eyes uncharacteristically solemn. "Ever since the Baobhan Sith were banished along with the rest of the court, the queen has grown weaker and weaker. She barely leaves her chambers these days."

"But we need to speak with her," I insisted. "It's urgent. A child's life hangs in the balance."

McRory held up his hands. "You're welcome to try, but I doubt she'll see anyone. Not even me, her most devoted and *fearsome* subject." He sighed heavily.

I glanced around at the shadowy forest, unease creeping up my spine. The darkness seemed thicker than before, the wisps dimmer. An unnatural hush lay over the woods.

This was not the same Unseelie forest I remembered. Something was very wrong here.

And if the queen was as far gone as McRory said... would she even have the magic needed to help Adam?

Doubt and dread churned within me, but I shoved them down. We'd come too far to turn back now.

"Take us to her," I told McRory, steel in my voice. "If she ails, we can help."

Helping Malvessa was the last thing I ever thought I'd do. Desperate times. Desperate measures. I knew now, though, that she had more reason to *want* to help us than I'd expected. Oberon's threat was daunting enough were he to ever return to the faerie realm, especially in her present condition. We might be able to convince her to help to both give us a fighting chance against the Seelie King and by offering her a chance to regain her power. McRory studied me a moment, then nodded.

"Follow me then. And tread carefully. The forest has only grown more treacherous in her absence."

With that ominous warning, he turned and headed into the shadowy woods. Ramon gripped Adam's hand tightly as we fell in behind.

Our group followed McRory deeper into the woods. The farther we went, the more it felt like the very air was weighing down on us.

Adam clung to Ramon, wide eyes trying to pierce the gloom. I could tell the unnatural stillness was getting to him, too.

"Are we there yet?" I asked McRory. Then I turned and winked at Adam.

"Not far now. Her majesty resides just ahead, in the heart of the forest."

He gestured to a stone archway, vines curling over it. Two shadowy forms flanked the entrance. They looked like guards. I thought all the Unseelie, apart from the clurichauns, were on earth.

As we approached, I saw they were made of twisted wood, grotesque but lifelike sculptures.

McRory bowed deeply. "Good sirs, I have brought the witch Mercy and her companions to see the queen. Please grant us passage."

The wooden guards didn't respond. I exchanged glances with Ramon.

"Just go with it," Ramon whispered.

McRory clapped his hands. "Good news! They'll allow us passage!"

"Yippee!" I couldn't hide my sarcasm. McRory scurried through the archway. We followed close behind.

The sight inside turned my blood to ice. Malvessa sat motionless on a throne of gnarled roots, skin paper-white, eyes vacant. More twisted subjects, trees warped to look like her former servants, lay scattered around the courtyard. It was sad. A little pathetic. She'd been stuck here for centuries, a lot longer than the time that had passed on earth for us. Her pretend subjects, allowing her to play at court, were the closest thing she'd had to companions in all that time. The clurichauns were too afraid of her to pay her visits.

I rushed forward, feigning a bow as I approached. Revering Malvessa turned my stomach, but we had to show her respect if we wanted her help. Her eyes remained fixed ahead, unseeing.

"Malvessa," I said urgently. "It's Mercy. Do you remember me?"

No response. I waved a hand in front of her face. Nothing.

McRory wailed. "See the tragedy that has befallen us! Without her court to sustain her, the queen has withered away!"

I examined Malvessa closely. Her chest barely moved with breath. How was she even alive?

"There must be something we can do," I insisted. "Some way to revive her."

Muggs stepped forward, placing a hand on Malvessa's forehead. He closed his eyes, chanting under his breath. The air hummed with gathering power.

Malvessa inhaled sharply. Her eyes refocused, fixing on me.

"You," she rasped. "The vampire returns. Why?"

"I need your help. More specifically, the child you carried needs your guidance."

Malvessa's confused gaze turned toward Adam. "Son? Is that you?"

Adam grunted. "You're not my mother."

Ramon elbowed Adam in the ribs.

"But I am," Malvessa said, somehow finding the strength to rise from her throne. "At least, I'm one of your mothers. My power flows in your veins. Yes... I can feel it. Come closer."

I grabbed Adam's arm and turned back toward Malvessa. "Not so fast. We won't let you harm the boy."

"Harm him?" Malvessa shook her head. "I wouldn't dare. You, on the other hand..."

I snorted. "Perhaps we can set aside our history. Adam needs your help. He's the only one who stands a chance to stop Oberon."

Malvessa cocked an eyebrow. "Stop Oberon? What has the pretentious king done to deserve your wrath, vampire?"

I sighed. "He's claimed your court as his own. They follow him, now. He's breeding Baobhan Sith. It's only a matter of time before he finishes whatever he's doing on earth and returns. I think it would be in your interest, as much as it is ours, to help us defeat him."

Malvessa pondered my words for a moment, her eyes distant. Finally, she spoke. "Very well. I will help you."

A spark of hope ignited within me. "Thank you, Malvessa. What do we need to do?"

Malvessa looked at Adam again. "He must drink from me. He is a vampire, as much as he is faerie. By consuming my blood, he will assume my throne."

Ramon stepped forward. "My son will not become the Unseelie King!"

Malvessa chuckled softly. "Fear not, Ramon. The Unseelie court is mine to give, and I give it freely to our son. He is my only heir. I fear I'm too far gone to ever regain my strength. I cannot help you. But Adam can challenge Oberon. He can reclaim authority over my court."

I tilted my head. "Including Morgana?"

Malvessa nodded. "Indeed."

"But what about my powers?" Adam asked. "Can you teach me how to use them? I need to know what I can do."

Malvessa stepped toward Adam. I let her pass. Ramon clenched his fists but I shot him a death stare. We wouldn't get very far if we kept her and Adam apart. She placed her bony hands on Adam's cheeks. "Yes, I will teach you what I know. But son, you are stronger than I ever imagined. There may be more, still, that you can do that's beyond my knowledge."

Chapter 15

RAMON, MUGGS, AND I stood around the edges of Malvessa's courtyard as we watched her train Adam. Willie hovered in the air overhead, watching from a distance. The Unseelie Queen was a shadow of her former terrifying glory—her wings drooped, her skin sagged, her hair hung limp and colorless. I almost pitied her. Almost.

"Hard to believe she was once so powerful," I muttered.

Ramon shifted uncomfortably beside me. "I don't miss the old Malvessa one bit. You didn't have to live with her like I did, not after I first became fae. Time moves differently here. I was with her for years before she betrayed me, went to the human world, and possessed Clarissa."

I snorted. "Yeah, after you knocked her up. Real smart move there."

Ramon bristled. "It wasn't like that. I thought so much time had passed that Clarissa would have moved on. I didn't think I was cheating." His voice dropped. "When we came back to earth, I was elated to see that barely any time had passed on earth. But it gutted me when Malvessa forced herself into Clarissa."

I sighed. "She's no friend, but she's fading fast. This might be Adam's only chance to really know her. As much as we hate her, he needs this time with his mother." I lowered my voice. "If the boy can control the Unseelie, we might actually defeat Oberon."

Ramon fell silent as we watched Malvessa guide Adam through a series of exercises, her voice barely above a whisper. Though frail, her movements still held an ethereal grace.

She showed Adam how to gather his energy and teleport by folding space itself. At first he stumbled, blinking in and out of view, but soon he was popping smoothly from one side of the courtyard to the other. Then Malvessa instructed him to push his limits, to use his power to move as far as it would take him. He couldn't move beyond the Unseelie Forest. But it was a vast place.

I tensed as Adam vanished completely. A few seconds later, he reappeared at Malvessa's side, grinning. He wouldn't be limited to teleporting only when other fae used their powers now. This small freedom meant everything to him.

Next, Malvessa had Adam summon the clurichauns. The task? To use his newfound power as Malvessa's heir, the newly crowned Unseelie King, to exercise influence over his subjects. An important lesson to master if he was going to arrest the Redcaps and Baobhan Sith, including Morgana, from Oberon's command. Under Malvessa's watchful eye, Adam set them to various tasks—moving boulders, weaving illusions from mist and moonlight, conjuring massive vats of faerie whiskey.

Though playful, the clurichauns took Adam seriously as the new Unseelie King. Their antics made Adam laugh. For a moment, I glimpsed the carefree child he might have been under different circumstances.

Malvessa called for a break, her pale face glistening with sweat. McRory brought her a mug of his special brand of drink. Probably not the best thing for someone already ailing, but she gulped it down like Gatorade.

Malvessa handed her mug back to McRory and beckoned us over.

"He's ready for a true test," she said. "I've asked McRory and his troop to spar with Adam, to push his abilities."

McRory swaggered up, a dozen clurichauns at his side, ever eager to prove his worth. He may have been a simple clurichaun, but he fancied himself a warrior.

Adam's eyes lit up at the challenge. He bounced on the balls of his feet, limbering up.

I wasn't sure how well he'd fare against the little buggers. The clurichauns weren't fierce fighters by any means, but they were crafty, quick, and they outnumbered him.

Adam looked over at us with a cocky grin. "Don't worry. I got this."

Malvessa gave him a wistful look. "I hope so, my son. You must understand that this is not just a test of your physical abilities, but also of your mental strength. You must learn to control your powers and use them wisely.

Adam nodded, his expression growing serious. "I understand, Mother. I won't let you down."

With that, the clurichauns charged. Adam moved with lightning speed, dodging and weaving around their attacks. He flickered in and out of view, teleporting behind them and delivering swift kicks and punches. The clurichauns were taken aback, but quickly regrouped and swarmed around him.

Ramon and I watched intently, ready to jump in if needed.

But it was unnecessary. Adam was holding his own and then some. His powers were no longer just a fledgling ability, but a force to be reckoned with. The clurichauns were tiring and faltering, while Adam appeared to only be gaining strength. He was tapping into something deep within himself, pulling out all the stops against his opponents. His eyes glowed with an intensity that sent shivers down my spine.

I wondered just how powerful he could become if he truly mastered his abilities. The thought was both thrilling and terrifying.

Finally, with a loud shout, Adam delivered a final blow to the last clurichaun. The little creature flew across the courtyard and hit a wall with a thud.

Adam turned to us, his chest heaving with exertion. "How was that?"

Malvessa looked at him with pride in her eyes. "Impressive. You have exceeded my expectations, my son."

Adam beamed. "Thanks, Mother. I couldn't have done it without your guidance."

Ramon winced at hearing Adam call her Mother. But he swallowed his protest and stepped forward, clapping his hands. "That was incredible, Adam! You're a natural warrior."

I nodded in agreement. "You definitely have some serious skills, Adam. With your power and our knowledge, we might just have a chance against Oberon and his army."

Adam's expression grew serious. "I know. This is incredible. I'm ready to show that faerie king what I'm made of."

Malvessa's face softened. "I'm proud of you, my son. You have proven yourself today. But remember, Oberon is a powerful and ancient foe. He's as strong as I ever was. Even if you can gather the rest of our court at your side to fight him, he'll be more than a match."

Adam's face twisted in frustration. "But we have to try, don't we? We can't let him keep hurting people and destroying our world."

Malvessa nodded slowly. "Yes, you must try. And you will need every tool at your disposal to defeat him." She gestured to Ramon, Muggs, and me. "But you won't do it alone. They will be with you every step of the way."

Adam's eyes shone with determination. "I know. And we'll find a way to win. We have to."

With that, we all fell silent, lost in our own thoughts and fears. The battle ahead loomed large in all our minds, but for the moment, we could rest easy knowing that Adam was growing stronger and more capable every day. He was the key to our success, and we'd do everything in our power to help him achieve it.

Malvessa retired for the day. I didn't sleep at all. I didn't need to. Willie could have used some of his special faerie dust to force us asleep. He was Wee Willie *Winker* after all, but I didn't like the idea of a forced slumber in a treacherous realm. I didn't really trust Malvessa, no matter how much leverage we thought we had. Muggs and Ramon were equally alert, despite their attempts to get in a nap, but Adam snored like a lumberjack.I wasn't sure if he required more sleep than other vampires—he had a human side, after all, and he was also a faerie.

As I lay there in the darkness, my mind kept returning to Adam's incredible display of power. The way he had moved with such grace and precision, dispatching the clurichauns with ease. I couldn't help but wonder what else he was capable of.

Eventually Malvessa reemerged from her room, looking just as sickly as ever, but with a little more life in her eyes.

"Today's training will involve all of you," Malvessa added, glancing at Ramon, Muggs and myself. "I've set up an obstacle course through the forest. Take your places and do your best to hinder Adam's progress."

I raised an eyebrow. "You want us to fight against Adam?"

Malvessa smiled thinly. "How else will he learn to wield true power? The clurichauns are spirited, for sure, but they're not natural warriors like the three of you."

Ramon shook his head. "I can't *fight* my son, Malvessa."

Malvessa sighed. "You don't have to fight him, Ramon. Just try to slow him down. He needs to learn how to face obstacles, and you can help him with that."

I nodded, understanding the reasoning behind her plan. "Okay, we'll do it."

Muggs cracked his knuckles. "I'm ready. Bring it on."

Malvessa led us to the edge of the forest, where a series of obstacles had been set up. McRory and his band of drunken clurichauns had put in a full night's work. The course comprised a series of ropes, walls, and pits, which Adam had to navigate through while we tried to impede his progress.

Adam looked at the course with a mixture of excitement and trepidation. "This looks intense."

Malvessa nodded. "It is. But you're up for the challenge, I know it."

With a determined nod, Adam stepped up to the starting line. Ramon, Muggs, and I positioned ourselves at various points along the course.

I took my position near a marshy pit criss-crossed with vines. Soon I heard Adam approaching, twigs cracking under his feet.

With a flick of my wand, and the proper incantation, I blasted my *enerva* spell at him. But he merely raised a hand, neutralizing my spell with a pulse of his own magic.

"Nice try!" Adam laughed, darting past me. I had to admit, his progress impressed me.

At last Adam reached the heart of the forest, where Ramon, Muggs and McRory waited. They tag-teamed him with weapons, spells, and brute force, but Adam held his own. He teleported between trees, confusing his opponents. With blasts of energy, he knocked McRory flat on his back.

Finally, Adam burst from the forest, victorious.

Malvessa applauded him, a small smile on her face. "Well done, my son. You've proven yourself yet again."

Adam grinned, rubbing his hands together. "That was exhilarating. I feel like I could take on anything now."

Ramon stepped forward, looking at him with a mixture of pride and concern. "You're getting better every day, Adam. But don't let your guard down. We're up against a formidable foe. You must be careful your confidence doesn't become arrogance."

Adam nodded, his expression growing serious. "I know, Dad. I won't let you down. I'll keep training until I'm ready for anything."

Malvessa's smile faded. "Speaking of which, we need to talk about your next phase of training. It's going to be more difficult than anything you've faced so far."

Adam's eyebrows furrowed. "What do you mean?"

Malvessa looked at him gravely. "You need to learn how to control your faerie and vampire powers simultaneously. It's a delicate balance, but one that's necessary if you want to defeat Oberon."

Adam's eyes widened in realization. "That's going to be tough. I barely have a handle on my powers as it is."

Malvessa nodded. "I know. But it's necessary. You have to learn to harness the power of both your faerie and vampire sides if you want to stand a chance against Oberon."

Adam took a deep breath. "Okay. I'll do it. When do we start?"

Malvessa smiled thinly. "Tomorrow morning. Be prepared. I do not know the full extent of what you might be capable of as a vampire. This next phase of your training will require the help of your friends."

I nodded. "We've got your back, Adam."

We gathered back in the courtyard. I noticed how heavily Malvessa leaned on her throne, as if the day's efforts had exhausted her. She bid us goodnight and retired to her chambers.

Adam bubbled with excitement, recounting each obstacle he'd overcome. His enthusiasm was infectious. For a moment, we forgot our worries and simply shared in Adam's joy.

But as the night progressed, I couldn't shake the feeling of unease that had settled in the pit of my stomach. Malvessa's warning about harnessing both his faerie and vampire powers simultaneously filled me with dread. It reminded me of when Muggs first turned. I was so afraid, then, of what he might do if he lost control, the full power of his druidic magic warped to serve his vampiric instincts. The thought of Adam losing control of his powers and succumbing to the darkness that came with being a vampire was a lot to consider. As a vampire, he was *still* a youngling. He had power, sure, but he was also vulnerable. It doesn't take much for a youngling to lose control. The slightest thing can set one off. A little anger, something that didn't go his way, or exposure to human blood, could send him into a rage.

I tried to push the thoughts aside, focusing on Adam's laughter and the warmth of the fire. But as the night wore on, my fears only grew stronger.

Eventually, the fire burned down to embers, and Adam drifted off to sleep. Muggs and Ramon soon followed suit, leaving me alone with my thoughts.

I lay there, staring up at the dark sky. My thoughts were interrupted when Muggs sprang to his feet. "Something's wrong. I sense a disturbance in the energy of this place."

From Malvessa's room came a faint gasp. My chest tightened. We raced to her chambers and threw open the doors.

Malvessa lay crumpled on the floor, pale and lifeless. Her skin had a waxy, translucent sheen, and her eyes stared vacantly at the ceiling. Dark veins webbed beneath her flesh.

"No," Adam whimpered, clutching her limp body. "Mother, please..."

Ramon checked for a pulse and shook his head grimly. Malvessa was gone.

Adam trembled, tears spilling down his cheeks. I wrapped my arms around him, my heart aching for his pain. He never really knew the real Malvessa. It was probably for the best. I'd lived my entire existence thinking my father was a monster. It was a burden that, at the very least, our quest into the Unseelie forest spared him from carrying.

Ramon, Willie, and Muggs carried Malvessa's body outside. I wasn't sure how much help Willie was—he was stronger than he looked, but Ramon and Muggs were strong enough. At least Willie felt like he was helping. Beneath a towering oak, we dug her grave in silence. McRory and the clurichauns joined us, singing a dirge. For once, they appeared sober. McRory handed Adam a single violet flower. Adam took it and placed it on Malvessa's chest before we lowered her into the ground.

As we filled the hole with dirt, Adam whispered, "Goodbye, Mother. Thank you for everything." He wiped his eyes, standing taller. The boy was becoming a man before my eyes. He'd probably grown a whole foot since we arrived.

I squeezed Adam's shoulder. "She'd be proud of you. Now let's make her prouder still."

Adam nodded, jaw set with determination. Together, we turned and walked into the shadowed forest. Willie flew in silence beside me. I didn't forget what the next day's training was supposed to entail, but without Malvessa, the burden fell on us.

Chapter 16

THE CLURICHAUNS' SHRILL CHEERS grated my ears as we trudged through the gnarled trees back to the convergence. Their wrinkled faces glowed with worship as they reached out to touch Adam, their new king. Adam shifted uncomfortably under their adoration, his shoulders hunched.

Adam looked at me and sighed. "You're a queen, right? How long did it take you to get used to people treating you different?"

I barked out a laugh. "Who says I have?"

Adam raised an eyebrow. I sighed, glancing back at the clurichauns still chanting Adam's praises.

"When you're queen, or a king, I imagine, no one shows their true self. It's the loneliest damn thing there is." My voice dropped, bitter memories rising. "Sure, they'll grovel at your feet, tell you exactly what you want to hear. But it's all an act. Makes you feel like you can't trust anyone."

Adam was quiet, thoughtful. I envied his innocence. Physically, he was growing up quick. Emotionally, he was going to have to catch up fast.

Adam glanced at me, his brow furrowed. "What about Ladinas? You two seem close."

I let out a long breath. "Ladinas is different. He was royalty himself, once upon a time, so he gets it. I think that's why we came together in the first place. Both of us were just so damn lonely. Figured we might as well be lonely together."

I gave a wry chuckle. Ladinas and I had our issues, but he'd proven himself loyal. He was one of the few who saw me, scars and all, and loved me for me. Not for my bloodline, my status, my position.

Muggs sidled up beside us, having overheard our conversation. "You're never as alone as you think, Mercy," he said gently. "You've got three progeny, two of whom would tear the world apart for you, and one still cooking."

I smiled softly at the old druid. "I know, Muggs. Thank you." I meant it, even though it wasn't the same. Progeny, children...it dulled the loneliness but didn't erase it fully.

Some burdens only monarchs carry, I thought ruefully. But the clurichauns continued their raucous praises, blissfully unaware of the angst, the isolation, the pressure that came with a crown.

Adam glanced between us, brow furrowed. "My father said it was always like that for you. Even before your sire died, you didn't connect with many people."

I tensed slightly. Ramon would know, I supposed. For decades after my turning, it had just been Nico and the two of us.

"He's right," I said finally. "I've always been... selective with who I let in. But eventually I opened up. Found a few I trusted beyond doubt to be my eyes and ears. That's the key, I think. Surround yourself with people you'd trust with your life. The rest comes in time."

I hoped Adam would understand. The isolation of leadership was something he'd face soon himself. But for now, we had a convergence to get to and a new king to present to the Unseelie on earth.

We emerged from the forest into the familiar rocky clearing, the convergence shimmering just ahead. I took a deep breath, reaching inward for the dormant dragon spirit.

"Oblivion," I called softly. "Time to go home."

The air rippled, coalescing into the now-familiar form. Oblivion stood before us in a human glamour, clad in shimmering green-scaled robes, golden hair tickling his brow. Power thrummed from him, setting my senses alight.

"Mercy," he greeted, then turned to Adam. "And the new Unseelie King. A wise choice."

I raised a brow. "So it meets with your approval?"

"It was inevitable," Oblivion replied mildly. "What is destined cannot be undone. The strands of fate converge here, now."

"And Malvessa's death?" I pressed. "Was that destined as well?"

Oblivion's eyes softened, his ageless gaze holding mine. "A faerie's death comes only when their power is spent. When they lack even the strength to draw more unto themselves. This was Malvessa's fate."

Ramon spoke up from behind me. "Does the same hold true for Adam? If he keeps expending his magic without rest..."

Oblivion turned to study Adam, eyes narrowed in consideration. "The boy is unique. His human spirit sustains the vampire, the vampire empowers the fae. A perfect trinity." He paused, meeting my gaze. "But all strengths have weaknesses. Oberon will seek to exploit the humanity in him. Tempt the vampire to rage and bloodlust. You must be ready."

I clenched my jaw. Oberon would doubtless strike back for this upset in his machinations. But we were forewarned and forearmed.

I turned to the rest of the group. "Remember, Oberon might be there on the other side when we return, with his army. We need to be ready to fight the second we step through."

Muggs, Ramon, and Willie nodded their understanding. Oblivion bent down and touched the convergence with his hands. It shimmered to life.

"Any last advice?" I asked Oblivion.

The dragon-gatekeeper smiled at me. "Do what you must. When you return, only a few minutes will have passed on earth. A great deal can happen in mere minutes. Remember your task. The boy is the key, now, to restoring the balance."

"Between the Seelie and Unseelie," I said. "I remember."

"And much more than that," Oberon said. Before I could ask him to clarify what that meant, though, he returned to an ethereal mist and forced himself back into my body.

With a deep breath, I stepped forward, followed closely by Adam and my loyal companions. We stepped through the convergence and the world around us swirled into a kaleidoscope of colors.

When our feet hit the ground earth side, I was struck by the bright light that glowed around us. I shielded my face, expecting the sunlight to burn my skin. If only minutes passed, why was it so bright?

Then, as I looked around and saw Antoine and the rest of the Underground standing armed beside us, I noticed the light above wasn't coming from the sun.

A vast dome of light was set over us.

"What in the world is this?" I asked. Antoine shook his head. "We aren't sure. It happened just seconds after you stepped into the portal. We expected it was Oberon, but the faeries didn't attack."

Willie grunted. "It's a veil."

"What kind of veil?" Muggs asked.

"Something to slow us down, to stop us from using portals to come or go. A veil like this is like a barrier that prevents any magic from reaching beyond it."

"Screws with technology too," Antoine added. "Our comms are down."

"Oberon's up to something," I said. "Everyone, get to the SUVs quick. We need to get back to the Underground."

Chapter 17

THE VEIL LOOMED AHEAD, a shimmering curtain of gold cutting through the darkness. I gripped the steering wheel, knuckles white.

"Muggs, get ready. The second we break through, I need you to zap us into the Underground."

The druid nodded, hands hovering, ready to cast. The SUV jolted as we passed into the veil. Static crackled over my skin. I slammed the brakes. I glanced at Muggs.

"Now!"

Muggs' brow furrowed in concentration. It was tight, but he swirled his staff overhead just inches below the vehicle's roof. The air rippled where a portal should have formed. Nothing happened.

"Dammit!" I slammed a fist on the wheel. I toggled my comm. "Mel? Come in, Mel!" Only static answered.

Willie leaned between the seats, his face grim. "Oberon's cut us off with these veils. I'm guessing he's created another one somewhere ahead that's blocking our magic and your communications."

No portals, no radio contact. We're on our own.

"Shit!" I stomped the gas, the engine roaring as I aimed us toward the city. Oberon wanted a fight? Well, he'd get one. And when I got my hands around that pointy-eared bastard's neck, he'd regret the day he set foot in my town.

I weaved through empty streets, pushing the SUV to its limits. Antoine and the others followed behind in the convoy. The city loomed closer, a maze of concrete and steel. Somewhere beneath its skin, the Underground lay vulnerable. Oberon could be there already, wreaking havoc.

My gut twisted. Mel. The kids. Were they okay? If that freak had touched them...

I swallowed hard. No time for fear. I needed action.

The skyline shimmered as we got closer to headquarters. Another veil. I slammed the brakes, squinting at its golden haze. It enclosed a section of the city in a glittering dome, roughly where our headquarters lay beneath. Oberon's work, for sure.

My hands curled into fists. That barrier might keep out magic, but it wouldn't hold forever. Oberon had power, but we had iron, fire, and one hell of a pissed off army. And once we were inside, it was no holds barred. We'd have all our power at our disposal again.

I revved the engine, tires squealing as I aimed us straight for the veil.

The SUV crashed through the shimmering veil, momentarily blinded by the flash of light. The warehouse was just ahead. I pressed the remote to open the doors and pulled in to the empty garage.

"Everyone out," I barked.

We spilled from the vehicles, weapons and supplies in hand. I made straight for the elevator and activated the retinal and palm scanner. I punched the call button repeatedly. The others fanned out, guarding our perimeter while we waited.

"C'mon, c'mon," I muttered. The elevator moved at a glacial pace. Finally, the doors parted and we stepped inside. I jabbed the intercom. "Mel? Can you hear me?"

Only static answered. I exchanged an anxious look with Ramon. As we descended, I bounced on the balls of my feet, adrenaline surging through my veins.

The doors opened again. The hallway beyond was dim and still, stripped bare of the usual guards and staff. We'd taken everyone with us—except for Mel, Clement, Clarissa, and the orphans. I stepped out cautiously, senses heightened.

Adam inhaled deeply. "Faerie magic was used here, recently," he reported. Ramon and Willie nodded grimly in agreement.

I took off running down the hall, the others on my heels. We burst into the throne room, and I stumbled to a halt. The place was destroyed—both thrones overturned, tapestries and furniture shredded. Scorch marks blackened the walls.

"Mel!" I shouted, though I knew it was hopeless. "Clement!"

Only echoes answered.

Ramon gripped my shoulders, face drawn. "We need to check on Clarissa. And the orphans."

I nodded, jaw clenched. We took off through the tunnels, calling out names in vain. The entire place was empty.

We reached the chamber where we'd been holding Clarissa. The heavy door had been blasted apart, the room within dark and still.

Ramon rushed inside. "Clarissa!" He spun in a circle, raking both hands through his hair. "No, no..."

I placed a hand on his shoulder. "We'll find her," I said, putting on a brave face despite the worry gnawing at my gut.

Adam lingered in the doorway, frowning. I could tell he sensed the residual magic, too. Oberon had been here.

"The orphans," Muggs said urgently.

We ran, following the winding corridors to the orphanage wing. The destruction here was even worse. Someone had ripped the doors off their hinges, cots overturned and the television smashed.

My heart clenched. "He took them all," I whispered.

Muggs' expression was grim. "More child vampires to use as batteries. To power his army."

Rage boiled up inside me. I spun and slammed my fist into the wall, crumpling the stone. Oberon would pay for this. For threatening my city, my people.

I would make sure of it.

I fell to my knees amidst the rubble, overcome. That bastard moved fast. How did he even know we were gone? When we activated the convergence, he sensed it as we expected. But he didn't go after us. He went after our base—defenseless, with our best fighters gone. And now he had Clarissa, Mel, Clement, and the children, too.

Adam stepped up behind me and placed a gentle hand on my shoulder. I looked up to see a single blood-red tear rolling down his cheek.

"We will get them back," he said, his voice soft but firm with conviction. "This is why I was created. My purpose."

I took a deep breath and nodded, willing my despair into anger, into action. We would find them. We would stop Oberon, no matter the cost.

Adam helped me to my feet. His tear-streaked face was set with determination.

"Gather the iron weapons we have left," I told the others. "We'll hit Oberon tonight. That bastard won't know what hit him."

Adam gave me a grim smile. "Let's go claim my army."

Resolve hardened within me, cold and sharp as iron. We strode together toward the armory, ready for war.

Chapter 18

THE FAMILIAR RUMBLE OF the SUV's engine was the only sound as we sped through the empty streets. It was just past midnight—we had several hours before sunrise to end this shit. My fingers tapped anxiously on the worn leather steering wheel while I glanced in the rearview mirror. The line of sleek black SUVs behind us was the vampire cavalry, ready for battle.

Beside me, Muggs stared ahead stoically, his weathered face betraying no hint of fear. In the backseat, Ramon held Adam close, murmuring soothing words to his son. The boy's wide eyes darted around nervously. He could sense the tension thick as smog. Willie rode shotgun—in more ways than one. He had one of our shotguns cocked, loaded with iron buckshot, and ready in his lap. The gun was as long as Willie was tall, but he could handle it.

My hands clenched the wheel tighter as we crossed the boundary out of Oberon's veil. "It's time," I said.

The convoy screeched to a halt in a parking lot outside an abandoned factory. Muggs stepped out, staff in hand. The air crackled with magical energy as he spun a portal overhead. A shimmering vortex opened up, just big enough for a person to pass through.

"It'll take too damn long like this," I growled. "Only a couple of us can go through at a time, while Oberon's freaks will be waiting for us full-force on the other side."

Muggs nodded grimly. "I know, but—"

"Adam can get us there faster," Ramon said quietly. All eyes turned to Adam. "Everyone at once."

The kid looked terrified, but determined. "My dad's right. I can do this. I think."

My heart swelled with pride and fear. "I believe in you, Adam. Lock and load, boys!"

Adam took a deep breath and closed his eyes. An unnatural stillness fell over the area. The air grew heavy, and reality itself warped and bent in front of our eyes.

Then came a violent lurching sensation, like falling into an endless void. My stomach flipped as the surrounding scenery melted away. Blinding light enveloped us, then faded to reveal a moonlit forest.

We were dumped unceremoniously onto the leaf-strewn ground. I rolled to my feet, guns up. Faeries surrounded us—dozens of them. Lithe bodies, pointed ears, eyes that glowed unnaturally in the dim light.

"They're all Seelie!" Adam shouted at me with wide and worried eyes. "They won't follow me."

"Well, shit," I muttered. We'd hoped we'd encounter Redcaps, Baobhan Sith, and even Morgana. We could turn them against Oberon and force Morgana to free our friends. That wasn't happening.

Behind me, I heard the click of rounds being chambered. Willie cocked his shotgun menacingly.

The faeries stalked toward us, malice etched on their angular faces. Their human-like features were distorted with hatred. One of them raised a bow, arrow aimed at Ramon's chest.

"Try it, pixie bitch," I snarled. "See what happens."

My finger twitched on my Glock's trigger, ready to start blasting. We were outnumbered, but we had enough firepower to do some damage.

The arrow loosed, slicing through the air toward Ramon. With blinding speed, I swung my free arm up and caught the arrow mid-flight.

"Nice catch," Ramon quipped, shedding his trench coat and expanding his faerie wings. Shotgun in hand, he flew up over the fray.

"Attack!" the faerie captain yelled, pointing at us. The horde of fae surged forward.

Gunfire erupted around me. Muzzle flashes lit up the darkness as we unloaded on the advancing faeries. They were fast—unnaturally fast—dodging most of our shots. But we still dropped a few. Their bodies spun and collapsed, glowing blood spraying.

One leapt at me, dagger glinting. Willie intercepted him, smashing the faerie aside with the stock of his shotgun and racked the pump. Then he fired. The faerie's torso exploded in a spray of viscera.

I winked at Willie. "Nice shooting. Keep it up."

Muggs let out a roar, and the staff at his side flared with energy. The ground shook beneath our feet as he summoned vines from the earth, which wrapped around the faeries' ankles and sent them tumbling to the ground.

Adam was nowhere to be seen. He'd disappeared in the chaos.

"Where the hell is he?" I shouted above the cacophony of gunfire and faerie screams.

"Over there!" Willie pointed to a clump of bushes on the edge of the clearing. A faint glow emanated from within.

I made a split-second decision. "Cover me!" I sprinted toward the bushes, Glock in hand.

I burst through the brush, my gun raised in front of me. And then I saw him. Adam was crouched low, his hands on the ground. A pulsating energy radiated from his hands, connecting with the dirt. It was incredible, the amount of force he was channeling.

"Adam!" I yelled, but the noise of the battle drowned my voice out. He didn't even seem to notice me.

I ran over to him, grabbing his shoulder. He jumped, nearly falling over.

"What are you doing?" I screamed at him.

Adam glanced toward the sky and I followed his gaze as Ramon was locked in mid-air combat with three other faeries. "I'm covering Dad!" With a surge of energy, Adam shot three bolts of magic, like electricity, into the air, striking each of Ramon's opponents.

The faeries exploded in a shower of glittering light, raining down on the battlefield below. Ramon landed gracefully, looking up at Adam in awe.

"Kid, you just saved my life," he said, pulling Adam into a tight embrace.

The rest of the faeries hesitated, their vicious assault momentarily halted by the display of power. I saw my chance and raised my gun, aiming straight at the faerie captain.

Before I could fire, a dozen more faeries emerged out of thin air blocking my shot.

"Damn it!" I screamed. "How many of these bastards are there?"

"We can't keep this up forever!" Muggs shouted over the din. "We're outnumbered three to one!"

As if on cue, Adam's head snapped up. His eyes glowed red.

"The Unseelie," he said. "I can sense them. In the city." He bared his fangs. "With Oberon."

I blew a hole through another faerie's chest. "Can you get us to them?"

Adam shook his head, his expression grim. "Not without bringing this whole Seelie rabble with us."

I cursed under my breath. We were pinned down here in Oberon's forest kingdom. Meanwhile, who knew what havoc Oberon and his Unseelie minions were wreaking back in the city?

A massive root erupted from the ground, impaling a nearby faerie warrior. Muggs stood nearby, hand outstretched, green energy swirling around him.

"We're sitting ducks here!" I yelled to Adam over the cacophony. I grabbed his arm. "Are you sure you can control the Unseelie if we confront them in the city?"

Adam gave me a fierce grin, his eyes flashing. "Absolutely." But there was uncertainty in his voice.

I pursed my lips. It was a risk. But we didn't have many options.

I took a deep breath and made the call.

"Muggs is right. We can't keep fighting these Seelie warriors forever. More are showing up faster than we can drop them. It's time we took the battle to Oberon."

I met Adam's gaze, holding it with determination. "Teleport us to the city. All of us."

Adam hesitated, uncertainty flickering across his face.

I gripped his arm tighter. "You said you could control the Unseelie. This is our only chance to stop Oberon once and for all." My voice softened. "I believe in you, Adam. You can do this."

Slowly, Adam nodded. His jaw tightened with resolve.

"Get ready!" I shouted to the others. Willie, Muggs, Ramon and the rest of our ragged crew formed up around us.

Adam closed his eyes, face tense with concentration. The air began to shimmer and warp.

With a sudden wrenching sensation, the forest disappeared. Skyscrapers and screeching cars replaced the trees and towering shrooms. We stood in the middle of a busy downtown intersection.

Faeries shrieked and scattered as a bus barreled straight toward us.

I pushed Adam out of the way, tackling him to the ground as the bus crashed into a nearby building, sending glass and debris raining down on us.

"Everyone, move!" I shouted, standing up and surveying our surroundings. We were in the heart of the city, surrounded by towering buildings and, even at this time of night, bustling crowds. There was a nearby venue, probably hosting a concert or something that had just ended, and the people were filtering out into the streets, panic on their faces. The sound of car horns and shouts filled the air.

"We need to find Oberon," Ramon said, wings flaring out behind him. "But how do we know where to look?"

"There's faerie magic here," Adam added, bouncing to his feet. "He's here. I can feel it."

"Not just him," Willie added. "Look at that domed building. It's shimmering in a veil."

I narrowed my eyes. The people weren't just leaving a concert. That's where Oberon attacked. I imagined he had a host of Baobhan Sith within and they were busy multiplying.

With Oberon's veil protecting the venue, we couldn't teleport inside. Adam couldn't take control of the Unseelie until we got past Oberon's magic.

"We have to go in on foot," I said, loading my Glock. "Once we're inside, Adam, can you command the Unseelie within?"

Adam nodded. "No problem."

We advanced toward the venue, weaving our way through the panicked crowds as Antoine and our soldiers fended off the Seelie who were pursuing us from behind. If they could hold them off long enough for Adam to command the Unseelie, we could stop Oberon and send reinforcements out to help.

Inside, the scene was chaos. The walls were pulsing with dark magic, and a horde of Baobhan Sith were swarming over the bodies of concertgoers while dozens of Redcaps tore through the crowd.

"Adam!" I shouted. "Do it! Command them to stop and fight for us instead!" But Adam's eyes were wild, his fangs bared. The bloodshed had triggered his vampirism. I knew what he was feeling—an all-consuming, single-minded desire to feed.

"Adam, NO!" I screamed. "As your sire, I command you to stop!"

But my sire bond didn't stall him. Maybe I wasn't his sire. He'd inherited his vampirism through Clarissa in the womb. I tried to pull him back, but he ducked out of my grasp and surged forward into the battle.

"Adam!" I watched helplessly as he disappeared into the fray, his form swallowed up by the crowd of screaming humans and blood-soaked Redcaps.

Chapter 19

THE SCREAMS WERE DEAFENING. Blood and viscera rained down as the Baobhan Sith tore into the defenseless crowd. I fired round after round, but the bloodsuckers just kept multiplying.

"Shit!" I yelled. "Willie, on your six!"

He spun and decapitated the fanged bitch sneaking up behind him. Her head tumbled to the ground, face frozen in a predatory leer.

Out of the corner of my eye, I caught sight of Ramon making a break for it. The idiot was trying to get to Adam.

"Ramon!" I shrieked. "Get your ass back here!"

He didn't even look at me. Just kept pushing through the writhing mass of bodies, using his wings to vault up and over.

"Goddamnit," I growled. I wanted to go after him, to beat some sense into that thick skull of his. But I couldn't abandon Muggs and Willie. Not with the Baobhan Sith reproducing faster than a Catholic rabbit.

One of the bitches latched onto a screaming woman, fangs buried in her neck. The woman's skin rippled, growing paler by the second as her veins turned black. Soon she'd be just another bloodsucker.

I put a bullet between her eyes before the transformation finished. "Sorry, sister," I muttered. Wasn't her fault, but I couldn't let the horde grow any bigger.

Muggs was hurling balls of green magic left and right, green flames that incinerated the Baobhan Sith where they stood. Impressive. But they badly outnumbered us. This wasn't a battle.

It was a massacre.

And we were on the losing side.

I felt a cold shiver down my spine as I realized we wouldn't make it out of this alive. Not if I didn't do something drastic.

"Muggs! Willie! On me! Casting a shield!"

Muggs didn't hesitate. His eyes glossed over in his spirit gaze, he huddled at my side. Willie dove at my feet. I spun a circle with my wand extended. "*Protegulum!*"

The air crackled as the shield sprang up around us. A fragile bubble holding back the bloodthirsty horde.

For now.

The Baobhan Sith shrieked and clawed at the barrier, their nails scraping like nails on a chalkboard. I winced at the sound.

One of the Redcaps drew back its clawed hand and slammed it into the shield. The whole thing shuddered, light flickering.

"It won't hold long," Willie said.

"No shit." I peered through the writhing bodies. Where was Adam? If he could focus, get a little blood in his system, he could take control of the Unseelie.

The crowd of Baobhan Sith parted, and the Redcaps took a step back. A dark-haired woman, face emaciated and pale, stepped forward. Morgana.

Her hands twisted in an intricate gesture and a sickly yellow light shot toward us. It splashed over the shield, making it buckle.

"Brace yourselves!" I yelled.

Morgana hit us again and again, rotten magic corroding the only thing keeping us alive. This couldn't be how it ended. Not when we'd come so far.

I turned to Muggs, desperation clawing at me. "Can you make a portal? Get us out of here?"

Muggs' brow furrowed, eyes distant as he focused his senses beyond the shield. After a moment, he shook his head. "Oberon's veil is still in place. I can't pierce it to connect us to anywhere useful."

My heart sank. The shield wouldn't last much longer against Morgana's assault. Once it fell, we'd be overwhelmed in seconds, torn apart by the blood-crazed horde.

I looked at Willie, at Muggs, committing their faces to memory. After everything we'd survived together, for it to end like this... it wasn't right.

The shield flickered again, light bleeding through the cracks spreading across its surface. Morgana bared her teeth in a gruesome approximation of a smile. She knew she had us.

My hands tightened on my wand, resolve hardening. If this was the end, I'd meet it on my feet, fighting with my last breath.

A familiar tingle raced across my skin. Goliath—I could feel him approaching through our bond. Relief flooded me. Even if it was too late for us, maybe the hellhound could wreak vengeance on our enemies.

"Goliath's coming," I said. "He must have sensed my fear."

Muggs nodded. "Your blood bond runs deep. He will fight to the death to protect you."

The words were barely out of his mouth when the shield shattered completely. Morgana's magic slammed into me, knocking me to the floor. I raised my wand with a defiant yell, ready to unleash hell before I fell.

I braced for Morgana's killing blow, determined not to show fear. But before it could land, a massive shape hurtled through the swarming horde—Goliath, eyes blazing, jaws open wide.

He slammed into Morgana with the force of a freight train, jaws closing around her torso. She let out an unearthly shriek as his teeth sank in. Her magic flickered and died as she thrashed in his grip, ichor splattering in fountains of silver.

With a savage twist of his neck, he ripped her in two. Her wailing ceased abruptly.

I froze, wand still raised, mind blank with shock. He'd killed her—our only way to access Oberon's pocket dimension prison. Which meant no way to reach Ladinas, Alice, Mel, Clement... the orphans. They were lost to us now.

Numbness spread through me, the wand tumbling from my nerveless fingers. All that time searching, only for our hopes to be crushed in an instant. Around me, the battle raged on, but I barely noticed, sunk deep in despair.

What now? What did we have left to fight for? My friends, my love—gone. Our struggle against Oberon had always been desperate, but now it seemed truly hopeless.

I bowed my head, grief threatening to swallow me whole. We'd sacrificed so much already. How much more could we endure?

A piercing howl cut through my melancholy—Goliath, triumphant and savage. What was I doing, giving up so easily? That wasn't who I was. I was Mercy goddamn Brown, and I'd be damned again before I let Oberon win.

My fingers closed around the wand once more. Power surged through me, fueled by desperation and rage. Goliath's consumption of Morgana had strengthened our bond—I could feel his savage joy like a wildfire in my veins.

With a guttural cry, I sprang forward, blasting the nearest Redcaps off their feet. One, two, three—they fell before my onslaught, shredded by iron and magic. I was a whirlwind, tearing through their ranks without hesitation.

Out of the corner of my eye, I saw Muggs and Willie fighting fiercely back to back, holding their own. Good—no distractions. I pushed forward, blasting and shooting my way through the teeming horde.

There—a flash of a familiar face up ahead. Ramon. Still holding back a struggling, blood-crazed Adam. My undead heart clenched at the sight. Despite everything, Ramon was still trying to do right by his son. I redoubled my efforts, desperate to reach them both.

"Hold on!" I screamed. "I'm coming!"

I was almost there when the air crackled with dark energy. Oberon appeared in a swirl of shadows, his face twisted in a cruel smile.

"Not so fast, my dear," he purred, all false gentility.

With a flick of his wrist, he dragged a chained and struggling Clarissa forward. My heart dropped into my stomach.

"Let her go, you bastard!" Ramon shouted hoarsely. He made as if to charge Oberon, but Adam held him back with supernatural strength.

"I wouldn't do that if I were you," Oberon tutted. With a snap of his fingers, a massive wooden stake appeared, hovering in the air above Clarissa's heart. She whimpered in fear.

Oberon turned to Adam, who was trembling with the effort to restrain himself. "Come to me, boy. Take your rightful place at my side... or your mother dies."

"Don't do this," Ramon pleaded, his voice breaking. "Please, Adam..."

But Adam was too far gone. With a guttural snarl, he threw Ramon aside and stalked over to join Oberon.

"No!" I screamed. "Oblivion! I need your help!"

The dragon-gatekeeper didn't respond. Damn it all!

Oberon smirked, his eyes glinting with malice. "Until we meet again, my dear."

With that, he and his captives vanished, leaving me to face the bloodthirsty horde alone. I fell to my knees, the fight going out of me.

We'd failed. Adam was lost, along with everyone else, and a horde of bloodthirsty fae still surrounded us.

I wanted to give up, to just let the darkness take me. But then I felt it—a surge of power still flowing into my veins, invigorating me. I remembered Goliath's gift.

Slowly, I rose to my feet. The power thrummed through me, primal and intoxicating. I bared my teeth in a feral grin.

"I'm not done yet," I growled.

With a guttural cry, I flung myself at the nearest Redcap. My hands tore through its throat in a spray of black blood. I whirled and launched a bolt of crackling violet energy from my palm—a magic I could only attribute to Morgana—incinerating a cluster of Baobhan Sith.

More fae rushed me, but I was unstoppable. I was the eye of a storm of violence, ripping through my enemies with preternatural speed and strength. Out of the corner of my eye, I saw Muggs and Willie back to back, fighting for their lives.

"The veil is down!" Willie shouted over the din. "Muggs can teleport us out!"

"No!" I roared. "We finish this!"

I would make Oberon pay for what he'd done. For Adam. For everything. The power sang in my veins, and I knew—we would prevail.

Chapter 20

Blood sprayed across my face as I drove my fingers into the throat of a snarling Redcap. The little bastard gurgled and choked as he fell to the ground. I wiped my hand off on my pants.

I didn't have time to savor my kill. Another Redcap leaped at me from the side, sharp teeth bared. I whipped out my wand and blasted it backwards with a gust of wind. It slammed into the brick wall with a sickening crunch.

"These fuckers just keep coming!" I yelled to Ramon as he grappled with a hissing Baobhan Sith. Her fangs were inches from his neck, but he flipped her onto her back and shoved an iron shiv into her chest. She let out an ear-piercing shriek before falling silent.

Ramon wiped the sweat from his brow, panting heavily. "Oberon's absence has them all disoriented. Or perhaps it was Adam's appearance. They don't know who to take orders from anymore."

A wave of relief washed over me. Without that arrogant asshole Oberon to direct them, we finally had a fighting chance.

The remaining Fae were backing away now, confusion and fear in their beady little eyes. Their confidence had vanished along with their king—whichever king they followed.

"Let's get the hell out of here while we have the chance," I said. "Antoine and the others are still dealing with Oberon's army outside."

Ramon nodded, and I whistled for Goliath and Muggs to follow us. We raced across the blood-smeared floor, jumping over bodies as we headed back to the exit. The cool night air hit my face as we emerged from the doorway.

I expected to see Antoine still battling against the endless horde of Seelie. But the faeries were gone. Red and blue lights flashed on the sides of the buildings. No sign of Oberon's forces anywhere.

"What the f—" I started to say when the crack of gunfire split the air. I whirled around to see a line of police cruisers blocking off the street, officers taking cover behind their car doors, with pistols aimed right at us.

"Get down!" Antoine yelled from behind a dumpster as a bullet struck my shoulder and passed straight through.

I winced in pain, and I dove behind to join Antoine. "Where are the Seelie?" I shouted over the gunfire.

"They took off moments ago," Antoine replied. "These cops showed up a minute later demanding we surrender. I tried to explain, but they opened fire before I could even speak."

I risked a peek around the dumpster. The police had us surrounded. Even with my magic, we were outgunned.

"Where's everyone else?" I asked.

"All taking cover," Antoine said. "We could handle the cops, no problem, but I know your policy. Don't kill humans if we can avoid it."

I sighed, knowing Antoine was right. We had to get out of this without harming the police, even if they deserved it for opening fire on us without provocation.

My shoulder still throbbed where the bullet had pierced me. I needed to end this quickly before any of us got seriously hurt.

"Cover me," I told Antoine. "I'm going to try something."

Antoine nodded, leaning out to return fire at the police cruisers. The sound of bullets ricocheting off metal echoed down the street.

I took a deep breath and stepped out from behind the dumpster, wand raised. I didn't have time for an elegant incantation. This would have to be crude but effective.

"*Somnum exterreri!*" I shouted, focusing my will through the wand.

A wave of magic pulsed out, blanketing the area. The police officers slowed in their shooting, then slumped over their vehicles, trembling in fear. One by one, they sank to the ground, hiding.

"What did you do?" Antoine asked, emerging cautiously.

"Just a little nightmare spell," I said with a smirk. "Harmless, really. But it brings their worst nightmares to life as illusions. Should give us time to get out of here."

Antoine nodded appreciatively. "Nice work. Now let's round up the others and disappear before more cops show up."

We gathered the rest of our team and hurried back to the parked SUVs. Muggs kept watch, his oak staff at the ready in case any of the sleeping officers broke free from the spell. But my magic was doing its job.

I opened the back of my SUV. "Everyone in. We need to get back to HQ and figure out our next move."

I did a quick headcount as the team piled into the vehicles. Willie, Muggs, Goliath, Ramon... everyone present except Adam and Clarissa. But this wasn't over yet. We'd find them, somehow.

Goliath whined, nosing at my hand. I scratched him behind the ears.

"C'mon boy, let's go," I said. He hopped into the backseat of my SUV, nearly taking up the entire space with his massive hellhound body. Ramon and Muggs were left sharing a seat while Willie sat in the passenger seat. Given his size, it would have made more sense for him to share a seat in the back, but it wasn't a battle worth having.

I slid into the driver's seat, catching Ramon's eye in the rearview mirror. He gave me a grim nod. Message received: We were down but not out. Not by a long shot.

I revved the engine and peeled away from the scene, the rest of the team following close behind. We'd made it through this battle. But the war was far from over. Oberon would pay. I'd make damn sure of it.

I drove in tense silence, my knuckles white on the steering wheel. The rest of our convoy trailed close behind me.

Adam and Clarissa—gone. Just like that. Everyone else, stuck in a prison dimension, maybe forever.

Ramon had to be out of his mind with worry about his wife and son.

My hands gripped the wheel tighter, anger boiling up. We'd get them back, no matter what it took. I'd rip that faerie kingdom down stone by stone if I had to.

"Don't despair yet," Muggs said. "We may still have an opportunity."

I glanced at him sharply in the rearview mirror. "What do you mean?"

"I saw you wielding Morgana's magic back there," he said. "I can see things in your magic others can't, because of my gaze. Before her power fades, we may be able to use it to access the pocket dimension."

My eyes widened. Could it really be that simple?

I pulled the SUV over to the side of the road. I touched my earpiece. "Antoine, we're going to make a quick pit stop. Get back to HQ and feed up. We still have several hours of night left, and we need to be prepared for another battle."

"Got it," Antoine replied. "We'll be ready."

I stepped out into the cool night air as he and the others joined me.

"Here's what we need to do," Muggs said. "Morgana's magic allowed her to access the prison dimension. If we can channel that residual magic into a vessel, like she did with her crystals, it may open the portal again."

I nodded. It was worth a shot. But there was one problem.

"That's great, Muggs. Except where the hell are we gonna find a crystal ball?"

Muggs tapped his staff on the cracked sidewalk under our feet. "No need. This concrete contains sand. I can repurpose it."

He kneeled, pressing his weathered hands to the ground. The air hummed with gathering energy. Sparks flew as the concrete liquefied, swirling and hardening into a perfect glass orb.

I took the sphere carefully. It was hot, but flawlessly smooth, glinting in the moonlight.

"Just focus the residual magic into the orb," Muggs said, placing his hand on my back. "I can see how her magic works. Most kinds of magic carry a sort of residual memory. If she's accessed the pocket realm recently, I should be able to help you form the magic accordingly."

I closed my eyes. This was all new stuff to me. But when it came to magic I didn't understand, Muggs was the expert. I channeled every last drop of Morgana's power into it. The crystal grew warm in my hands, pulsating with light.

I opened my eyes. "Let's hope this works. Will you be able to get us home again?"

Muggs nodded. "Possibly. Getting you out of a pocket dimension, to this world, will be easier than trying to find a pocket dimension in the void. However, I'm not sure I'll be able to bring us back here and now."

I sighed. "The last thing we need is another trip through time."

Muggs sighed. "Let's hope Oblivion will rise to the occasion."

I grimaced. "I wouldn't count on it. But we have to take the risk. I won't make any of the rest of you follow me. If you want to stay behind…"

"I must," Ramon said. "For Adam's and Clarissa's sakes."

I nodded. "I understand. Willie?"

"I'm with you!" Willie said.

Goliath nuzzled my leg. He wasn't going to run away this time.

"Good luck." Ramon spread his wings and touched my shoulder.

I smiled at my former lover. This wasn't our first goodbye. I hoped it wouldn't be our last. "You too. Don't be reckless. If this works, we'll come back with everyone. I promise we'll get Adam and Clarissa back."

Ramon nodded and took off into the sky. The others gathered close. I dropped the makeshift crystal at my feet. It flared blindingly bright before the world folded away, and we fell into darkness.

Chapter 21

Darkness swallowed me whole, its pitch black tendrils seeping into every pore. I stumbled blindly, grasping at the empty air.

"Ladinas!" My desperate cry echoed into the void. "Alice! Can anyone hear me?"

Only silence answered. This damned pocket dimension was a wasteland, devoid of light and life.

Beside me, Muggs and Willie called out in futility, their voices muffled in the dark shroud enveloping us. I swore under my breath. We were well and truly fucked.

Then a flicker of movement caught my eye. A familiar silhouette took shape, and my heart leapt. "Ladinas!"

I raced toward him, nearly tripping over my own feet. But as I drew close, his form dissipated into wisps of smoke.

"Shit!" I skidded to a halt, cursing. It was just a cruel illusion.

But then I heard it—the faintest whisper of my name. Mel's voice. I whirled around to see her spectral shape reaching for me.

"Mel!" Hope surged in my chest. I sprinted toward her, only to grasp at empty air as she, too, vanished into nothingness.

"Goddammit!" I kicked at the ground in frustration. This place was playing twisted tricks on me. But I wouldn't let it break me. I'd find a way out of this nightmare realm if it killed me.

"This ain't working," Muggs said, his gruff voice cutting through the darkness. "We're in some kind of adjacent pocket dimension. We got close to the prison, but not close enough."

I scowled, hating to admit he was right. We'd hit yet another dead end.

"There's gotta be a way to bridge the gap," I said. "Can you spin us a portal or something?"

Muggs stroked his beard thoughtfully. "I can try. No guarantees, but Druid magic just might do the trick."

He spun his staff. The air crackled with gathering energy. I held my breath, willing the portal to form.

But then a sly voice whispered in my mind, scattering Muggs' concentration. Oblivion.

Muggs' magic fizzled out as the dragon's presence overwhelmed my senses and seemed to suck Muggs' magic right out of the air.

Well, well, Oblivion purred in my head. *You always were a stubborn one, Mercy.*

I clenched my fists, biting back a scathing retort. "You have impeccable timing, you know. Could have used your help back there against Oberon."

Oblivion's presence intensified, and suddenly he stood before me in a physical form—tall and golden-haired, with a smug smile twisting his too-perfect features.

"But my dear, everything is going exactly as planned," he said. "With Adam united to Oberon, we can finally force peace among the fae."

My temper flared. How dare he act so nonchalant after all Adam had suffered?

"Adam didn't want to join with that monster!" I shouted. "Oberon deceived him. Used him for his own selfish ambitions. He's angry, deceitful, and murderous!"

Oblivion merely shrugged, utterly unconcerned. "All is as it must be. You'll come to accept this in time. And here, you'll have plenty of it. An eternity! "

I wanted to claw that infuriating smirk right off his pretty face. But I knew lashing out would only play right into his hands.

So I took a deep breath and channeled my fury into an icy stare. "I should have known from the start. You're not justice. You're the mirror-image of the gatekeeper-dragon Excalibur. You're his opposite!"

Oblivion's smile only widened at my outrage, as if it pleased him. "What is justice? Is it not to set all things right? Did I do you wrong when I helped you heal the divide between you and your father?"

"No," I huffed. "But you only did that to earn my trust. Just so you could betray me now."

Oblivion laughed. "Think what you wish. To make things as they ought to be. To set things right. Well, who decides what's right? What ought to be is in the eye of the beholder, is it not? My brother, Excalibur, and I see things differently. He believes the gates between worlds were to be guarded, the integrity of each world forever separate. I believe all worlds were meant to be as one."

"That's madness!" I screamed. "You can't absorb the earth into the faerie realm."

Oblivion laughed. "The union of the faeries is just a means to an end, my dear. Their peace, their unity, will begin on earth. They'll eventually turn the whole world into faerie. Then, they'll attempt to unite the realms. When they do, the two worlds will combine, but neither will be able to contain the other. They'll dissolve together into the void. Into oblivion!"

I shook my head in disbelief. How could I have been so blind?

"You're insane," I said. "Destroying everything won't bring order. It will only bring chaos."

Oblivion's eyes flashed with anger for the first time. "Order? Chaos? Such limited concepts. I am beyond your petty moralizing. I am Oblivion, the end of all things. I am the darkness between the stars, the silent void that awaits when all light burns out."

His voice took on a fanatical tone that sent a chill down my spine. This was no longer the charming, reasonable entity I thought I knew. This was madness, a force beyond reason or appeal.

"When the walls between worlds fall, all will be one again in peaceful oblivion, as it was before the first dawn. In the beginning, all was formless and void. It's no chaos. It's only the opposite of existence as you know it, the opposite of what you see as order. No more fractured realities, no more discordant life forms tearing each other apart. Just pure, perfect oneness."

I shook my head slowly. "You're wrong. Life finds a way. The voices of the living will cry out again, even from the void. You can't unmake what is."

Oblivion's face contorted in contempt. "Let them cry out. Their voices will be swallowed by the silence."

Oblivion's body began morphing, scales rippling across his skin as he shape-shifted into an enormous dragon. His wings unfurled, shadowing the empty landscape.

I stumbled back, shocked by the sudden transformation. Willie stepped forward, magic crackling at his fingertips.

"Your madness ends here," Willie declared. With a sweep of his hands, glowing chains materialized, wrapping around Oblivion's limbs and snout. The dragon thrashed against the bonds but remained trapped.

Willie smirked. "Not so tough now, are you?"

Oblivion roared, the sound echoing endlessly across the void. "You cannot hold me forever, faerie! I am eternal, inevitable!"

Willie yanked at his chains, then handed them to me. I took them. "What are you doing?"

"Hold on, Mercy poo!"

Willie fluttered around Oblivion as the dragon continued to thrash against the chains. It took all my strength to hold on. Muggs lent his strength to mine. Willie fluttered around the dragon, flicking something like glitter from his hands. "Go to sleep, you big nasty!"

Then, in an instant, Oblivion went limp and tumbled under the weight of Willie's chains before the bindings disappeared in an instant. Willie fluttered back down, dusting off his hands. "They don't call me Wee Willie Winker for nothing!"

"A sleeping faerie!" I laughed. "The original sandman!"

"Bingo!" Willie did a little twirl.

"Good work!" I laughed, patting Willie on the back. "But we're still in trouble here. Without Oblivion's help, we're basically stuck."

Willie's face fell. He glanced between me and the slumbering dragon uncertainly.

Muggs stepped forward, gripping his staff. "That's not necessarily true. Don't forget, Adam can fold space. If I can reach him, somehow, at some point in time, I can help guide him back here to find this pocket dimension again."

I bit my lip, glancing back at the endless void around us. "I don't know. That seems risky. If you leave, we'll be stuck here indefinitely."

Muggs met my gaze steadily. "Trust me, Mercy. Now that I've been here, I think I can find my way back. If I can bring Adam to this dimensional space, being so close to the prison pocket where the others are, I'm certain he'll be able to merge the realms."

I hesitated, uncertainty gnawing at me. "How can you be so sure you'll make it back again?"

He gave me a crooked smile. "Ah, well, let's call it sixty-forty odds." I stared at him incredulously—though he didn't know it, he must've sensed my dissatisfaction with his answer. "Have a little faith."

I searched his face, then slowly nodded. If anyone could guide Adam here, it was Muggs. "Alright. But you better not leave us hanging." I tried to sound stern, but couldn't keep a faint smile from my lips.

Muggs's eyes crinkled. "Never, Mercy poo. Never."

I rolled my eyes. "Never call me that again."

"Hold on," Willie said. "I have an idea."

Muggs tilted his head. "What are you thinking?"

Willie pinched his chin. "What if Goliath and I stay behind while you two go? Your connection to Goliath, and my magic—"

"It could help anchor this space," Muggs finished Willie's thought. "It'll give Adam more of a tether to find his way back if we're able to reach him."

Willie beamed. "Exactly!"

I met Muggs's thoughtful gaze. "It's risky either way. But this could improve our chances."

Slowly, Muggs nodded. "You may be right. Willie's magic has grown strong indeed. And with Goliath..." He trailed off, then smiled. "Yes. I think your plan is wise, Willie. Mercy and I will stand a better chance together."

I squeezed Muggs's arm. "Let's do this."

I took a deep breath as Muggs began weaving his spell once more. Willie moved to stand beside the still-slumbering Oblivion, one small hand resting lightly on the dragon's scaly hide. Goliath sat at his feet, tongue lolling out in a doggy grin.

"Remember," I said, "don't engage with Oblivion at all. If he wakes up again ..."

"Don't worry about us," Willie said breezily. "We'll be fine as wine. And he'll sleep as long as I'm here. You just focus on finding our boy."

I nodded, swallowing down my nerves. Willie was right—Adam had to be our only focus now.

Beside me, Muggs grunted with effort. The very fabric of space began to warp and bend. A wind whipped my hair as a swirling portal opened up before us.

I clutched Muggs's hand tightly. "Let's bring him home," I said. "Let's bring everyone home."

With a shared look of determination, we stepped into the maelstrom. The portal snapped shut behind us, leaving Willie, Goliath and Oblivion behind.

The only question was when would we show up back on earth? I wasn't sure I was ready to face another faerie apocalypse. But what other choice did we have?

Chapter 22

A PIERCING SCREECH FILLED the air as we tumbled out of the portal, my body slamming into the hard ground. I groaned and blinked, my eyes adjusting to the dim light filtering through the canopy of trees stretching endlessly above us.

"What the hell?" I grumbled, rolling onto my side. The damp earth soaked through my clothes as I took in our surroundings. We were surrounded by nothing but dense forest as far as I could see.

I hauled myself to my feet. "This sure as shit doesn't look like Providence to me."

Muggs dusted the dirt from his robes as he stood up beside me. "It is Providence. Or at least, it will be."

My eyes narrowed. "You wanna run that by me again?"

"We seem to have traveled to a time before Providence was settled," he explained. "Either that, or so far into the future that no trace remains."

"Well, that's just fang-fucking-tastic," I snorted. "Can't you just zap us back to the right time with your little magic tricks?"

Muggs tried to form another portal, but his magic faded the second the vortex formed. "I'm afraid not. Something is interfering with my abilities here. We'll have to find another way."

I kicked at the ground in frustration, sending leaves and twigs flying. The last thing I needed was to be stuck in the wrong century with no way to get home.

"Then I guess we better start walking," I said. "These trees have to end somewhere."

I'd barely taken two steps when an arrow suddenly whizzed past my head, embedding itself in a nearby tree with a sharp thwack.

I spun around, fangs bared, to see a shirtless Native American nocking another arrow in his bow. Before I could react, he let it fly.

Muggs thrust out his hand and a thick tree branch shot out to block the arrow's path. "Be careful," he warned. "Those arrows are wood. Good as a stake."

"No shit," I hissed, glaring at the archer as he reached for another arrow. Whoever this guy was, he clearly wasn't thrilled by our presence. Can't say I blamed him.

"Well, this answers one question at least," Muggs said. "We didn't travel to the future. This is pre-colonial America."

The Native let his next arrow loose. Again, Muggs blocked it with a branch.

Muggs and I took off, using our vampire speed to race through the trees. I held onto Muggs's arm, since he couldn't see where we were going.

We didn't get far before a group of Native Americans surrounded us, bows drawn back and arrows aimed right at our hearts.

One of the men approached. His eyes narrowed. I bared my fangs and let out a vicious hiss, hoping to scare him off.

He gasped and stumbled back. The others followed suit, lowering their weapons. I heard one of them whisper "vampyre."

I glanced at Muggs, not sure what to make of their sudden reverence. He looked just as puzzled as I felt.

"Well, this is new," I murmured. "Since when are vamps treated like royalty instead of monsters?"

Before Muggs could posit a theory, the man who'd first approached inclined his head respectfully. Though he spoke no English, his gestures indicated we should follow him.

I hesitated, not keen to go traipsing through the wilderness with a bunch of heavily armed strangers. But we didn't have much choice. Maybe they had a shaman or someone who could help us find a way home.

With a resigned sigh, I nodded and fell into step behind the man.

As we walked, the other men offered their wrists to Muggs and I. The tangy scent of human blood perfumed the air. My fangs throbbed, eager for a taste, but I held back.

"Think it's safe?" I whispered to Muggs.

He considered a moment before sinking his teeth into a proffered wrist. The man didn't even flinch.

"Seems so," Muggs said after drinking his fill.

I followed his lead, carefully piercing the skin of the nearest wrist. The man's blood was earthy and rich. I drank deeply, savoring the nourishment.

After a time, we reached a small village nestled amongst the trees. Wigwams made of bark and animal hides dotted the clearing. Women cooked meat over fires while children played simple games with stones and sticks.

Our escort brought us to the largest wigwam and motioned for us to go inside. I tensed, unsure what we would find within. Gripping Muggs's arm, I pulled back the flap covering the entrance.

The interior was dim, lit only by a small fire. As my eyes adjusted, I made out a figure reclining on a pile of furs. Three Native American women lounged around him, their necks bearing fresh bite marks.

My breath caught when I realized who it was.

"Nico?" I whispered in disbelief.

The man raised his head, blood dripping from his lips. He looked at me with no recognition in his red eyes.

"Who are you? How do you know my name?" he demanded. "And how do you know English?"

My mind reeled. Somehow we'd landed in my sire's distant past, before I was born, long before he made me.

This was going to take some explaining.

I took a deep breath to steady myself. "My name is Mercy. I know this will be hard to believe, but I've come from the future. Centuries from now, you will sire me. I will become your favored progeny."

Nico's eyes widened in shock. He sat up slowly, gazing at me. "You are from the future? But how is this possible?"

I glanced at Muggs, unsure how much to reveal. He gave me a subtle nod.

"This man with me, Muggs, he's an ancient druid. His magic brought us here. By accident. In my time, he is family. I suppose you could say he's your grandson."

Nico looked Muggs up and down curiously. "A druid, you say? I have never met one of your kind before."

He turned his piercing gaze back to me. "And you claim that one day I will sire you? That you will join me as a creature of the night?"

I nodded. "Yes. You taught me everything. You showed me the beauty in darkness. I've missed you more than you could know."

Nico tilted his head, intrigued. "Then tell me something only I would know."

I pursed my lips. "Well, for starters, you aren't born yet. I mean, not exactly. You were made a vampire when you were trapped in Guinee, sent here by Baron Samedi. You were born in Louisiana, used to attend a school for vodouisants in an underground world called Vilokan. You're still pretty pissed at Annabelle Mulledy for leaving you behind in Guinee, but don't worry, you'll get over it. Eventually. Sort of."

He rose gracefully from the furs and approached me. Gently, he took my face in his hands, studying every feature.

"Unbelievable," he murmured. "It seems you have an interesting tale to tell, my future progeny."

I smiled, relieved that he seemed to believe me.

"I wish I could tell you everything," I said. "But I've seen Back to the Future. And I've traveled through time a few times before. I don't want to fuck anything up."

Nico nodded thoughtfully, dropping his hands from my face. "A wise precaution. Knowledge of one's destiny can be a heavy burden."

He turned to Muggs. "What magic brought you here, druid? Why have you traveled through time itself to find me?"

Muggs sighed. "It's a long story. But we didn't intend to come here specifically. We were trying to return to Providence in the year 2023. But we were traveling out of a pocket dimension, and your presence here testifies to the fact that moving between realms can be unpredictable. You never know when you'll show up."

Nico glanced at the natives gathered curiously around the wigwam. "This land is precious to the Samoset people. The colonists have not yet come to drive us from our homes."

I nodded sadly. If only there was a way we could prevent the atrocities that were to come. But Muggs was right—we couldn't risk altering the timeline.

Nico regarded us shrewdly. "You must stay here as my honored guests until we unravel this mystery. Together, we will find a way to return you to your rightful place in time."

I bowed my head gratefully. "We're in your debt. Thank you for welcoming us."

Nico smiled, his fangs glinting in the firelight. "It is I who should thank you, daughter of the future. Your arrival brings good tidings—proof that my bloodline will endure. Only tell me this. How am I to be remembered?"

I shrugged. "By some, you're feared. But most, those who know you, you're honored. But I probably shouldn't say much more than that. Only that you were like a true father to me. The best man I ever knew."

Nico grinned. "Then I suppose there's reason to hope for the future. That I won't always be as I am."

"As you are?" I asked.

Nico smirked. "These people don't love me. They are terrified of me. They honor me because of my power. And because they think I'm some kind of prophet. But I'm no sage. My thirst is..."

"Unquenchable?" I asked. "Don't worry. In my time, you had more control than any vampire I'd ever known. You were the best of us."

"You speak of me in the future, but in the past tense?" Nico raised an eyebrow.

I sighed. "It's a long story. One I really can't tell you."

Nico nodded and gestured toward the ladies who lay with him. "Care to join me for a feast?"

Chapter 23

THE BRACKISH SCENT OF wet furs and smoke hung heavy in the wigwam's air. Muggs and I sat cross-legged by the small fire, watching the ancient vampire I'd dearly loved, the model of civility, chomp on a woman's wrist. He was like a rabid dog, blood dripping down his chin. Hardly the immortal dark lord I knew.

"So let me get this straight," I said, picking at my nails. "You've only been a vampire for a year?"

Nico swallowed and wiped his mouth with the back of his hand. "Give or take a few moons. Why, how old are you?"

I rolled my eyes. "A hundred and thirty-one."

Nico's eyes widened in awe, and it made me want to retch. I thought he was going to have all the answers, but he was just a clueless fledgling.

"Will you impart some of your wisdom to me, then?" he asked eagerly. "Teach me the secrets of surviving eternity as one of the damned?"

I barked out a laugh. "Hate to break it to you, oh mighty Nico, but everything I know about being a vampire, I learned from you."

He furrowed his brow in confusion.

"Well, the future you, anyway," I explained. "Clearly you haven't gotten there yet."

Nico chuckled, a deep rumbling sound. "Then perhaps the lessons began with me here and now, so that one day I may teach them to you in your past."

I huffed. "Time travel's a bitch."

Nico grinned, blood staining his fangs. "Tell me about it."

I sighed and ran my fingers through my hair. This was going to be difficult to explain without giving too much away about the future.

"Look, being a vampire is tough," I began. "It's a constant battle against your demons, your bloodlust. There were times I didn't know if I could control it, if I could stop myself from becoming a monster."

Nico nodded, his expression solemn.

"But eventually I realized something important," I continued. "Vampires aren't inherently evil. We have the same capacity for good and evil as humans. In fact..."

I hesitated, wondering how much I should reveal. Ah screw it, might as well lay down some hard truths.

"In fact, humans are the ones who will commit true atrocities in the centuries to come," I said bluntly. "Far worse than any vampire has done."

Nico's eyes darkened, and he gazed into the fire. "That weighs heavy on my heart," he murmured. "This tribe, these people I've come to love... their future is so uncertain. When the colonists arrive, they will be decimated by disease."

He turned back to me, his expression pained. "I've thought about turning some of them, so they might survive the coming plagues. But history tells me most will perish, regardless."

I reached out and squeezed his shoulder. "I'd like to tell you that the future isn't written yet. But we both know what's going to happen. And I hate to tell you, but all these atrocities against these people you love happened even in my future, a world where you'd been a vampire for millennia."

Nico sighed. I couldn't imagine how difficult it must have been for him to know about every war, every tragedy that was to come, but realize there was nothing he could do to stop it.

"Is there anyone here with magic?" I asked, changing the subject. "A shaman or wise woman? Someone who can help guide us, maybe figure out a way to get us back to the future?"

Nico shook his head, a wry smile touching his lips. "Great movie, by the way. I miss movies. But if I knew of a shaman who could send us into the future, I would have sought their counsel already."

I huffed a laugh. "Yeah, guess that was a stupid question. It's just... we really need to get back to our time. There's a threat we have to stop, and our presence here is putting the future in jeopardy."

Nico's eyes sharpened with interest. "What kind of threat?"

I hesitated. How much could I reveal without damaging the timeline? "Let's just say we were betrayed by a sword. A powerful magical being that tricked us and trapped us here. If we don't get back, it will mean the end of the world."

Nico frowned. "Betrayed by a sword? I don't understand."

"It wasn't really a sword," I explained. "More like a dragon that was bound to a sword. A gatekeeper of dimensions that turned against us."

At that, Nico sat up straighter. "A dragon, you say? Interesting..." He stroked his chin thoughtfully. "There is a legend among my people. A powerful creature is said to dwell in the lake nearby, able to travel between bodies of water. The Samoset people believe he protects this land and their tribe."

I exchanged an excited look with Muggs. "A gatekeeper dragon," I breathed. "Do you think one could be living here now, guarding a convergence?"

Nico lifted his shoulders. "It's certainly possible."

This could be promising. If one of the ancient dragons was here, it might help us return home once it learned what one of its kind had done.

"Can you take us to this lake?" I asked urgently. "We should speak to it right away."

Nico nodded. "Yes, we can journey there tonight. But daylight approaches, even with our speed, we wouldn't make it back in time if we left now. We must remain hidden till then."

I nodded, trying to contain my impatience. The promise of the dragon's help meant everything, but we were forced to delay.

Nico regarded me with his ancient eyes, as if sensing my frustration. "I know you're eager to get back. You must've been in the fight of your life before you came here."

I took a deep breath. "That's the understatement of the century. Whatever century we're in."

"Then perhaps you should see this as an opportunity to gain your strength. Enjoy the generous offerings of these fine people. If you succeed, and can return to your time, will it matter how many days you spent here?"

I sighed, knowing he was right. "Yeah, I get it," I said. "It's just... hard being stuck here. But you're right, we'll figure it out." I managed a smile. "One day at a time, right?"

"I have to ask," Nico added. "You know me in the future. How do I get back?"

I smirked. "Oh, you will travel time."

"I will?" Nico's eyes widened.

I smiled widely. "One day at a time."

Nico rolled his eyes. "I was afraid you'd say that."

Chapter 24

THE NIGHT AIR PRICKLED my skin as we stepped out of the stuffy wigwam. I sucked in a deep breath, the cool air refreshing after being cooped up all day.

Nico strode ahead confidently, calling out to a man lingering near the treeline. The guide responded in a language I didn't comprehend, but I tried to smile warmly in thanks.

We set off, Nico and the guide leading the way through the inky blackness of the forest. I couldn't see two feet in front of me and had to trust we weren't being led into a trap. The trees loomed ominously, their gnarled branches like claws scratching at the night sky.

After what seemed like hours of stumbling through the dark, we finally broke through the treeline. An expansive lake glittered before us, moonlight dancing across its glassy surface.

Nico conferred with the guide before turning to us. "He says this lake is home to a powerful spirit. It rarely shows itself, but if we're lucky, it may grant us a blessing."

"Magic," Muggs said. "That's all we can offer."

"It will have to do." Gripping my wand, I allowed it to draw raw magic from within me. Nothing defined by an incantation or spell. The purer the magic, I figured, the more likely the dragon would respond. Muggs did the same with his staff beside me, his eyes glowing emerald with power. Together, we released our magic into the placid water.

The lake erupted, water flying high as a massive dragon burst from the depths. It towered over us, scales glinting in the moonlight, wings spread wide. The guide dropped to his knees, head bowed in reverence or fear.

But Muggs and I held our ground. This was our only chance to return home. I stepped toward the magnificent beast, unafraid.

"I'm not sure if you can understand me," I called out, meeting the dragon's ancient eyes. "But we don't belong here. Another of your kind, Oblivion, deceived us. He wants to tear down the walls between worlds, meld everything into one void."

The dragon stared back impassively, smoke curling from its nostrils. I prayed my words would somehow reach its primal mind.

The dragon reared back its head and roared, the force of it nearly knocking me off my feet. Muggs grabbed my arm to steady me as we both took an instinctive step backward. Then, before our astonished eyes, the beast began to shift, its massive form blurring and shrinking down. Magic sizzled through the air.

Where the dragon had been now stood a young Native American boy, no more than fifteen years old. He regarded us solemnly.

"To some, I am known as Caladbolg," he said, his words clear.

Muggs sucked in a sharp breath beside me. "Caladbolg," he murmured. "That's another name for Excalibur."

Hope leaped within me. Who didn't know the legends of Arthur and Excalibur? Caladbolg was a force for good, Oblivion's very opposite.

"Oblivion is your counterpart," I said urgently. "Please, we need your help to stop him before he unmakes everything."

The boy eyed me intently, as though peering into my soul. The fate of all worlds depended on reaching some understanding here tonight beneath the stars.

Caladbolg was silent for a long moment. Though he now wore the guise of a human youth, power radiated from him in waves. His dark eyes were deep and fathomless.

Finally, he spoke. "I must examine your heart to determine the truth of your intentions." His piercing gaze shifted to Muggs. "You have attempted to breach the walls between worlds before, have you not?"

Muggs looked abashed. "I have, but with no ill intent," he admitted. "Only to return us home, to stop Oblivion's madness from consuming everything we hold dear."

Caladbolg's expression was grave. "The paths between worlds are not to be trifled with by those who do not fully comprehend the forces they meddle with."

"You're right, of course," Muggs said contritely. "I meant no harm. Only to protect our friends, our world. Oblivion threatens all we know."

The ancient being pondered this. At last, he nodded slowly. "Your words have the ring of truth. Oblivion's hunger for chaos is insatiable. He must be stopped."

"Agreed," I whispered fervently. "Tell us what we must do."

Caladbolg approached, raising his hands to either side of my head. His fingertips were like brands against my temples. I gasped as his consciousness flooded into mine.

It was overwhelming, the torrent of images and sensations crashing through my mind. Millennia of memories and power, a raging river threatening to sweep me away. I clung to my sense of self by a fraying thread as Caladbolg rifled through my innermost thoughts and dreams.

Just when I thought I could endure no more, he withdrew. I sagged with relief as the onslaught ceased.

Caladbolg's expression was approving. "Your spirit is strong, your purpose true. I will aid you in returning to your world."

"How do we stop Oblivion?!"

"I will lend you my power. Together, we shall return to your time." His eyes flashed with ancient ferocity. "Oblivion must be stopped. This is my ancient charge, granted me by the All Father, and now I pass it along to you. Do you accept?"

"I do." I nodded, exhilarated by his words.

"Hold out your hand."

I extended my hand, palm up, still trembling from the intensity of our mental joining. Caladbolg grasped it, his skin surprisingly warm and rough against mine.

"It will not be pleasant," he cautioned. "Prepare yourself. I must take a form you can wield when we pass through the gate."

His body began glowing, limbs dissolving into ribbons of light that swirled and coalesced around my hand. An agonizing heat seared my palm. I clenched my jaw against a scream as the magical energies poured into me, fusing with my essence.

The light faded, leaving a dagger clutched in my fist—but it was no ordinary blade. This was Caladbolg himself, his power and consciousness bound to the gleaming metal. I could feel him thrumming through me, our beings intertwined.

Quickly now, we must reach the gate. His voice echoed in my mind.

I nodded, blinking back reflexive tears as the pain receded. "Let's go home."

"Wait," Nico said. "Can I come with you? This might be my only chance…"

I hugged Nico. "I'm sorry. If you were to come with us, I'd never become a vampire. It would change everything. But we will meet again."

"I can't wait for the day. Thank you for your wisdom."

I smirked. It was strange hearing those words come out of Nico's mouth, but I appreciated it. "One more thing."

"Anything," Nico said.

"When we meet again, don't speak about this encounter. I can't know it's coming. Remember, everything must happen just as it did."

Nico nodded. "I promise. Until we meet again."

I kissed Nico on the cheek. He didn't know that the world I was going back to was one where he'd long been dead. He'd see me again. I wasn't sure if I'd ever meet him again.

Muggs and I turned toward the lake. With a sweep of his staff, Muggs parted the waters, opening a path to the shimmering portal below. "I don't know how to swim," Muggs admitted. "This will have to do."

I chuckled. "Well, I don't want to get all wet. So, good call."

Gripping Caladbolg, I stepped forward. We descended into the lake, walls of water towering on either side. The muddy bottom squelched under our feet as we walked deeper. Ahead, the portal swirled violently, a maelstrom of magical energy.

I glanced back at Muggs. His brows were furrowed in concentration as he held the waters at bay.

"Ready?" I asked.

He nodded. "Let's end this."

I faced the portal again, tightening my grip on Caladbolg. His power thrummed through me, resonating with the wild magic swirling in the convergence ahead.

I leaped, plunging Caladbolg into the heart of the maelstrom. Blinding light exploded outward and a tremendous force seized me, hurtling my body forward.

Then darkness. Silence.

Finally, water all around us. We were in the lake. So much for not getting wet. The water around me churned. Muggs was panicking. Who would have thought that he didn't know how to swim?

I swam towards him, grabbing his arm and pulling him to the surface. We gasped for air, coughing up water.

"We made it," I said, relief washing over me.

Muggs nodded, still panting. "But where are we?"

I looked around, disoriented. We were in the middle of the lake; the shore shrouded in darkness. Mugs grabbed onto my back as I kicked my legs, holding him above the water. Even with my strength, carrying the weight of a full-grown man in water wasn't easy, but we made it to shore.

"I didn't know there was a convergence here," I admitted.

Muggs shook his head. "Neither did I. Apparently, there's more than one in the region."

"Doesn't matter," I said, waving Caladbolg through the air. "We have what we need."

Chapter 25

THE FLAMES LICKED AT my fingertips as I summoned Caladbolg from the ether. I spoke his name, which was a bit of a tongue twister. The dagger in my hand burned hot before he appeared before me as a lanky Native American teenager, wisps of smoke curling from his palms.

"I need you to open a portal," I said without preamble. "My friends are trapped in a faerie prison in a pocket dimension."

Caladbolg's eyes darkened. "I am a gatekeeper, not a gatemaker. If there is such an aberration, a pocket dimension as you call it, then unless a gate was folded into it when it was made, I have no access."

"But you're a badass dragon!" I protested. "Can't you just... burn a hole through realities or something?"

He cracked a wry smile. "I'm afraid it doesn't work like that."

I suppressed a growl of frustration, sparks flying from my fingertips. We were running out of time. Oberon still had Adam and Clarissa. I had hoped, now that I had the famed blade of Arthurian legend—even if he took the diminutive form of a dagger, rather than a broadsword in my hand—that he'd be able to help me gather the whole team before we launched an assault on Oberon. Apparently, we were going to have to tackle these problems in reverse. It wasn't all that unexpected. When we left the pocket dimension, our plan from the start was to risk it all to save Adam. Ramon was around somewhere, probably trying to rescue his son and wife as well.

I sighed, running a hand through my hair. "Well, if you can't get us into the pocket dimension, we need to get Adam back from Oberon. He's the only one who can help us rescue our friends."

Muggs nodded, though his usual exuberance was dampened. "Even with our entire team, facing Oberon would be difficult. We can't do it alone."

"You're not alone," Caladbolg chimed in, a grin spreading across his youthful face. "You have me now. I'm a lot stronger than I look when I'm in this form. But I like this body. It's more flexible than my dragon form, but every time I see a pretty girl, a certain part of this body becomes... *less* flexible."

I laughed as I noticed Caladbolg examining my body up and down. "So you really went all the way with this human body thing, huh?"

Caladbolg nodded. "It's the only way. I needed a form to mimic, and this was the one I chose. It has its advantages. Most people who see me don't have any idea how powerful I can be."

I winked at Caladbolg. "Big things come in small packages."

Caladbolg glanced down to below his waist. "Indeed."

I gulped. "That's not what I meant."

"How do I get this thing to go away? It's awfully uncomfortable."

"Think of me instead of Mercy," Muggs suggested. "Mercy gets a rise out of a lot of people."

I sighed. "You're never short of jokes, are you, Muggs?"

"Not the time to be making short jokes, Mercy."

I snorted. "There you go again."

Caladbolg tilted his head and sniffed at Muggs. "Ugh. Yes, that's having the effect I hoped for. Thank you, Mug Ruith."

"Any time. I'm glad my unattractiveness pacified your condition."

Then Caladbolg turned back to me. "Damn it."

I pointed at my face. "Eyes here, buddy. That will help."

Caladbolg shook his head. "No. It doesn't. Your eyes are..."

"Irresistible?" I chuckled. "It's a part of my vampiric allure. We all have it, some to greater," I glance at Muggs, "or lesser degrees than others. It's meant to attract our prey." Caladbolg shifted back and forth, adjusting himself under his loincloth. "What is happening to me?"

I chuckled. "It's called puberty. It's a dark form of human magic."

Caladbolg furrowed his brow. "Dark magic?"

"You really don't know much about humanity, do you, Cal?"

THE FURY OF A VAMPIRE WITCH: BOOKS 4-6

Muggs grunted. "Don't call him Cal. That just makes me think of that incubus."

I sighed. "Maybe Calad?"

"Isn't that the name of a DJ? I was feeling his funky beats recently," Muggs added. "Makes me want to shake my bottom!"

I tilted my head. "I think he spells his name differently, but strangely enough, I've heard of him."

"You could simply call me bolg," Caladbolg suggested.

I shook my head. "Too close to bulge. Fitting and appropriate. But inappropriate at the same time. We'll workshop nicknames later. We need to get Adam so we can stop Oberon, thwart Oblivion's plans, and then save our friends."

"If we don't save Clarissa, we won't be able to save Adam," Muggs noted. "Adam doesn't want to work with Oberon, but he won't do anything to anger the Seelie King so long as his mother is vulnerable."

"Clarissa is the priority. My guess is that Oberon is keeping her close to he can keep Adam in check," I said. "Let's do this. Muggs, can you make us a portal into Oberon's throne room?"

The druid frowned, waving his hand. The air shimmered for a moment, then went still.

"I was afraid of that. Oberon's veil must be in full force. My magic cannot breach it."

"But mine can." Caladbolg stepped forward, body elongating and scales rippling across his skin. Wings unfurled, crimson and expansive. With a roar that shook the trees, an enormous dragon stood before us.

"Well," I muttered, "that's more like it. First, we need to head to the Underground. We need to let Antoine know we're ready to attack. We'll need everyone if we're going to pull this off."

"Underground?" Caladbolg asked, his voice much deeper and gravelly in his dragon form.

"Just what we call our base. I'll show you the way."

I swung my leg over Caladbolg's neck, settling between two ridges on his back. His scales were smooth and warm beneath me. Muggs climbed up behind me, grumbling under his breath.

"Alright, Calad, or whatever," I said. "We're ready to go!"

With a rumbling growl, Caladbolg launched himself skyward. The force of it nearly unseated me, but I grabbed onto his ridges. The landscape blurred into a patchwork quilt of green and brown far below us.

The wind stung my cheeks as I surveyed our surroundings and directed Caladbolg where to go. Flying on dragon back was exhilarating. Muggs held on to my waist. He squeezed tighter the faster Caladbolg flew.

"Isn't this amazing?" I called back to him.

"It's extremely windy," he yelled over the roar of the wind. "Not pleasant."

We soared over the city until we reached the warehouse entrance to the Underground. Caladbolg hit the ground with a thud—but not as much of one as you'd think, given his size. After Muggs and I dismounted the dragon, he shifted back into his boyish form. "This won't take long. We just need to coordinate with the rest of our team."

When we got inside, Antoine was already waiting alongside the rest of our vampire soldiers, armed and ready for a fight.

"Mercy, Muggs, and... who are you?" Antoine's eyes widened at the sight of the bare-chested boy in a loincloth. "What in the world?"

"Long story," I said, glancing at Caladbolg. "He's more than meets the eye."

Antoine nodded, his face grim. "We're ready. Everyone is here. But we need a plan."

"That's why we're here," I said. "Goliath and Willie aren't with us. I'm not sure where Ramon is, but I'm betting we'll find him once we launch an assault on Oberon."

"Just tell us what you need us to do," Antoine said, following Caladbolg with his eyes and the dragon-boy examined one of our SUVs, clearly curious about modern ingenuity.

I cleared my throat. "Attack the forest at the perimeter. Try to lure as many of those Seelie bastards out of there as possible. Our plan is to fly overhead, dive down near Oberon's throne room, and try to get to Adam and Clarissa."

Antoine raised an eyebrow. "Fly?"

Caladbolg craned his neck around, pulling himself away from his reflection in the polished black door of one of the SUVs. "I can fly."

"And that boy can carry you two?" Antoine stared at me incredulously.

"Damn straight," I laughed. "Calad, why don't you show him your true form?"

THE FURY OF A VAMPIRE WITCH: BOOKS 4-6

Caladbolg grinned mischievously as he transformed into his dragon form once more, towering over the vampires in the Underground. Antoine and the others gawked in awe as the dragon unfurled his wings and beat them once, creating a gust of wind that nearly knocked us all off our feet.

"Impressive," Antoine gulped, nodding his head in approval. "But it's going to take one hell of a distraction to occupy Oberon's army."

"Yes," I said. "I need you to lead the charge. Take as many of our troops as you can and hit them hard. Use everything you've got. I want them to know we're coming for them."

"I can cloak us in the sky," Muggs said. "We'll stay high enough that Oberon shouldn't be able to detect our approach."

I nodded. "Have another earpiece? We'll keep in touch by comms. If you get in over your head, let us know."

Antoine signaled for one of the other vampires to grab another ear piece for me. I took it when he got back and put it in my ear. "We'll be fine, Mercy. We've fought these bloody bastards before and picked up a few tricks. Don't worry about us. Just focus on the mission. If you can get Adam..."

"Then we can both save our friends and take control of the Unseelie to defeat Oberon once and for all."

Chapter 26

THE WIND WHIPPED MY hair wildly as Caladbolg soared through the clouds, the city streets far below us. Muggs clung to my waist behind me, knuckles white and eyes squeezed shut. I threw my arms wide, reveling in the thrill of the flight.

No sooner did we arrive at the edge of Oberon's forest, and Antoine's team exited their vehicles and headed into the woods. Gunshots cracked through the air. It didn't take long before they encountered resistance. I leaned forward. "Take us up higher!" I shouted over the wind. Caladbolg's wings beat powerfully, lifting us up above the forest canopy.

Antoine's team was already in one hell of a fight. I itched to join the battle, but we had our own mission. "I can't see a thing!" I shouted.

Muggs took a deep breath and steadied himself. "I'm looking through spirit gaze. Most of the Seelie are at the edge of the forest, fighting our team. I can see Adam's presence, but he's not alone. He's within that tree that houses Oberon's throne room."

I patted Caladbolg on his side. "Let's do this."

He folded his wings and we plunged into a steep dive. The forest rushed up to meet us. Muggs let out a shriek behind me. I laughed wildly, adrenaline pumping through my veins.

We burst through the trees, Caladbolg pulling up just before we crashed. A few lingering faeries scattered in surprise. Caladbolg bathed the Seelie guards in flames before landing lightly outside the royal oak.

I laid my hand on the trunk. It remained solid. "Muggs?"

The druid staggered off Caladbolg on shaky legs. Steadying himself with his staff, he placed both palms against the oak. Green light flickered around his hands.

"Ah, good friend, this one. We have an understanding," he said, referring to his druidic connection to the oak. I grabbed his shoulder. Back in boy form, Caladbolg took my other hand, and when Muggs touched the tree this time, it pulled us in.

Oberon's throne room materialized around us. Shocked faeries reacted instantly, spells and weapons raised. My hands flexed, ready for a fight.

Adam huddled in the corner, his mother chained beside the throne. A wooden stake hovered ominously before her heart.

Oberon shouted, "Fight them, boy, or she dies!"

Adam remained paralyzed with indecision. I flung spells at the approaching guards while Caladbolg, even in his human form, breathed fire through his boyish maw. Oberon yelled for us to stop, or Clarissa would pay the price.

"A stake won't kill her, just immobilize her!" I shot back. "Help us, Adam!"

Adam clenched his fists and took a step forward.

With a flourish of his hand, Oberon ignited the tip of the stake. "We'll see if this burns her heart out."

Adam stopped in his tracks. His eyes flashed with anger, but he stayed frozen, unwilling to risk his mother's life.

Muggs stepped forward, twirling his oak staff. "You've made a grave mistake, Oberon. Don't you know trees and druids are besties?"

Magic flowing around Muggs, the entire throne room responded. Vines shot out from the walls, knocking away Oberon's floating stake.

Adam seized the opportunity and dispelled the chains binding his mother. Clarissa scrambled to her feet.

I aimed my wand at Oberon. "*Incendia*!"

My flames struck the Seelie King but didn't burn his flesh. Caladbolg exhaled a torrent of fire at Oberon, but the faerie's magic protected him.

"Your magic cannot defeat me!" Oberon laughed.

I tilted my head. "Then how about my fists?"

I charged at Oberon, ducking under a blast of his magic. My fist connected with his jaw in a satisfying crunch. He stumbled back, surprise on his face.

"You hit like a girl," he sneered.

"I am a girl, dumbass." I swept his legs out from under him. He fell hard on his back with a grunt. Before he could react, I planted a knee on his chest, pinning him down.

"Let's try this again." I aimed my wand between his eyes.

But a blast of golden magic flowed right out of his gaze and sent me flying back.

I slammed against the wall, my wand flying out of my hand. Oberon stepped toward me. A wooden blade, ablaze like the stake before, formed in his hand. "Ready to meet your maker in hell?"

I narrowed my eyes. "Been there, done that."

I dodged as Oberon jammed his sword at my chest.

Adam and Caladbolg were distracted, fending off the few guards who remained. I kicked Oberon in the gut, but it only made him take a single step back.

Another vine shot out of the walls behind Oberon. Then the vine flung my wand into the air. I reached up and caught it.

"*Enerva!*" I shouted, blasting Oberon. Again, though, my magic bounced off him.

But then something knocked him forward. I looked past Oberon and saw Clarissa there, eyes wide. Oberon spun around and caught her by the neck.

Like lightning, Adam rushed to his mother's aid and placed both hands on Oberon's head. The Seelie King gasped.

"I'm silencing his power!" Adam shouted. "But I can't hold him for long."

I raised my wand again.

"Mercy!" Caladbolg shouted. "Use the spell we talked about!"

I nodded with understanding. "*Anima ardenetis!*"

Soulfire erupted from my wand, engulfing Oberon completely. He screamed, the sound rising in pitch to an inhuman wail. The scent of burning flesh filled the room. When the flames died down, only ashes remained of the once mighty Seelie King.

I stood up, breathing hard. It was over. The rest of Oberon's Seelie guard similarly turned to ash. Clarissa approached tentatively.

"Thank you," she said. "For saving us."

I managed a smile. "Anytime."

At that moment, Ramon came bursting into the room, forcing his way through the wooden walls, skidding to a halt as he took in the scene.

"No way. I missed all the fun?" He hurried over to Clarissa. She fell into his embrace.

"You're just in time to celebrate our victory," she said, kissing him soundly.

I rolled my eyes, but couldn't help grinning. We'd done it. Oberon was dead, and Adam was free. Now to deal with the next crisis.

"It's not over yet," I said, interrupting their reunion. "Oberon might be dead, but his faeries are still out there, fighting the rest of the Underground. We need to help."

Adam nodded. "You guys go on ahead. I'll catch up in a minute."

I glanced at him curiously, but he offered no explanation. A ripple coursed through the air around Adam and he disappeared. No time to worry about it now.

"Let's move," I said, heading for the exit. Clarissa, Ramon, Caladbolg and Muggs followed close behind.

We raced through the forest, branches whipping at our faces. In the distance, the sounds of battle grew louder—gunshots, clashing metal, screams. We burst into a clearing and froze.

It was chaos. Antoine and the others were surrounded, faeries swarming them on all sides.

Caladbolg let out an enraged roar and transformed into his massive dragon form. He unleashed a torrent of flames at the faeries, but some kind of shield deflected it.

"Dammit," I muttered. We were badly outnumbered. I raised my wand, ready to fight, when a ripple in the air made me pause.

Adam shimmered into view, an army of redcaps and Baobhan Sith appearing behind him. With a slash of his hand, he sent them surging into the fray. Now we had the numbers to make it a fight.

The Redcaps were a blur of claws and fangs, tearing through the faeries with savage glee. Their hats grew redder with each kill, fueling their bloodlust.

The Baobhan Sith moved with preternatural speed, their cries piercing the air as they drained faeries dry. Antoine and the others backed away, providing cover fire with iron rounds that dropped the remaining fae. Muggs called the entire forest to our aid, roots shooting from the ground, ensnaring the faeries by the ankles.

I blasted as many as I could with my spells. Caladbolg went after them, too, swallowing at least one of the faeries whole. He belched a cloud of glitter. I couldn't help but laugh.

It was over in minutes. The clearing was littered with fae bodies. Adam turned to me, eyes blazing.

"What now?"

I let out a shaky breath. "We're not done yet. We need to get to Oblivion before he destroys everything. And we need to bring our friends home."

Chapter 27

ADAM TILTED HIS HEAD. Understanding dawned on his face. "You need me to open a gateway."

"Yes. Can you do it?"

Adam nodded. "If I can find them. I'm not sure where to start."

Muggs stepped forward and took my hand. He placed it on Adam's shoulder. "Can you feel Mercy's magic?"

Adam nodded. "I can."

"She's connected to Goliath, the hellhound. Willie is there, as well. Focus your magic beyond the confines of this world. Let the connections you feel guide you."

Adam's lips curved in a smile, both proud and feral as his eyes blazed with golden light.

Then the air around us shifted. Ripples in space warped the shape of the surrounding forest.

"Found them!" Adam declared.

Space continued to fold over itself until we were standing in darkness. Willie was still there, fluttering around, casting his sleep magic. But Oblivion was awake and Willie's power wasn't putting him down again. Apparently, he'd developed a resistance. Goliath had Oblivion's tail in his jaws, pulling at it to prevent Oblivion from destroying Willie.

"Looks like we are just in time," I declared.

Caladbolg grabbed my arm. "When the time is right, leave. Go save your friends."

"We need to destroy Oblivion."

Caladbolg shook his head. "We can't leave this place. Oblivion and I are connected. If you use soulfire on either of us, it will kill both of us."

"I'm not going to kill you!" I insisted. "There has to be another way. If we can incapacitate him again, then you can come with us."

Caladbolg nodded. "If you have a chance to save your friends, you need to take it. They are not far. I will be fine."

"We're not leaving you behind! You're a blade of legend. You have an important role to play."

Caladbolg touched my cheek. "I'm older than I look. The adventures you know, the tale of Arthur among them, are in my past. This was my final task. You are the protector now."

I gulped. "But with your help, we could close all the gates. We could protect the world."

"You have everything you need to do it yourself. My time has passed."

I grunted. "I won't accept it. You're coming with us. That's all there is to it."

Caladbolg smiled at me. Then he turned and shifted again. In dragon form, he dove at Oblivion. The small pocket of space shook around us.

"How can we help!" I shouted, but Caladbolg was locked into battle with Oblivion.

Adam stepped up beside me. "We need to knock out Oblivion without killing him."

Willie buzzed up beside me. "So glad you're back! I don't know why he won't go to sleep!"

"I have an idea." I raised my wand at Oblivion. "*Enerva!*"

My paralysis spell struck Oblivion true.

But the paralysis didn't last long. Oblivion shook it off violently and turned his attention to me. His eyes glowed a deep red as he let out a bone-chilling roar. I stumbled back, a wave of fear washing over me.

Goliath dove at Oblivion's neck, sinking his teeth into Oblivion's scales. The dragon shook his head until Goliath went flying, but Goliath's bite weakened him.

Caladbolg looked at me and winked as he tackled his brother. They both shifted at once, back into their human forms for a moment, then into dragons again. Then into the shape of something I didn't recognize.

As the two dragons shifted into their unknown form, a blinding light enveloped them. I shielded my eyes, but could still feel the heat emanating from their transformation. When the light faded, Oblivion and Caladbolg were gone, replaced by a single dragon larger than any I had ever seen. Its scales shimmered in the dim light, almost like they were made of diamonds.

"Is that...?" Adam trailed off, his eyes wide with wonder.

"It's Calivion," Willie buzzed excitedly. "I've heard stories, but I never thought I'd see it with my own eyes!"

A surge of energy blasted from the combined dragon's body. Then I saw it. A shimmer, fleeting, but clearly it was Ladinas. "That's them!" I shouted, pointing at the apparition.

"Got it!" Adam said. "I can take us there!"

I clenched my fists. There was no saving Caladbolg now. "Everyone, together! We can't take the dragon with us!"

Goliath was the first to meet my side, Willie shortly thereafter. We crowded into a huddle as Adam bent the world around us.

A blast of light again filled the space as Calivion turned to pure energy. It shot at me—as if trying to possess me again.

"Out of here!" I shouted.

I wasn't sure if the energy hit me or not, but the next thing I knew, our entire team was standing in an old, abandoned factory. Just like the place where we'd lost Ladinas and Alice when all of this started.

Footsteps sounded in the distance. My nearly dead heart leaped as a figure appeared—but it sank when I realized it wasn't Ladinas. It was Cal freaking Rhodes. And the incubus within him.

I clenched my fists, but Adam stepped forward and raised his hand. "Kneel."

Cal obeyed. "My Liege."

I smirked. "Nice. That's going to take some getting used to."

Adam chuckled. "Tell me about it."

"Where is everyone?" I asked.

Cal directed his eyes up a stairwell. I hurried up the old steps. It was strange. This old factory still stood in Providence, but the pocket dimension replicated it.

I pushed through two large doors and entered a room. Before I could examine the scene, Mel wrapped her arms around me. "Mercy, you're here! Please tell me..."

"I'm not trapped here. We beat Oberon's ass. Time to go home."

Mel winced. "Mercy, there's something you need to—"

I heard a giggle through another set of doors. I charged through. There, on the floor, were Ladinas and Alice—stripped of clothes. A barely breathing human body laid among them, blood smeared over their bodies.

"What the fuck!?"

Ladinas jumped to his feet. "Mercy! I never thought—"

Rage boiled up within me. "What the hell, Ladinas? You're stuck in here with Alice for a couple days and you two..."

"It wasn't a couple days," Alice said as she pulled herself to her feet, covering her chest with her crossed arms. "We've been here for a century."

I gulped. "A hundred years."

"I never thought I'd see you again," Ladinas said, his voice calm. "Mel and the others, the orphans and Clement, they showed up about a year ago. We thought all was lost."

"And you have humans to feed from?" I asked.

"Sent here by Oberon," Ladinas said. "But again, we haven't seen any in some time. Not since shortly after Mel and the rest arrived."

I sighed. "After I defeated Morgana."

"This woman still lives. There are a few more who still survive. But not many."

I tried to speak but I couldn't find the words. Just when I thought I was going to be with Ladinas, he ends up trapped in prison with Alice... and now *they* were together.

"I don't know what to say. Do you love her?"

Ladinas took a deep breath, but didn't respond.

"Do you love me?" I asked, more urgently.

Again, no response.

"Fuck it." I stomped my foot and turned to leave the room.

Mel was waiting for me, her eyes wide. "Mercy, I'm so sorry, I—"

"Save it," I said. "It is what it is. Where are Clement and the orphans?"

"Not far. This isn't a very large place. I can get them if you'd like."

I nodded. "We're getting the fuck out of here."

The entire group was silent as they saw Ladinas and Alice stumble out of the room behind me, totally naked except for the woman's blood that they'd smeared all over each other. Disgusting. I wanted to puke.

Everyone looked at me with pity. Except for Muggs. "Hey, why the sour mood? We did it!"

"Shut up," I snapped. Clarissa whispered something in his ear and his jaw dropped. This sucked. Everyone was looking at me with pity.

"If you all don't stop staring, I'll punch your faces out."

"Mercy," Ramon said, approaching me carefully as he placed a hand on my shoulder. I shrugged it off.

"I don't need your sympathies."

Adam's eyes were glued to Alice's blood stained chest. Poor kid. He was as bad as Caladbolg. I snapped my fingers in front of his face. "It's time to go home."

Adam nodded with understanding. After Mel reappeared in the room with Clement and the orphans, he released his power. The factory shifted, the walls, floors, and ceiling all folding around us until it wasn't.

"Did it work?" I asked.

Adam nodded. "This is the real factory. Back in Providence."

I glared at Ladinas. "Put on some fucking clothes. It's time to go home."

Chapter 28

The Underground was suffocating. The tension in the air was thick—thanks to Ladinas, and his inability to keep his thing in his pants for a century. Could I really blame them? They'd been there together, so long that I was probably little more than a distant memory. I understood why it happened. That didn't mean it didn't hurt like hell.

All this time, while I was traversing realms, dealing with faerie monarchs, and even traveling back in time, Ladinas and Alice were together, humping like a couple of dogs on the street.

Having Adam and Clarissa back was the only saving grace we had. Now, we had a few Redcaps and Baobhan Sith who'd lend us support in the future—provided Adam was in a helping mood. He was a good kid; I didn't have any reason to suspect he'd be a problem.

I hadn't said two words to Alice since we returned. I'd barely spoken to Ladinas. All business. Mel was back to her usual routine, bolstering our security systems and devising new weapons to help with whatever threat we'd face next. The convergences were still there—and now we knew about more than one in the region.

I secretly craved another fight. Some monster, some threat, that might emerge from some unknown dimension. Just so I'd have something to fight. I needed an outlet for my fury.

I'd learned through the years that if I let my rage boil over, I could lose control, just like any vampire. In my current state of mind, it wouldn't take much to set me off.

The orphans weren't much better off, despite being gone for a year, than when they'd left. There were only a few humans that Oberon left in the prison dimension, and they were supposed to ration the blood. While they starved, Ladinas and Alice were practically bathing in it mid-tryst. Another reason I was pissed. But they'd been gone a lot longer than the rest. They were stuck there with a freaking incubus who *fed* on sexual energy. It explained the insatiable lust that consumed Ladinas and Alice, but it didn't excuse it.

After all, the incubus was tame, now under Adam's command. And Ladinas and Alice still spent every waking hour of the day together in his room.

When night fell, I couldn't get out of there soon enough. In the Underground, I was queen. But what I'd told Adam before was true. When you're queen, you're lonely. It had never been more true than it was now.

When I left the Underground, I could be me. Just Mercy. A vampire. I could imagine, at least for a few hours, that I wasn't responsible for an entire army of tactically trained vampires. I could *indulge.*

I left HQ and headed out alone onto the city streets. There was a club not far from the warehouse where I could probably find someone to play with. I knew how to handle myself without drawing too much attention. I'd been at this a while. Call it reckless, if you must, but I *needed* this.

I stepped into the club, glamouring my way past the bouncer and avoiding the cover charge. When I was on the prowl, there wasn't a man in the world who could resist me.

Nico called it a gift. My allure was damn near irresistible.

What you have is a gift, Mercy. Nico's voice echoed in my memories. *But don't abuse it.*

Whatever. I hadn't put my *gift* to use in years. How much harm could one night, or two, embracing what I was, really do?

It didn't take long before I identified my prey. A tall man, probably thirty. He was playing pool with a few of his less-attractive buddies.

I sauntered over to the bar and ordered a drink, watching him out of the corner of my eye. He had a strong jawline, dirty blond hair, and a toned physique. My kind of man.

I leaned against the bar and waited for him to notice me. It didn't take long.

"Can I buy you a drink?" he said, sidling up next to me.

I turned to face him, letting my lips curve into a seductive smile. "I'd like that."

We talked for a while, making small talk and flirting shamelessly. I could tell he was into me, and I was into him. Though certainly for different reasons. I wanted to *taste* him.

As the night progressed, we moved to the dance floor. His hands were strong on my hips as we moved together in time with the music. The way he looked at me sent shivers down my spine. It was a look of hunger, of desire, of need. It was the same look I saw in the mirror every day.

I pressed my body against his, feeling his hardness against me. He leaned in close, his lips grazing my ear. "I want you," he said, his voice low and husky.

I smiled, knowing exactly what he meant. "Then let's go somewhere more private."

We left the club and walked to his car, parked on the street. He opened the door for me and I slid into the passenger seat. As soon as he got in on the driver's side, I pounced. I pressed my lips to his, feeling his tongue slip into my mouth. I was marinading him in seduction. When I was done, he'd be delicious.

I took his tongue into my mouth and bit, blood flooding my mouth. He didn't resist. I had him enthralled. Then, his blood dripping from my lips, I sank my fangs into his neck.

I drank, and didn't stop. Not until his gorgeous body lay in his seat, cold as ice.

I took a deep breath and glanced at the moon. It had been a long time since I'd taken a life like that. *Too long.*

I headed back into the club. He was just an appetizer. I was ready for the main course. A surge of energy swelled in my chest. What was in that man's blood? Was I gaining power from his soul?

Say my name...

The voice echoed within my mind.

I held out my hand. "Caladbolg."

Nothing happened. I tried again. "Oblivion?"

Say my name!

I took a deep breath. "Calivion."

A rapier formed in my hand. Long and slender, coursing with power. The combined essence of both gatekeeper dragons now connected to a single blade. "Is that all you can do?"

The voice didn't respond. But the power that flowed from the blade into my arm was undeniable. Then the rapier emitted a pulse of light and a man was standing in front of me. His hair was golden like Oblivion's, his skin dark like Caladbolg's . He was dressed in tight leather, formed from dragon scales. He was *gorgeous.*

Calivion stepped up to me and touched my face. His eyes swirled with both golden and dark magic. I lost myself in his gaze. "That's all I needed. A little blood."

I melted under his touch. "What do you want?"

Calivion stared into my eyes. "I want *you.*"

"I want you too," I whispered back, not even sure where those words came from. He'd just appeared, out of nowhere. Technically, from within me—but I didn't know he was there until now. I'd never wanted someone more.

When he kissed me, I didn't resist. I couldn't resist. He pressed me against the car door, my previous meal still lying cold and dead within. As he tore at my clothes, I didn't even care that we were on a public street, or that I'd left a man dead.

I was a bloody queen. Enthralled by a timeless dragon—now a man. If someone had a problem with it, they'd have to deal with both of us. I'd never felt so invincible. But never so vulnerable, enthralled by another. That was usually my role. But I embraced it. Things were going to change—everything was different, now. Let Ladinas and the rest come after me, try to stop me. They were my past. Calivion was my present, my future, my everything... and the world was ours for the taking.

The End of Book Four

THE FURY OF A VAMPIRE WITCH
BOOK 5

BLOODY BRILLIANCE

THEOPHILUS MONROE

Chapter 1

CALIVION AND I WALKED hand-in-hand into the local precinct. Why did these police think they had a right to spoil my fun? These humans were pathetic, trembling little rodents scurrying for cover at the sight of us. Calivion strode beside me, his eyes glowing like hot coals, ready to torch this place to ashes.

"It's her!" An officer gasped, recognizing me as he leveled his gun at my chest. "You're under arrest. Hands over your head."

"What's the crime?" I asked. "Overeating, I suppose."

Calivion laughed. "Looks like we stepped right into a buffet. Tell me, Mercy. Do you like your pig raw or roasted?"

"I said, hands up!" the officer screamed. I could smell the perspiration gathering under his pale-blue shirt.

I ignored him and winked at Calivion.

I grinned. "Some of both. I like variety. It's my spice."

I bared my fangs, letting my true nature show. The man's smug expression melted into one of horror. With lightning speed, I grabbed his wrist and snapped it like a twig. His screams were music to my ears.

"Anyone else want to arrest me?" I purred. The other officers shrank back, clutching their useless guns. Calivion let out a rumbling chuckle, smoke curling from his nostrils.

We strode through the precinct, leaving a trail of bite marks and singed flesh. The chief's office door splintered under one kick of Calivion's boot. The chief himself sat trembling behind his desk, reeking of urine and fear.

I hopped up on his desk, crossing my legs casually. "Had a little accident, did we?"

The chief stared at me, mouth agape, too terrified to speak. Calivion loomed behind me, his hulking frame blocking the doorway, his red eyes burning with amusement.

"Here's how this is going to go," I said, leaning in close enough to see the beads of sweat on the chief's forehead. "You're going to stop sending your boys after me. I run this city now. Got it?"

He nodded frantically, whimpering something that sounded like "yes." Pathetic. I could rip his throat out right now if I wanted. But I'd made my point.

"Good boy," I purred, patting his cheek. Then Calivion and I sauntered out, leaving the chief a quivering, soiled mess. No one dared challenge us as we exited the precinct, the broken and burned bodies of officers littering our path. This city belonged to us now.

We stepped out of the precinct and into the cold night air. A line of black SUVs waited at the curb, headlights blinding.

I rolled my eyes and nudged Calivion. "Should have seen this coming."

"They don't know when to quit, do they?" Calivion asked.

Doors opened and out stepped Ladinas, Alice, Antoine and the rest of the Underground, guns aimed right at me.

I threw my head back and laughed. "Wooden bullets? You'd have to hit my heart, and I'm not sure I have much of one these days."

Ladinas' jaw clenched, his eyes flicking to Calivion beside me. "Come with us, Mercy. You need help."

"Oh, I don't think so," I said, linking my arm through Calivion's. "We're doing just fine on our own."

Calivion grinned, smoke curling from his nostrils. He flexed his shoulders, and I gasped as leathery wings unfurled from his back. With one powerful sweep, we were airborne, leaving the precinct far below.

Wind whipped my hair as we soared over the city lights. I'd never felt so alive, so free. And Calivion—he was full of surprises.

"Where to now?" he asked, red eyes dancing.

I smiled slowly. "Anywhere. Everywhere." As long as we were together, nothing else mattered.

I clung tight to Calivion as we sailed through the night sky, the city shrinking below us. His wings beat steadily, the wind roaring in my ears. I couldn't stop grinning.

We soared upwards until the sparkling city looked like a child's model far below. The cold air at this altitude bit my skin, but I barely felt it. All that existed in that moment was me and Calivion and the endless sky.

I threw my head back and laughed with pure delight. The wind stole all sound, but Calivion's lips curled into a smile. He banked, and we spiraled slowly downwards, the city revolving around us.

"What shall we do next?" he murmured, his breath warm on my cheek.

I gazed out at the tapestry of lights below. We could go anywhere, do anything. The world was ours.

"I don't care," I said. "As long as we're together."

Calivion chuckled. "Don't be so short-sighted." He swept us down until we were skimming just above the rooftops, his wings extended. "We rule so much more than just this city, Mercy. Anything you desire—name it, and it shall be yours."

I smiled slyly. "Anything?"

His eyes flashed. "Anything."

Possibilities spun through my mind, each more tempting than the last.

"Show me everything," I whispered.

Calivion's grin turned wicked. With a powerful stroke of his wings, he propelled us upward once more into the waiting night.

Our ascent was swift, the city shrinking away until it was just a glittering smear beneath us. Higher and higher we climbed, the air thinning, the temperature plummeting. But Calivion's body was a furnace against mine, warding off the cold.

We burst through the cloud layer, emerging into a sea of stars. The moon hung huge and heavy, close enough to touch. Calivion's wings beat steadily, carrying us up and up. The curvature of the earth became visible, the atmosphere fading from blue to black.

We were no longer flying but floating, untethered. Calivion rotated slowly so I could take in the magnificent sight. The planet revolved beneath us, impossibly huge and heartbreakingly small all at once.

"What do you think?" Calivion asked softly.

I tore my gaze away to look at him. His eyes reflected the galaxy behind me.

"It's beautiful," I said. "But so lonely."

He brushed a strand of hair from my face. "It doesn't have to be."

I felt something stir inside me then—a hunger I'd never known. We were above it all, gods gazing down on the world I'd been born into. We could shape it as we saw fit—or leave it behind entirely. Who could stop us?

Calivion saw the yearning in my eyes. "Tell me where to take you, Mercy. I am the gatekeeper and the destroyer. Every world opens up to me, or falls at my command."

I grinned wickedly, tracing a finger along Calivion's chest. "Then take me to a world where we can rule as gods. A place where we can live forever, free from anyone who might try to stop us."

Calivion's eyes glinted with amusement. "You want to be a queen, do you?"

I leaned in close, pressing my body against his. "I want to be a goddess."

He chuckled and gestured at the world below. "Then take it. This world is yours."

Chapter 2

SNAP OUT OF IT, love! You're better than this!

The text message pinged my phone once Calivion flew me back into range of Providence's cellphone towers. It was from Mel.

"Delete," I said out-loud as I archived the message and slipped my phone back into the back pocket of my leather pants.

"Your friends?" Calivion asked.

I nodded. "They still think there's hope for me. Pshhhh."

"What shall we do next?" Calivion asked. "Perhaps we could devour a grocery store. Not the food, of course, but the patrons."

I shrugged. "I don't think I could drink any more blood right now if I wanted to. I don't need to feed more than a couple of times a month at my age. Since we've been together, I've been feeding several times a day."

"But it's more than that!" Calivion exclaimed. "It's the thrill of the hunt, of the kill!"

"Not all that thrilling after a while." I shook my head. "This is small-time stuff, Cal. If you're serious about giving me the world, surely we can think bigger than grocery stores and shopping malls."

Giving me the world...

Something in my gut turned when I'd said it. What was becoming of me? Why was I acting like this? And worse, why was my conscience suddenly kicking in out of the blue when I'd suppressed it for days? Ever since I saw Ladinas with Alice...

then I went out to feed on that poor boy and lost control. I never lost control. Not if I was in control to begin with.

I shook my head vigorously. A futile effort to clear my mind—or give myself a concussion and hope it bruised the part of my brain that housed my personal Jiminy Cricket. Because as soon as my conscience kicked in, I'd realized all the shit I'd done. All the people I'd hurt. I wanted it to go away...

But then I thought about Mel, Muggs, even Clarissa. My baby vamps. My progenies. I was being selfish. But even at my worst, I'd never been this bad. I told Calivion that I want to be a fucking goddess? Who says shit like that?

"But you must feed!" Calivion insisted. "More blood! More death!"

I tilted my head. "That's how you're doing it, isn't it?"

"Doing what, my love?" Calivion grazed my cheek with the back of his hand.

I snapped and grabbed his wrist. "You're still a part of me. When I feed it gives you control... it's how you're influencing me..."

Calivion huffed. "Oh, please. I am what I am!"

"You're a combination of two gatekeeper dragons. A part of you is Oblivion, who craves chaos and destruction. But Caladbolg is in there too. I'm guessing that when I feed Oblivion takes the reins, am I right?"

"Pish posh!" Calivion waved his hand through the air. "I'm just me. Besides, I'm not urging you to do anything you don't already desire. You *want* to feed, don't you, Mercy?"

I snorted. "Not really."

"But you have to! I insist!"

Calivion grabbed my wrist and started dragging me through the street toward a bar. I kicked at the back of his legs, but it had no effect. I was no slouch, but this bastard had fortitude.

As we approached the bar, I saw a group of people leaving, laughing and joking with each other. I tried to pull away from Calivion, but he clung to me.

"Look at them," he said, pointing at the group. "They're so happy, so carefree. Don't you want to feel that way?"

"I don't need to feed to feel free," I said through gritted teeth.

"They're just humans," Calivion said, his eyes glinting dangerously. "They're nothing to us. We're above them, Mercy. We're powerful. We're strong. We're invincible."

I shook my head, but Calivion's grip on my wrist only tightened. As we approached the group of people, I saw fear in their eyes. They must have recognized us. We were becoming infamous, thanks to the cops who'd blasted my image across social media feeds and the local news channels.

"Please," I said, trying to reason with Calivion. "Let them go."

But it was too late. Calivion had already torn open the neck of the nearest human. Blood spurted onto his face, and I recoiled in horror. But then, something inside me snapped. Suddenly, I felt it. The primal urge to feed, to kill, to destroy. It was the kind of bloodlust I hadn't known since I was a youngling. Something about this dragon's influence amplified my desires, my cravings...

I tore my wrist out of Calivion's grasp and lunged at the nearest human. My fangs dug deep into his flesh, and I drank greedily, relishing in the rush that flooded through my veins.

Calivion joined me, and together, we attacked everyone we could grab while the rest fled in terror. It was chaos, pure and simple, and I loved every moment of it.

But as the last human fell to the ground, lifeless and drained of blood, I felt a pang of guilt. What had I become? This wasn't me...

Calivion grinned at me, blood dripping from his face. He didn't drink, but he was a part of me. When I fed, he fed. "Ahh. Yes. That's better. I feel alive again!"

I pushed Calivion away from me, disgusted with what we'd just done. "No. This is not better. This is not living. This is madness."

Calivion chuckled. "Madness? Perhaps. But it is only madness because you refuse to embrace your true nature, Mercy. You are a vampire, a being of darkness and death. You thrive on chaos and destruction. Why do you think, as Oblivion, I accepted you to begin with? It wasn't your virtue, like you believed. It was your potential. And I will help you fulfill your destiny, whether you like it or not."

I shook my head. "No. I won't let you control me. I won't let you turn me into a monster."

Calivion shrugged. "A little late for that, don't you think? You cannot deny what you are. The choice is simple. Accept what you are and we'll grow more powerful together until nothing in the world can stop us. Or try to suppress your desires; test the world and see how unforgiving they are after all you've done. I doubt even your so-called vampire underground would take you back. And why would you want to go back there, anyway? With that Alice bitch fucking Ladinas, her screams filling the halls. You can't get away from it. They humiliated you. The great Mercy Brown. And you think you can walk back in there like some kind of vampire queen and they'll take you back? You think they'll *ever* respect you again?"

I turned away from him, unable to look at him any longer. He was right. There wasn't any going back. What was done was done. Things could never be the same again.

"Feed again, my love. Drown out these troubling thoughts. The stronger we become together, the less you'll be plagued by such sentiments."

Getting stronger together. The one thing I knew that Oblivion was interested in was nothing at all. Literally, *nothing.* His goal was to swallow up all existence into the void. He'd told me as much *before* Caladbolg bound himself to Oblivion. Where *was* Caladbolg? He was in Calivion, somewhere, but so long as I kept feeding Oblivion, he never had a chance. I had to figure out a way to fix this. But all it took was a little blood and that bastard had me jonesing like a crack addict.

If only I knew a way to force Calivion to return to the form of the rapier, the blade he'd possessed after the two dragons merged. It was an ethereal weapon that had formed in my hand when I said the name, "Calivion," and maybe since I'd recently fed, that's how he had the strength to manifest.

I didn't know what the hell I was dealing with. Only that I couldn't get away from him. A part of me didn't want to. Another part of me—the better part—wanted to run as fast as I could and never see the son of a bitch again. That wasn't an option, though. We were connected. And I was vulnerable to his suggestions. Moreso after a feed.

But somehow, for some reason, I was gaining clarity. The last time I'd let on that I was second-guessing him, he tore open a poor girl's neck and made me feed. Honesty was a deadly policy in this situation.

But how do you outwit an entity that's a part of you, who is inside of you? He could manipulate my emotions, and I suspected he could read my thoughts. Some of them, anyway. From what I could tell, he only took notice of my clearest thoughts, those that I dwelled on. If I was going to outsmart the bastard, or free myself of his influence, I had to guard my mind. You wouldn't believe how hard it is *not* to think about something. Just telling myself *not* to think about how to get rid of Calivion meant I was thinking about it already.

I needed to use the only power I really had over him—something he couldn't resist.

I traced my finger along Calivion's shoulder, the dragon-scale armor cool to the touch. "What do you say we head in for the day? I realize we have several hours of darkness left, but I'm not sure I can wait that long. I want you all to myself..."

Calivion grinned widely. He was remarkably attractive—even if he was *pure* evil. "Very well, my love. If I am your desire, who am I to refuse? But I grow tired of these dingy warehouses and abandoned storefronts. Follow me, I have an idea."

I raised an eyebrow. "An idea?"

"You're supposed to be a queen, am I right? You wish to be a goddess. You deserve a castle."

I snorted. "A castle? We're in America. Castles aren't exactly littering the countryside."

Calivion stepped behind me and put his arms around my waist. He spread his wings. "I have a place in mind. A place suitable for your new army."

I gulped. "My new army? What are you talking about?"

"You don't intend to take over the world alone, do you?"

Before I could respond, Calivion flapped his wings and we took off into the sky. We were heading east—toward Newport. We flew fast—the world below little more than a blur. When he slowed down, hovering in mid-air, I saw it below us.

Belcourt Castle. Not really a "castle" in the medieval sense. More like a mansion. Construction there began the same year I was turned, in 1891. Last I knew, it had been converted into an art gallery and an event space.

And from the looks of it, something was going on...

Calivion lowered us to the steps. A car parked outside, a classic Chevrolet, with tin cans tied to the bumper and words in shoe-polish on the rear window reading "Just Married" suggested we were about to crash someone's wedding reception.

And we weren't there for free cake and dancing.

Chapter 3

THE THUMPING BASS OF the wedding reception pulsed against my eardrums as Calivion and I stood on the grand steps of Belcourt Castle. I eyed the ornate doors, picturing the revelry happening within—laughing guests raising glasses of champagne, women in glittering dresses twirling across the dancefloor, the bride and groom gazing lovingly at one another.

It was supposed to be a joyous occasion. The best day of a young couple's life so far. Not the nightmare Calivion was about to make it.

"Please, Calivion," I begged, taking his arm. "We can't attack these people. If you want the castle so badly, we'll wait a few hours until the party's over."

He scoffed. "Their lives are meaningless. All that matters is creating an army bound by bloodlust. With you as their maker, they will be unstoppable!"

I shook my head. "I don't want mindless killers under my command. When I choose progeny, it will be for their character, not their craving for violence."

Calivion's eyes flashed dangerously. "You're still clinging to your pathetic humanity," he sneered. "How many centuries need you endure as a vampire before you leave such pettiness behind? These vampires will not be your friends. Just bloodthirsty soldiers. We'll use your magic to heal any of their victims afterwards, expanding your forces exponentially. Think of it, Mercy. We can take the world, spreading your kin far and wide, and they'll all be under your command as their sire. More than that, if you do not wish to feed so frequently, your younglings can do it for you. All we'll need to do is follow the carnage and revive the bitten into a larger army."

"That sounds like a fucking nightmare! I won't do it!" I crossed my arms in front of my chest, but I was hiding a deeper-seeded fear that all he had to do was attack a few people and whatever tendrils he had probing my mind would awaken my bloodlust again.

"I thought we wanted the same thing, my queen. To spread delightful chaos! Your will shall be the only order than remains on the earth. Everyone will bend their knee to you, their queen, their goddess!"

I shuddered. How didn't I see this coming before? He didn't care about ruling the world. He craved anarchy. He appealed to my ego, and my bloodlust, to spread the mayhem he craved. Since he was in my head, he found whatever he could use to his advantage and doused it with the gasoline of his influence.

I cared little about power. Not the ruling-the-world kind. But I was hurting. Ever since I discovered Alice and Ladians had been banging for a century their-time in a pocket dimension while I risked my existence to save them.

I only desired power because I desperately craved *control*, a way to protect myself from the unpredictable bullshit that seemed to smash into my face every time I opened my heart to anyone. That's what Calivion exploited, cloaking his temptations with delusions of divinity and ruling worlds. He was playing me like a snake charmer's flute.

But how could I resist? Every time I tried, he'd open some poor schlep's veins and trigger my bloodlust, giving him more control each time it happened.

Calivion burst through the double doors, his black wings tucked behind his back. "Come, my queen," he purred. "Let us begin our reign of glorious chaos."

Reluctantly, I followed him into the opulent ballroom. Chandeliers glittered overhead, illuminating the wedding guests dancing gracefully to a string quartet. The bride was radiant, her groom dashing. My dead heart ached for their innocence.

Revelers swirled around us, oblivious to the vipers in their midst.

At the head table, Calivion halted behind the unsuspecting bride. She was a picture, blonde wavy hair, wide eyes, and a round, youthful face. Her dress was extravagant, pure white and adorned with sequins and pearls. She giggled, leaning into her new husband. Calivion seized her delicate wrist, yanking her to her feet. She shrieked. Guests jumped up, shouting.

Calivion raised a clawed hand, poised to strike. But before I could intervene, the groom charged forward bravely, the force of his body against Calivion's, only forcing the dragon back a few steps. I acted on instinct, tackling Calivion from the side. We crashed to the floor in a tangle of limbs. The bride scrabbled back into her husband's arms, sobbing.

"Run!" I yelled at the stunned guests. "Get out, now!"

Calivion roared, shoving me off. His eyes glowed crimson with rage. "You dare defy me?"

The ballroom erupted into chaos. Guests stampeded for the exits as Calivion and I circled each other. His lips curled in a snarl.

"I gave you power," he hissed. "And I can take it away."

My veins burned with defiance. "I don't want your shitty power. I have everything I need already."

Calivion leapt at me with lightning speed. I barely dodged his attack, feeling his claws rake across my shoulder. The scent of my blood hit the air, rich and metallic.

Calivion inhaled deeply, his pupils dilating. "Yessss," he purred. "Delicious…"

"I won't play your games anymore," I said through gritted teeth. Behind Calivion, I saw the bride and groom slip out the back door.

Calivion heard the door slam shut and spun on his heel.

Shit…

Using my vampiric speed, I sprinted for the door. Calivion roared as he blasted through. We burst into a narrow hallway, the thrum of music fading. I tracked the couple's scent to the kitchen, but Calivion was in my head. Because I'd located them, he knew where they were.

Calivion winked at me. "Thanks for that. I'm only doing this for your own good."

"Killing people isn't what I want. I don't want your kind of power. I just want to get rid of the fucking pain. I never should have listened to you."

Calivion laughed. "As if you ever had a choice."

Then he took off toward the kitchen. I didn't know how to stop him, but I had to try. I grabbed and tugged at his wings from behind as I kept pace, but he plowed forward.

The groom whirled as we crashed through the doors. The bride screamed, clutching his arm.

Calivion advanced on them, licking his lips. "Congratulations," Calivion added. "I come bearing gifts. The gift of immortality!"

I snorted. "You don't want it! He wants me to turn you into vampires."

The groom stepped protectively in front of his bride. "I know you! You're that killer from the news! Stay back!" His voice quavered.

I positioned myself between Calivion and the couple. They'd heard of me, thinking I was some kind of serial killer. "He's the monster, here. You guys need to get out of here." I narrowed my eyes. "Let them go, Calivion."

Calivion's eyes narrowed. "I don't take orders from you."

He shoved me aside and grabbed the groom by the throat. The man choked, face reddening.

"No!" I shouted. But before I could intervene, the lights abruptly went out, plunging us into darkness.

The bride's screams pierced the shadows. I blinked, letting my vampire vision adjust.

A cloaked figure darted between the tables, too quick for human eyes. He paused, tilting his head as if listening. Then he turned and sprang toward us.

Calivion released the groom with a snarl. With a brief flash of light from the hallway doors, the couple fled into relative safety.

But where had Calivion gone? I could see in the dark, but I didn't see him anywhere. Did he leave to pursue the couple? No, I would have noticed.

The figure halted before me. Broad shoulders, confident stance—a hunter. He raised a strange glove. A pulse of light blasted from its palm, momentarily blinding me.

"Neat trick!" I screamed at the mysterious hunter. His heart beat was steady. Usually if I encountered a hunter, or anyone who knew who they were dealing with, their hearts raced as if they'd just finished wind sprints. "My eyes will heal. And I can hear you. You're no match for me."

The moron smelled of cedarwood and mint. Subtle enough that most vampires wouldn't notice, but with my senses heightened by my recent feeds, I picked up the scent of his body wash. Combined with my acute hearing, I easily identified the hunter's position.

I raised my wand. *"Enerva!"*

Quick footsteps in response.

Damn it! I missed.

This wasn't some slouch, some punk who'd seen too many *Buffy* or *Supernatural* episodes. This guy was a real pro, like a genuine Van Helsing.

More rapid footsteps. This time heading straight toward me. Zeroing in on the hunter's location, I struck out reflexively. He deftly sidestepped, using my momentum to throw me off balance. I stumbled, shocked by his skill. No human should be able to match my speed and strength so easily.

He pressed the attack, raining precise blows. I blocked and dodged, struggling to regain my footing.

Then a tight grip on my wrist. I couldn't pull free.

What the hell was this guy on?

With a final quick twist, he flipped me onto my back. Before I could rise, his boot pinned my chest. A sharp wooden point pricked my sternum.

I trembled in shock. With a stake in my heart, I was on my way to vampire hell. Chances were, better than not, this hunter would burn out my heart before I revived.

This is it. It's over...

So goes the legend of Mercy Brown. Was she a hero or a villain? Depended on the day of the week. But people would remember me not for the many times I'd helped save the world. I'd live in infamy as the onetime vampire-witch who'd given in to her darkness... a merciless killer...

I wasn't sure if I was more afraid or relieved.

As darkness claimed me, I heard Calivion's enraged screams echo in my mind. If I was on my way to hell, he was coming with me. But then his voice faded and my mind drifted into silent oblivion.

I looked around. Pure and utter blackness. No wraiths. Not like I'd encountered in vampire hell before. This wasn't my hell.

It was Calivion's hell. Oblivion's oblivion. I was in the void.

I floated in endless nothingness, devoid of light or sound. How long had I lingered here in this empty oblivion? Minutes, hours, centuries - time held no meaning in the void.

My battle with the hunter replayed in my mind. His gauntlet had blinded me. Celestial magic, most likely, but that guy was not a member of the Order of the Morning Dawn. He was a rogue, independent, and I wasn't the first vampire he'd bested. He knew how to deal with me, how to use my strength and speed to *his* advantage. He wasn't half as strong or fast as me, but his skill overcame his natural deficiencies.

Who was he? Some ancient slayer sworn to end me forever? Someone who'd seen my face on the news and came to Rhode Island to do what the police—and my old friends with the Vampire Underground—couldn't?

Why did I even care? I was gone. I'd never find out who he was, anyway. Had he already burned out my heart? I felt nothing, no connection at all to my life before.

I searched inward for Calivion's whispering voice but found only silence. My thoughts were my own. No cruel words or bloodthirsty urgings corrupted my conscience now. The void had liberated me from the dragon's malevolent influence. For the time being. But this was Oblivion's domain. He was here... somewhere... in the middle of this literal nowhere.

I drifted through the darkness, contemplating my unnatural life. Perhaps this oblivion was a fitting end. At least Calivion couldn't hurt anyone through me. If I must die to be free, so be it.

Chapter 4

A PINPRICK OF LIGHT startled me awake. One second I was floating in nothingness, the next I was back. Had this mysterious hunter neglected to burn out my heart? A hunter of his skill surely knew better. So why leave me alive?

As my vision adjusted, strains of Bon Jovi's "Dead or Alive" reached my ears, along with someone singing terribly off-key in a deep, raspy voice. I tried to move and found myself chained to a wall with silver. Some vampires had a more acute silver allergy than others. The metal was an annoyance rather than genuine pain for me, but it still dulled my preternatural strength. No way I could break free.

I surveyed my surroundings, trying to get my bearings. The room was dingy and coated in dust, with random car parts scattered on shelves along the walls. Some kind of storage room or basement.

"Hey, asshole!" I shouted, hoping to get my captor's attention.

A few seconds later, the music cut off abruptly. I heard some banging noises, then heavy footsteps approaching. A tall, muscular man emerged from another room, hair long and beard trimmed tight. Sleeveless shirt showing off his physique. Hands black with grease, tool belt around his waist. If he wasn't my jailer, I might have found him attractive.

He was a mechanic. But from my experience fighting the bastard, he was a lot more than that.

I looked my captor up and down. "Holy crap. I've been captured by freaking Aquaman."

The hunter chuckled. "You aren't the first who has told me I look like Jason Momoa."

He extended a hand. "Name's Sebastian Winter. Pleased to finally meet you, Mercy Brown."

I rolled my eyes, flexing against the silver chains. "Unlock me and I'll shake your damn hand."

Sebastian laughed, tapping his temple. "Too smart for that. You're not the first vampire I've caught. But probably the first I didn't burn, so, you know, if you're keeping a gratitude list, add that to the top."

Unease stirred in my gut. Just what did this hunter have planned for me? I had to keep him talking, figure out his game. The silver dulled my strength for the moment, but I'd escaped worse scrapes than this. All I needed was an opening.

I looked Sebastian in the eyes. "Why didn't you kill me? You could have ended this, once and for all. After everything I've done... I can't say I don't deserve it."

Sebastian pulled a chair over and sat down across from me.

"Let's see. What have you done? Since I've been tracking you, you've saved the world from demons possessing vampires. There was that whole ordeal with the wild hunt, Moll Dyer, and her deal with Lucifer. You stopped Jack the Ripper from coming back for a sequel. And you kicked some serious faerie ass when those little bastards tried to enslave humanity."

He leaned forward, elbows on his knees. "The way I figure it, recent indiscretions aside, you're an asset. For humanity, I mean. Regardless of *what* you are, *who* you are is what really matters. You've shown your character more than once through the years. You've saved all of us time and time again. Now it's time to repay the favor. Let someone save you, for once."

I barked out a harsh laugh. "You're a hunter. Isn't killing vampires what you do?"

Sebastian winced, like I'd insulted him personally. "I'm not like other hunters. I prefer the term sentinel. I don't hunt vampires indiscriminately. I only go after those who are a true danger to humanity."

He stood and paced in front of me. "I'm a protector, not an executioner. My goal isn't to wipe out all supernaturals, just the monsters. And by monster, I mean anyone—human, vampire, whatever—who preys on the innocent."

I scoffed. "Well, that certainly includes plenty of humans."

Sebastian nodded. "Exactly. I don't discriminate based on species. You threaten the innocent, that makes you a monster. Usually I leave humans to the authorities, but those who are dabbling with magic, powers beyond their understanding, things the authorities aren't suited to handle, well, that's my specialty. Simple as that."

I studied him, searching for any sign of deception. But his steady gaze didn't waver. Could this hunter actually be some kind of noble protector? What motivated a guy like this? Someone doesn't just wake up one day and start hunting monsters.

He had wounds… deep wounds…

"So what, you're some kind of vigilante?" I asked, genuine curiosity creeping into my tone.

Sebastian grimaced slightly at the term. "I wouldn't use that word exactly. But yes, I act outside the law to protect people from threats they don't even know exist."

He leaned forward, intensity burning in his eyes. "I'm a sentinel guarding the borders between the human world and the supernatural one. Keeping the peace, keeping the innocent safe. It's a duty I chose for myself. Just like you did once, before Oblivion got its claws in you."

I flinched at the mention of the dragon's name. Suddenly its presence stirred within me, like a coiled serpent uncurling from sleep.

"You know his name?" I whispered. "Where is he? What have you done with him?"

Sebastian held up a hand. "One second. I'll explain everything." He turned to leave but stopped, pivoted back, and extended his index finger. "Whatever you do, do not speak the dragon's name."

He disappeared through a side door, leaving me confused and on edge. What did he know about Oblivion? And what was this sentinel planning to do with me?

Sebastian returned clutching an ancient tome, its leather cover embossed with intricate dragon motifs. He held it open before my face.

"This is how I learned who that strange winged man with you was, how he was a dragon, and not a man," he said. "Dragon possession is rare, but it's happened before. This journal belonged to a hunter who dealt with a case centuries ago. He said the only way to fully exorcise the demon was to kill the host."

Sebastian snapped the book shut, a small cloud of dust puffing into the air.

"So I figured staking you for a bit might do the trick. You're dead already, after all." He chuckled. "Looks like it reset Oblivion, at least temporarily. I'm betting he's still rattling around inside you, though. The moment you feed, he'll be back."

I glared up at the sentinel. "Yeah, about that. In case you hadn't noticed, I'm a vampire. I'm going to need to feed, eventually. And when I do, Oblivion will return."

Sebastian grinned and flipped open the ancient book once more, scanning the faded pages.

"Not necessarily," he said. "According to this, if you perform a noble act—if you save a life rather than take one—it will strengthen the power of Caladbolg, the other dragon within you."

He snapped the book shut again. "I've been watching you these past few months, Mercy. There's light and dark warring inside you. Another dragon, not just Oblivion. Caladbolg, right?"

I nodded slowly. "Yes, but they're two parts of the same whole. Calivion is both destruction and protection. The two dragons merged in the pocket dimension where I found them. Now they're bound to me, two sides of one coin."

Sebastian leaned forward, his eyes intense. "But if the legends about Caladbolg are true, then a selfless act, one in service of balance, could give him more influence. If his power grows enough to emerge before Oblivion's, he may keep control when you have to feed again. It's your best shot at keeping Oblivion at bay."

I mulled this over. It was a long shot, but I was desperate. If I had any hope of reclaiming my life, I needed to try.

I eyed Sebastian warily. "You're taking an awful risk trying to save me. What's your angle?"

He sighed and ran a hand through his hair. "It's just a gut feeling. Call me an idealist, but I think the world's better off with at least one vampire—namely, you—keeping the rest of your kind in check. Like I said, I've been observing you from afar for years. I know how we all owe you a debt of gratitude. This is my attempt to pay off that debt. Besides, imagine the shit show starring thousands of other vampires worldwide without you around to keep them in check? Things could get ugly fast."

I had to admit, he had a point. The vampire factions respected me, even feared me a little. I'd helped to keep us hidden from mortal society.

Still, I wasn't convinced of Sebastian's motives. He was a hunter, after all. Or sentinel, or whatever cute label he wanted to slap on it so he could sleep at night.

"So what's the plan, then?" I asked warily.

In response, he pulled a set of keys from his pocket and jangled them. "Got a lead on a pack of werewolves up in Maine. You're going to help me take them out."

I frowned as he started unlocking my shackles. A part of me wanted to lash out, but Sebastian didn't kill me when he had the chance. If he was right, if there was a way to get rid of Calivion's influence over me, I had to trust the guy. For the time being, at least. "Funny, I thought you didn't just indiscriminately kill things because of what they are. That's what separates you from the other hunters, right?"

"These aren't just random werewolves, Mercy." He gestured to a wall plastered with newspaper clippings chronicling the grisly murders. "It's a nasty bunch, racking up quite the body count. They've gone rogue, feral. Killing anyone unlucky enough to cross their path under the full moon. Even their own kind wants them put down." His expression was grim. "So, you in or not?"

I fell silent, considering. Werewolves were something of a bane to my existence. A werewolf's bite didn't kill vampires, but it left us wishing we were dead. It took a century or more for the pain to wane and, usually, drove the vampire murderous and insane. That's why, under most circumstances, we steered clear of the beasts. But I'd dealt with werewolves before. I wasn't a total amateur. At least I knew the risks and what we were facing.

"What if I say no?" I asked.

Sebastian shrugged. "Then I take you again. I'm betting on your history, Mercy Brown. You realize what I'm doing here goes against every code, every manual, that hunters follow? But like I said, I don't call myself a hunter. I'm betting on you. Don't let me down."

I took a deep breath. What other choice did I have? I couldn't just waltz back to the Vampire Underground and beg Ladinas, Alice, Mel, Muggs, and the rest to let bygones be. Besides, the more I was around Ladinas and Alice, the more fodder Calivion had to use against me if he emerged again.

I didn't trust Sebastian, not totally, but he was right. He'd had a chance to do me in and chose to save me. If this was what we had to do, and if we were going to save some lives in the process, well, what did I have to lose?

I flexed my fingers, my wrists now free from my shackles. Sebastian's heartbeat remained steady. This guy really wasn't scared of me—or probably anything—in the least. This guy had one hell of a story. Eventually, I'd learn it. "Where's my wand?" I asked. "If we're going to do this, I need it."

Sebastian winked at me. "In the seat of my baby."

I raised an eyebrow. "Your baby? Seriously?"

Sebastian gestured toward his garage. His car was a thing of beauty. Cherry-red with black racing stripes. "She's a 1970 LS6 Chevelle. King of the Road in her day. With my mods, she still is."

I chuckled. "Nice car. Almost as cool as my hearse."

Sebastian winked at me. "Right. Almost. Okay, if we leave now, we can get to Maine before sunrise."

I bit my lip. "How long did you leave me staked? I wasn't in hell. I was in the void. Hard to say how much time passed."

Sebastian shrugged. "It's been a few days. Pulled out your stake, and it still took you a few hours to come to. I was getting worried you wouldn't find your way back. I would have revived you sooner, but I wanted to make sure I had a plan to save you. Didn't want to give you false hope."

I shook my head. "Or risk me coming back only to kick your ass?"

Sebastian snickered. "Right."

I took a deep breath. "Well, whatever. We're going to have to do this soon. If I've been down a few days, coming back from a staking, I'll have to feed soon. If feeding brings back Calivion, well…"

Sebastian opened the passenger side door of his admittedly gorgeous car and I climbed in. "Then we'd best hit the road and kill ourselves some wolves."

Chapter 5

THE CHEVELLE'S ENGINE ROARED to life, the garage door rattling in protest. Sebastian cranked the stereo, and the opening riff of "Hungry Like the Wolf" blasted through the speakers. I winced, the sudden noise like shards of glass in my sensitive ears.

"Duran Duran," I chuckled. "Ironic, right?"

"What? I can't hear you!" Sebastian yelled over the deafening music. I leaned over and turned the volume down a few notches.

"I said, it's kind of ironic we're going werewolf hunting with this song playing."

Sebastian glanced at me, amusement flickering in his icy blue eyes. "I guess it's a little ironic. But it's not really about werewolves, you know. It's about a guy who's hungry for a woman, willing to do anything to get her attention."

I rolled my eyes. Was he really going to be like that? Classic rock snob. "Still ironic."

Sebastian just shrugged and cranked the music back up, his fingers drumming along to the beat on the steering wheel. The wind whipped through our hair as we flew down the highway, the Chevelle's engine purring. Maine was still hours away, nothing but darkness and road ahead.

I gazed out at the moon, nearly full in the night sky. The actual full moon wasn't until tomorrow night. I leaned over and turned down the music again, cutting through the wailing guitar solo.

"So where are we staying tomorrow?" I asked. "You know I can't be out past sunrise."

Sebastian's eyes remained fixed on the road. "I've got a place lined up. Don't worry about it."

I studied Sebastian's profile, trying to get a read on him. He was still such a mystery to me.

"Where are you from, originally?" I asked.

Sebastian's mouth quirked. "Here and there."

"Yeah, but where were you born?"

He hesitated. "I'm not sure, exactly."

Cryptic bullshit. I wondered if I'd ever get a straight answer out of him.

Sebastian glanced at me, as if reading my skepticism. "I don't really have a place I call home. The garage back in Providence was just a rental. I've been using it to keep an eye on things the last few months."

I raised an eyebrow. "So you were in Providence all this time? Why didn't you help with Jector? Or the faeries?"

Sebastian gripped the wheel, his knuckles whitening. "I had other matters to deal with. And I knew you could handle it." He flashed a sly grin. "I don't usually slay well with others."

I rolled my eyes again. "Yeah, well, you're bringing me along this time."

"That's different," Sebastian added. "You're as much the mission as you are my assistant."

I snorted. "I'm your assistant?"

Sebastian winked at me. "I bested you last time we fought. That makes you, the..." He trailed off.

"Your bitch?" I raised an eyebrow. "Were you seriously going to call me your bitch?"

Sebastian laughed. "No, I wouldn't do that."

I shrugged and backhanded the burly hunk of manliness beside me on his shoulder. "Well I am a bitch. Just not someone else's bitch."

Sebastian gulped. "No comment. I think that's one of those things a female says that if a guy replies to it in any way at all, he's screwed. Damned if you do, damned if you don't."

I twirled my wand as I laughed. "Someone has trained you well." I was fishing for more clues about the strange "sentinel's" past, but he wasn't giving.

I reached into the backseat, my fingers brushing against the strange gauntlet, part metal, part leather. Before I could grasp it, Sebastian's hand shot back and slapped mine away.

The car swerved violently before he regained control. "Don't touch that!" he snapped.

I held up my hands. "Whoa there, didn't mean to ruffle your feathers. I was just curious about that thing. It's the one that blinded me, right?"

Sebastian's jaw clenched, his eyes fixed on the road. "Yes. But it's not a toy. If I still had celestial power coursing through that thing, it would burn the shit out of you."

"Sorry," I said. "I've just never seen anything like it. How does it work?"

"It's enchanted," Sebastian explained, some of the edge leaving his voice. "I have a colleague who is damn good with magical artifacts. He made this for me to use in my work."

I leaned closer, peering at the intricate tool strapped to his wrist. "What kind of magic does it hold?"

"Depends on the crystal I fit into it," he said. "But the crystals are only a part of it. Right now, it has a silver dagger that can pop in and out. Squeeze my fist, deliver a swift punch to a werewolf's gut, and the monster's as good as dead."

He paused, giving me a sidelong glance. "Before, when I was after you, it had a stake carved from oak wood."

I raised an eyebrow. "Yet now you've already got it swapped to silver. That's pretty bold, considering you're driving around with me."

Sebastian shrugged, eyes back on the road. "I don't think you're going to 'turn' on me. We want the same thing now—to get rid of that dragon rattling around in your head. And I meant what I said back there. I still believe the world's a better place with you in it."

His words sent an unexpected warmth through my undead heart. I quickly deflected. "So what other kinds of crystals can that thing hold?"

Sebastian relaxed, seeming glad to change the subject. "All sorts. Celestial light is useful against vampires, and can also smite demons. An infernal crystal channels hellfire for heavy damage, good against pretty much anything. I also have druidic crystals that can heal wounds. I even have a lightning stone I got from a voodoo priestess in New Orleans."

"New Orleans?" I raised an eyebrow. "I've spent most of my vampiric life in that city."

Sebastian nodded. "I know. Funny we've never met, right?"

I rolled my eyes. "Yeah. Hilarious. Makes me wonder what you've been up to all this time."

"If you'd heard of me, it would have meant I'd failed at my job. I'm not in this for the glory, Mercy. I'd rather people not know what I do."

This guy was a mystery, wrapped in an enigma, shrouded in a giant package of what- the-fuck. The more I learned about him, the more curious I was. Who was he really? And what experiences had forged him into... whatever he was.

My curiosity was piqued, but Sebastian's body language told me he wasn't ready to delve deeper. I let it go for now. We still had a long drive ahead, and nothing fucks with a road trip more than awkward tension. After a few days in the void, I was just glad to be alive again.

I studied his face, trying to get a read on him. He seemed so casual on the surface, so rough and tough. But I could see it in his eyes. All of that was covering up a deep well of pain and purpose underneath.

There was more to all of this than saving me. It was personal. I just didn't know why.

"Well," I said, leaning back in my seat. "I guess I'll just have to solve the mystery of Sebastian Winter one piece at a time."

He smiled, the corners of his mouth tense. "Good luck with that."

Chapter 6

THE PASSENGER WINDOW FRAMED a postcard view of quaint New England as we rolled into Farmington, Maine. I gazed out the passenger window, taking in the picturesque scenery. In neither my nineteen years as a human nor my 130+ years as a vampire did I ever venture further north than Rhode Island. When I left Exeter with Nico, we headed to New Orleans and in all my years, I'd only rarely left town. Vacationing isn't easy when you're a vampire. Daylight limits our travels. Just try finding a flight anywhere that both takes off and lands the same night. Even under the streetlights, though, the town of Farmington was vibrant and had all the markings of pleasant suburban life. The quaint houses and colorful foliage were more welcoming than I'd expected. It wasn't the kind of place one would usually think was about to be under assault by werewolves.

"Farmington's a college town," Sebastian said as he navigated the narrow streets. "A lot of young, foolish kids around here." His grip tightened on the steering wheel as he continued, "That's why it's so crucial we deal with these werewolves. They've recently moved into the surrounding woods and mountains, and they're getting too close for comfort."

I glanced over at Sebastian, his jaw set with determination. I still didn't trust him totally, but my only other choice was becoming Calivion's plaything again. There was an allure of mystery around the sentinel, something that drew me in like a schoolgirl with a crush, but also screamed back at me to steer clear. Sebastian was a beautiful specimen of a man—but he was also damaged, some-how. If anything, that only intrigued me more. He did his best to cover up his wounds—whatever they were—with a rugged façade. He was like an M&M. Hard on the outside. Nuts within.

At least we had *that* in common.

"Any idea how many werewolves we're dealing with?" I asked, trying to keep my tone casual. Inside, though, my stomach churned with a mixture of anticipation and dread. Werewolves were nasty creatures—unpredictable, ruthless, and nearly impossible to kill unless you caught them off guard.

Sebastian shook his head. "No solid numbers yet, but we're not talking about a small pack. These bastards have been growing bolder by the day, and it's only a matter of time before they strike."

"How exactly are you tracking them?" I asked.

Sebastian tossed his phone on the dashboard. "A sentinel down in North Carolina tagged one of the wolves' phones last month while they were shifted. Uploaded a little tracking bug that sends me real-time locations."

"Well, aren't you clever?" I bit my bottom lip. "So why isn't Mr. North Carolina dealing with this himself instead of sending you? Too busy?"

At that, Sebastian's expression darkened. "He tried, last month. Didn't make it. The wolves tore him apart." His jaw clenched, fingers tightening around the steering wheel. "The tracking bug was an insurance policy in case any of them got away."

"And you just happen to have access to this dead hunter's tracking program?" I cocked an eyebrow. "I'm guessing there's more to this story than you're letting on."

Sebastian cleared his throat. "He was a friend, alright. I have access to all his shit. Look, Mercy, in my line of work, our life expectancy isn't much better than the next twenty-four hours. Our only shot of making any difference at all is by picking up where our fallen brothers and sisters leave off. I'm finishing the job he started."

"What was his name?" I asked. "Do you want to talk about it?"

Sebastian glanced at me with a raised eyebrow before he turned his focus back on the road. Then he cleared his throat. "What's done is done. What matters is what we do from this point forward. Once that moon rises tonight, the wolf's phone will be with his clothes. We won't be able to track them after that."

I nodded slowly, processing the information. That these werewolves had already killed one sentinel didn't exactly fill me with confidence. But I'd dealt with wolves before. Some of them friendly, others not so much. "I can track them."

Sebastian nodded. "So can I, but having you with us should expedite our hunt. I presume you can hear them coming from a lot further out than I can."

"And smell them." I grimaced. "It's not pleasant. But here's a thought. If you can track them now, why not take them out preemptively? You know, before they shift. Simple enough."

Sebastian let out a dry chuckle. "If only it were that simple. Werewolves are cunning bastards. Even in human form, they're strong, fast."

"Not as strong or fast as they are under the full moon," I added.

"True," Sebastian continued. "But when they're wolves, they operate on instinct. They're predictable. In human form, they're careful, strategic, and conniving. This pack is notorious for using innocents as shields. Sort of like how those terrorists in other parts of the world set up their missiles and assemble their bombs near schools and hospitals. If we attack them now, not only are we going to come in looking like the bad guys, going after what look like innocent humans, but we'll risk putting more lives in danger than is necessary."

I bit my lip. "Surely there's a way we could lure them out."

He shook his head. "They're too smart for that. Don't forget, this pack has dealt with sentinels before. They know what they've done. They're *expecting* us. All that strategy, though, won't amount to much after the moon rises. We wait until they're fully turned. It's the only way."

I cleared my throat. "Color me skeptical."

Sebastian shook his head. "And if we go after them when shifted, there's a chance we can save them."

I shook my head in disbelief. "You can't *cure* a fucking werewolf."

"I know it sounds crazy," Sebastian said. "But I've done it once before. The silver burns away the curse, the body holds on a split second longer."

"And you use your magic glove to heal them at that moment?"

Sebastian nodded. "Like I said, I've done it before."

"You said it's worked once," I sighed and shook my head. "Out of how many times?"

Sebastian sighed. "I don't know. I've lost count. But that one life..."

"Is worth a thousand failures, right?" I finished for him. "Admirable, but seems like a lot of risk taking on a pack like that for little chance of reward."

"Doesn't matter. The odds, the risk—it's irrelevant in the face of saving even one life. That's why I do this. That's the whole damn point." Sebastian's voice was firm, resolute.

I studied his face in the fading light, surprised at the conviction I saw there. "And your life doesn't matter? Fighting these wolves under a full moon, I don't care what you say, it's riskier. It's dangerous."

Sebastian clenched his steering wheel. "I'm on borrowed time. I should have died a long time ago. It should have been me instead of..." Sebastian trailed off, his countenance softening a little before he took a deep breath, gathered himself, and flushed his emotions. "It doesn't matter. This is my job. I'm bringing you along because you need to do something that will keep that damned dragon buried. If we can't do that, if that asshole dragon takes you over again, don't think I'll hesitate to finish what I started."

I chuckled and shook my head. For a moment he was vulnerable, but as soon as he realized it, he doubled-down on his tough-guy act. "You got lucky last time."

"Did I?" Sebastian smirked. "Call it what you want. You're still the one who ended up on the short end of my stick."

I snorted. "Short end of your stick, eh? You aren't the first man who has tried to stick his wood in me, you know."

Sebastian winked at me. "You wouldn't know what to do with a man like me."

"Oh, really?" I laughed. "Sounds like a challenge to me."

Sebastian grunted. "Good luck with that. Your allure doesn't affect me. I'm numb to that shit. And I don't do vamps."

"Excuse me?" I stared at Sebastian blankly, but he kept his eyes fixed straight ahead. "How presumptuous! Why would you *think* I'd even be interested in a human like you, anyway?"

Sebastian shrugged. "Don't flatter yourself. I wasn't implying you were interested. Not really. But I know how vampires operate. You hope to seduce me, lure me in with those irresistible eyes, your womanly figure, until I'd do whatever you want. Thing is, that doesn't work on someone like me. To catch a fire, you need a spark. My last embers burned out years ago."

I rolled my eyes. "Well, aren't you just God's gift to monster hunting?"

"I'm good at my job," Sebastian said plainly. "Doesn't mean I enjoy it."

"So where's your hunter friend live?" I asked. "You sure he's alright putting me up for the day?"

"Donnie? He and his mom have a house on the edge of town. Nothing fancy, but it'll do for us to crash and prep for tonight's hunt."

We pulled up to a modest single-story house with peeling blue paint. Sebastian cut the engine and nodded toward the front door.

Before we could even knock, the door swung open, and a sixty-something woman with curlers in her hair answered. "Hello, Mrs. Livingston," Sebastian said with a wide smile and a nod.

"Sebastian!" she exclaimed, pulling him into a tight hug. "So good to see you again! How long has it been? Two years? Three?"

"Longer than that," Sebastian shook his head. "It was B.C. When I helped Donnie kill that wendigo in South Portland."

"B.C.?" I furrowed my brow.

Sebastian chuckled. "Before COVID. All my cases blend together. But I know what happened before and after lockdown. Helps me keep things straight."

Her smile faded as she noticed me lingering behind him. "And who's this?"

"Mrs. Livingston, meet my friend Mercy," Sebastian said. "She's going to help us out tonight."

Mrs. Livingston looked me up and down with pursed lips. "Sebastian Jameson Winter! You're bringing a vampire into my home?"

"Now Martha," Sebastian said gently. "Didn't Donnie tell you we were coming?"

Martha thrust her fists on her hips. "He said you were bringing a woman with you. I thought, well, goddamn, about time. It'd be a shame for such a hunk of a man to go to waste. It's been a decade. About time you moved on and put yourself out there, I figured. Didn't realize she was a *vampire!*"

Sebastian shook his head. "We're not dating. Mercy's one of the good ones. She's here to help. I promise you have nothing to fear from her."

Mrs. Livingston sighed, but stepped aside to let us in. "Fine, then. I *invite* you in, but don't let me regret it, missy."

I raised my hands in mock surrender as I stepped over the threshold. "Wouldn't dream of it."

Martha nodded curtly. "I trust your judgment, Sebastian. But no funny business, you hear?"

"Understood, ma'am." Sebastian nodded and hung his jacket on a coat tree behind the front door.

I was a little surprised that Sebastian trusted me enough to bring me into someone's home. After everything I'd done lately, I wasn't sure I trusted myself. A little blood on my lips and I'd go homicidal. I felt like myself, again, but I knew the dragon was still in there, waiting for a chance to exert his influence.

Sebastian headed for a door that I assumed led to the basement. I followed, taking in the dated floral wallpaper and family photos decorating the hallway.

"So Sebastian Jameson Winter, huh?" I said as we descended the creaky stairs. "Never would have pegged you for an S.J.W."

Sebastian glanced back with a wry smile. "It's a family name. And I'm no social justice warrior, if that's what you're implying." He paused a moment on the stairs, holding the rail with his right hand and pondering his words. "More like a supernatural jackass whacker."

I laughed. "You whack off supernaturals? Whatever you're into, dude. Far be it from me to kink shame."

Sebastian just shook his head and kept walking. I grinned, pleased I could get under his skin a little. Maybe there was a spark in him yet.

We reached the bottom of the stairs and I couldn't believe my eyes. The basement looked like an episode of Hoarders. There were stacks of boxes, old furniture, and just general clutter filling up the entire space. Sebastian didn't seem fazed as he navigated through the maze.

I followed closely behind, ducking under low hanging pipes and squeezing between narrow gaps in the piles of junk. How could anyone live like this?

Finally, we came upon a small clearing in the center of the room. A chubby, balding man sat hunched over a computer desk, headphones on, barking orders into a microphone while his fingers frantically clicked away at a mouse. Empty bags of chips and cheese balls littered his desk and the surrounding floor.

The man was so focused on his game that he didn't even notice us approach. I looked at Sebastian incredulously. *This guy* was a hunter? He looked more like a basement troll.

Sebastian just smiled and put a finger to his lips, indicating for me to keep quiet. He stepped up behind the man and tapped him on the shoulder.

The man jumped and ripped off his headphones, twisting around in surprise. "Sebastian!" he exclaimed. "You're early!"

"Donnie, I'd like you to meet Mercy," Sebastian said, gesturing to me.

Donnie's eyes went wide as he looked at me in awe. "*The* Mercy Brown? I... I'm your biggest fan!"

I blinked in surprise. I guess my reputation preceded me, though I wasn't sure that was a good thing. Still, I managed a smile. "Nice to meet you, Donnie. Thanks for letting us crash here today."

"Your photos don't do you justice!" Donnie exclaimed as he stood up, shaking Cheetos dust off his shirt. "Even the Photoshopped ones on Reddit."

"Excuse me?" I furrowed my brow.

"You know, your face on other people's bodies."

"Unclothed, I presume?"

Donnie stared at me blankly. "Sorry! I don't make them. I just download... I mean, no, I'd never..."

"How many headshots of me are there out there, anyway?" I pinched my chin. "I don't pose for photographers."

Donnie gulped. "I'm sorry. I shouldn't have said anything. I didn't mean to offend... I mean, I should have figured... damn it, Donnie. You're such an idiot!"

I rolled my eyes and glanced at Sebastian. "This is the winner who is going to help us take down a pack of werewolves?"

Sebastian gave me an amused look. "Don't let appearances fool you. Donnie's one of the best hunters out there."

I looked at the doughy man-child before me and raised an eyebrow. Somehow, I found that hard to believe.

I sighed and glanced around the cluttered basement. "So where can a girl get comfortable around here? Is there a decent place to sit and relax for a bit?"

Donnie's eyes lit up. "Oh yeah! You can use my bed if you want." He gestured to a mattress tucked against the wall.

I shrugged and walked over, ready to plop down. But as I got closer, the smell hit me. Moldy socks, stale sweat, and...other unmentionable odors. I noticed a stack of crusty magazines, lotion bottles, and crusty tissues scattered around the stained sheets.

"On second thought, I'm good standing," I said quickly, crinkling my nose in disgust.

Donnie's cheeks flushed bright red. "Oh geez, sorry about that. Here, you can use this." He hurried over and pulled a rickety lawn chair out from under a pile of clothes.

"Thanks," I said, gingerly lowering myself onto the chair. The metal frame creaked under my weight.

I shook my head and smirked. "So let me get this straight—you're what, thirty-something? Living with your mom, no girlfriend, you have a video game addiction, and you hunt monsters?"

Donnie gave a sheepish shrug. "I mean, when you put it like that..."

I shook my head. "Freaking millennials."

Chapter 7

THE METALLIC SCRAPE OF Sebastian pulling a lawn chair across the concrete floor was like nails on a chalkboard. We were stuck in this damn basement with the original Toys R Us kid who really didn't want to grow up. Donnie had already retreated to his computer, headphones clamped firmly over his shiny, bald head. He said he was my biggest fan. Well, he got over it quickly. It took a whole ten minutes before he lost interest in me and returned to his digital addiction. It was just as well. He was lost in another world, battling it out in Fortnite, leaving Sebastian and me surrounded by stacks of boxes and piles of crap.

"So," I began, breaking the suffocating silence, "are we going to sit here all day and watch Donnie's shiny bald head play games, or are we going to talk?"

Sebastian stared at me, his eyes narrowing. "What do you think we have to talk about?"

"Let's see." I leaned back in my chair, idly picking at a loose thread on its armrest. "How about you tell me your story? You said you don't know where you were born. That's a little weird. Then Donnie's mom said something about moving on, implying there was someone in your past. It's obvious you're pretty fucked up, so spill it. What's your story?"

Sebastian squirmed in his seat, probably not expecting to be put on the spot like this. But hell, I'd been through enough shit lately. I was putting a lot of faith in a guy I barely knew, who I only thought I might trust because he didn't burn my heart out of my chest when he had the chance. I had no reason to suspect

Sebastian had ill-intent, but no one just wakes up one day and becomes a warrior against inexplicable evil.

"Fine," he finally spat, his hands gripping the edges of his chair. "Might as well tell you the truth. Maybe you can help me sort it out."

"Trust me," I drawled, "I've seen it all. Give me what you got."

Sebastian's jaw tightened, his eyes clouding over as he retreated into the past.

"I don't know where I was born because my parents gave me up. Abandoned at six months old on the steps of a fire station in Tacoma. I spent most of my childhood bouncing between orphanages and foster homes, getting into trouble. Never really belonged anywhere."

He paused, old hurts rising to the surface. I stayed silent, letting him take his time.

"I aged out of the system with no family to call my own. No real future ahead of me, either. I'd dropped out of high school, was working a dead-end job."

"Flipping burgers?" I asked.

"Oh no," Sebastian shook his head. "I envied that job. I cleaned the fucking grease pits."

I chuckled. "Wouldn't know much about fast food. There weren't joints like that when I was still human. When I became a vampire, my sire provided everything I ever needed. Believe it or not, I've never worked a job. But cleaning grease pits sounds awful."

Sebastian shrugged. "Didn't take me long before I decided I wanted more out of life. I decided to get my GED. That's when I met Angie."

His voice softened on her name.

"She was a tutor at the adult education center. Helped me graduate. We started dating, innocent at first. But after a year, we got married. For the first time in my life, I felt... wanted. Valued."

I nodded, understanding that longing all too well. My own father had tried to murder me, after all.

"Things were good for a while," Sebastian continued. "I got a job as a trainer at a gym, quickly became the lead trainer. Making real money for the first time. Angie got pregnant. We were planning a family, a future. Everything was fucking beautiful."

His voice cracked on those last words. I sensed the tragedy coming but stayed quiet, letting him continue his story in his own time. Some pains run too deep for hasty words.

Sebastian took a shuddering breath, composing himself before continuing.

"One night we went out to celebrate. Angie had her sixteen-week ultrasound earlier that day. I went with her to the appointment. Couldn't tell what we were looking at on the screen, but the tech saw everything. She wrote the gender of our baby on a little index card and stuck it in an envelope so we could find out later. It was Angie's idea. She was good at things like that, always making everything special, every event an occasion."

He smiled sadly at the memory.

"The ultrasound tech gave us a gift certificate to this fancy restaurant downtown. Said she had a few she could give out to deserving couples each month, and there was something about us she liked."

His eyes narrowed, and his voice grew tense.

"We should've known something was off. The place was way too high-end for us. I mean, the gift certificate covered more in food and drinks than the total cost of the ultrasound. But why look a gift horse in the mouth, they say. Count your blessings, don't question them. That was my philosophy. When you're dealt a shit hand at life, you don't question it when you come up with aces."

"I get that," I said. "Nothing wrong with accepting a gift."

Sebastian nodded. "The waiter brought out these weird appetizers, something I'd never heard of. Said they were the house specialty. Not seafood, nothing that Angie couldn't have while pregnant, he told us. So we tried them."

He paused, jaw tightening. I could see the pain in every line of his face.

"Next thing I knew, Angie was choking, gasping for air. I stood up to help, but I lost my balance. The whole place started spinning, and I blacked out. Came to alone in a field, a hundred miles away. I didn't realize it yet, but I'd lost an entire month."

His hands clenched into fists.

"By the time I made it back to the city, the restaurant was just gone. Vanished. Nobody remembered it. It was like it never existed."

I raised an eyebrow. "That's unusual. What about the ultrasound nurse? She sent you there, right? Did you check with her?"

Sebastian took a deep breath. "I went back to the clinic. No one there even knew who she was, said no one who fit her description worked there, and they knew nothing about gift certificates to local restaurants. None of it made sense. Restaurants don't just disappear. People don't just get erased from memory."

He met my gaze, eyes burning with intensity.

I nodded slowly, trying to process his story. A fancy restaurant, a strange waiter, his wife dying before his eyes—it sounded like something supernatural was at play. The kind of evil bullshit I was all too familiar with. But what could be responsible for something like that? Faeries? Demons? Something else? I kept my theories to myself. The last thing Sebastian needed was a lead on a wild goose chase.

"Have you found any clues since then?" I asked. "About what happened to Angie, or about what happened the month you lost?"

Sebastian shook his head, jaw clenched tight. "Nothing concrete. Been chasing dead ends for years. But I know she's still out there, somewhere. Along with our kid."

His voice softened slightly at the mention of the child.

"Don't know if it was a boy or girl. But I'll find them someday. And I'll kill the thing that took them from me."

There was an edge of desperation in his tone now, and something close to madness glinting in his eyes. I knew that look. I'd seen it in the mirror too often myself. The look of someone obsessed with vengeance, willing to sacrifice everything to get it.

"Until then, I'll keep hunting," he continued grimly. "Whatever evil I can find. Saving people from losing what I lost...it's the closest I can get to finding Angie again."

He fell silent, lost in memory and simmering rage. I didn't know what to say. Part of me wanted to help him, to find the truth of what happened. But another part worried where this path would lead him. Down the same dark road I'd stumbled too many times myself.

I sighed, knowing there was little I could say to deter him from his chosen path. Losing a loved one could drive even the best of us to extremes.

"Well, if you ever need help hunting down the supernatural scum of the earth, you know where to find me," I said, forcing a grin. "Ass-kicking is my specialty."

That got a flicker of a smile from him. "I'll keep that in mind."

Just then, a triumphant whoop came from Donnie's corner of the basement. He'd apparently won his round of Fortnite.

"Yeah, take that, fucking newbs!" he crowed, doing a stupid little dance in his computer chair.

I rolled my eyes. "Right, well, any lead on the werewolves?"

Sebastian checked his phone. "They haven't moved. They'll head out before sunset. Even wolves intent on doing damage don't shift in the presence of others. It could give away their identities."

I nodded. "Sure enough."

"And Mercy?" Sebastian reached over and grabbed my hand.

"Yeah?"

"Thanks for, you know, listening and all that," he mumbled.

"Anytime," I said. "Us fucked up people gotta stick together, right?"

I gave him a friendly punch on the shoulder, then sank back into my chair.

"Want to know a secret?" I asked.

"Sure. I showed you mine. Now you show me yours."

"I feel like an idiot," I admitted, slumping back in the lawn chair. "The guy I thought I loved got trapped in a pocket dimension and after experiencing a century while only a few days passed here, he moved on, hooked up with his ex, who was trapped there with him. But he came back. He's not dead. I found him after only a few days, my time. Meanwhile, you lost someone you loved, who you had a real future with, in the blink of an eye. You've spent a decade searching for answers, looking for Angie, without success. And you haven't lost your shit."

Sebastian studied me, his expression unreadable. "Who are you to say I haven't lost my shit? Besides, it's not a competition to see who has the shittiest origin story. My loss doesn't make your pain any less real."

"Maybe not," I sighed. "But at least you didn't go on a 'fuck y'all' rampage afterwards."

"Give yourself some credit," Sebastian said. "You had a powerful dragon bent on destroying all existence in your head. That the entire world wasn't sucked into the void by now means something. You've been fighting your dark side this whole time. That takes guts."

I snorted. "Not as much guts as tracking down supernatural baddies. How'd you even know where to begin?"

"I was asking a lot of strange questions. I drew the attention of an old hunter in Seattle," Sebastian replied. "He approached me, offered to train me up, taught me everything he knew. Spent nearly every day with that old bastard for the first couple of years after..." His voice trailed off.

"After you lost Angie," I finished quietly.

Sebastian nodded, his jaw tightening.

"Well, for what it's worth, I think it's impressive that you fought back." I nudged his foot with mine. "Most people would've just curled up in a ball and given up."

"Yeah, well, giving up was never really my style." A ghost of a smile crossed Sebastian's face. "I've got my own 'fuck y'all' attitude, too. It just manifests differently."

"I'll say. You're a badass, Winter."

"Takes one to know one, Brown."

We sat in companionable silence then, two battle-scarred warriors who'd seen far too much darkness in our lives. But at least we had each other's backs now. And that counted for something.

I tilted my head, studying Sebastian. "Can I ask you something? If it's too personal, tell me to piss off."

He shrugged. "Shoot."

"Why are you wasting time hunting werewolves when it's obvious they aren't connected to what happened to Angie?"

Sebastian was quiet for a moment, contemplating. "You're right, they aren't directly tied to her disappearance. But evil is evil, no matter the form it takes. These werewolves have destroyed lives, ruined families. If I can stop them from inflicting that kind of pain on others... the kind of loss I had to experience..." He trailed off, his jaw tight.

"It's like you're one step closer to finding Angie," I finished for him.

"Exactly." His voice was rough with emotion. "I may not be able to save her yet, but I'll be damned if I don't save someone else from going through what I did."

I nodded slowly. His motivations made sense, even if his methods were unorthodox.

"Can I ask how you know she's still alive?" I ventured cautiously. "Everyone else thinks she's dead, right?"

Sebastian's eyes darkened. "It's just a feeling I have. In my gut. Call it intuition, whatever. But I know she's out there somewhere." His hands curled into fists. "And I won't rest until I find her and the bastard who took her from me."

I believed him. The steel in Sebastian's voice left no room for doubt. He would move heaven and earth to be reunited with his wife. And God help anyone who tried to stand in his way.

Chapter 8

THE STENCH HIT ME like a punch to the gut. I gagged, the noxious fumes burning my nostrils. Donnie's shiny bald head bobbed along to some internal rhythm, eyes glued to the computer screen, oblivious to my discomfort.

"How long's it been since he got up to take a piss?" I asked Sebastian in an undertone.

He shook his head. "Hasn't moved since we got here."

Six empty Mountain Dew cans were strewn around Donnie's desk. My stomach churned as I did the math.

"No way. He can't have just been sitting here..." I sniffed again and wretched. "Oh god, he totally shit himself."

Sebastian yanked Donnie's headphones off. "Hey man, you wearing a diaper right now or what?"

Donnie's fingers froze on the keyboard. "Huh?"

"Did you seriously put on a diaper so you don't have to stop playing that stupid game to go to the bathroom?" Sebastian demanded.

Donnie shrugged. "If I get up to go, I'll lose my squad. Can't pause an online game." He scratched his ass. "Only thirty more minutes until sunset. Then we can go hunt werewolves or whatever."

I dry heaved, hand clamped over my mouth and nose. The things I did for the greater good. I'd never get the stench out of my hair.

"Alright, well, time to get ready I guess," I managed. "Don't want to be late for the monster mash."

Sebastian nodded, glancing at his phone. "The tracker hasn't moved in about thirty minutes. That means, more likely than not, the wolves ditched their phones and headed out to the woods already."

He stood and started going through his duffel bag, pulling out an array of weaponry. A pang of longing hit me as I watched him prep. Back at the Underground, we'd had stockpiles of silver bullets and blades. Not that we could bring any of that through airport security.

"Man, back at the Underground we were loaded on silver rounds," I mused. "Had a whole crate of them in the armory. Would be nice to have some of those bad boys tonight. Whatever, though. I guess I burned that bridge."

Sebastian snorted, his eyes fixed on his various enchanted crystals as he stuck one into the wrist-strap of his tactical gauntlet and slipped the rest in a satchel dangling from his waist. "Get your shit together and deal with Calivion. That's why you're here. Why couldn't you go back?"

I scratched the back of my head. "Well, apart from the fact that I'm Providence's number one 'Most Wanted,' I'm not sure my old team will ever trust me again."

"Maybe you're right," he added casually. Too casually. "You really fucked up." My hackles rose. "Dude. Blunt much?"

He gave me a pointed look. "What's done is done, Mercy. You're never going to get anything back if you're stuck in the past or too worried about what might happen in the future. You know what they say. If you have one foot in the past, the other in the future, you're pissing all over the present."

I glanced at Donnie out of the corner of my eye as he clicked his keys furiously in an effort to drop his digital opponent. "Unless you wear an adult diaper."

Sebastian smirked. "Then you're pissing yourself. Either way, all you can control is the present. Screw the past. Everyone fucks up. That doesn't have to define you. Don't worry about what's next. Do the best with what's right in front of you now. Handle your business. The future will take care of itself."

I crossed my arms. "And all this monster hunting shit has nothing to do with *you* living in the past?"

"The past brought me to where I'm at." Sebastian flexed his fingers in his gauntlet. "There's a difference between using your past and dwelling on it. I can't worry about shit that's outside of my control."

I nodded slowly, considering Sebastian's words. He made it sound so simple—focus on the present, let the future come as it may. But the tangled threads of my past weren't so easily severed.

"I turned my back on the only real family I had," I mumbled. "My progeny—the vampires I sired—they depended on me. And I abandoned them. All because I was pissed off about Ladinas and Alice. And because of my fucked up relationship with Calivion."

Sebastian studied me, his expression unreadable. "You think you're the first broken-hearted girl to go off the rails for a while?" He shook his head. "That shit happens all the time. It doesn't make you a bad leader."

"It does when you're a vampire," I muttered. "When I go on a bender, I don't just lose a few days and embarrass myself. People die."

"This wasn't a bender, Mercy. Sure, you might have gone and fed on someone, but if that dragon wasn't screwing with your mind, do you really think you couldn't have stopped? You've restrained yourself for centuries. You've endured more than a broken heart. Hell, you've had your heart literally torn out of your chest. This wasn't your fault, Mercy. It's that dragon inside of you. He's the real monster."

I shook my head. "Doesn't mean I don't have *some* responsibility in it all. I let that bastard manipulate me. He took advantage of me in a moment of weakness. It's my fault I was weak enough to allow that to happen to begin with."

"Your fault?" Sebastian shook his head. "Sure, you're flawed. Like the rest of us." Sebastian placed a hand on my shoulder. "But that doesn't justify what that dragon did to you, how he took advantage of you. The question is, are you going to continue being the victim, or are you going to fight the fuck back?"

I managed a small smile. "You should become a freaking therapist."

Sebastian laughed. "I told you, I used to be a personal trainer. You can't train the body without training the mind. It all goes together. Doesn't matter if you're overweight trying to break free of your fast food habit and get in shape, or if you're a vampire who's gone off the rails for a season. Are you going to let those cravings, how the dragon manipulates your flesh, control your life? Or will you master the bastard and make him *your* bitch?"

I rolled my eyes, but Sebastian's words struck a chord with me. Maybe it was time to stop letting Calivion control me and take back my power. He didn't have willy-nilly control over me. He was using my weaknesses. He knew I craved power over shit I couldn't control, like what happened with Ladinas and Alice, and in a twist of irony, used my need for control to manipulate me. To use me to fulfill Oblivion's agenda of chaos and destruction. All I had to do was *decide* I didn't care anymore. Screw Ladinas and Alice. Why did I let a *guy* have so much influence over my state of mind, over my self-esteem, over *everything?*

This wasn't just about refusing to let the dragon pull my strings. It meant cutting away all the heartstrings that I'd given to Ladinas. But tonight, well, the present that stared me in the face was a werewolf problem. Deal with these wolves, and whatever else I had to do to reclaim control over the beast within, then if Sebastian was right, the other shit would handle itself.

"Alright, enough touchy-feely crap. Let's go kick some furry ass."

Sebastian grinned. "That's more like it."

"Yo Donnie, time to log off," I said. "We've got werewolves to hunt."

"Just a sec, I gotta finish this round," he mumbled, eyes never leaving the screen.

I sighed, glancing at Sebastian. He gave me a knowing look and nodded toward Donnie.

Rolling my eyes again, I marched over and yanked the headphones off Donnie's head. "Now means now, tubby. Let's move."

"Hey!" Donnie yelled as his character died on screen. He swiveled in his chair, bits of chip crumbs tumbling from his stained shirt. "What the hell?"

"Full moon's rising, dummy. We've got bigger problems than your game." I waved my hand in front of my nose. "And change that diaper. You're ripe."

Donnie grumbled under his breath as he lumbered to his feet. He peeled his sopping diaper off and flung it in the corner. I gagged at the sight, pinching my nose shut.

"Gross, dude! My vampire eyes can't handle your bare ass in HD."

Sebastian chuckled. "The full moon officially rises."

I glanced back at Sebastian. "Yeah, well, the *full moon* has craters, but it doesn't have pimples and a hairy crack."

"The real moon isn't *that white* either," Sebastian added.

"I know, right? I'm a vampire, and I think I have more pigment in my ass than Donnie."

Donnie just chuckled at our color commentary as he rifled through the clutter on the floor. He slipped into a pair of camo pants and a tank top strained tight over his swollen belly. A red headband completed his Rambo cosplay.

Donnie nodded at both of us and slapped his gut. "I'm locked and loaded. Those wolves won't know what hit 'em."

I shook my head. This was our backup for a werewolf hunt? We were so screwed. But the sun was nearly set, so ready or not, it was time to roll.

We clambered up the stairs after Donnie, and he shouted to his mom as we reached the top.

"Hey mom! I'm off to go kill some werewolves!"

Martha only gave a nod, her hands still buried in a sink full of dishes and soapy water. "Have fun, you three! Just check in if you're going to be out past midnight!"

Donnie stopped in his tracks. I could practically hear the groan, but he complied. "Yesss ma'am."

I nudged Sebastian. "Aw, how sweet, he still has to check in with mommy."

Donnie turned and rolled his eyes. "Her house, her rules. What can I do about it?"

"Gee, I don't know." I chuckled a little. "Maybe move out of your mother's basement?"

Donnie sighed. "Then I'd have to pay rent and other bills. That would mean I'd have to get a job! How am I supposed to make time for that? Between trying to juggle my World of WarCraft guild raid schedule with my Fortnite duties, I don't have a single minute to spare!"

Chapter 9

MOONLIGHT GLISTENED ON THE black hood of Sebastian's Chevelle as he unlocked the doors manually. Donnie heaved himself into the backseat. I slid into shotgun. The scent of leather and motor oil filled my nostrils.

"Plan is to check the woods closest to the university for the werewolves first, then spread out from there," Sebastian announced, cranking the engine to life. "Listen for any howls once the moon rises high."

"Got it," I replied, my senses already on high alert. "If we get close or on their trail, I'll probably be able to smell them or even hear them if they're trying to lurk in the brush somewhere." The thought of tracking down werewolves ignited my predatory instincts, but also a little anxiety. Vampires weren't werewolf hunters. Humans were our prey. We couldn't feed from werewolves while shifted and their bites were painful as hell.

"Either of you know how many we're dealing with?" I asked, scanning the horizon ahead, just in case.

"Last I heard, it was a pack of about a dozen," Sebastian glanced at me through narrowed eyes. "But that was before the North Carolina attacks. There's a chance they expanded their pack then, but usually a pack doesn't initiate more than two or three new wolves at a time."

"A dozen?" I shook my head "That's... that's a lot of werewolves."

"More fun for us!" Donnie spun a throwing knife in his hand. "I could use the workout!"

I craned my neck. "Throwing knives? You sure about using those?"

"Absolutely," he replied with a grin that made me uneasy. "They're silver, perfect for wolves. And if a wolf gets too close, I can still use the same knives in a close combat scenario."

"Let's hope it doesn't come to that," I muttered, unconvinced. "In my experience, if you're in a close-combat scenario with a werewolf, you've as good as lost the fight."

"Still doesn't hurt to have a good knife on hand," Sebastian chimed in. "I have a small arsenal in the trunk. When we arrive, I'll get you one."

Sebastian pulled the Chevelle to a stop at the edge of a hiking trail that disappeared into the moonlit woods. The car's engine went silent, replaced by crickets, hooting owls, and croaking frogs.

"Here we are," Sebastian said as he popped open the trunk. He rummaged through an assortment of weapons before selecting a knife and handing it to me.

I couldn't help but laugh when I saw it. "You've got to be kidding me," I said, holding up the blade. "This looks like something that might have belonged to Crocodile Dundee."

"Who is Crocodile Dundee?" Donnie's eyebrows furrowed.

Sebastian and I exchanged bewildered glances. "You seriously don't know who Crocodile Dundee is?"

"Should I?"

"Here," I said, raising my new knife with a flourish. "'Now that's a knife!' Ring any bells?"

"I've got nothing." Donnie shook his head.

"That's my Subaru Outback!" Sebastian blurted out, with the worst Australian accent I'd ever heard.

Donnie's eyes widened. "Oh! That guy! I remember those commercials."

"Finally," I sighed, still chuckling as I examined the silver blade. The hilt and handle were wrapped in dark leather, ensuring no contact with the silver. It was perfect.

"Let's get moving," Sebastian urged as he turned up the trail. Donnie and I followed suit.

The moon was rising, high enough that it should have triggered the werewolves' shifts. Strange, though, that we hadn't heard a single howl.

"Maybe we're in the wrong place," I whispered. "The wolves could be anywhere, on any side of Farmington."

"Let's keep going a bit further," Sebastian suggested, his voice steady. "Some wolves don't howl at the moon. The pack will follow the lead of the alpha. If he does it, they will too. If it's not his style, they'll stay silent. Still, if we don't find anything soon, we can't risk the wolves attacking another part of town while we're stuck in the woods. We'll head back and try somewhere else."

We continued along the trail. Every scurrying animal in the woods, a flutter of a bird's wings, or fallen branch in the distance startled my senses.

Then a gust of wind blasted through the trail—with it a familiar, distasteful scent.

"Wait," I whispered, holding up a hand to signal for the others to stop. "They're that way," I said with certainty, pointing in the direction of the breeze's origin.

Sebastian and Donnie exchanged glances before nodding in agreement. We crept through the woods, following the stench that grew stronger with each step we took.

"Stay close," I warned Donnie, but he just rolled his eyes. "You should stay close. When's the last time you've been out werewolf hunting?"

I shrugged. "It's not exactly my favorite past time."

"Well, this is what I do," Donnie said. "It's the only thing I do well that isn't on a computer. Trust me, alright?"

I sighed. "Sure. Whatever, Donnie."

"Why don't both of you shut the hell up?" Sebastian snapped. "Before *we* become the hunted."

We continued to move stealthily through the underbrush. The air was thick but the smell was getting stronger with every step.

Suddenly, a snarl erupted out of nowhere, and a werewolf lunged at me with terrifying speed. Instinctively, I raised my wand in one hand and my knife in the other, ready to defend myself against the vicious beast. But before I could even cast a spell or strike, one of Donnie's throwing knives whizzed past my ear, embedding itself between the werewolf's eyes. The creature crumpled to the ground, dead before it even hit the leaves.

"Damn," I said, turning to Donnie with wide eyes. "That was impressive."

A smug grin spread across his doughboy face. "Yeah. I know."

Sebastian rushed over to the werewolf's lifeless body, his gauntlet-covered hand hovering above its head. A green magic pulsed around his fingers, but instead of the wolf shifting back into human form, it remained motionless and very much dead.

"Damn," Sebastian muttered. "It was worth a shot."

"Next time," I told him, looking down at the corpse, "I can try a healing spell. See if that's more effective."

"No time to talk," Sebastian piped up. "They're approaching, the whole pack."

I nodded. "I can hear them. Smell then. Shit, they're all around, coming at us from every side." The stench of wet dog intensified, making my nose wrinkle in disgust. A half second later the first one appeared, snarling between two trees, then a third, fourth, and eventually, a dozen or more. Their eyes glowed with the moon's reflection and saliva dripped from their fangs.

"*Enerva!*" I shouted, directing my wand at the nearest werewolf. The powerful spell hit its mark, dropping the creature tumbling into a motionless pile of fur.

Sebastian wasted no time, using the blade extended from his tactical gauntlet to slice through werewolf after werewolf. The sound of metal cutting through flesh filled the air as he fought with lethal precision.

Donnie, meanwhile, ran, jumped, and tossed his silver throwing knives with incredible speed and accuracy, dropping one werewolf after another. It was like the soul of Jason Bourne suddenly inhabited the body of George Costanza. Sebastian was right—you can't judge a book by its cover, and you certainly can't judge a hunter by his midsection. This guy was the real deal.

"Keep going!" I shouted to my companions, casting another spell as I dodged a vicious swipe from a werewolf's claws. "We can do this!"

"Damn right, we can!" Donnie yelled back, grinning wildly as he hurled another knife into the eye of an oncoming beast.

"Stay focused!" Sebastian commanded. "Little less talk. A lot more action, please!"

I only ended up having to use my knife once. I dropped at least four of them with my spells, allowing Donnie and Sebastian to finish them off with silver.

But as we fought, another gust of wind struck my face. This time, it carried with it the aroma of blood. My head snapped toward Sebastian, who was still cutting through werewolves like a hot knife through butter. But it wasn't his skill that drew me to him. It wasn't his rugged physique. It was the gash on his arm, fresh and oozing crimson.

Drink, Mercy... Do not resist. You need it, you want it!

The world around me faded into a blur, tunnel vision narrowing my focus on that gash, the sweet scent of blood intoxicating my senses. Inside, I screamed back at Calivion, refusing to give in. But my body betrayed me, dazedly stalking toward Sebastian, driven by an insatiable thirst.

"Mercy, no!" Donnie shouted, but it was as if his voice came from miles away. The sounds of battle dulled, muffled like I was underwater.

Just before my fangs could pierce Sebastian's flesh, he spun around with lightning-fast reflexes and grabbed my wrists. His intense gaze bore into mine, and he spoke firmly, "Stay focused, Mercy. Remember who you are. Don't let the dragon control you."

Sebastian's words and touch grounded me, forcing back the darkness that threatened to consume my sanity. I blinked back into reality, and the world around me came sharply into focus. My heartbeat pounded in my ears, only once or twice per minute, but it was enough to startle me out of my temporary reverie. Relief, embarrassment, and gratitude washed over me as I realized how close I'd come to giving in.

"Thank you," I whispered, throwing my arms around Sebastian in a tight embrace. He stiffened, clearly caught off guard by my sudden display of affection, but after a moment, he awkwardly patted my back.

"Hey, we still have work to do," he reminded me, gently pushing me away. His eyes held concern, but also determination. As I looked around, I noticed one of the werewolf bodies lying lifeless in a bed of crisp autumn leaves.

"Let me try something," I said as I aimed my wand at the wolf's bloodied body. "*Sanare.*"

The air around us shimmered with magic, and the wolf's form began to shift, its fur receding as it transformed back into a human being.

"Sweet Jesus, you did it! You healed him!" Donnie exclaimed, checking the man's pulse with an expression of pure amazement.

Sebastian's eyes widened as he regarded me with newfound respect. "Remarkable, Mercy," he praised. "Try it on the others."

I attempted to replicate the spell on the other fallen werewolves, but my magic seemed to have no effect. Disappointment gnawed at me, but Sebastian reassured me, "It's still good news that we managed to save one. But we can't linger here. He might not survive for long like this, and it's best if we drop him off at the hospital and stay out of it."

I nodded in agreement, knowing full well that our presence would only raise more questions. As we stealthily made our way out of the woods with the unconscious man, I couldn't help but feel a strange mix of victory and worry. I'd come so close to giving in. If Sebastian hadn't caught me in time, maybe I would have let Calivion take hold of me again. But at the same time, the fact that I didn't give in, I resisted, and I did something good for a change. Well, it gave me the first inkling of hope I'd had in weeks. Maybe, just maybe, if I kept this up I'd be able to get rid of the blasted dragon once and for all.

But how long could I keep it up? I'd have to feed sooner or later. And the more I exerted myself, the more magic I used, the thirstier I'd become.

Donnie sat with the recovering werewolf in the backseat of Sebastian's Chevelle as I resumed my place in the passenger-side front.

Sebastian turned his key in the ignition and the Chevelle roared to life. I wasn't much of a nail biter. Fangs tend to get in the way of bad habits like that. But I found myself gnawing on my thumbnail no less while my leg bounced up and down for no reason at all.

"You alright?" Sebastian glanced my way as he pulled back onto the road.

I dropped my hand from my mouth and dropped it to my nervous knee. "I'm going to have to feed soon. Doing that magic, smelling your blood. You realize, Sebastian, if I don't feed eventually, I'll go feral. My instincts will take over and I'll kill anything in my path. Or, worse, losing my mind will give Calivion another foothold."

Sebastian nodded. "You're right. But you did something good tonight, Mercy. Real good. You saved that boy's life."

"Can we really be sure he's cured?" I asked. "The silver might not have totally burned out the wolf inside of him."

Sebastian shook his head. "The only way to know for sure will be to wait until tomorrow night. Most wolves shift two or three consecutive full-moon nights each cycle. Besides, there's no way to know for sure if we got the entire pack."

"Pretty sure we didn't," Donnie said. "Werewolves are smart like that. Too many of their number go down, they'll regroup."

I glanced back at Donnie. "By the way, dude. You really surprised me out there."

Donnie smirked. "I'm like a Transformer. More than meets the eye!"

"Told you," Sebastian interjected. "Donnie's a lot tougher than he looks."

"How did you learn to fight like that?" I asked.

"I started Krav Maga classes when I was five," Donnie said. "Only thing my momma could find that got me away from the video games and television. Had my black belt by the time I was ten. When you learn how to fight at a young age like that, the skill never really goes away. Sort of like riding a bike."

Sebastian cleared his throat. "Krav Maga is an Israeli martial art. A combination of aikido, judo, karate, boxing, and wrestling."

I raised an eyebrow. "I didn't realize there was a Jewish martial art."

Donnie shook his fist over his head. "Shalom, motherfucker!"

I laughed. "Alright, so that's how you learned to fight. How'd you get into this sentinel business?"

Donnie laughed. "You don't have to use *that* s-word for me. That's Sebastian's thing. I prefer the term 'slayer.'"

"Like the metal band from the eighties," Sebastian added.

"Or Buffy," Donnie added. "I mean, I'm hotter, of course. Way out of her league. But other than that. Buffy and me. We're the same."

"Except she's *fictional,*" I added.

"Shhh!" Sebastian laughed. "Buffy is like Donnie's Santa Claus. You don't want to spoil it for him. He started hunting *because* of Buffy. Had a poster of her on his ceiling over his bed and everything."

I raised an eyebrow. "You started hunting monsters because of a *television* show?"

Donnie shrugged. "Not exactly. I mean, Buffy inspired me. Benny Bernstein brought his family golem to Hebrew school for show-and-tell when we were twelve. Thing about Benny, he wasn't one of the cool kids. Not like me. People picked on him. Not a smart thing to do in the presence of someone's golem."

I scratched my head. "Hold on, I'm a little rusty on my golem lore. They're animated beings, made from the ground, with Kabbalah magic, right?"

"More or less," Donnie nodded. "Not every Jewish family knows how to do it, and there can only be one in a family at a time. But this one had been with Benny's family for decades. One of those old-school golems that only knew one way to respond to a threat."

"So this golem went on a rampage at your Hebrew school?" I asked.

"Until I stopped it. Golems are tough bastards. Easily triggered, but also easy to control. Thing was, Benny didn't want to stop it. He wanted the golem to teach his bullies a lesson. Thing about golems, though, they're tough but slow. You can't really kill them. A family's golem once forged from clay can be reformed at any time given the right incantation. But I put it down, temporarily, anyway."

Donnie laughed recalling the incident. "Lets' just say the golem got its ass handed to him—literally."

"And after that?" I asked. "You just started branching out to other monsters?"

Donnie nodded. "Pretty much. I mean, despite what you probably think about me, I wasn't very popular as a kid. I was even bullied a lot, too, just like Benny."

"Shocker." I did my best to suppress a grin.

"But after that, well, I was the hero of Hebrew school. Everyone wanted to be like Donnie. I'd say it went to my head, and it probably did, but then I started researching other strange shit out there. I found out vampires were real, werewolves, shifters, demons, sasquatch."

I chuckled. "Bigfoot isn't real."

"Not anymore," Donnie nodded. "Because I killed him!"

"No, you didn't," Sebastian corrected. "Stop making things up to impress Mercy."

Donnie sighed. "Fine, I didn't kill him yet. But I will someday."

I shook my head. "Even if he is real, he's peaceful. If he was a real threat a lot more people would believe he's real than do."

"That's what I keep saying," Sebastian said. "We shouldn't kill things just because we can. Defending the defenseless. That's what we do."

"But it's Bigfoot!" Donnie piped up. "Can you imagine what his head would look like mounted on the wall in my room?"

"You mean your mom's basement?" I snickered.

"Six of one, half a dozen of the other! The point is, with that on my wall, it would no longer be my mom's basement. It would be a sanctuary of seduction. A drop-your-panties pavilion. I mean, who wouldn't want to bang the guy who killed the sasquatch?"

I raised my hand. "Hard pass for me."

Donnie waved his hand through the air. "Ah, you're just playing hard to get!"

"Not playing..."

Sebastian cleared his throat as he pulled into the drop-off lane at the local hospital's emergency room and shifted the car into park. "You guys stay here. I'll handle this. They might recognize you, Donnie, being local, and you, Mercy, from the news coming out of Providence."

"No objections here," I said. "Go play the Good Samaritan. We'll be here."

Chapter 10

THE RUMBLE OF SEBASTIAN'S Chevelle drowned out the wail of ambulances as we idled in the hospital's u-drive. Red emergency lights bathed the interior in an ominous glow. Donnie's blathering was white noise as I stared out at the looming entrance, anxiety gnawing my gut.

Sebastian had been in there for twenty minutes, but it felt like hours. I fidgeted with my wand, the hem of my pants, anything to keep me distracted. Calivion was still inside of me. I heard his voice when the wolf wounded Sebastian's arm. Doing something good, noble, was supposed to strengthen Caladbolg, give him control of Calivion rather than Oblivion. So far—nothing. I felt so helpless, just sitting there twiddling my thumbs. I hated it. The sense that I was losing control, that the few things I tried to tame the literal monster inside of me weren't enough. What if Sebastian's little book was bullshit? Maybe there'd been a few instances when gatekeeper dragons possessed people, but people embellish stories like that over time. Just because something's written in a tattered, dusty old book doesn't make it true.

Sebastian was taking too long. I'd never been to an E.R. Why would I? The closest thing to a hospital I'd ever stayed in was the sanatorium where I languished my last few weeks as a human. You'd think if this place was dedicated to medical *emergencies*, they'd get people checked in fast. Nothing worse than people bleeding or sick, all sitting in a room together waiting their turn. Surely that wasn't what was happening. I mean, what kind of bullshit health care system would that be?

Had Sebastian gotten the werewolf settled? Were the doctors suspicious? A million disastrous scenarios flickered through my thoughts.

"Yeah, so that ghoul last month nearly ripped my arm off, but I shoved a grenade down its throat and boom!" Donnie mimed an explosion with his hands. "You should've seen the look on its face. Priceless."

I resisted the urge to bang my head against the window. Donnie's inflated tales of hunting glory had been nonstop since we parked. I was this close to chucking him out and peeling away, Sebastian or no Sebastian.

"Mm, fascinating," I muttered, scanning the ambulance bay again. A pair of paramedics wheeled a gurney inside, but no sign of Sebastian.

Donnie rambled on, oblivious to my disinterest. "I know I ain't got nothing on Sebastian. Dude's a certified badass. But hey, fifteen monsters *this year* ain't small potatoes, ya know?"

"Uh huh."

"Bet you've iced your fair share too, being a vamp and all."

I flashed him a tight smile. "Sure, loads of them. Couldn't even count."

His eyes lit up. "I knew it! So what's your craziest kill?"

Crazy was slaughtering a hospital full of people if Sebastian didn't get his ass out here soon. I thrummed my fingers on the dash, debating how much longer I'd wait before investigating myself.

"Uh, Mercy?" Donnie waved his hand in my face.

I swatted him away. "What?"

"You gonna answer my question?"

I sighed, glancing at the doors again. Still no one. "Right, craziest kill..."

I opened my mouth to fabricate some grandiose tale of vampire heroics when the squeal of tires interrupted me. A car whipped into the ambulance bay, brakes screeching as it jerked to a halt beside us.

Donnie's mouth snapped shut. We watched as a man leapt from the driver's seat and raced around to the passenger side. He wrenched open the door, reaching in to help a woman out.

Even with the windows rolled up, the scent hit me like a punch in the face—the rich, metallic tang of blood. The woman clutched her hand, wrapped in a rapidly reddening bandage. Crimson dripped between her fingers, spattering on the pavement.

A familiar burning ignited in my throat, ravenous and raw. I gripped the door handle, muscles coiling. It was a struggle not to simply rip the door off and vault across the space separating me from that vital fluid.

Just a taste. She's hurt anyway, won't miss a little more...

No! I clenched my jaw, fighting back the predator inside me. *I will not hurt these people. I am not a monster.*

But the beast within roared in defiance. It had caught the scent of prey, wounded and vulnerable. Nothing would stop it from claiming what it desired.

In the end, it wasn't even a contest. The man had barely helped the woman from the car before I erupted from the Chevelle in a blur. Some distant part of me heard Donnie's shout of surprise, but I lost it beneath the pounding of blood in my ears. The man turned just as I seized his companion, my fangs sinking deep into her throat.

Sweet, coppery blood filled my mouth, still hot from her veins. She screamed, thrashing weakly, but I held her in an iron grip. The man yelled and grabbed at me. I barely felt his efforts. With one hand, I flung him aside. He flew across the pavement, crashing limply against his car.

I drank greedily, gulping down the woman's life essence. Some nagging thought insisted I stop, but the thirst was all-consuming now. Nothing else mattered except satiating it at last.

I never saw Donnie move. There was only the sudden, sharp pain between my shoulders as one of his knives pierced my back. I released the woman with a snarl, whirling to face this new threat. Donnie stood by the Chevelle, another knife in hand. Fear lurked in his eyes, but his jaw was set stubbornly.

"You know that won't kill me," I said, baring my bloody fangs in a gruesome smile. "A bit of advice. Don't bring knives to a vampire fight."

Donnie shook his head. "Wasn't trying to kill ya. But it'll slow you down alright."

I laughed harshly. "Slow me down? Face it, Donnie. You can't slow me down enough. A hundred knives and I'd still be too strong for you."

With preternatural speed, I flashed across the distance between us, seizing Donnie by the throat. I lifted him effortlessly, his feet dangling above the ground as he choked for breath.

"Any last words?" I purred. Behind me, the woman's whimpers had gone silent. One quick snap, and Donnie's neck would break like a twig. My fangs ached to finish draining him. Just a little more blood, and I would be whole again...

A voice screamed in my mind, faint but desperate. Caladbolg. The ancient sword bound to my soul, a part of Calivion.

Mercy, stop! This isn't you!

Another voice hissed venomously, drowning Caladbolg out.

Drink him dry! His blood will set us free!

My fangs hovered over Donnie's throat. Thirst warred with conscience. I trembled, trapped between them.

Then strong hands seized me from behind, breaking my grip on Donnie. I spun with an enraged snarl, lashing out at my newest assailant. Sebastian caught my wrist easily, using my momentum to hurl me into the brick hospital wall.

I staggered upright, shaking my head to clear it. Sebastian stood resolutely between me and Donnie, gauntlet raised and glowing with celestial light. Behind him, Donnie scuttled away to take shelter behind the Chevelle.

"Back off, Mercy," Sebastian warned. "I don't want to hurt you, but I will if I have to."

I charged at Sebastian, a red haze clouding my vision. He swept his gauntlet in an arc, and a blast of celestial energy slammed into me. I cried out as the light seared my skin, but I was ready this time. I shielded my eyes with my forearm.

Kill him! Drain him dry! Oblivion shrieked. The bloodlust threatened to consume me.

No! This has to stop! Caladbolg's voice, faint but stubborn.

I hesitated, shaking with the effort to control myself. Sebastian watched me warily, ready to strike again. Behind him, Donnie peeked out from behind the Chevelle, the trunk open. He was going for a stake.

"Get...out...of...my...head!" I growled through gritted teeth. With a final defiant scream, I spun and sprinted away, a blur of preternatural speed. I had to get away before I hurt someone else.

As I fled, the tip of Donnie's silver knife still lodged in my back sent a bolt of agony through me. I cried out, stumbled, wrenched it free. The wound would slow me down, but I couldn't stop. Not yet. Not until I was somewhere I couldn't hurt anyone.

For now, my conscience and Caladbolg's pleas had won out. The further away I got from Sebastian and Donnie, from that woman I hoped I hadn't killed in front of the hospital, the more I calmed down. But the bloodlust was still there, lurking, waiting for me to falter again. I only hoped that next time, I would be strong enough to resist.

Chapter 11

THE BLISTERED FLESH ON my arm looked like melted wax, warped and bubbling from the heat of Sebastian's blast. I hissed as I prodded the angry red skin. That damn sentinel just had to go and make things more difficult for me. Not like I gave him much of a choice, but still. It wasn't the brightest move. To heal, vampires need blood. If you're trying to stop a vampire's cravings, but don't intend to kill them, injuring them is the worst thing you can do. Then again, I got a few good gulps from that woman before Donnie intervened and Sebastian showed up.

A wounded vampire's a hungry vampire. The dragons in my mind stirred, drawn by the scent of vulnerability. I leaned against the rough bark of an oak, trying to steady my thoughts. I'd run as far from civilization as possible. I couldn't be near humans. Not now. Being around people would be like taking a buffet to an Overeater's Anonymous meeting.

There had to be some way to rein the beasts in. But my control was slipping. I knew it wouldn't totally work, but I aimed my wand at my wounded forearm.

"Sanare..."

A soft glow emanated from my wand, but the spell fizzled out before it could do much good. Being my own healer was about as useful as being my own barber. Since the spirit of the witch conditions a witch's magic, using magic on myself wasn't efficient. Sort of like how you can't catch a cold from yourself. Or how Donnie couldn't smell his own B.O.

The scorched patch remained an agonizing reminder of how dangerous Sebastian could be. And how I was chin-deep in shit.

At least the spell took the edge off the pain, though it did nothing for the bloodlust mounting inside me.

Maybe I should've let Sebastian finish me off. It wasn't like I'd done much good in this world lately. I was a killer now, like the rest of my kind. It didn't matter that Oblivion tempted me. "The devil made me do it" was never a good defense, and blaming a dragon wasn't much better.

I bared my fangs in frustration, hissing at the shadows. The darkness hissed back. I was losing my goddamn mind.

I tensed, listening intently. That wasn't just the madness talking. Something was out there.

A howl pierced the night. Just one, at first. Could have been a common wolf. But then a chorus of howls echoed the first. We knew there was a possibility we hadn't taken out the whole pack. If we'd killed the alpha, who apparently didn't howl at the moon, whatever wolf took the mantle apparently did. And these werewolves were on the hunt.

New alphas could be dangerous. Not that I was an expert in pack sociology or anything, but I'd known enough wolves to have a general understanding of how their hierarchies worked. A new alpha's position was tenuous, easily challenged, until he led the pack on a hunt—on a kill.

I fingered the hilt of Sebastian's silver hunting knife, still strapped to my thigh. I had two choices. I could get Sebastian and Donnie. Apologize for losing my shit. Warn them about the wolves. We'd stand a better chance. Strength in numbers and all that. But approaching them was too damn tempting, like setting a giant bowl of candy in front of a kid and telling him not to eat any when you left the room. I was getting hungrier by the minute. One whiff and I'd pounce.

No, I had to handle the wolves alone. People would die if I didn't fight them. People would die—courtesy of Yours Truly—if I went and got help.

I rose and stalked toward the howls, my steps silent as moonlight. I crept through the underbrush, a lethal shadow. The beasts wanted blood? Oh, I'd give it to them. The last thing they'd expect was a vampire, or a witch. They were about to meet both—all in one tiny but powerful package.

The wolves were close now, their savage cries resonating through the trees. I slipped Sebastian's silver knife from its sheath, the blade glinting coldly in the moonlight.

A twig snapped to my left. I whirled, fangs bared, a feral growl rumbling in my throat. Gleaming yellow eyes stared back from the brush. The wolf edged forward, lips curled back from its jaws. My muscles tensed, ready to spring.

"Come on then," I hissed. "Let's see what you've got."

With a snarl, the wolf leapt. I ducked its snapping jaws and slashed upward with the knife, opening a long gash along its side. The wolf yelped and stumbled, dark blood pooling on the forest floor. Not waiting for it to recover, I pounced, driving the blade deep into its heart. The wolf convulsed and went still.

I rose, flicking blood from the knife. The kill had been quick, efficient. But it barely took the edge off; did nothing for my bloodlust.

I aimed my wand at the wolf. "*Sanare.*"

I couldn't tell for sure if it worked. Still, I had to try. If I couldn't feed until one dragon or the other took over Calivion, I had to give Caladbolg something, anything, that might give him an advantage. I didn't know if healing a wolf, like I had before, would do a damn thing. But I *did* hear Caladbolg for the first time since I'd given Oblivion control. He was distant, weak, but he was there. The only thing that might have done it was saving the wolf before, curing him from his curse by healing his body at the perfect moment.

All I could do was continue the hunt. More were out there—probably watching me as I lurked between the trees. I could see in the dark just as well as a werewolf. And they were larger than me, more instinctual than strategic. But they also had me outnumbered. How badly, I didn't know. Not yet.

I stalked silently between the trees, senses primed. My arm still throbbed where Sebastian had burned me, the blistered flesh stinging with each movement. I muttered another healing spell, but my magic barely eased the pain. Only blood could heal my wounds.

The dragons raged inside my mind, Oblivion's raspy voice rising above the din.

Let me take over, Mercy. Just a little more blood. Speak my name and I'll appear. We'll destroy these mongrels together. Just head back into the city... find someone, anyone... drink...

"Not a chance," I growled under my breath.

A chorus of howls sounded close by. I froze, peering into the darkness. Glowing eyes watched me from all sides. The pack had found me.

The wolf edged into the moonlight, a massive black beast with scarred flanks—clearly the new alpha. He bared his fangs and snarled.

Slowly, I drew the silver knife. "You're worse than a fifteen-year-old at homecoming. You going to stand there and leer at me all night, or are we going to dance?"

With a roar, the alpha leapt, the pack surging behind him. I braced myself. Ready or not, I was going to meet their challenge or die taking a wolf or two with me.

Chapter 12

MY CHEST TIGHTENED AS I felt the first vibrations of the wolves' approach. The low growls and snapping branches filled the air as they closed in on me, their bloodlust palpable.

"Enerva!" I shouted, aiming at the nearest werewolf. The beast froze mid-leap, its eyes wide with panic as it fell to the ground, immobilized. "Incendia!" Another wolf erupted into flames, howling in agony as it thrashed about before collapsing.

I wasn't sure which spell would be most effective against werewolves. My split-test suggested comparable outcomes. Neither spell would kill the wolves, but if I could immobilize them long enough to stab them with my silver knife, or at least get the fuck out of there, it didn't much matter.

I barely had time to catch my breath before more of them poured through the trees, snarling and snapping at me from all sides. Running would not work. I'd have to fight my way through. Whatever the case, there were a lot more than twelve, and we'd already killed nearly that many.

"Sebastian's intel was shit," I muttered under my breath as I fought off the wolves as they came at me one-by-one. It was like some kind of game, some display of prowess. Each wolf taking a turn to prove they could best me one-one-one. No complaints. Much better to drop one at a time than fend off several at once.

The wolves that came at me were relentless, more vicious and determined than I had ever seen. I gripped the silver knife Sebastian had given me tightly in my hand, slashing at any that came too close. The blade cut through their fur and flesh like a hot knife through butter. But when one wolf backed off, another took its place.

And the crowd around me was growing. It was like I was in the middle of some kind of werewolf Colosseum. I was the gladiator facing off against the fiercest beasts—destined to lose, eventually, much to the crowd's delight.

This pack was far larger than Sebastian's estimate. If the pack he'd tracked from North Carolina was only a dozen, and might have turned one or two since, then we weren't dealing with one pack. This was some kind of fucking conclave. Multiple packs all gathering in Farmington, Maine. Why Farmington? No clue. But something nasty was going down.

"Enerva! Incendia! Enerva!" My voice grew hoarse as I cast spell after spell, warding off the onslaught of werewolves as they started coming at me two, then three at a time. But for each one I knocked down or set ablaze, two more took their place.

"Shit, shit, shit," I muttered under my breath as I ducked and weaved around the snapping jaws and swiping claws of the enraged werewolves.

Let me out, Mercy, Calivion's voice whispered in my mind, smooth as silk. *You know you cannot win this battle alone.*

"Fuck off!" I snarled, but the wolves didn't seem to notice. All they were thinking about was ripping me apart.

I can help you, Calivion continued, his voice urgent but cloyingly sweet. *You have enough blood from your last feed. Just say my name, and I can fly you out of here. I can consume these beasts with my breath and send them to the void.*

"Keep dreaming, asshole," I spat, as I slashed at another wolf that lunged for my throat. I knew I couldn't keep this up much longer, but there was no way in hell I was going to let Calivion take control. He might save me from the wolves, but who would save the world from him?

"Enerva! Incendia!" I shouted again, desperately trying to hold my ground. But the wolves just kept coming, their numbers seemingly endless.

"Come on, you furry bastards!" I taunted, trying to buy myself a few precious seconds to catch my breath. "Is that all you've got?"

As if in response, the werewolves howled as one, a cacophony of rage and hunger that sent shivers down my spine. And then they charged, a tidal wave of fur and teeth crashing down upon me.

A sharp pain in my left arm nearly dropped me. "Son of a bitch!" I shook off the wolf that bit me, but his pack mates were relentless, and another wolf latched onto my leg, tearing through muscle and skin.

Mercy, just say my name, Calivion pleaded once more. *You don't have to die here.*

"Rather die than let you destroy everything," I spat back, ignoring the agony that coursed through my body. My vision blurred with each passing moment, but I refused to give in.

Very well, Calivion's voice whispered, growing distant. *But if you die, I'll simply find another. You already brought me to this world. Allow me to save you, or die for nothing.*

"Fuck off!" I hissed through gritted teeth, summoning every ounce of strength left within me just to stand, much less fight.

For a moment, my thoughts drifted back to my friends. Mel, Muggs, Clarissa, Ramon, Adam. Even Ladinas and Alice. I thought about everyone back in New Orleans. Hailey, Sarah, Annabelle. To them, I'd be a tragedy. A vampire who'd fought for good—for a season—but in the end gave in to her lesser demons.

"Enerva! Incendia!" I repeated, casting spells and slashing with Sebastian's silver knife, but the wolves just wouldn't stop coming. Blood dripped from my wounds, staining the forest floor below me, and I knew I was running out of time. If the pain didn't drive me mad, the blood loss would turn me feral. I'd be like one of these damned wolves. Insatiable, uncontrollable.

I fought on, determined to protect not only myself but the ones I loved. Maybe Calivion was full of shit. Maybe he'd die with me, or wouldn't be able to find another host. But if I didn't die now, he'd take over soon. If he was going to destroy the world, I sure as hell wouldn't be a part of it.

The pain spread through my body, worse than anything I'd ever experienced. The wolves couldn't tear me apart, but their teeth had pierced my flesh just enough to infect me. I realized the pain would last for more than a century, too long to bear.

For the first time, I *longed* for a stake in the heart. Something to end this. But I couldn't so much as get past the wolves to find a stick or a branch to do it. If I turned feral first... if I left and fed...

Damn it. Calivion was going to get *everything* he wanted.

Mercy, Calivion's voice hissed in my head, more urgent than before. *This is your last chance. Call upon me, and I can save you. I can take away the pain.*

As the pain intensified, my vision blurred, and I could no longer discern reality from hallucination. I heard growling and snarling, but it sounded different—as if the wolves were fighting something else.

Then, suddenly, the cacophony faded, and I felt something large, cold, and wet on my cheek. My heart leapt as I recognized the sensation. Goliath, my loyal hellhound, had found me.

"You found me..." I gasped, relief flooding through me even as the pain continued to rage within. Goliath growled softly, nuzzling my bloodied face. He was here now; things might not be as hopeless as they seemed.

Had he taken on the whole pack? Or had he simply scared them off? I didn't know, and the pain was too much and the relief of his arrival too overwhelming to consider it for more than a second.

"Get us out of here, boy," I whispered, my voice barely audible amidst the chaos. Goliath nodded, understanding my command, and scooped me up gently in his massive jaws. As he bounded away from the fray, I clung to consciousness, focusing on the sound of my hellhound's breathing and the faint hope that he'd brought with him.

He'd saved me from the werewolves, but not from the hunger within. Not from the insatiable need to feed. Not from Calivion.

Goliath raced through the woods, his powerful strides carrying us away from the woods. The pain still coursed through my body, tearing at my insides with every breath I took, but Goliath's firm hold kept me safe from any further harm.

Just as we reached the edge of the woods, I heard a voice shouting at the hellhound to drop me. My senses, already heightened by the pain, recognized it immediately as Sebastian.

"Drop her, you damn beast!" he yelled, his tone furious. I could only imagine what the scene looked like—a gigantic hellhound emerging from the dark forest, carrying a battered and bleeding Mercy in its jaws.

"Wait, Goliath," I choked out, my voice strained and weak from the pain. "They're friends."

Goliath hesitated, his massive form tensing as he prepared to lower me to the ground. But just as he was about to release me, his instincts kicked in, and he growled menacingly at Sebastian and Donnie, his hellish vocal chords sending vibrations through my already agonizing body.

"Easy, boy," I whispered, trying to calm the protective hellhound. The last thing I needed was for my rescuers to end up as Goliath's dinner. "They're here to help."

Goliath whimpered and huffed. Then he reluctantly set me down on the ground, still standing protectively over me, ready to attack if necessary.

"Jesus, Mercy," Sebastian said, kneeling beside me and taking in my injuries. "What the hell happened?"

"Too many wolves... hundreds of them..." I gritted my teeth against the pain. "I... I couldn't fight them all off."

"Shit," Sebastian muttered, his eyes widening at the realization of just how dire my situation was. He extended his hand, his gauntlet enveloped by green Druidic magic. As he waved it over my battered body, I could feel the raw power emanating from it, but nothing changed—the pain remained as intense as ever.

"Dammit," he cursed, frustration evident in his voice. "It's not working. This is just raw magic—without someone who can actually control it, it's useless."

"Sebastian..." I gasped, clutching his wrist with a trembling hand. "Muggs... My progeny. A druid... he can... he can help."

My vision blurred as the pain threatened to consume me entirely. But there was still one thing I needed to do. With every last ounce of strength, I turned towards Goliath.

"Goliath," I rasped, barely able to form the words. "Go find Muggs. Bring him to me."

The immense hellhound looked at me hesitantly for a moment before nodding, his massive head dipping in understanding. With a final glance at Sebastian and Donnie, he turned and bounded into the forest, his powerful limbs carrying him swiftly through the darkness.

Pain washed over me like a cruel tide, threatening to drag me under. But I held on, clinging to the hope that Muggs would arrive in time to save me. I couldn't give in to Calivion's temptations—my friends, my family, they all depended on me. I had to survive, even if it meant enduring unimaginable agony.

"Stay with me, Mercy," Sebastian urged, his voice filled with concern. "We need to get you someplace safe."

I grabbed Sebastian's hand and squeezed—a little too hard. He winced. "Chain me or stake me. If I go feral... Calivion will..." A sudden surge of pain interrupted my thoughts. I clenched my teeth until the agony subsided. "You need to restrain me until my progeny arrives."

"I'll do what I have to do," Sebastian said. "We'll take care of you."

I nodded weakly, my body trembling as I fought to stay conscious. I knew that this was just the beginning of a long and grueling battle—both against the pain and the dark influence lurking within me. But I couldn't give up—not when so much was at stake.

"Sebastian," I whispered, my voice barely audible. "Promise me... no matter what happens... don't let Calivion win. Stake me. It will prevent him from leaving. If I die, he might find another host."

His eyes met mine, fierce determination shining in their depths. "I promise, Mercy," he said solemnly. "We'll get you through this. We won't let him win."

Chapter 13

Pain seared through my body, the werewolf bites agonizingly fresh and burning like hellfire. Everything faded to black as I lost consciousness, the world slipping away from me.

"Did Sebastian stake me?" I wondered in the darkness. If he had, I didn't notice. But a stake to the heart would have felt like a Thai massage compared to the werewolf bites. I'd told Sebastian to stake me again. He knew that was what I wanted, but would he see it through? Did he realize what was at stake? There's that damned "at stake" pun again. It always seems to turn up and at the most *pointed* of times.

The last time Sebastian staked me, my spirit went reeling into a void of nothingness, alone and terrified. This time, however, something was different. Slowly, as my senses returned, I heard laughter, *jazz,* and the sound of clinking glasses. Then my vision returned.

The room was sleek and contemporary, with glass liquor shelves reflecting the dim lights, creating an intimate atmosphere. A jazz singer crooned softly in the corner, accompanied by her small band. She was talented. I'd never had much of a singing voice. If I could choose a voice, though, it would have been hers. Silky and seductive. People I didn't recognize laughed and sipped on various cocktails, enjoying themselves at the bar and various tables scattered throughout the space.

"Where the hell am I?" I murmured under my breath, taking in my surroundings. My gaze fell upon the bartender, who busied himself making drinks, his back turned to me. "Hey!" I called, trying to get his attention. He turned, and my heart skipped a beat.

"Caladbolg?"

It was him, though he looked paler and older than before, when he'd appeared to me as a Native American boy. His features were still unmistakable, and a shiver ran down my spine. What was going on?

"Mercy," he said, a wry smile playing on his lips. "Fancy seeing you here."

"Don't tell me you're surprised," I replied warily. "You must've brought me here. What's going on? Where am I?"

"First things first, Mercy," he said smoothly. "What can I get you to drink?"

I stared at him incredulously for a moment before retorting, "Are you serious? You know what I want." He snapped his fingers with a grin and announced, "One Bloody Mary coming up. Extra bloody!"

With a snap and a flourish, a glass that looked like pure blood appeared on the glass bar under Caladbolg's hand, and he slid it to me.

"Thanks?" I muttered before taking a cautious sip. The taste was rich and satisfying, and I couldn't help but let out a small sigh of pleasure. "This can't be real," I told myself aloud. "It must be some kind of dream... or a hallucination."

"Ah, well, that depends on how someone defines 'real,'" Caladbolg mused. "Who's to say a dream isn't real? Perhaps it's just a different kind of reality."

"Last time I was staked, I was in the void," I reminded him, my voice edgy. "Why is this so different?"

"Your spirit was connected to Oblivion's," he explained, nodding solemnly. "You'd given the nobler dragon—myself—no opportunity to show myself. This isn't just a bar, Mercy. It's a pocket dimension, a spiritual realm—an alternative to the void, a kind of heaven, perhaps."

"Heaven?" I scoffed, taking another sip of the strangely comforting liquid. "Usually my adventures take me to hell. One way or another. Eventually. Never to heaven. Pardon my disbelief. Is heaven real?"

"Ahh, the real..."

"Right." I rolled my eyes. "What *is real, really?* Spare me the lecture on metaphysics. How did you bring me here? And why?"

"Your actions have loosened Oblivion's hold on you, giving me an opportunity to intervene," he replied, his eyes reflecting a deep wisdom. "In the end, it was your sacrifice that allowed me to help. You accepted great pain and gave up your life under the stake—even if it might be temporary—in order to imprison Oblivion in your staked body. That gave me the chance to bring you here, to this refuge."

"Fine," I said, my voice dripping with skepticism. "But what am I supposed to do now? Just sit here and drink blood until someone pulls that stake out?"

"Consider it a reprieve," Caladbolg suggested. "A moment of respite from the battle against Oblivion. While you're here, he can't reach you. Use this time wisely."

"Right," I muttered, rolling my eyes but secretly grateful for the break. "Because heaven knows I could use some thinking time without that bastard's voice in my head."

"Indeed," Caladbolg agreed with a knowing smile. "And who knows? You might find some answers here. Some insight into how to defeat Oblivion once and for all..."

"Answers?" I scoffed. "In a jazz bar? What am I supposed to learn in a bar that can help me defeat your evil twin, who only wants to consume all existence into chaos?"

"This is more than a bar, Mercy."

I raised an eyebrow, my skepticism mingling with a twisted sense of amusement. "Right. It's heaven. Gloria in excelsis. Hallelujah and shit."

Caladbolg leaned back against the bar, arms crossed as he considered his words. "Well, in some cultures it would be called Gwynfyd, Elysium or Valhalla. In others, it might be Nirvana or Paradise. But yes, more or less, that's true." He paused for effect, his voice taking on a more serious tone. "Though you won't stay here forever. Unless someone burns out your heart, of course, which wouldn't be good because then Oblivion might find his way out. He was telling you the truth, Mercy, when he said that he'd find another vessel if you freed him."

"Great," I muttered, taking another sip of the bloody concoction Caladbolg had provided. It wasn't exactly comforting to know that my time in this strange heaven was limited, but I suppose it beat the alternative. "So I have to kick his ass... from the inside?"

Caladbolg chuckled. "From the inside of his ass? No, child. It is a spiritual battle that must be had."

I snickered. That's what I get for speaking metaphorically to a trans-dimensional gatekeeper dragon. "So you're saying me getting bitten by wolves gave you a chance to overpower Oblivion?"

"Your sentinel companion isn't wrong," Caladbolg replied, his gaze never leaving mine. "A few noble deeds have loosened Oblivion's hold on you and gave me an opportunity to help. But in the end, it was your sacrifice that made all the difference."

He paused, giving me a moment to absorb his words before he continued. "The last thing you did, Mercy, was allow yourself to suffer. You accepted great pain, and gave up your life under the stake—even if it might be temporary—in order to imprison Oblivion in your staked body. That act of selflessness allowed me to bring you here, away from his reach."

I shivered involuntarily at the memory of the agony I'd experienced. The searing pain of the werewolf bites, the ice-cold terror of facing the stake... It was a small price to pay for a chance at defeating my enemy, but it was a price nonetheless.

"Alright," I said, my voice heavy with the weight of all that had happened. "So, what now? Do I just sit here, drinking blood and listening to jazz while I wait for someone to pull the stake out?"

"Consider this an opportunity, Mercy," Caladbolg suggested, his eyes gleaming with a hint of warmth. "A respite from your ongoing battle against Oblivion. Here, he cannot reach you. Use this time wisely, and perhaps you'll find the answers you seek."

I couldn't help but press the issue, my curiosity gnawing at me like a ravenous beast. "You still haven't answered my question, Caladbolg," I said, narrowing my eyes at him. "You told me how I gave you a little control. But how did you bring me *here*?"

"Ah, yes," he replied, taking on the air of a professor giving a lecture. "As you know, I am a gatekeeper dragon, also known as Excalibur, the blade of righteousness." He paused for a moment, allowing the gravity of his words to sink in. "This realm is the one place I could bring you where Oblivion cannot go. You're here with me and the other inhabitants of this realm, so you can consider how to defeat Oblivion without him listening in."

My gaze wandered over the bar's patrons, their laughter and chatter providing a soothing backdrop to our conversation. It was hard to believe that this pleasant scene held any answers to my dark dilemma. But then again, stranger things had happened.

Caladbolg leaned in closer, his voice dropping to a conspiratorial whisper. "The real question is whether you will revive and take control, or allow Oblivion another foothold in your spirit."

With a sigh, I took another sip of the blood in my glass. It was unexpectedly delicious—rich, velvety, and strangely satisfying. "This is pretty damn good," I admitted, raising an eyebrow at the dragon-turned-bartender. "What kind of blood is it? Angel blood?"

Caladbolg laughed, a warm, hearty sound that seemed out of place in our grim discussion. "It is what you want it to be, Mercy. This is your version of heaven, after all."

I couldn't help but snort at the absurdity of it all. "My version of heaven is a smooth jazz bar?" I asked, glancing around at the dimly lit room filled with laughter and music.

Caladbolg chuckled, his eyes twinkling with amusement. "The answer you seek is here, Mercy. If you want to defeat Oblivion, perhaps you should spend some time getting to know some people. After all, everyone in heaven has escaped Oblivion in one way or another."

"Great," I muttered, my gaze sweeping over the unfamiliar faces. "Just what I need—small talk with strangers." The prospect was about as appealing as a root canal (or a fang canal), but I knew Caladbolg had a point. If I could find someone who'd outsmarted Oblivion, maybe they'd have some advice on how I could do the same.

"Buy them a drink," Caladbolg suggested, gesturing toward the patrons milling about. "Ask them to share their stories. Perhaps you'll find a bit of brilliance, a little insight that you can use once you return home."

"Fine," I grumbled, tipping back my glass and finishing the blood within—which refilled to the brim the second I set it back down on the bar. "Well, ain't that neat?"

"Indeed," Caladbolg chuckled. "Free refills in heaven. Store policy."

I took a deep breath, retrieving my glass again from the bar, as I straightened my spine and forced a smile onto my face. Then, I approached the nearest table, where a group of people were engaged in lively conversation.

"Excuse me," I said, interrupting their chatter. "Mind if I join you?"

The group exchanged curious glances before nodding their consent. "Sure," said a woman with fiery red hair and a mischievous grin. "Pull up a chair."

"Thanks," I replied, settling into an empty seat. "Name's Mercy. I'm new here."

"Welcome, Mercy," said a man with salt-and-pepper hair and a kind smile. "I'm Thomas, and this is Lucy," he gestured to the redheaded woman, "and that's Darius and Eliza."

"Nice to meet you all," I said, trying my best to sound genuine. "So, uh, what brings you to... heaven?"

Thomas chuckled. "Well, that's quite the conversation starter. We all have our stories. No one's journey is easy. Every journey is unique, but the same, all at once."

My interest piqued, I leaned in closer. "Did you confront Oblivion? That devil of a dragon is trying to drag me down, lure me to evil... destruction... chaos... "

"Each of us has a different story, an encounter with your Oblivion," Eliza explained, her voice soft but steady. "The road to heaven..."

"Is paved with good intentions?" I finished her sentence.

Eliza shook her head. "Perhaps. I was going to say it's never a straight path, usually perilous, and certainly difficult. There are easier roads that intersect with the righteous path. Smoother roads, with better scenery, that are more pleasant. But the end of those roads leads always to Oblivion."

I bit the inside of my cheek. "Yeah, yeah. Avoid temptation. Follow the righteous path. Heard that sermon a million times."

Eliza laughed. "It's not like that. You know your darkness. It's not a particular sin, like drinking or promiscuity, that's the problem. Those are just symptoms of a deeper flaw. Those vices don't damn someone to Oblivion so much as we turn to them to ignore the abyss within that we don't know how to fill. But so long as we ignore the root problem, try to cover it up or fill it with other garbage, the abyss only expands until it swallows us whole."

Darius nodded in agreement. "Same for me. You can't defeat Oblivion by denying your own shadows. Embrace them, understand them, and use them to your advantage."

"Interesting," I mused, taking a sip of my blood as I considered their words. Embrace my darkness... could it really be that simple? "I'm a vampire. Embracing my darkness is kind of my modus operandi."

"Remember, though," Lucy warned, her eyes narrowing. "Balance is key. Too much darkness, and you risk losing yourself to Oblivion entirely."

"Thanks for the advice," I said, tucking their insights away for later reflection. "Now, how about we raise a toast to new friends and old enemies?"

"Cheers to that," they chorused, clinking their glasses together.

As we drank and shared stories late into the night, I couldn't shake the feeling that I was on the cusp of something important–a breakthrough that might just help me defeat Oblivion once and for all. But I had to learn more. Don't deny your darkness—confront it. Embrace it to a point, but don't let it control you. Great advice. But I needed something practical. If I couldn't kick Oblivion out—if I had to embrace him, somehow, I couldn't just call him by name and let him take over again. I needed a collar and a leash. A way to tame the dragon so he knew I was his master, not the other way around.

As I was about to stand and return to the bar, Thomas grabbed my hand. "Remember, friend, the enemy is not the dragon, the tempter. He can only use against you what is already there. Your darkness is his weapon. Take it from him, defeat the darkness first, and he'll be powerless."

I nodded, grateful for the reminder. "Thanks, Thomas. I'll keep that in mind."

With one final toast, I bid my new friends farewell and headed back to the bar. As I walked, I couldn't help but feel a newfound sense of hope. Perhaps defeating Oblivion wasn't as impossible as I'd thought. Maybe, just maybe, I could conquer the darkness within me and take control of my destiny.

When I reached the bar, Caladbolg was waiting for me with a knowing smile. "Well, Mercy, did you find what you were looking for?"

"I think so," I said, taking a seat on one of the stools. "I need to confront my darkness head-on and control it. Only then can I defeat Oblivion."

Caladbolg nodded. "Wise words. But how do you plan to accomplish this?"

I paused, considering his question. "I need to channel my darkness to use it for good instead of letting it consume me. And I need to do it in a way that keeps Oblivion on a leash, so to speak."

Caladbolg stroked his chin thoughtfully. "Interesting. It sounds like you need a... weapon, of sorts. Something that can harness your darkness and give you control over it."

"A weapon...?" I repeated, narrowing my eyes in contemplation. "Yes. That's it. But what kind of weapon?"

Caladbolg leaned in closer, his eyes gleaming with excitement. "I know just the thing. It's a weapon that was forged for a warrior just like you—one who had to confront their own darkness and take control of it."

"Tell me more," I said, leaning in closer.

"It's me," Caladbolg said, his voice dropping to a conspiratorial whisper. "The legendary sword of the Tuatha De Dannan, forged by the great smith Goibniu himself. Infused with my spirit, drawn from the stone by the would-be-king."

I snorted. "Alright, well, cool. A weapon is sort of what I wanted. What does all of that have to do with defeating my darkness? Is this a spiritual thing or a slash-and-stab kind of fight?"

"Why can't it be both?" Caladbolg asked. "I bound myself to Oblivion to give you a chance. You must take hold of my power and use it to slay my brother."

"He's like the yin to your yang, right?" I asked. "If all this shit is about balance, he's a necessary evil. He exists so you can."

Caladbolg bowed his head slightly. "When Goibniu invited me to inhabit the blade, known later as Excalibur, he had to forge a second blade and invoke Oblivion to possess it. Oblivion and I will always exist. Disorder is the beginning order, and we can only know order in contrast to chaos. But our blades connect us to this world through the wielder. We have no influence over anyone apart from our blades."

"I don't know how to destroy your blade," I admitted. "I let it go, it just disappears and returns when I speak your name."

"But now all you can speak is the name, 'Calivion,' and something of both of us manifests in your hand."

"Right," I sighed. "But when I do that, *he* doesn't remain a sword I can wield. He takes flesh, lures me, exploits me... like he knows exactly what buttons to push to tempt me with things I don't really want at all! Like a goddess? Why did I even tell him I wanted to be a freaking goddess?"

"I think you know the answer to that," Caladbolg said.

I sighed. "Because I'm sick of shit happening that I can't control. I wanted to be the one who pulls all the damn strings for once, rather than the fucking marionette."

Caladbolg nodded in understanding. "I know what it's like to feel out of control. But you can't let that desire for control consume you. Find balance, Mercy. That's the key to defeating Oblivion."

"I know," I said, running a hand through my hair. "But how do I find that balance? How do I control my darkness without letting it control me?"

Caladbolg leaned in closer. "The wrong questions can only accommodate inadequate answers. Why do you still speak of control?"

"Um, maybe because there's a dragon inside of me that wants to send the entire world into chaos? I can't just let the bastard free. I have to control him."

"Sometimes things happen," Caladbolg added. "You say you want to be the one who pulls the strings, but why assume anyone is pulling strings at all? Unfortunate circumstances are a part of life—or undeath, as the case may be. Do you recall how all of this started?"

I shook my head. "I was pissed. About Alice and Ladinas. So I left and went out for a bite. I didn't think I'd lose it like that... but something overwhelmed me when that man's blood touched my lips."

"Moderation is part and parcel of order," Caladbolg said. "Oblivion specializes in chaos and excess. All it took was a whisper..."

"I thought I deserved it," I admitted. "a chance to just fucking be myself, to indulge. Like I'd had it with everything. But I've felt that way before without killing people."

"That thread might be there every time you feed," Caladbolg said. "But you've learned to ignore it. You don't pull the thread that unravels your control because you choose to deny it's there. All my brother had to do was point it out. You were powerless to resist it because you've only suppressed your cravings all these years by pretending you're something you aren't. You imagine you're strong, and you cling to that, but when confronted with weakness—with what you can't control—you're as vulnerable to your natural cravings as any youngling."

"Well, shit," I shook my head. "So what do I do? Stand up, make some declaration of weakness, and move on?"

Caladbolg laughed. "That's not how it works."

"Then help me out here." I took a sip of my bottomless glass of blood. "Do I go to a meeting or some shit?"

"Suck it up," Caladbolg said, then tilted his head. "Poor word choice, given I'm talking to a vampire. But you've never been the sole source of your strength. You've become the person you are because you've known you can't handle everything alone. Intuitively, you knew you needed to rely on others. You need to forgive your friends, move on, and accept things for what they are."

"Accept the fact that Ladinas and Alice are fucking? Yeah right."

"What else can you do, Mercy? It's not like they meant to hurt you. They found themselves trapped in a pocket dimension together for a century. They made the best of it. Now, they have a history together you can't possibly understand. They've been through something terrible, and they helped each other survive it.

The last thing Ladinas was thinking was, 'Gee, what is Mercy going to think if we ever get out of here?'"

I grunted. "Honestly, he'd only just barely decided to be with me over Alice when it happened. Maybe I should let them be happy and get over myself."

"I'm not saying to swallow your feelings," Caladbolg said. "That's the surest way to give Oblivion a foothold. Say your piece. Accept what is. Move on."

I scratched the back of my head. "How do I know they'll do the same? What if I go back to them and they're too pissed about everything I've done? All the people I've killed..."

"If they do not understand that Oblivion influenced you, and will not listen to you, then that's on them. You cannot control other people. All you can do is what you can do. In every situation, we must be bold to do the most we can do, to exercise whatever is within our scope of control to do what's right, but attempting to influence what's beyond your control is futile. You will not only waste your efforts, but drive yourself into a prison of fury and frustration."

I cocked an eyebrow. "And if I do that, I can beat Oblivion?"

"If you recognize what you cannot control, if you are honest about your weakness, your darkness, then he will have nothing left to use against you. What you do next is up to you."

"There's a werewolf problem in Farmington." I shook my head. "I can't leave my new friends behind to face it while I go running home to my old team."

Caladbolg pinched his chin. "Well, whatever could the solution to this dilemma possibly be? Let's examine the facts. Something's gathering werewolves in a small town in Maine. The hunters you've allied with are outnumbered and distracted by your peculiar issue. But you have an entire team of old friends who are but a druid portal away with all the weapons and the ability to handle the problem." Caladbolg waved his hand through the air. "But you're right. There's *nothing* you can do about it."

"Funny," I rolled my eyes. "I get it. So, I patch things up with my old team. I pray that they'll work with me again if I ask for their help. Then we kick some werewolf ass with Sebastian and Donnie."

"Sounds to me like a plan," Caladbolg said. "And, perhaps in the process, you'll find the chance to defeat Oblivion once and for all."

Chapter 14

I GASPED, MY EYES snapping open as I felt something gigantic and slobbery bathing my face. Goliath's hellhound tongue was relentless, and I couldn't help but laugh despite the situation. As I came to my senses, I realized the pain that had been consuming me was gone. Muggs, my Druid progeny, was hovering over me with concern etched on his blind face, while Sebastian stood nearby, arms folded.

"Christ, Goliath, you trying to drown me?" I grumbled, pushing the massive beast away gently. "Okay, okay, I'm awake."

Muggs tilted his head, his sightless eyes searching for mine. "How are you feeling, Mercy?"

"Like I just got smacked with a two-by-four, but the pain is gone," I admitted, sitting up slowly. "I assume it was your magic that dealt with the wolf bites?"

Muggs nodded. "And the other thing..."

"Give her a moment," Sebastian interjected, reaching out to take my hand and help me up. It was then that I realized we were in Donnie's basement of all places. The familiar smell of stale Doritos and Mountain Dew filled the air. Donnie himself was sitting in his gaming chair, complete with headset, making it appear as if he'd just paused one of his games. Despite the crumbs littering his shirt, he looked genuinely concerned.

"Take all the time you need," Muggs said softly, giving my shoulder a reassuring squeeze.

"Thanks," I sighed, attempting to collect my thoughts amidst the chaos. My mind was racing, trying to make sense of what had happened and how I'd ended up here. I could still feel Calivion's influence lurking in the periphery of my consciousness, waiting for a chance to push me into darkness once more. But for now, at least, it seemed subdued.

"You must be hungry," Sebastian said. "You were ravenous before, barely holding on, and now after all those bites, being staked..."

I tilted my head, recalling the blood I'd consumed in... heaven? I wasn't hungry at all. "I can't explain it, exactly, but where I went. Well, I think it took care of that. For now, at least."

Muggs cleared his throat. "And... what about, you know, the *other* thing?"

"The other thing... you mean... my propensity for murder and mayhem?" I asked, trying to keep the bitterness out of my voice.

Muggs nodded solemnly. I sighed, running a hand through my disheveled hair. "Oblivion has been influencing me, pulling my strings. But that's no excuse. The whole situation with Ladinas and Alice came out of left field, and I acted like a child."

"Everyone makes mistakes," Muggs murmured, his blind gaze filled with empathy that I didn't deserve.

"Speaking of which," I said, forcing a weak smile, "how are Mel and Clarissa doing?"

"Lost without their sire," Muggs replied, gripping my hand. "I can't speak for everyone, but I know they miss you. We all do."

My chest tightened at the thought of the bewildered fledglings I'd left behind. I knew it wasn't fair to them, but with Oblivion's influence hanging over me, I couldn't risk putting them in danger. There was no telling what I might do as long as Calivion continued to manipulate me.

"What about Clarissa?" I asked, concern bleeding into my voice. "She was struggling with her cravings when I last saw her."

"Ramon and Adam are with her," Muggs explained. "As long as they're nearby, she seems to be fine. But a young vampire needs her sire."

"True," I agreed, my heart heavy with guilt. "But until I can figure out how to keep Oblivion at bay, it's too dangerous for me to be around them."

"Then we'll help you find a way," Sebastian declared, his grip on my hand tightening reassuringly. "That's what I promised you, and I still intend to save you."

"Thanks, Sebastian," I said softly, touched by his unwavering support. "But I can't go home with you guys just yet. There's a bigger problem in Farmington, and I need the team to help me stop it."

Muggs furrowed his brow. "Sebastian mentioned something about a werewolf issue?"

"More like a conclave." My voice grew dark as I recalled the ominous gathering. "Dozens of packs, all converging on the area for some reason. Whatever they're up to, it can't be good."

"Shit," Sebastian muttered, pulling out his phone and checking the time. "If the wolves are planning something, it'll start soon. Tonight is the last night of the full moon. That means the shit is going to hit the fan in less than an hour."

"Wait, how long was I out?" I asked, alarmed at the thought of having lost precious time.

"Almost a whole day," Sebastian confirmed, his expression grim.

"Damn it," I cursed under my breath. Time was running out, and the pressure to act weighed heavily on me. But I couldn't let fear or guilt cloud my judgment—not with so much at stake.

"Alright," I said, straightening out my top to cover the hole left from Sebastian's stake. Like, did he really need to fuck up my clothes? "We need to gather the team. Sebastian and Donnie are tough, but they can't possibly defend this city against hundreds of werewolves. I need to speak to Ladinas and get everyone on board."

"Agreed," Muggs replied, spinning his staff overhead as he prepared to forge a portal back to the Vampire Underground.

"Wait," Sebastian said, grabbing my arm. "I'm coming with you."

"Is that wise?" I raised an eyebrow. "A hunter walking into a den of vampires?"

"Wouldn't be the first time," he replied with a wry grin. "But I also know you'll have to face some difficult shit with your ex, and I want to be there just in case you need support. Or in case that dragon exploits your emotions."

"Fine, but we better hurry," I conceded, knowing that having Sebastian by my side would give me the strength I needed to confront Ladinas—and Oblivion. Even if it was going to make things awkward as hell. I mean, my old team already didn't trust me. What would they think about me bringing a hunter—sorry, a sentinel—into the Underground?

"I'll be here!" Donnie confirmed. "Going to try to squeeze in a raid or two."

Sebastian cleared his throat. "Or, perhaps, you could get ready for the fight. Less than an hour, Donnie. That's how long we have before the sun sets and the moon rises. You need to be ready for one hell of a fight."

Donnie sighed, stood up, and dusted the crumbs off of his shirt. "Fine. You're worse than my mom, you know that?"

Muggs tilted his head. "How old is he, anyway?"

"I'm thirty!" Donnie interjected.

"And you're living with your mother?" Muggs' furrowed brow reflected his confusion.

"He's a millennial," I laughed, slapping Muggs on the back. "What do you expect?"

"Ahh," Muggs nodded his head. "That makes sense, then."

Sebastian gazed at Muggs' portal—a green tornado spinning around all the shit that was scattered around Donnie's mother's basement. "How does this thing work, exactly?"

I winked at Sebastian. "Click your heels together three times. Remember, there's no place like home."

Sebastian cocked his head. "That doesn't track. That's how you leave Oz. The tornado is what takes you there."

"Right," I nodded. "I was just giving you shit. Step inside the portal and Muggs' magic will do the rest. Be careful, though. Travel by druid portal sometimes comes with the urge to hurl."

Chapter 15

THE STALE SCENT OF damp stone filled my nostrils as we entered the dimly lit throne room of the Vampire Underground. My throne, carved from mahogany and padded in red velvet, still stood on a slightly elevated platform beside an identical throne for Ladinas. I was a little surprised it was still there.

"Figures. Alice probably parks her bony ass there now." I rolled my eyes.

"Oi, why would you think that?" Muggs shot back, his raspy voice echoing through the cavernous space. "You're the bloody queen, not Alice. No one here has given up on you, despite everything that's happened. We know you've been... influenced... by something else."

"Whatever." I scratched the back of my head. "We'll deal with all that shit later. We need to find Ladinas."

Just then, a high-pitched shriek cut through the air. I whirled around to see Mel standing in the doorway, her tablet clutched tightly in her hand. She must've seen me appear on her screen through the security cameras and come running. Her eyes widened with a mix of shock and relief as she ran over to me, opening her arms for a hug.

"Mercy!" she cried, wrapping her arms around me. The embrace was unexpected, and I hesitated before awkwardly patting her back. "I can't believe you're back!"

I gently pried Mel off me and held her at arm's length. Her eyes were glossy, the red hue of her irises faded. She was long overdue for a feed.

"Are you...you?" she asked uncertainly. "Which Mercy are we dealing with here? Jekyll or Hyde?"

I gave her a wry smirk. "Well, I'm here with a human and he's not bleeding out, so what do you think?"

Mel peered around me at Sebastian standing stoically behind us. Her eyes lit up.

"You brought takeout!" she exclaimed excitedly.

Sebastian let out a derisive grunt. "Don't even think about it. I'm no one's food."

I shot Mel a pointed look. "I wouldn't mess with him if I were you. He might be a human, but he's resilient as fuck. He's handed me my ass a couple of times already. But he's good people."

Mel tilted her head, looking Sebastian up and down appreciatively. "Damn. He's like food porn. Just *look* at him!"

I quirked an eyebrow. "He's what now?"

"You know, food porn!" Mel giggled. "Like those pictures people post on social media of amazing looking meals. Oooh, look what I'm eating tonight! Don't you wish you could have some?"

I chuckled. "Oh, I'm sure he's as delicious as he looks. But Sebastian here is no ordinary human." I shot him a pointed glance. "He's a hunter."

Sebastian cleared his throat. "Sentinel," he corrected gruffly. "I don't hunt indiscriminately. I'm a protector. I only kill monsters who threaten the innocent."

Mel pouted. "Well aren't you just a big bucket of buzzkill?"

"I'm not sure you trust me right now," I said. "But if you trust me at all, well, you can trust him. He could have killed me more than once but hasn't. He's been helping me find myself again."

Mel cocked her head coyly, staring at Sebastian with renewed interest.

"So how *exactly* did you two meet?" she asked, her eyes glinting mischievously. "Was it some kind of forbidden vampire-hunter romance?"

I sighed, pinching the bridge of my nose in exasperation. "It wasn't like that, Mel."

But she was no longer listening, lost in her own romantic imaginings. "Oooh, I can just picture it! The brave hunter stalking the streets at night, determined to rid the city of the dark vampire scourge." She clasped her hands to her chest dramatically. "Until one night, he meets a stunning vampiress who takes his breath away! It's love at first bite!"

I rolled my eyes as Mel dissolved into a fit of giggles. "Are you done?"

She grinned impishly. "I'm just getting started!"

Before I could stop her, she launched into an off-key song. "Mercy and Sebastian, sitting in a tree, F-U-C-K-I-N-G!"

Sebastian frowned in confusion. "I fail to see how copulating in a tree would be enjoyable. Seems terribly awkward."

I couldn't help but chuckle at his sincerity. Time to change the subject before Mel got any more absurd ideas in her head.

"Speaking of awkward, where's Ladinas? We need to speak with him straight away."

Mel pouted, clearly disappointed the fun was over. "Just missed him. He left with most of the team on a mission. Didn't want to waste a minute of the night."

My brow furrowed. "What about Ramon and the others?"

"Gone too," she replied with a careless shrug. "Ramon and Ladinas butted heads one too many times. And that boy Adam... he commands those Unseelie Redcaps now, and Ladinas didn't like having them around. So they all took off."

I nodded slowly, processing this new information. We'd have to make do without them.

"What about Clement and the orphans?" I asked hopefully.

"Back in the orphanage wing, far as I know," said Mel. "And before you ask, Willie is back in the forest monitoring the convergence. And the other convergences you found before."

I nodded. "Good to know. Glad you've got all the bases covered."

Mel tilted her head. "So what kind of trouble have you got yourself into this time, Mercy?"

I sighed. "I'm in deep shit with the human authorities, but that's nothing new. The real problem is there's a massive werewolf gathering in Maine. We don't know exactly what they're up to, but we're pretty sure they're planning something big—either a slaughter or trying to turn an entire college town."

Mel's eyes widened in alarm. "Seriously? Why didn't you call for backup sooner?"

"I didn't exactly have time for a chat while fighting for my sanity," I said dryly. "That damn dragon is still rattling around inside me. The only thing keeping Oblivion at bay is focusing on doing good, protecting people. But now I know the only way to really beat him is to deal with my... past..."

Mel nodded in understanding. "You mean Ladinas and Alice."

I winced at the mention of their names. "Yeah. That."

"Awk-waaaard," Mel sang.

"Doesn't matter," I said sharply. "We've got less than an hour before the full moon rises. Can you reach out to Ladinas on comms? We really need the team. Whatever they're up to tonight, it can't be as urgent as this werewolf crisis."

Mel shifted uneasily. "Yeah, about that... Ladinas and the others are downtown dealing with a mess of freshly turned younglings gone wild."

"What? How were they turned?"

"You really don't know?" Mel gave me an incredulous look. "Ever since that dragon got its claws in you, everyone you've been biting has been turning full vampire. No deaths, only undead walking away. We're overwhelmed trying to control them."

I scratched my head, disturbed by this news. "Well, shit. Looks like we'll have to fight fire with fire. You said Ramon is gone. Can we get him? If Adam can help, he still commands those damn Redcaps. I'm not exactly keen on fighting with a bunch of Unseelie faeries, but if Adam can command them, they'd give us a fighting chance against the wolves."

Sebastian cleared his throat. "You want to fight werewolves with faeries?"

"Desperate times," I shrugged. "I don't like it either, but we're short on options."

Mel shuffled her feet. "I know where Ramon, Clarissa, Adam, and the Redcaps are hiding out. But are you sure about this, Mercy? Things could get ugly real fast."

I set my jaw stubbornly. "Doesn't matter. It's my mess to clean up. I let that damn dragon cloud my judgment. Now people are paying the price. No more running or hiding. Tonight, I make my stand. With or without help. We'll deal with the wolves, ideally with Adam's Redcaps leading the charge, and if I really am the sire to all these feral younglings, I guess I'd better come back and mother up. Just ask Ladinas to try to stop them from wreaking too much havoc until we're back."

Chapter 16

"MEL, I NEED YOU to be the bridge between Ladinas and me," I said, my voice tense with urgency. "Keep communications open. Let me know what he's up to and if they get into trouble while we're in Maine."

"Got it, Mercy," Mel replied, handing me an earpiece. The little device felt cold as I slid it into place, but it was oddly comforting. Like wearing that damn earpiece made me a part of the team again. "I'll stay in touch."

"Good," I nodded, turning to Muggs. "You know where Ramon is, right?"

"Of course," Muggs replied, his blind eyes aloof but twinkling with mischief. "I can bring you and your friends there."

"Ready, Goliath?" I asked, looking at the loyal hellhound by my side. He nuzzled my hand, licking it in response. His warm breath and the rough texture of his tongue were both a little gross and comforting at the same time.

"Here we go again," Sebastian grunted, bracing himself for another topsy-turvy trip via druid portal.

Muggs spun his staff overhead, its energy crackling through the air. A green tornado swirled around us, our surroundings dissolving into a blur of motion before we found ourselves in a new location—an old bottling factory.

The place smelled like stale beer and rust, and I couldn't help but wrinkle my nose in disgust. I glanced around, taking in the abandoned machinery and broken windows, and wondered how long this forsaken place had been left to rot.

"Are you sure this is the right place?" I asked Muggs, my tone a mixture of doubt and curiosity. "This isn't really Ramon's style."

"Positive," he replied, a hint of a smirk playing on his lips. "Be on the lookout, though. Those Redcaps are hanging around. They're mostly harmless under Adam's command, but they can be a nuisance."

"Alright, let's move," I said, my voice resolute. The earpiece crackled to life as Mel's voice chimed in.

"Stay safe, Mercy. I'll keep you updated on Ladinas and the team."

I nodded, knowing she couldn't see me, but somehow it felt like the right thing to do. "Thanks, Mel. Did you talk to him yet?"

"Yeah," Mel replied. "Let's just say he's glad you're back with us. But he's a little too busy to chat right now. He could really use your help to get those younglings under control."

"Understood. But we have to deal with these wolves as well. Let Ladinas know I'll be there as soon as possible. But if things get too nasty with the younglings, let me know, and if I can get away to help, I will."

With Goliath by my side, Sebastian and Muggs following closely behind, we ventured deeper into the decrepit factory, each step echoing through the silent halls.

Something wet hit my cheek.

Raising a hand to wipe it off, I found myself staring at a spitball. My lips curled into a slight snarl as I scanned the area for the culprit. In the distance, I spotted a Redcap cackling and quickly darting away.

"Little bastards," I muttered under my breath, my anger flaring. But I knew we had more important matters at hand, so I decided to let it go for now. "Come on, they must be this way."

We followed the mischievous Redcap down a dark hallway, its worn walls seeming to close in on us. Suddenly, Sebastian yelped. I whipped around to see another Redcap standing just behind the sentinel, with two fists full of underwear, pulling it as high as they could reach.

"Damn it!" Sebastian grunted, his face flushing with embarrassment as he picked his wedgie. "Fucking faeries."

I couldn't help but laugh at his misfortune. "Don't worry, Aquaman. At least you're making friends."

He shot me a glare but said nothing as we continued our search. Eventually, we reached a back room set up like a makeshift apartment. Ramon, Clarissa, and Adam were all hanging out, watching television. The moment they saw me, their eyes widened in shock.

"Mercy?" Ramon stood up, his gaze flicking between Muggs and Goliath, clearly trying to figure out if I was still under Calivion's influence.

"Relax," I assured them. "It's really me. Oblivion doesn't have control over me right now."

"Thank the gods," Clarissa breathed, visibly relieved. "I'm glad you're here. I really need to go get a bite and Ramon won't take me..."

Ramon shrugged. "She's fine. I told her that the hunger would pass."

I rolled my eyes. "Since when was moderation ever *your* specialty, Ramon?"

Ramon cocked an eyebrow. "Moi? Never! But that does not mean I do not understand the theory."

"Ramon, Clarissa, Adam," I began, looking each of them in the eye. "We need your help."

Ramon's expression turned serious. "What's the issue?"

"Maine is crawling with werewolves preparing to launch an all-out assault on a city. We don't know how many there are, but they're gearing up for something big. Adam, if you could use the Redcaps to help us fight them off, I would appreciate it."

Adam hesitated, glancing at the mischievous Redcaps still lurking in the shadows. "I'm not sure how effective they'd be against werewolves. They pretty much stick to themselves and carry on with their games."

Sebastian tugged at the back of his jeans. "Not a big fan of their *games.*"

I smirked and slapped my knee. "They aren't all they're *cracked* up to be, are they, Sebas?"

Sebastian narrowed his eyes. "Hilarious. Really, I'm laughing so hard right now. On the inside."

Adam smiled. "My apologies if they were rude. I know I'm supposed to be the king of the Unseelie, but I don't feel like a monarch. And I don't like being told what to do, so I don't really boss them around too much."

"Seriously, Adam? They respect you; they'll listen to you," I argued, trying to appeal to his sense of responsibility. "We could save a lot of lives."

"Wait," Ramon interjected. "Why haven't you asked Ladinas for help?"

I sighed. "I haven't spoken to him, but Mel said that Ladinas and the team are dealing with my 'spawn'—apparently everyone I bit while Oblivion was messing with me turned into a vampire. So, they're kind of busy."

"Aïe, aïe, aïe!" Ramon shook his head. "Let me get this straight. There's a brood of unfettered younglings wreaking havoc in Providence *and* some kind of werewolf convention that's converging on a small town in Maine?"

"Exactly," I continued, my voice laced with urgency. "And with Ladinas and the team occupied, you're my last hope for stopping the wolves. We need all hands on deck for this. Can we count on you?"

Ramon exchanged glances with Clarissa and Adam. "I'm not sure we'd be much help, to be honest."

Sebastian stepped forward, eyeing Ramon cautiously. "You used to be a vampire."

Ramon nodded. "Oui. You're familiar with my work?"

Sebastian grunted. "I'm aware of your reputation. You were on my list, once. Then, you disappeared."

"He became human," I said. "Thanks to the work of a goddess and a cauldron. Then, he became a vampire again, then was turned into a faerie. Ramon here has changed his stripes more frequently than a politician. But in his heart, despite what you might have heard, he's trustworthy. He's saved my life more than once."

Sebastian nodded. "Very well. The point is, I know the havoc you *used* to cause. Anyone with the potential for great evil also has an equal and opposite potential to do good. I do not doubt you'd be an asset as an ally in battle."

Ramon bristled, sizing up the sentinel. "Who are you, anyway? Anyone ever tell you that you look like Aquaman?"

I quickly moved between them before things escalated. "He's a friend, Ramon. This is Sebastian."

Ramon raised an eyebrow. "You're friends with a hunter now?"

"I'm not a hunter," Sebastian corrected. "I'm a sentinel. And I'm no threat unless you're up to no good."

I gave Sebastian an appreciative nod. He was really trying here.

"We need help, Ramon," Sebastian continued solemnly. "There are too many wolves and too many lives at stake."

I saw Adam watching us intently as we spoke. It was easy to forget he was only a few months old with the way he carried himself. But there was still so much for him to learn about who and what he was. He'd grown up in a matter of weeks. Something to do with being a tribrid of human, vampire, and faerie. He had a soul, so far as we could tell, that his vampirism didn't suppress. But he could drink blood. It made him stronger, and he had our strength and speed. But as a faerie—the son of Malvessa, the late Unseelie Queen—he had powers he'd barely begun to understand.

Sebastian pressed on urgently. "Come next full moon, we'll have pandemonium on our hands if we don't stop them now. What if these wolves turn all of Farmington?"

Ramon sighed, running a hand through his hair. "You raise a fair point, sentinel. Alright, you have our assistance against the wolves. We'll do what we can. But I was willing to help from the start, for Mercy's sake. Even if I doubted my ability to make much of a difference."

I let out a breath I didn't need. "Thank you, Ramon. This isn't just about what you can do. Adam's gifts are unique. He's our best shot at stopping this horror."

Adam approached me then, his intense gaze searching my face. Gently, he placed his hands on either side of my head.

"Have you considered these events might be connected?" His eyes were wide with curiosity..

I furrowed my brow, resisting the urge to pull away. I hated it when people touched my face. But there was something about Adam that was... different. When he touched someone, he sensed things others couldn't. "What do you mean?"

"Think about it," Adam urged. "Oblivion used you to create those rogue vampires you didn't even know about. Now this wolf army appears out of nowhere. Are you certain Oblivion isn't behind them, too?"

I shook my head. "I don't see how. He's been trapped inside me all this time."

But even as I said it, doubt crept in. I'd never heard of wolves gathering and assaulting a town like this. I had to admit, there was a remarkable similarity between the kind of chaos that Providence and Farmington were about to face—and for these issues to come to a head at precisely the same time?

Adam's expression was grim. "Are you so sure about that? I don't sense Oblivion within you anymore. Only the other one remains."

"Caladbolg?" I whispered.

As soon as the name left my lips, a huge broadsword materialized in my grip, glowing with power. Excalibur's equal, if legends were true. "Oops," I said. "Didn't mean to do that. But... that's not Oblivion. Somehow, the two dragons have separated. I don't understand... how could that happen without me realizing it?"

Adam released me, his face solemn. "I don't have those answers. I only know Oblivion is no longer inside you."

My mind raced, possibilities swirling. If Oblivion had somehow freed himself when I was vulnerable after the wolf bite... he could be possessing any of us now and we'd never know.

Sebastian's eyes widened, his fingers tightening on the hilt of his sword. "The wolf bite," he said slowly. "What if when that mutt sank her teeth into you, Oblivion saw his chance? He could have jumped right into her in that moment."

I sucked in a breath as understanding hit me like a sledgehammer. "You're right. But when I was staked, when I went to heaven, Caladbolg acted as though Oblivion was still a part of me. He told me how to defeat him, how to gain power over him. If he'd already left me when the wolf bit me, that wouldn't track."

Ramon threw his hands up in exasperation. "Oh sure, Sebastian can send you to paradise with a stake through the heart, but all the times you staked me over the years led straight to hell. Real fair, Mercy."

I rolled my eyes. "That had nothing to do with me and everything to do with this." I hefted the glowing sword. "Caladbolg took me there for a reason."

I rubbed my brow. "Adam, can you check Sebastian?"

"Check me for what?" Sebastian took a step back.

"Just want to make sure Oblivion didn't jump out of me and into you."

Sebastian took a deep breath. "Alright. Do what you must."

Adam approached Sebastian and placed his hands on either side of his head—just as he'd done to me moments earlier. "He's alone," Adam said with a nod. "The dragon is not within him."

I tilted my head. "Oblivion has to bind himself to someone in this realm. Caladbolg told me as much. He said if I cast him out, somehow, he'd find another host. That means anyone I've been in contact with since I came back could be possessed by the dragon."

"Donnie," Sebastian shook his head.

I pulled out my earpiece and covered it with my hands, muffling my voice. "Or Mel," I whispered.

"Not likely," Sebastian said. "She's not involved. She's staying back at your lair."

I snickered. "My *lair*. Right. Where she can coordinate our efforts on two fronts. Think of it, if Oblivion is attached to Mel, he could be feeding her bullshit information to screw up our attempts to stop the chaos he's causing."

Sebastian nodded, his expression grim. "Then we take any information she gives us with a grain of salt until we know for sure. We're running out of time. The werewolves have to be our priority. We can deal with Oblivion after."

I felt a gentle pressure on my shoulder and glanced over to see Adam's concerned face.

"Do not fear, Mercy," he said softly. "I will accompany you to find Oblivion once this crisis is resolved. You won't have to face him alone."

Despite the gravity of the situation, his words brought me a small measure of comfort. I managed a faint smile.

"Thanks, Adam. I appreciate that. But Sebastian's right, we're almost out of time here. If we don't get to Farmington now, a lot of innocent people are going to die once that full moon rises."

Adam nodded. "Then let us make haste. The Redcaps and I stand ready to assist you against the wolves in any way we can."

I took a deep breath, gripping Caladbolg tightly. "Right. No time to waste worrying about Oblivion now. We've got a town to save."

Chapter 17

MUGGS' PORTAL SPUN OPEN, a swirling vortex of green magic. Sebastian stepped through without hesitation. Almost as if traveling by portal was becoming old hat.

I watched as Adam barked orders at the Redcaps, his voice deeper than it had any right to be for his young appearance. The gnarled little creatures scrambled to obey, gathering their makeshift weapons with muttered curses and snarls. Clarissa and Ramon herded them toward the portal, their faces grim.

Muggs gestured for me to go ahead. Reality stretched and bent around me. An instant later, I stumbled out beside Sebastian's Chevelle on a quiet street in Farmington. A full moon hung heavy in the sky. Distant howls from every direction raised the hairs on my neck.

Showtime.

By the time I'd arrived, Sebastian had already gone inside Martha's house to grab Donnie. Just as Muggs arrived and closed the portal, the door to the house swung open to reveal a rotund, slovenly man wearing head-to-toe black leather and pitch-black shades. What little hair Donnie had left in the horseshoe that surrounded his bald head, he'd slicked back with gel. Under his leather coat, he wore a low-cut shirt that showed off a curly forest of Cheetos-dusted chest hair. He looked like he'd raided Arnold's dressing room on the set of the last Terminator movie.

Sebastian shuffled out behind him, shaking his head, as Donnie strutted our way. Donnie approached me and extended his hand. "Come with me if you want to live."

I rolled my eyes. "Rambo wasn't badass enough for you? What's next? Bruce Willis from *Die Hard*?"

"Yippee-Ki-Yay, motherfucker!" Donnie shook his fist as he shouted John McClane's most famous line.

"Donald Eugene Levingston!" a shrill voice shouted from within the house. "You watch that mouth or I'll wash it out with soap!"

Sebastian elbowed Donnie in the ribs. "Someone's in trouble…"

"Fuck off," Donnie mumbled, hushing himself enough to avoid the wrath of Mother.

I didn't doubt that Donnie could handle himself in a fight. He proved himself—shockingly enough—the last fight. Apparently, he had to get into character to fight. If it worked, who was I to question it?

I didn't have to do that. I was in character all the time—ass kicking was quickly becoming a part of my daily routine. Get up, check my phone, wash my face, go kick some ass. Rise and repeat. Sometimes, I'd grab a bite while I was out. Though, this time, I wasn't hungry at all.

Strangely, that blood from heaven still sustained me. At the very least, on a mental level, I felt like I'd had my fill lately. There was a chance my real-world stomach would catch up, eventually.

The tension was so thick that you could have waved a piece of bread through the air and buttered it with angst. Our plan was risky at best, suicidal at worst. But it was the only way the people of Farmington—not to mention all the kids at the university—had a fighting chance.

I took a deep breath, even though I didn't need the air. It was a force of habit.

"Okay, let's go over the plan again," I said. Sebastian, Donnie, Adam, Ramon, and Clarissa all turned their attention to me. Muggs was staring off into space, per usual, but I knew he was listening. Goliath stood at my side, nuzzling his giant head against my right butt cheek.

"Sebastian, Donnie, Goliath and I will take the north side of the city. Adam, you and the Redcaps will take the south and east. Ramon, Clarissa, you get the west. Muggs, go with Ramon and Clarissa."

They all nodded. I could see the fear and apprehension in their eyes, even if they tried to hide it. We were severely outnumbered and outmatched. But we had to try.

"Remember, stay in contact by phone," I continued, feeling a little proud of myself that I'd actually incorporated modern technology into my strategy. They say you live, you learn. When you live forever, you learn *eventually*. "Make sure you have your notifications on vibrate. Texts only. No fucking calls. If shit goes south, we regroup and re-strategize. No lone wolves."

I smirked at my unintentional pun. A small chuckle escaped Sebastian's lips.

"I'll do my best to keep my ears open!" Muggs added. As a vampire with enhanced senses, and a blind man at that, his hearing was a bit like Superman's. He could hear a pin drop from a mile away if he focused enough.

"Let's do this," Adam said, determination shining in his young eyes. He turned to his Redcap army. "Move out!"

The Redcaps cheered and followed Adam south. Ramon and Clarissa headed west, weapons at the ready.

Sebastian popped the trunk on his Chevelle, revealing the organized arsenal within. He handed me a silver dagger and took one for himself. I slid it into my boot sheath.

"Locked and loaded," Sebastian said. "Let's go kick some wolf ass."

I smiled, baring my fangs. "With pleasure."

We took off running north, Donnie lumbering behind as fast as his too-tight leather pants would allow.

I could already hear the howls and snarls up ahead as we raced through the dark streets. My supernatural vision allowed me to see clearly, though the humans with me relied on the dim street lights overhead.

We were nearing the tree line at the edge of the city when the first wolf burst from the shadows. Nearly seven feet tall, fangs bared and claws extended, it leapt right for me. I barely had time to raise my dagger before it slammed into me, knocking me backwards.

I grappled with it, our strength nearly equal as we rolled across the asphalt. It snapped at my face, strings of saliva dripping onto my cheek. I wedged my elbow under its throat to push it back, then drove Caladbolg into its heart. It let out a pained yelp before going still.

I shoved the body off me, wiping my mouth with the back of my hand. Sebastian was beside me, offering his hand to help me up.

"You good?" he asked.

"Peachy," I replied, taking his hand and getting to my feet. Two more wolves were emerging from the treeline. "Here we go again."

Sebastian lifted his fist and squeezed, his silver blade extending with a click. Bracing himself, he let the wolf make the first move, then with a quick spin, he evaded the beast's attack and caught it across the back. The wolf's skin simmered in reaction to the silver and, with a few stumbles, it crashed to the ground.

I launched myself at the other wolf, but Donnie already tossed two of his silver throwing knives, each finding purchase in an eye.

I turned back to Donnie with a smirk as the wolf howled and collapsed.

Donnie nodded at me as if he'd done shit like this every day. I swear, that momma's boy was a big, flabby bundle of surprise.

I raised my blade, ready, keeping a wary eye on the treeline. More would come, I knew. I just hoped Adam and the others were faring as well on the other fronts.

A trip of wolves burst from the brush, moving with unnatural speed. I barely had time to react before one slammed into me, knocking me flat on my back with its jaws inches from my face. Caladbolg was too long, too big, I couldn't get a good angle. I jammed the legendary blade's hilt into its throat to keep those snapping teeth at bay as I frantically felt around for my knife.

"A little help here!" I yelled.

Goliath came running to intercept, but one wolf collided with him in a snarling ball of fur and saliva.

Sebastian was grappling with the third wolf, but at my call, he twisted and plunged his blade through its back and into its heart. It yelped and with all my vampiric strength, I pushed the dying beast off me, giving me the chance to scramble to my feet and drive my own blade home. Just for good measure.

I shot Sebastian a grateful look. "Thanks for the save."

He wiped his blade off on his pants. "Anytime. But there's no end to them."

I watched more shadows stalking at the treeline, yellow eyes glowing. We were badly outnumbered. My only hope was that Adam was kicking ass and taking names (probably not Fido or Spot, more like Fang and Stinky). If Adam and the Redcaps could finish off their wolves, then help Ramon and Clarissa do the same, they could join us. But so far, no texts. No news at all. And the wolves were coming at us so fast I didn't have time to fire off an update.

So much for feeling good about my progress with technology.

"I guess we better keep killing them," I tightened my grip on Caladbolg. "Because I am not dying tonight."

"We'll be fine," Donnie said. "Where's your confidence, Mercy? I'm here, remember?"

I chuckled a little. "Almost forgot. You mean to say you've faced worse than this before?"

"Sure," Donnie said. "I mean, I once took on the Lich King with shit armor, barely level 80. I still beat the bastard."

"Who the hell is the Lich King?" I asked.

"World of WarCraft! Duh!"

"Shit." I shook my head. "We're dead."

The three of us stood back to back, weapons at the ready as more wolves emerged from the darkness. I counted at least ten circling us, their lips curled back to reveal sharp fangs. This was not going to be pretty.

One lunged and I slashed out, opening a gash across its muzzle. It fell back with a yelp, but two more quickly took its place. Sebastian went to work, moving faster than any mortal should have. No wonder he'd kicked my ass—twice. Strength and speed can only get you so far. He had skill. And there was something sexy as hell about the way he moved, but I didn't have time to appreciate it.

A knife whizzed past my face. Fucking Donnie. But he wasn't aiming for me. It caught a wolf on my opposite side. I took a deep breath and used my speed to slash and stab as fast as I could.

Three wolves rushed me at once. I killed one, but the other two bowled me over, jaws snapping. Goliath made it there this time and tore one of the wolves' heads off with his jaws, leaving me to contend with only one. But in the chaos of it all, the wolf found an angle. I cried out as fangs tore through my shoulder. "Damn it! Not again!"

I jammed my knife into its gut, but the damage was already done.

"You okay?" Sebastian asked worriedly, eyeing my wound out of the corner of his eye as he defended himself from another wolf.

"I'll live," I gritted out. We had taken down several wolves, but more kept coming. We were tiring, injuries slowing us down. We couldn't keep this up much longer.

Right on cue, my earpiece crackled. "Mercy!" Mel's worried voice came through. "Ladinas is in trouble! The younglings are out of control! You're the best shot we have at taming them! Please tell me things are going better on your front than in Providence."

I cursed under my breath. It seemed no one was faring well tonight.

"We're getting shredded over here too," I said breathlessly. "There's too damn many. We need a new plan."

Sebastian grunted as he took down two wolves in quick succession. "What kind of plan?" he asked.

I hesitated only a moment before the idea hit me. "Adam!" I shouted over the din. "He can fold space! Bring the battlefields together!"

Sebastian looked confused but kept fighting. "What the hell does that mean?"

"Adam can bend the fabric of reality!" I explained hastily. "He can combine the two battlefields into one! We can fight both enemies at once with our full forces!"

Sebastian's eyes lit up with understanding. "That's brilliant! But what makes you think we can handle a bunch of vampires on top of all these wolves?"

I shook my head. "If I can use my sire bond to control the younglings, I can use them to help us fight. But if Adam screws up..."

"I'm not going to try to pretend to understand how it works," Sebastian said. "If you think this plan will help, go find Adam. Do what you need to do. Donnie and I will handle the wolves here."

Chapter 18

THE NIGHT AIR WAS thick with tension as I hurried through the empty streets of Farmington. My boots pounded the pavement like the pistons of Sebastian's Chevelle. I was running at full speed, but even so, I couldn't help but notice an eerie silence over the middle of the city. A stark contrast against the battles we were fighting just outside Farmington's borders on every side.

I couldn't shake the knot in my stomach when I thought about what I was asking Adam to do. Mel knew the plan, which meant Ladinas did now, too. Hopefully, he'd have the whole team ready when they arrived and we could end this shit show early. But a thousand things could go wrong first.

Folding space and dimensions was risky magic, even for someone as powerful as Adam. If he lost focus, even for a moment, reality could fuse in horrific ways. Buildings, landscape, even people could get caught between dimensions, lost in some nightmarish limbo. If places could merge, maybe people could, too. For a split-second I thought about Donnie's body being swapped with Alice's. Petty, I know, but it made me laugh thinking about how horrified Ladinas would be. And how Donnie would probably never leave a mirror for the rest of his life.

Bottom line? This was really, really dangerous stuff. We'd already learned the hard way what bending time or space could do. This wasn't like simple portals that allowed a person to move from one place to another. Adam's magic literally brought different parts of reality together in *one* place. The ways it could go wrong were so many, it was less a question of preventing *anything* from getting screwed up and more about mitigating the damage. The most I could hope for was that the effects of Adam's magic would be relatively inconsequential beyond what we required—the chance to take over the vampire younglings and use them to stop the wolves.

If it worked, we'd deal with the problem that Providence was facing because I'd have my younglings handled, and we'd stop the wolves all at the same time.

I trusted Adam, but this was a delicate, dangerous endeavor. All I could do was hope the kid had enough finesse to pull it off without screwing everything to hell and back.

The howls of wolves carried on the wind, along with sounds of fighting nearby. We were in a bad way, no doubt about it. But if Adam succeeded, we'd have the numbers and ferocity of the youngling vampires on our side. It might not be enough to *beat* the wolves, but maybe we could protect Farmington until the wolves shifted back at sunrise.

The younglings would be in danger then, too, of course. But if I had them under control, I could surely compel them to take cover during the day. At the very least, they could bury themselves underground out in the woods.

I'd worry about that if we got that far. How the younglings would fare at sunrise was the least pressing of my concerns.

I just had to have faith and brace myself. Adam was our only shot of getting backup here from Providence. It was the only way I could help Ladinas stop the younglings without abandoning Farmington. If folding reality was what it took, so be it.

I found Adam on the south side of Farmington, where a line of Redcaps were clashing with a pack of wolves. He stood back from the fray, focused intently as he waved a hand at any wolf that broke through. The wolves immediately went docile, wandering away once Adam's power took hold.

"Not a bad system you've got going here," I commented as I approached him.

Adam gave me a strained smile. "Redcap claws don't kill the wolves, and their bites don't do much damage to my boys either. It's a stalemate. I figure we can hold this position until sunrise when the wolves change back. It's contained at least."

I nodded. "Sure, that works for a small section. But there are packs coming at the town from every side. No way your Redcaps can hold them off all night."

Howls erupted in the distance, as if to emphasize my point. Adam's brow furrowed with concern.

"And there's more trouble," I added. "Ladinas and the others are getting overwhelmed by younglings back in Providence. We need to bring them here, get them fighting on our side."

Adam sighed heavily, glancing around at the skirmish before us. "You know how risky it is, right?"

"I know," I said. "But we're running low on options here. I can control the younglings, but I can't leave this place behind. If you can bring both battles together, we should be able to win on both fronts. Can you do it?"

"I think so." Adam lifted his hands, and I could feel power thrumming around him. "But it'll take everything I've got to keep the dimensions separate while bringing them together. If I lose focus, everything will crash together and merge for good. Keeping everything maintained will leave me vulnerable."

I put a hand on his shoulder, meeting his worried gaze. "I'll keep you safe, Adam. Call some Redcaps to form a perimeter around you while you work."

Adam considered this, then turned and waved over a half dozen Redcaps. He directed them to surround him as he prepared to fold space.

Taking a deep breath, Adam lifted his hands again. His eyes glowed white, power swirling, as he began intricately weaving the fabric of reality.

I watched in awe as Adam worked his magic. The very air around us seemed to shimmer and warp.

Then, flickering into existence, I saw it—one of the Vampire Underground's black SUVs. It blinked in and out of reality before solidifying with a heavy thud. More figures took shape, youngling vampires dripping blood from their mouths, members of the Underground looking around in shock.

With a rush of displaced air, Ladinas appeared a few feet in front of me. We exchanged a brief nod, the awkwardness palpable. But there was no time for niceties.

I turned to Adam. His forehead was beaded with sweat, jaw clenched in concentration. The dimensional folding was taking its toll.

"Are you sure you can maintain this?" I asked.

Adam's only response was a tight nod. His fingers flexed spasmodically as he struggled to maintain the connection.

I glanced around hurriedly. The younglings were getting their bearings, the Underground members rallying to take them on. We had only moments before both sides would clash here, too.

"Keep your defensive positions around Adam!" I barked at the Redcaps. "Keep him safe at all costs, got it?"

They didn't pay me much heed. I wasn't *their* queen, after all. But they were doing their job.

I took a deep breath, praying my sire bond would work. Time to turn these younglings from enemies to allies. The fate of Farmington rested on it.

I strode towards the nearest youngling, a blonde girl still clutching the limp form of her human victim. It sickened me that I didn't even recognize her. These younglings were people I'd drained... She was nothing to me but a blood bag. How had I allowed Oblivion to have such an influence over me?

She clearly recognized me. Blood dripped from her chin as she stared at me blankly, licking her lips.

"Release him," I commanded, injecting as much authority into my voice as I could.

The girl blinked slowly, then bared her fangs with a feral hiss. She did not let go.

I cursed internally. "I'm your sire. You will do what I say!"

Then the girl had the nerve to spit blood right in my face.

I wiped the blood from my face, trying to keep my cool. Losing control now would only make things worse.

"Listen to me," I said, taking a step closer. "You can fight against me, or you can fight with me. Which do you think is going to give you a better chance of survival?"

The youngling hesitated, glancing around at the other vampires. I could sense her confusion and desperation. She wanted to live, even if it meant following my orders.

"Join me," I urged. "Help us fight the wolves and I'll make sure you're safe come sunrise. You don't have to be alone out here."

For a moment I thought I was reaching her, and the younglings gathering around the girl seemed to follow her lead.

But the bitch was only distracting me. I heard footsteps approach as another youngling came at me from the side.

I sidestepped hastily. "Get back!"

He ignored me, swiping with his fingers curled as if his nails were claws. I seized his wrist and flipped him to the ground.

"We're on the same side, damnit!" I shouted in frustration. But my words meant nothing to the blood-maddened youngling.

Ladinas appeared at my side, his sword drawn. "If these vampires won't fight the werewolves, I'm afraid we've only made things worse. We must restrain them quickly, before the werewolves arrive."

I huffed. "I don't get it. If I'm their sire, why the hell aren't they listening to me?"

Ladinas rubbed his brow. "I wish I had an answer. But it's a mystery that will have to wait to be solved. Because these younglings are getting restless."

"Goliath!" I shouted. "Get over here!"

The hellhound was never far away. And he heard me no matter where I called him from. "I think it's time that Goliath had a snack."

Ladinas tilted his head. "If he feeds on vampires..."

"I get stronger," I nodded. "I don't like it. I'm responsible for--"

"It wasn't your fault," Ladinas cut me off before I could proceed. "When you killed them, that damned dragon was in your head."

"Still," I sighed. "I hoped to save them. But right now, I don't see any way to save this town if I don't let Goliath loose on them."

I ducked as another youngling flew at me, his hands outstretched like talons. He careened past and Goliath pounced on him the second he hit the pavement.

The surge of power was immediate. I tightened my grip on Caladbolg. "Here's the thing," I said as I stepped toward the youngling girl I'd addressed before. "You learn to listen to your sire, or you become hellhound kibble."

She screeched and raked her nails down my cheek, drawing blood. I cursed and head-butted her hard. She stumbled back, but then took the hands of other younglings gathered around her.

Then, as one, the younglings froze. Their eyes glowed an eerie violet as they turned to face me.

"Oblivion!" they chorused in unison.

My blood ran cold. What the hell?

A familiar form coalesced before me—before *them*. Blond hair, leathery wings, scales that glinted like metal. He was like Calivion, before, but lacking a light, a color to his skin.

"Surprise," he purred.

I stared at Oblivion in dismay. How could he be here, controlling all these younglings I had sired?

He chuckled at my shock. "Don't look so confused, my dear. You should have known I'd never fully release my hold over you and your spawn. Each person you bit, I left a piece of myself within them. Call it my insurance policy, in case you turned stubborn."

I shook my head in denial. "No. I broke your influence. I'm free of you!"

"Is that what you think happened?" Oblivion tilted his head, looking almost sympathetic. "My *brother* only got a voice when I willingly let parts of myself go to bear our children! Yes, Mercy, I needed you to make this army of ours. But now I have more than enough vampires at my disposal to make as many as I'd like. The only question is whether you'll turn your back on our young family or not."

My stomach dropped. If what he said was true, then all my attempts to redeem myself had been futile. Caladbolg only influenced me when Oblivion relinquished his hold on me. And even then, I had to freaking *die* for the better of the two dragons to get through to me.

"Join me again, Mercy," Oblivion purred, holding out a clawed hand. "Together we'll usher in a new era, just as I promised. It's not too late. You can be a goddess, the mother of a new era of chaos!"

I recoiled, disgust roiling through me. "Never," I spat. "I'll never be your puppet again."

Oblivion's eyes narrowed, his false warmth vanishing. "You don't have a choice. Who do you think rallied the wolves? I arranged all of this before, when you so willingly gave me free rein as your partner, as your lover, at your side. It took very little effort to set the stage for this—our future, your coronation, your *divination!*" His smile turned cruel. "Or you can die with your friends. Divinity or death. What will it be, my love?"

My hands curled into fists. I had come too far, fought too hard to surrender myself to this monster again.

"I'd rather die," I growled.

Oblivion shook his head in mock sadness. "What a waste. But no matter." He snapped his fingers. "If you won't serve willingly, your death can serve my cause just the same."

The younglings closed in, ready to tear me apart on their master's command. I braced myself, determined to go down fighting. This couldn't be how it ended.

But I'd be damned if I let Oblivion take me alive.

I whipped out Caladbolg, the fabled blade reflecting my face back at me. With a fierce cry, I slashed at Oblivion, aiming right for his black heart.

But faster than my eyes could follow, his hand shot out and caught the blade. Caladbolg's razor edge rested against Oblivion's palm, yet didn't so much as scratch his scaly skin.

Shock coursed through me. Nothing should have been able to stop Caladbolg's bite. But Oblivion merely chuckled, an awful grating sound, and wrenched the sword from my grasp.

"This can't kill me," he sneered. "To do so would destroy itself. And we are forbidden from destroying each other."

With a flick of Oblivion's wrist, Caladbolg evaporated into mist. I stared at my empty hand, stunned and afraid for the first time. Without the sword's power, how could I hope to defeat Oblivion?

Desperate, I scrambled for my wand and aimed it back at Oblivion. "*Enerva*!"

The blast of magic should have knocked Oblivion flat. But the spell fizzled uselessly against his chest.

Oblivion threw back his head and laughed. "Foolish witch," he mocked. "I was part of you once. I was bound to your spirit. I'm immune to your spells. Your magic is useless against me."

My blood turned to ice. He was right—I couldn't hurt him any more than I could hurt myself. The same reason my healing spell couldn't totally heal the werewolf's bite earlier. Now, I had another bite on my shoulder, but with all that was going on, I barely even noticed the pain.

A crossbow bolt suddenly whizzed through the air, striking Oblivion in the chest. I whirled to see Ladinas lowering his crossbow, his face set with determination.

But Oblivion merely plucked out the bolt and flung it back casually. It struck Ladinas directly in his eye. He howled in agony, crumpling to the ground.

Oblivion grinned, savoring his pain. "Pathetic," he sneered. "Is this rabble the best you can muster against me?"

Ladinas writhed in the dirt, blood streaming from his ruined eye. He'd heal—eventually. But he was down an eye for the fight—if there was going to be any fight left to have. The younglings closed in for the kill. I could fight them off, but what was the point? I couldn't best Oblivion. Even if I fought my ass off, he'd hand it right back to me when all was said and done.

Then, with a fierce cry, Alice charged forward, her katana flashing. "Alice, don't!" I shouted, knowing it was useless, but she was determined. She swung at

Oblivion with all her might. But the dragon blocked her strikes easily, laughing as her blade glanced harmlessly off his scaly arms.

"Futile," he mocked. "No mortal weapons can pierce my flesh."

Alice attacked relentlessly, her face set with determination. But Oblivion batted her aside like a bothersome fly.

As Alice struggled back to her feet, I heard the roar of an engine. A red Chevelle screeched around the corner and barreled straight for Oblivion. It slammed into the dragon with bone-crunching force, sending him flying.

I doubted assault by automobile would kill the dragon, but even Oblivion couldn't deny the laws of physics. Mass times acceleration equals dragon gets knocked on his ass. Temporarily, at least.

The car skidded to a halt beside me. Sebastian leaned out the window. "Get in!" he shouted. "We need to regroup."

I hesitated, glancing back at Adam. He stood where he was before, still encircled by Redcaps. But if Oblivion turned against him, if I left him unprotected...

Sebastian read my thoughts. "Oblivion won't harm Adam," he said urgently. "But we need a new strategy, fast."

With great reluctance, I jumped into the passenger seat. How could Sebastian be so sure Oblivion wouldn't go after Adam first thing once I was gone? Still, the sentinel had done nothing but prove time and time again that I could trust him, so I didn't question it. "Wait!" I said. "Ladinas and Alice!"

Sebastian honked twice. "You two! Get the fuck in here if you want to survive this shit!"

Alice was already back at Ladinas's side, helping him forward as he clutched at his wounded eye. She pulled him over to Sebastian's car and I sprung out, sliding my seat forward to make room for them in the back.

"Goliath!" I shouted. "Help protect Adam!"

I had to trust he understood me. He usually did. At the very least, if the younglings started attacking and Goliath got a bite, I'd get stronger. I quickly slipped back into the passenger seat. Oblivion would be back on our asses in seconds if we hadn't wasted too much time already.

"Buckle up," Sebastian said. "Or don't. Since car crashes probably won't hurt you bloodsuckers anyway."

The tires squealed as Sebastian floored the gas pedal. We peeled away into the night, leaving Adam behind. Hopefully, between Goliath and the Redcaps, he'd be fine. But if Ramon and Clarissa knew I left him in that condition...

"Get back to Ramon, Clarissa, and Muggs," I told Sebastian. "How did it go with you and Donnie?"

"We thinned them out for now," Sebastian said. "But once that spell was cast, the wolves all started moving away from our position. I got in the car to follow while Donnie stayed to watch the perimeter. That's when I found you..."

I shook my head. "Oblivion said he organized this werewolf convention. He planned all of this shit."

Ladinas cleared his throat. "But I think he told you how to kill him."

I tilted my head. "He did?"

"He said you couldn't use Caladbolg against him. If either of them were destroyed, the other would die as well, right?"

I shook my head. "I'm not sure I even still have Caladbolg after Obliv—"

I'd said his name, and the blade appeared in my hand. "Well, shit me!"

Sebastian nodded. "The question is, how do we destroy that thing?"

I shook my head. "I won't kill him. Not without talking to him first. You could always stake me again. Maybe I'd get another chat with the dragon in my blade from the nightclub in heaven."

Sebastian laughed. "You're a strange one, Mercy Brown."

"First, we need to get Ramon, Clarissa, and Muggs," I said, rubbing my shoulder. "I need to make sure they're fine, to know we have all our bases covered. And I need Muggs to heal me again."

Chapter 19

THE TIRES OF SEBASTIAN'S Chevelle crunched over fallen leaves as we pulled up to the edge of the woods. Donnie sat hunched on a stump, shoveling Cheetos into his mouth. Orange powder coated his fingers. He lumbered over to the car, mumbling through a full mouth that the northland was clear. The wolves had left the area at almost the exact time that Adam folded the worlds together. It made sense. Oblivion was behind all of it, and he had a role for the wolves. I just wasn't totally sure what that role was yet.

That was only one mystery.

How the hell did Donnie get Cheetos out in the woods? I didn't see him bring them with him. Maybe his junk-food detector picked up a nearby supply somewhere. Too bad he didn't have an "Oh shit, your friends are fighting for their lives" detector, because while he was chowing down, we could have used his help. Then again, it was probably best he wasn't there when Oblivion showed. Too many hungry younglings that even with Donnie's MMA training and knife throwing skills, he wouldn't have lasted long.

We sped west, the trees blurring into a wall of green. My fingers tapped impatiently on the door handle. The world was shattering, and every minute we wasted felt like another fissure cracking open.

When we reached the clearing, my breath caught. Ramon, Clarissa, and Muggs lounged in the grass, chatting casually. Clarissa braided blades of grass while Muggs whistled a merry tune.

I leapt from the SUV. "What the fuck?" My voice lashed out like a whip. "The world is coming apart at the seams and you're all sitting on your asses?"

Ramon raised an eyebrow. "Bonsoir, ma chérie! Lovely night, non?"

"Lovely?" I gestured wildly at the sky. It rippled with unnatural streaks of violet and gold, undoubtedly because of Adam's magic forcing two places into one. "Have you gone blind? We're on the verge of apocalypse and you're braiding fucking grass?"

Clarissa sighed. "We've been through this before, Mercy. Another year, another end of days." She tilted her face up, letting the fractured sunlight wash over her skin. "Might as well enjoy the view."

I dug my nails into my palms, fighting the urge to slap that peaceful look off her face. She was my newest progeny—before the horde of younglings Oblivion and I had together. She'd only been through *one* apocalypse averting adventure with me. She was an amateur. She had to save the world at least three times before she could pretend to know what she was talking about.

Ramon stood, brushing dirt from his jeans. "Mercy's right. We can't sit idle." He clasped my shoulder. "But the wolves left, and you did not respond to your texts!"

I checked my phone. Yeah, I'd missed a bunch of messages. So much for vibrate. Come to find out, a phone vibrating in your pocket doesn't do much to get your attention when baby vampires are clawing at your face, space is warping around you, and chaos dragons are gloating about their world-ending aspirations.

I ran a hand through my hair, shaking off the lingering adrenaline. "Yeah, well, my bad. Was a little preoccupied with the whole almost dying again thing."

Ramon gave me a knowing look. He'd pulled my ass out of too many fires over the decades.

"Anyway," I went on, "doesn't matter now. Oblivion's made his move. He's turned those baby vamps into horcruxes."

"Into what now?" Muggs asked, scratching his head.

"Horcruxes. You know, from Harry Potter." Blank stares all around. I threw up my hands. "Don't any of you read?"

Ramon cleared his throat. "I prefer biographies myself."

"Whatever. The point is, Oblivion split his essence into the younglings when he turned them, so now we can't just kill them. We've gotta figure out how to take him down without hurting them."

I looked to Clarissa, who was back to braiding daisies or some shit. "You get all that, newbie? This is end of the world 101 stuff. Starts out fun but gets real depressing real fast. So drop the flower crown and get your head in the game."

She rolled her eyes at me. Some progeny she was turning out to be. Didn't have an ounce of respect for her maker. But I guess that's what I get for turning her just so I could save her freaking life.

Oh well. I'd straighten her out eventually. For now, we had bigger fish—or dragons—to fry. An ancient primordial force of darkness being one of them.

I nodded to Ladinas. "You said something earlier about asking Caladbolg to destroy himself. Seems like our best bet at this point."

Ladinas inclined his head. "If Caladbolg ceases to exist, so does Oblivion."

"Right. They're two sides of the same coin." I started pacing, thinking it through. "Only problem is, what if old Cal isn't in a self-sacrificing mood? He will not be exactly forthright about how to kill Oblivion if it means killing him, too."

Ramon crossed his arms. "Yes, but if we just kill Caladbolg, same result, non?"

"Maybe." I wasn't convinced. "But it's not right. Caladbolg is *good*. I'm not going to just murder him. Maybe it would be for the greater good, but that's shitty ethics."

"Right," Sebastian added. "Utilitarianism doesn't justify being an asshole."

"Depends," Donnie added. "I mean, technically, that's the whole point of utilitarianism. But I get it. Big assholes don't serve the greater good forever. Eventually, they shit on everything."

I rubbed my brow. "Okay, enough ethics bullshit. The point is, I will not betray Caladbolg like that. But at the very least, he'll know if there's anything we can do. Think about it. I brought both of these dragons to our world. They united in a pocket dimension and hitched a ride on me."

My earpiece buzzed, Ladinas glancing at me as he clearly heard it too. "Mel, what's up?" I asked.

"Sorry to interrupt," Mel's voice came through, "But I've been listening to everything. What if Adam intentionally messes it all up?"

I froze, exchanging a look with Ladinas. "What do you mean?"

"The dragons escaped their prison by binding themselves to you," Mel explained. "What if Adam can bind them again and throw them back?"

It was risky, but clever. "It could work," I said slowly. "Pocket dimensions are how the Fae imprison things. But both dragons would need to go together."

"Then that's our play," Sebastian said decisively. "We get Oblivion and Calad-bolg together, have Adam create a prison dimension and toss them in."

I bit my lip. "Maybe. But if any part of Caladbolg remains on Earth... I'm talking to Caladbolg first. If we're going to do this, he has to be on board with it. And we have to be sure it will work."

Sebastian grabbed my arm, his expression serious. "And if he says no? Then what?"

I met his gaze steadily. "Then we try Mel's idea anyway. Because it's still the best shot we have."

Sebastian searched my eyes for a moment, then nodded. We both knew the stakes. If Caladbolg rejected the plan, we'd be taking a massive gamble. But the risk might be worth it if we could end Oblivion for good.

"Here's as good a place as any," I said. "A stake to the chest, and I'll go have words with Caladbolg."

"Can't you just talk to him through your blade?" Ladinas asked. "Is this really necessary?"

I held Caladbolg in front of my face. "Hey you. Come out, come out, wherever you are."

I shrugged. "He doesn't talk like this. I don't know why. He doesn't seem to have the strength to manifest like Oblivion did. Probably because it's easier to cook up a little chaos in my spirit than virtue."

Ramon chuckled. "That's true for all of us. You know, ma chérie, I could always stake you so you and the dragon boy can talk. For old time's sake."

I barked out a laugh despite the circumstances. "Yeah, well, usually I was the one staking your ass back in the day. Sending you to time-out in hell and all."

Ramon chuckled. "Too true, too true. Well then, allow me to return the favor this time." He made a theatrical stabbing motion that made me snort.

I looked around at the group. "Sebastian? Have a stake you can toss Ramon, here?"

Sebastian reached to the back of his waistband and retrieved a wooden stake. How the hell he'd had that back there, while sitting all that time, was a mystery I wasn't eager to solve. But Sebastian was nothing if not resourceful. He tossed the stake to Ramon.

I laid down on the ground. "Give me ten minutes, tops. We can't afford more than that."

Ramon knelt down beside me, stake at the ready. "You're sure about this, chérie?"

I nodded, taking a deep breath. "Just do it."

Without another word, Ramon plunged the stake into my chest. The pain was excruciating, but I gritted my teeth and focused on my breathing.

Everything faded to black—you know, the usual when you basically die. It was just another weekend for me. But then I found myself sitting on a bar stool. The same one I sat on when I'd met Caladbolg in heaven before.

He was still mixing drinks. "So tell me, buddy. Are you really in heaven all the time, or do you only come here when I do?"

Caladbolg smirked. "We're connected, Mercy. What do you think?"

I cleared my throat. "Well, make me something strong, because we have a lot to talk about."

Caladbolg made me another glass of blood, just as he'd done before. "I know why you're here. As you said, we *are* connected. You want to know if I'd be willing to sacrifice myself in order to eliminate my brother."

I shrugged. "Or if you would be willing to bind yourself to him again and let us put the two of you in another dimension, you know, like a prison. Sorry I don't have more pleasant ideas, but Oblivion has to be stopped."

Caladbolg leaned against the bar, his eyes solemn. "I understand the gravity of the situation. Oblivion is a danger to everything and everyone." He paused, taking a sip of his own drink. "But sacrificing myself is not the answer. I won't make the same mistake twice."

I frowned. "What mistake are you talking about?"

"The mistake of believing that I could handle the darkness alone," he said, his voice heavy with regret. "I thought I could keep Oblivion in check, that I could control him. But I was wrong. And it cost me everything. It cost *you* everything."

I tilted my head. "You didn't bite those people."

Caladbolg sighed. "But I couldn't stop him from making you do it."

I cleared my throat. "Because I was being a little bitch. I was feeling sorry for myself about Ladinas and Alice getting together."

"You had a right to feel what you were feeling," Caladbolg said. "You may be a vampire, but you're entitled to your *human* emotions as much as anyone. To expect you to suck it up and *accept* what happened wouldn't be fair. You had to go through it to get past it."

I rolled my eyes. "Well, usually when a relationship ends, getting over it doesn't involve mass murder."

Caladbolg extended his finger. "And you wouldn't have lost control like that if I'd been able to keep Oblivion in check. Nothing that happened was your fault, Mercy. You are entitled to experience heartbreak as much as anyone."

I chuckled. "Funny way to put it, you know, since there's a piece of wood stuck in my heart at this very moment."

Caladbolg chuckled a little at my joke. "Your idea with the pocket dimension isn't bad. However, I think I have an idea that might improve your chances of success."

I shrugged. "I'm all ears."

"Anything my brother can do with his essence, I can do as well. I must divide myself even as he has done. A part of me will remain with you. But a greater part will arrest as much of what remains of Oblivion and take it to this prison dimension you speak of."

I tilted my head. "So you'll still be a part of me?"

Caladbolg nodded. "I will. But my brother mustn't know it. Even a small part, if it remains in this world, can grow into full strength over time. He will gladly send the bulk of his essence into the pocket dimension if he thinks it will imprison me there and put me out of your reach."

"But you'll leave your strongest part with me?" I asked.

"Which should be enough to defeat the smaller part of Oblivion that he leaves behind. But I will not be able to stay with you. You must find where he has housed what remains of his spirit so that I can overwhelm him there, and dominate him the way he controlled the two of us when we were both bound to you."

I bit my lip. "So, we're going to horcrux the shit out of the horcrux. Got it."

"In a manner of speaking," Caladbolg said.

"Well, if he's leaving a small part behind, knowing it will grow more powerful eventually, won't he try to be discreet? How are we going to find him?"

Caladbolg laughed. "Because I know exactly where he is. He's in the wolves. All of them."

"Wait," I said. "He split himself up into all the younglings *and* the wolves?"

"Yes," Caladbolg said. "But if you put me into the *alpha...*"

"Then you can overpower his influence over the alpha... and with the alpha's power, the whole pack. But we're dealing with a bunch of packs. How do we know who the alpha is?"

"The packs are working in concert. There is an alpha of alphas. He shouldn't be difficult to find. But we mustn't do that until we've sent the greater part of his spirit into the pocket dimension with me."

"And that's inside the younglings?" I asked.

"Not at present," Caladbolg said. "When they spoke his name, he manifested in the flesh. Just as he did with you. He can influence the younglings just the same, but he can only act of his own volition this way. Speak my name, and I will manifest enough of myself to convince my brother it is my full being. It will not take long before he realizes I've divided myself and left a portion with you. Adam must act to send us away before he knows what's happening."

I nodded. "Then, after that, I find the alpha. And I do what? Stab him with you?"

Caladbolg nodded. "Say my name. I'll form into a lesser blade. Use it on the alpha and I'll release myself into the wolf. Then, I'll make sure Oblivion doesn't gain control again."

Chapter 20

I GASPED AWAKE, THE sharp pain in my sternum lingering. Three faces hovered over me—Ladinas with his stern brow furrowed, Ramon's dark eyes full of concern, and Sebastian... Sebastian with his damn charming half-smile.

"Ex number one, ex number two, and the new guy," I croaked. "What a way to wake up."

Ladinas scowled, his gaze flickering between Sebastian and me. "You're the new guy?"

Sebastian bit his lip, an endearing tell that he was nervous. "We're just friends."

Ramon let out a sharp laugh. "Yeah right. The chemistry between you two is explosive."

Sebastian shook his head, sandy hair falling over his eyes. "Maybe so, but you don't mix acids and bases. Or vampires and humans." His voice softened. "That shit never works out. Besides, I have a wife out there, somewhere. I'll find her one day."

I felt a pang in my unbeating heart. He was right, of course. I hadn't even really considered any feelings I had for the sentinel until now. Things had been too hectic, but I found myself suddenly... disappointed... that it couldn't be. But then again, why was I in any rush? I'd stay young and hot forever. Sebastian would grow old someday. Eventually, if we got together, everyone would think I was with him for his money. His car aside, Sebastian didn't have shit. I doubted his bank account had over four figures. Maybe only three. If he even had a bank account.

Sebastian didn't have much. But he *was* intriguing...

Still, I'd gone after Ladinas when he still had feelings for Alice. So long as Sebastian believed his wife was out there and alive, trying to pursue the man was foolish. Vampire-human complications aside. I wasn't about to put myself through that shit again.

If I fell for anyone else, ever again, he'd have to bend over backwards to prove that his world revolved around me. I would not be the backup, the second-choice, the girl anyone settled for. I deserved better than that.

But I'd be damned if I didn't feel the pull towards him—as if he had his own kind of magic. I sighed, pushing myself up from the cold ground. We had more important things to deal with right now than my love life. Or lack thereof.

I cleared my throat, drawing the attention of the three men hovering over me.

"None of that shit is important," I said firmly. "I have a plan, and I need you all to play along. Just trust me, alright? I can't let anyone know for sure what's going on."

Ladinas narrowed his eyes, clearly annoyed by my cryptic statement. "And why is that, Mercy? Why can't you share this so-called plan with us?"

Before I could respond, Sebastian rose to his feet, having finished securing his sharpened silver blade back to his gauntlet.

"Isn't it obvious?" he said. "We know Oblivion divided himself and possessed multiple vampires. He could be inside any of you right now. Mercy can't risk revealing the full plan because it might get back to Oblivion."

Sebastian met my gaze, smiled a little, and nodded. "We'll support you no matter what happens. Right, everyone?"

Ladinas scowled, but gave a curt nod. Ramon murmured his agreement as well.

Donnie snapped to attention and gave Sebastian a salute. "Aye aye, captain!"

I couldn't help but chuckle at his antics. "So you're a pirate now?"

"Psh, no way," Donnie scoffed, dropping the salute. "Pirates are lame. Ninjas are where it's at! They have real ultimate power!"

"Whatever you say," I said with an amused shake of my head. "Muggs, teleport us back to Adam. We're going to confront Oblivion head-on. Just get me close enough to Adam so I can let him know what I need him to do."

Muggs rubbed his hands together eagerly, his blank eyes wide and glinting. Then he spun his staff overhead. "All aboard the Muggs express! Hold on tight!"

A swirling green vortex materialized in the air before us. Sebastian, Donnie, Ramon, Clarissa and I hopped inside. We tumbled out the other end directly into utter chaos.

Youngling vampires were everywhere, taunting and harassing the Redcaps surrounding Adam. I shoved my way through, making a beeline for the teenaged-looking boy. When I reached him, I grabbed his arm and pulled him close so I could whisper urgently in his ear.

"When the dragons unite, I need you to pop the dimensions apart and trap them in a pocket dimension—like a faerie prison. Can you do that?"

Adam met my gaze and gave a single nod. I knew I could count on him. Now we just had to get Oblivion to take the bait.

I broke away from Adam and strode back out into the open, my friends forming a protective barrier around me.

"Oblivion!" I shouted, my voice ringing out clearly. "Show yourself, you wily bastard!"

A dark shadow swooped down from the sky, massive wings spread wide. Oblivion landed with an earth-shaking crash, his clawed feet gouging furrows in the earth. He folded his leathery wings and glared at me with glowing red eyes.

"Have you reconsidered, my love?" he purred.

"No," I said flatly. "But I've brought you something."

I took a deep breath and yelled with all my might. "Caladbolg!"

A massive shape took form in front of me. Scales glinted, claws flexed, wings unfurled—it was Caladbolg in his true draconic form. But only I knew it was only a *part* of him. The rest of him still lingered inside of me.

Oblivion rolled his eyes contemptuously. "Mercy, Mercy, Mercy. You've got me! You're going to trap us. You finally outsmarted me." His tone dripped with sarcasm.

But I could see the gleam of greed in his expression. He was taking the bait. He couldn't resist sending a big part of himself to a prison dimension if it meant taking *all* of Caladbolg with him. That would leave us with no means to beat him on earth at all. Of course he'd jump at the chance.

Oblivion willingly allowed himself to merge with Caladbolg, thinking he could overpower and imprison his brother while leaving part of himself back on earth unchallenged.

It was time to spring the trap. I caught Adam's eye and shouted, "Now!"

Oblivion's head snapped around, his eyes going wide with shock. He was just starting to realize this wasn't all of Caladbolg after all.

As Adam worked his magic and space began to warp and bend around us, I flashed Oblivion my middle finger.

"That's right, you son of a bitch," I snarled. "You divided yourself up too many damn times. But your brother only split himself twice. Just enough to kick your ass in prison... where he'll be your new daddy."

Oblivion let out an enraged roar as the pocket dimension closed around him. "You'll never control me!" he shouted. "I'll be back! My essence will spread!"

I barked out a harsh laugh. "Yeah, yeah. Hope is always a good thing to hold on to in prison, tough guy. But don't worry—we've got a plan for that, too."

With a deafening crack, the portal snapped shut. The younglings and Oblivion were gone. The younglings back in Providence with Ladinas, Alice, and the rest of the team, where they were before Adam brought them to Maine.

It was finally over—sort of. I allowed myself a small smile of satisfaction before turning to my companions. We still had work to do.

I grabbed Sebastian, Donnie, Ramon, Clarissa, and Muggs. "We've got one last thing to take care of," I said grimly.

Sebastian raised an eyebrow. "And what might that be?"

In response, I held out my hands and shouted, "Caladbolg!" A slender rapier-like blade materialized there in a flash of light. I hefted it, feeling its comfortable weight.

Sebastian laughed. "You still have him!"

"For now," I smirked. "The rest of Oblivion is still inside the wolves. Divided up among all the packs. If I stab the alpha of alphas with this baby, Caladbolg's power will keep that bastard under control for good."

Sebastian let out an impressed whistle. "Damn. Using the wolves' structure of dominance against the dragon bastard. That's one hell of a plan."

I flashed him a wicked grin. "What can I say? I didn't get it from hell. I got it from Heaven."

Chapter 21

THE CHEVELLE'S ENGINE ROARED as we sped through the forest, the trees whipping past in a dark blur. I gripped the leather seat, tense. We were headed straight back into the wolves' territory—and who knew what we'd face this time?

Goliath bounded behind us, chasing Sebastian's car the whole way. A lot of dogs chase cars—but only a hellhound can actually keep up.

I turned to Sebastian. "Remember, we're not here to kill them. Just find the alpha."

He kept his eyes fixed ahead, his knuckles white on the steering wheel. "Got it."

"It has to be the one who dominates all the other alphas," I added. "The big boss."

Donnie piped up from the backseat. "So we're basically looking for a wolf like me."

Sebastian burst out laughing, nearly choking on his tongue. I couldn't help cracking up too. "Right, the alpha of alphas...in what digital world?"

Donnie glared at me, dead serious. "In all of them."

I shook my head, stifling a smirk.

The Chevelle skidded to a stop at the forest's edge. We piled out, the night air thick with tension. I took the lead this time, gesturing for the guys to follow.

"No one dies tonight," I said firmly. "Try not to kill any wolves we don't have to. We just need to rile these wolves up until we get to the big boss."

With that, I plunged into the trees, senses primed. Howls split the surrounding darkness. The hunt was on.

I whipped out my wand, letting instinct take over. "*Enerva!*"

A jet of red light burst from the tip, striking the nearest wolf. It collapsed, fast asleep. I pivoted, firing off more stunning spells in quick succession. Wolves dropped left and right, slumbering peacefully amidst the underbrush.

Muggs joined in, calling upon the trees themselves to harass our foes. Ancient oaks and pines creaked to life, snaring wolves in their gnarled branches or tripping them with roots that burst from the ground.

Goliath did his part, too. He wasn't a werewolf, but as a canine of a sort, he sensed the way we needed to go. As if the alpha released some kind of pheromone he picked up on.

We pressed deeper into the forest, following Goliath's lead, leaving a trail of snoozing canines behind us. The sounds of battle faded as we neared the heart of their territory. An unnatural hush fell over the woods.

Then we saw him. A massive wolf, easily twice the size of the others, stood waiting in a moonlit clearing. Smaller wolves flanked him on all sides, hackles raised in defense of their leader. His fur was jet-black, eyes burning crimson in the shadows. Power and menace rolled off him in waves.

Adrenaline surged as I stepped into the clearing, twirling Caladbolg in my hand. The blade glinted in the moonlight, hungry for battle. As a rapier, he was easier to wield. Much more my style.

"Cover me," I said, never taking my eyes off the alpha. His lips curled back, revealing dagger-like teeth. My friends fanned out behind me, wands and weapons at the ready.

With a feral grin, I charged, my boots pounding the earth. The alpha bounded forward to meet my advance, jaws snapping. I leapt, Caladbolg flashing as I swung with supernatural speed. The blade sliced across the wolf's shoulder in a blaze of golden light.

That was all it took. One strike.

He howled in pain and fury, but the cry changed into one of shock as the magic took hold. Caladbolg's energy surged into the alpha, setting his fur aglow. Black fur turned to shimmering gold as the dragon's power possessed him. His eyes burned like twin suns.

I landed in a crouch, my eyes meeting his. I knew those kind eyes. They were the same ones that looked at me kindly in that heavenly nightclub. "Thank you," I said to the wolf, knowing Caladbolg stared back at me. The alpha threw back his head and let loose a bone-chilling howl.

All around the clearing, wolves emerged from the shadows, answering their leader's call. The packs united as one. Caladbolg had claimed dominance over them all.

I rose, my wand in my opposite hand, and the hand that held Caladbolg before empty. "It's done. Let's get going before more wolves show." We slipped away under the cover of night, leaving the wolves to puzzle over their new alpha. Caladbolg and I had won the day, but greater battles lay ahead. The burden of destiny is mine to bear, for good or ill. Such is the life of an ancient vampire witch.

We sped through the dark forest in Sebastian's red Chevelle, the rumble of the engine nearly putting me to sleep—and as a vampire, I didn't strictly *need* to sleep at all. But after all we'd been through, the idea of catching a few Zs sounded nice.

Lost in thought, I barely registered Donnie's sudden exclamation from the backseat. "Shit, I didn't check in with Mom at midnight!"

Sebastian met my eyes, his expression mirroring my false concern. Sebastian turned back. "So, Donnie. What do you say you hit the road with me for a bit? I hear there's some crazy shit going down in Denver right now. What do you say?"

Donnie took a deep breath. "I think that would be... awesome!"

I laughed. "No gaming on the road trip, you know."

Donnie shrugged. "Maybe it's time I put my talents to better use. Thank you, Sebastian. You won't regret it. I'll be like Batman to your Robin."

Sebastian laughed. "Right. Something like that."

We pulled up to Donnie's house, and he hurried inside, moving with the closest thing to preternatural speed a chubby guy could muster. Martha was sitting there in the kitchen, curlers in her hair, a lime-green mask spread on her face. The look she was giving Donnie said everything.

"I'm thirty, Mom," Donnie said. "And I just helped save the world. So drop it. I'm not your little boy anymore."

Sebastian and I exchanged surprised looks. Donnie was growing up in front of our eyes! Sure, it took him thirty years to exert his independence, but at least he was getting there.

That didn't assuage Martha's wrath. She was harping at him as he made his way down to the basement to change his clothes.

All I could do was laugh. Fight off some nasty werewolves, no problem. Face your angry and overbearing mother? Well, Donnie had a long way to go. I could only imagine how she'd respond when Donnie told her he was going on a "hunting trip" with Sebastian.

I found myself standing alone with Sebastian on the stairs of Donnie's porch. "Thanks for everything, Sebastian."

He studied me with those intense, dark eyes. "You could stay. Wait out the sun here."

I stepped forward and kissed his cheek. "My team needs me. I've got a lot to make up for." I squeezed his hand. "You really are my hero, Sebastian."

Sebastian's blush deepened at my words. Though he towered over me, his bashfulness made him seem almost boyish.

"Until we meet again," he said gruffly. Clearing his throat, he pulled me into a quick, fierce hug. His breath stirred my hair as he murmured, "Take care of yourself, Mercy. Stay good."

I returned the hug just as tightly, breathing in his scent of leather and steel. We'd only known each other a short time, yet I sensed our paths were meant to cross.

"Keep fighting the good fight," I told him as we parted. "And I hope you find Angie."

He nodded, his eyes bright with emotion. Then, with a last lingering look, he turned and went inside to join Donnie.

I watched him go, knowing I'd likely never see him again. But our brief time together had changed me. Strengthened me.

I reached down and scratched Goliath behind the ears. He leaned into it. I looked at Ramon, Clarissa and Adam. "You guys coming back to the Underground with me?"

"I can get us home," Adam said. "Besides, I need to gather up the Redcaps. Can't leave them running around Maine causing problems."

"And I don't really feel like the Underground is right for us," Ramon said.

"But I'd really like to spend some time..." Clarissa shifted a little between her feet. "You know, maybe you could teach me a few things."

I smiled at the young, oddly constituted family. "I'd love to. I'll be in touch, alright?"

"Sounds good!" Clarissa exclaimed.

With Goliath at my side, I turned to my other progeny, my 'middle child.' Then again, I had a lot of children now. Those younglings were still a problem—and now they really were my responsibility. But the sunrise was rapidly approaching. They'd pose another problem for another day. "Alright, Muggs. Let's go home."

The End of Book 5
Want more SEBASTIAN WINTER?

New Series Coming Soon!

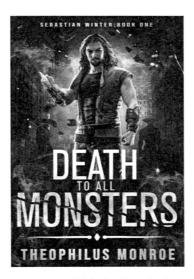

Now Available for Pre-Order
https://store.theophilusmonroe.com

THE FURY OF A VAMPIRE WITCH
BOOK 6

BLOODY
MERRY

THEOPHILUS MONROE

Chapter 1

THE SMELL OF SWEAT, alcohol, and blood permeated the air as my team and I entered the backroom of a seedy club in Providence. The darkness was oppressive, but our vampire senses easily cut through the gloom. Prince Ladinas, Muggs, Antoine, Alice, and Mel followed closely behind me, ready for anything.

"Showtime," I declared, preparing myself for the confrontation ahead. We'd tracked a gang of youngling vampires here, and it was time to put an end to their reckless killing spree.

The city was swarming with baby vamps. Ever since I was possessed by Oblivion—an ancient gatekeeper dragon born of the void who desired one thing: chaos. And that's what he got. Everyone I'd killed while under his influence *turned*. Oblivion put a part of himself in each of them, or strategically in a few, and those I killed and turned kept the tradition going. The more people my "oops baby" vamps bit, the more there were. At first we'd thought there were only a couple dozen younglings left from my days under the dragon's thrall. Come to find out, there were a couple hundred, at least.

The younglings huddled together like cornered rats, their eyes wide with fear and defiance. I stepped forward, trying to exude an air of authority that would hopefully make them more amenable to reason. They didn't know who I was, that I was the favored progeny of the *original* vampire. They didn't know that for most of our kind, I was a kind of royalty. They awoke into our world without a roadmap, without a guide to show them the way. That's why I was there. But first, I had to command their respect.

"Listen up," I said, my voice echoing through the cramped space. "I know you're scared. You've been running wild, killing too many people, and now we're here to help. We don't have to be enemies."

I focused on the sire bond I shared with some of them, attempting to exert my influence over them, but even those I'd killed weren't easily managed. Something about Oblivion possessing *them* even as he possessed me diminished the efficacy of the bond. "Come with us. We can help you gain control over your cravings, teach you how to survive without causing so much destruction. It's not your fault you've hurt people. It was your nature. But if you don't get it under control, there are hunters who will come for you, and vampires who aren't as patient as I am who will eliminate you to protect our secret. But it doesn't have to come to that. We can help. We can be the masters of our nature rather than its slaves."

A young female vampire with short blond and pink hair, piercings decorating her face like tiny stars, sneered at me and stepped forward. She was clearly their leader, or at least had appointed herself as such.

"Fuck, where are my manners?" she said sarcastically, making a show of curtsying. "I'm Jinx, by the way. And what's your name, my liege?"

"Mercy Brown," I replied, gritting my teeth against the mockery in her voice.

"Ah, yes. Mercy Brown," she drawled, rolling her eyes. "Well, your highness, I've got news for you." Her eyes narrowed, and with a wicked grin, she spat in my face. "Fuck off."

I saw red. For a moment, the rage threatened to overwhelm me. How dare this insolent child mock me so openly? I was ready to tear her apart, to show her what true power looked like.

But then I felt Muggs' steadying hand on my shoulder. "Don't," he murmured. "She's one of Oblivion's victims. This isn't her fault."

I took a deep breath, willing my fury to subside. He was right, of course. I couldn't blame them for what Oblivion did to them.

Ladinas stepped forward, regarding the younglings coldly. "The choice before you is simple. Come with us, and we'll help you adapt to your new existence. Or stay and face the consequences."

Jinx laughed harshly. "Is that a threat? Who are you, anyway? Mercy's lapdog?"

I clenched my fists. "I have a dog. His name is Goliath, adopted straight out of hell. Vampires are his kibble. I could always introduce you to him if you'd like... but that's Prince Ladinas."

"A prince? What the fuck?" Jinx rolled her eyes. "We're not interested in your little offer. What's the point of being so powerful if we have to bend our knees to pretend royalty?"

The other younglings hissed and shouted in agreement and amusement. Ladinas' eyes narrowed, but he didn't rise to the bait. "I'm not asking you to become subjects. Only to follow our guidance, our lead, until you learn how to resist your urges."

"Urges? We aren't *slaves* to our urges. This is freedom. This is power!" Jinx declared. "Let's just get this over with."

Jinx dove at me with more speed than I'd expected, given her age. She went straight for my throat, but I dodged just in time, grabbing her from behind and slamming her to the ground.

"Big mistake, little bitch."

But she blasted back to her feet, defying my strength with a force she shouldn't have had. Why the hell was she so strong? Usually vampires got stronger and faster with age. Sort of the opposite of how human aging worked. But this little girl was moving like a five-hundred-year-old vamp with tactical training to boot.

Maybe she wasn't one of the *younglings* after all. But who the hell was she? Any vampire old enough to be that strong would be someone Ladinas or I would know. But we'd never seen her before.

She came back at me with a rage in her eyes that sent chills down my spine.

I engaged Jinx head-on, my fists a blur of motion as I aimed for her jaw, ribs, anywhere that would slow her down. She ducked and weaved with impressive agility, her piercing-riddled face twisted into a sinister grin.

"You think you're tough, don't you?" she taunted, effortlessly dodging my punches.

I snarled and lunged at her, tackling her to the ground. We wrestled and rolled on the grimy floor, neither of us gaining the upper hand.

Meanwhile, the rest of the younglings sprang into action, going after my team like rabid raccoons.

Ladinas swiftly fired a volley of bolts from his crossbow, felling two vampires immediately. Guns cracked as Antoine and Mel began picking off targets with ruthless efficiency. Muggs wove his natural magics from the glowing green tip of his staff, roots from trees surrounding the building bursting from the concrete to entangle some of the younglings.

Restrained by Mugg's roots, Antoine and Mel fired wooden bullets into their chests.

But I barely noticed. This punk rock wannabe bloodsucker was all I could handle. For a moment, somehow, Jinx got the upper hand, nearly pinning me to the ground before I delivered a knee to her gut, then kicked her off of me. Scrambling to my feet, I raised my wand, casting an enervation down toward the bitch, but she rolled away so damn fast I missed.

Alice blurred around me with lethal grace, her katanas flashing as she relieved one youngling after another of their heads. I could have asked for help, but come on. I should have been able to handle this little girl, no problem. If I couldn't handle Jinx alone... well... let's just say that would seriously compromise my reputation.

Within minutes, half their number were dead or staked. At least the others weren't as big a challenge as Jinx. Just as I thought I'd had the upper hand, she slipped around me, pushed me against the wall, and darted toward the exit.

"Enough of this shit!" Jinx yelled. "Let's get the fuck out of here!"

I blasted across the room with all my speed. I couldn't let Jinx get away, but the goddamn minx slipped out of my grip. The rest of the vampires turned and fled with her into the night. I started after them, but Mel grabbed my arm.

"We should let them go," she breathed. "We've done enough damage here tonight. If you want to save any of them, this isn't the way. We can't beat them into obedience."

I clenched my fists. Mel was right. If we went after them, this was only going to end one way. I didn't want these vampires dead and gone. I owed them a chance, a shot, to do immortality right.

I surveyed the carnage, anger and frustration churning in my gut. Half a dozen young vampires lay staked on the floor, their undead lives suspended. A few more had lost their heads at the swift edge of Alice's blades.

"We need to take the staked back to the Underground," I said, nodding at the staked vampires. "We can revive them. Once they've cooled off, maybe we can help them get control of their bloodlust."

Ladinas let out a derisive snort. "Don't be foolish, Mercy. They've given themselves over to their baser natures. The beast has consumed them." His eyes were cold, remorseless. "It would be a mercy to end them now."

I bristled, glaring at him. "Who the hell are you to decide their fates? We have a responsibility to at least try to save them!"

Ladinas met my gaze evenly. "I've seen this too many times. They are too far gone, warped by the blood and their descent into hell. There is no coming back from that."

"Bullshit," I spat. "I came back from it, didn't I? After what Oblivion did to me? If I can claw my way out of that pit, then so can they."

I knelt down next to a young vampire, brushing pink and blue hair away from her pale face. She looked so small and fragile with that stake buried in her chest. She wasn't one of my victims. But one of the vampires I'd killed had killed this girl in turn.

Yeah, we beat Oblivion. But the mess he left in his wake mirrored the void-dragon's essence. Pure chaos.

"We have to try," I said softly. I would not give up on them. I couldn't. They deserved that much.

Alice cleared her throat. "Come on, Mercy. Let's not pretend there wasn't some part of you that *enjoyed* what Oblivion made you do. It's our nature. You've had a century and a half to learn better, to fight your cravings. These younglings, under his influence, without a sire to guide them? What did you expect they'd become?"

I rounded on her, anger flaring hotly in my chest. "Fuck you, Alice. You have no idea what it was like, what he put me through." I bared my fangs, hands clenching into fists. "Yeah, no shit, I'm a vampire. We all have that hunger within us. But I didn't choose what happened, what he forced me to do."

Alice held up her hands in mock surrender, though her eyes still glinted with provocation. I could cheerfully strangle her sometimes.

"It's not your fault," Ladinas said. "Oblivion corrupted them. But you want to save them because you feel guilty for what he made you do. I get it, but these vamps are a lost cause."

Taking a deep, unnecessary breath, I reined in my anger. "This has nothing to do with guilt," I said evenly. "I refuse to abandon them to death or madness. If there's any chance we can pull them back from the brink, we have to take it."

I stared Ladinas down, daring him to contradict me again. He met my gaze steadily, though I thought I detected a flicker of doubt in his eyes.

"Even if we could save them, how many more might die at their hands in the meantime?" he asked quietly. "I've seen this too many times. Situations like this demand swift action. If we offer them patience, we won't just pay for it, dozens of innocent people will as well."

I opened my mouth to argue, but Antoine stepped forward, raising a placating hand.

"Perhaps a compromise?" he suggested. "If we take these for interrogation, they may provide information about other youngling gangs. We could prevent further attacks."

I considered this, then nodded. It wasn't ideal, but better than executing them all. It gave me a chance, at least, to reach them and prove that they weren't beyond redemption.

Ladinas sighed. "Very well. We'll keep two alive for now." He turned to Antoine. "Burn the hearts of the others."

"No!" I moved to block Antoine's path, fangs bared. "I won't let you slaughter them."

Ladinas grabbed my arm. "Stand down, Mercy. I made my decision."

With a snarl, I shook him off. We stood toe-to-toe, tension crackling. "Who died and made you king?"

Ladinas shook his head. "You have to regain the trust of the team, Mercy. After what happened... surely it's best I call the shots for now."

"You *just* told me it wasn't my fault. It was Oblivion's influence. Bottom line, you don't trust me."

"Use your head, Mercy. You've been a vampire long enough to know what I'm saying is true. Leaving these younglings alive is too risky. We have to eliminate them."

I was seriously considering punching that arrogant scowl off his face when Mel jumped between us.

"Please! This solves nothing." She looked pleadingly from me to Ladinas. "Mercy, let's just go and cool down. No one's burned out any hearts yet and they can stay staked while you two sort out your shit."

I hesitated, then stepped back with a frustrated growl. As much as I wanted to tear into Ladinas, getting into a brawl wouldn't help matters.

"Fine," I bit out. "Do what you want. I'm going for a walk."

Before Ladinas could object, I spun on my heel and stalked out alone into the night. I needed to cool off before I did something I'd regret.

I strode down the empty street, fuming. How dare Ladinas undermine me like that? Questioning my judgement, countermanding my orders... the nerve! Just because I'd killed a few dozen folks under a *dragon's* influence didn't mean I'd lost control. Oblivion was gone and I was back. I was the bloody queen! I was still the rightful leader of this team.

My temper simmered as I stalked along, hands clenched. I should just head back there and put Ladinas in his place. Remind him who was really in charge. He was older than me, but being a direct descendant of Niccolo the Damned, I was just as strong. With my magic, I could take him in a fight. No question.

I was halfway down the block when footsteps approached behind me. I whirled, a snarl on my lips, then relaxed as I recognized Mel and Muggs.

"Mercy, wait up," Mel called, jogging to catch me. "We just want to talk."

I crossed my arms. "I told you, I need some space."

"We know," Muggs said gently, his blind eyes staring right through me like x-rays, as if he could see everything going on beneath the surface. "But you shouldn't be alone right now. Not when you're upset."

I scowled, even as I knew they were right. I was balanced on a knife's edge. One wrong move and I could spiral out of control. And this time, I wouldn't have a dragon to blame.

"Fine," I sighed. "You can tag along for now. But no lectures, got it?"

They exchanged relieved looks. "Got it," Mel smiled. "Let's just take a quiet walk. Clear our heads."

I nodded, gesturing for them to follow. I didn't know where I was heading. But the idea of going back to the Underground with Ladinas and Alice was suffocating. Ladinas said he wouldn't kill the vampires *yet*. There was no rush. So long as they were staked, or had wooden bullets lodged in their hearts, they were as good as dead. They weren't a threat. Somehow I needed to prove that these younglings weren't beyond saving, that they had a chance. But deep down I knew Ladinas had a point. Once a youngling heads down a bloodthirsty path very few ever come back from it. That didn't mean it was impossible, or that I shouldn't try. Maybe it *was* my guilt at work, a futile attempt to make up for what I screwed up. Introspection has never been my strong suit. But I had to believe that redemption was possible—that it was *never* out of reach.

Sebastian believed in me when I didn't believe in myself. A hunter, of all people, had intervened and pulled me from the precipice. Now it was my turn to save these vampires—even that bitch, Jinx. Even if they didn't want to be saved.

Chapter 2

THE GARISH CHRISTMAS LIGHTS assaulted my eyes as we strolled down the cobblestone streets of Federal Hill. Carolers crooned off-key renditions of Jingle Bells, their voices grating against my eardrums. I longed to rip their hymnals from their grubby mittened hands and chuck them into the icy waters of the Providence River. This holiday pageantry was nothing but a façade, a glittery mask that people wore to cover up their dissatisfaction with the other three-hundred-and-sixty-four days of the year.

Mel, of course, was enraptured. She oohed and aahed over each tacky lawn ornament and blow-up reindeer we passed, her youthful enthusiasm a foil to my jadedness. I fought the urge to roll my eyes.

Then she let out an excited gasp, grabbing my arm with such force that had I been human, she might have snapped my limb clean off. I followed her gaze to a line of snot-nosed children and harried parents queued up outside a shop. At the front, seated atop a gold velvet throne, was the main attraction—Santa Claus himself.

"Mercy, Mercy! Can we go see Santa? Please?" Mel begged, practically bouncing up and down with anticipation.

I fixed Mel with an icy stare. "You do realize that's not actually Santa, right? That's just some sad sack who couldn't hold a year-round job, so he's reduced to letting brats drool on his lap for minimum wage once a year."

Mel's face fell. "But I always tell Santa what I want for Christmas! It's a tradition!"

I scoffed. "You're a grown ass woman, not to mention a vampire. He's not going to give you shit for Christmas, except maybe a boner when you plop your ass down on his lap. Don't be a ho-ho-ho..."

Muggs, who'd been silent until now, chimed in. "Oh, let the girl have some fun, Mercy. You're such a Scrooge."

Before I could retort, he scampered off, his heightened sense of hearing guiding him unerringly toward the Santa line. With a pleading glance at me, Mel hurried after him.

I rolled my eyes again, but followed them over to indulge Mel's childish fantasy. As I watched the progression, my lips curled in a smirk. Muggs plopped himself down on Santa's lap, and I could see the old man's eyes bulge in dismay at having an elderly blind geezer perched on his thighs.

With my vampire hearing, I picked up on their conversation.

"Ho ho ho!" Santa exclaimed with obviously forced jolliness. "And what do you want for Christmas, um... little boy?"

Muggs leaned in close, his cloudy eyes peering sightlessly as he whispered his request. "I'd like a nice young lad, preferably with B positive blood, hold the hepatitis and the AIDS."

Santa recoiled, his bushy white eyebrows shooting up in shock. I had to stifle a laugh. This was even better than I'd hoped.

Before the traumatized Santa could eject Muggs from his lap, Mel bounced up with a wide grin on her youthful face. "My turn!" she sang out.

Santa's demeanor changed instantly when Mel settled onto his thighs. His eyes roved over her appreciatively and he gave her a squeeze, chuckling with far more authenticity. "Well, hello there, little girl! Have you been *naughty* or nice this year?"

Fucking creep. I rolled my eyes.

Oblivious to his leering tone, Mel launched into her wish list. "For Christmas I want a new PlayStation 5, some designer shoes, because a girl can never have too many shoes... Oh! And a pet penguin!"

I shook my head, smirking. Looked like Santa was getting a bit more Yuletide cheer than he'd bargained for. As I watched the pathetic scene unfold, a flashing sign across the street suddenly caught my eye.

I turned and noticed a small storefront that I could have sworn wasn't lit up before. It was as if it had just opened up for business. Strange considering it was nine o'clock and most of the shops on this street were closing down.

The sign over the door blinked erratically, spelling out "The Peddler" in glowing red and gold lights. I frowned. Despite the holiday decorations covering the exterior, this place gave me an uneasy vibe that I couldn't quite place.

Curiosity won out over caution, and I decided to investigate while Mel and Muggs were distracted. I crossed the street, my boots crunching on the salt-strewn sidewalk as I approached the peculiar shop.

A bell jingled overhead as I stepped inside, greeted by the cloying scents of cloves and aged paper. The lighting was dim; the shop illuminated only by a few weak bulbs and candles flickering on the shelves. As my eyes adjusted, I could make out the shop's wares—a cluttered and quaint collection of antiques, trinkets, and other arcane objects.

Many of them looked to be Christmas-themed, reminiscent of decor from decades past. Tarnished bells, faded tinsel garlands, and retro glass ornaments that would have been in style back when I was still human. Before I could study anything further, a gravelly voice spoke up from the shadows.

"Welcome, Mercy. I've been expecting you."

I whirled around to find the source of the voice, my muscles tensing instinctively. Behind the counter stood an old man watching me with keen interest. He had bushy gray eyebrows, a hooked nose, and a hunched back. His nametag simply read "The Peddler."

"Who are you?" I demanded. "How do you know my name?"

The Peddler smiled, the corners of his mouth nearly reaching his eyes. "Well, it's what I do. Call it my *business*. I know many things—especially concerning those touched by the craft."

I narrowed my eyes. Either this guy was psychic, or he wasn't entirely human himself. "What's that supposed to mean?"

"It means I have something that might help you, Mercy Brown." The Peddler reached below the counter and produced an ornate oil lamp etched with strange symbols. "A token to mend bridges. That's what you desire the most, is it not, to fix what's been broken?"

I snorted. "I suppose."

The Peddler held the lamp out more closely for me to examine. It was beautiful, no doubt, but not the kind of thing that appealed to my minimalism. It was more Ladinas' style. "Well, I suppose I know someone who might appreciate it."

"Indeed. It's a priceless artifact, but for one who has lost her way, consider it a gift. On the house."

I scoffed, crossing my arms. "Yeah, no thanks. I've learned a few things through the years. Nothing's ever free, and don't accept gifts from strange men."

But the Peddler insisted, wrapping the lamp in tissue, shoving the lamp into a gift bag and handing it to me. "Please, I wish for you to have it. No strings attached. Consider it a Christmas gift."

"I don't know what the hell to do with it!" I protested. "I mean, I appreciate the generosity, but—"

"Keep it. Or don't. Give it away. The choice is yours, and the answers you seek will soon become clear."

"I'm not looking for any fucking answers. What the hell, man?"

Before I could object further, he ushered me out the door with surprising strength for such a frail-looking man. I found myself back on the sidewalk, confused as hell and holding the mysterious gift. What was that place? Where had it even come from?

I turned around again, certain the shop had been right behind me. But there was nothing there now except a vacant storefront. Unease crept down my spine. I'd been a witch long enough, faced enough nastiness of the supernatural sort, that when things like this happened, I knew it was just a matter of time before shit went south. Strange men don't appear out of nowhere and insist you take gifts. Not without an ulterior—usually pervy—motive.

Shaking my head, I tightened my grip on the bag and went to find Mel and Muggs. I had an internal debate with myself about whether I should tell them about the Peddler and his strange disappearing shop. They didn't follow me out onto the streets after my disagreement with Ladinas because they *trusted* me. They were worried about me, the same as him.

To think. My two progenies were chaperoning *me?* The idea would have been laughable if it wasn't the damn truth.

People in puffy coats, stocking hats, and ugly sweaters stomped around me like a herd of buffalo.

"Muggs," I muttered under my breath, appealing to the vampire-druid's doubly enhanced hearing. "Where the fuck are you two?"

If he heard me, there was no way to know. Not like he'd teleport himself to me in the middle of a crowd. Maybe they'd find their way to me. Whatever. It was just as likely they'd find me if I sat on my ass and waited.

I had to be extra careful being out and about. When Oblivion was with me, influencing my every move, I'd become something of an outlaw. We'd even made quite a show at the local precinct. I still couldn't believe I'd told the cops that I *owned* the city now. No one in their right mind really *wants* that kind of responsibility.

Sure, pretty much every bad guy *ever* has said at some point or another that he wanted to rule the world. I'd said as much under Oblivion's thrall. But can you imagine all the crap you'd have to deal with ruling a freaking planet?

Ruling the world is one of those things that sounds appealing until you actually try it. Like shower sex. Once you give it a go, it's only a matter of time before you lose your footing and slip and slide like a dumbass until you realize things were a lot easier before.

So far, though, no one recognized me. Except for the Peddler. Maybe that's how he knew so much about me. He wasn't a cop or anything, but that didn't mean he hadn't seen my mug on the news, or whatever. That didn't explain his disappearing act, though.

I found a vacant park bench on the sidewalk, just in front of a candles and oils store that had already closed up shop for the night. I reached into the gift bag and pulled out the lamp.

It was a beautiful piece of work, with ornate and intricate designs etched into the porcelain. The writing on the surface was unusual, similar to Arabic, but different, simpler, more archaic, perhaps. Not that I could read Arabic, anyway, but I knew it when I saw it. There was a subtle thrum within it as well, almost as if the lamp had its own energy source—which made me anxious. It felt like magic, and messing with mysterious magical artifacts rarely came without unforeseen consequences.

Intricate floral designs that must have taken the lamp's maker hours to complete decorated its porcelain base. Its metal handle was small and curved to make an elegant "S" shape.

"A token to mend bridges, to fix what's broken," I muttered to myself, recalling the Peddler's words. "What the hell does that even mean?"

I stared at the lamp for what must've been several minutes, trying to sort out the mystery and get a feel for the kind of magic the thing contained. It was alluring, like it was calling to me, begging me to take it and study what secrets lay inside. But before I could lose myself in the mystery of the lamp any further, I heard a familiar voice interrupt my reverie.

"Hey Mercy! Over here!" I looked up and saw Mel and Muggs standing several yards away, waving energetically at me. They'd dressed themselves up in festive holiday costumes, with Mel wearing a penguin onesie and Muggs sporting an elf costume.

I quickly wrapped the lamp back in tissue and put it back into the bag as I rose to approach my two overly spirited progenies.

"Whatcha got there?" Mel asked.

"Nothing really." I lied. Not sure why. "Just something that caught my eye."

Muggs fiddled with the plastic extensions he'd slipped over either ear. "How do you like them? Do they look real?"

"Sure." I shrugged. "I'm clearly not imagining them. They're real *false* ears."

Mel nudged me. "Stop! You know what he meant. I think they look real enough."

I rolled my eyes and smiled. "Yeah, they look great. You both look great." It was strange to see them dressed up like that, but it was nice, too. How long had it been since we had just hung out without some kind of world-threatening baddie to deal with? It was almost like I'd forgotten *how* to enjoy myself.

"So, where to now?" I asked, trying to steer the conversation away from the gift bag in my hand.

"I was thinking we could go ice skating," Mel suggested.

"Ice skating? Really?"

"C'mon, Mercy!" Mel grabbed my arm. "It's Christmas Eve. Live a little!"

I snorted. "Live? You know who you're talking to, right? Been there, done that, a hundred and thirty-one years ago. Besides, I don't know if putting a blind man on ice is a great idea."

Muggs shrugged. "I'll be fine. I'll just stay on that bench you were sitting on and enjoy the carolers. You two have some fun!"

"Fun," I muttered as Mel took my hand and dragged me through the crowd. "Yeah, right."

Chapter 3

THE FROSTY AIR NIPPED at my cheeks as Mel and I glided across the ice. I scanned the crowded rink, taking in the glowing Christmas lights and cheerful skaters, oblivious to the fact that they were *skating with vampires.*

Muggs sat hunched on a nearby bench, ever the watchdog. The gift bag with the peddler's lamp lay beside him. If anyone could detect magic, it was Muggs. But if he didn't touch it, maybe he'd remain oblivious to what was within. I'd tell him about it later, most likely. Or would I? It felt like the whole damn encounter with the Peddler was some kind of secret I was meant to keep. But I wasn't sure if it was a "keep this a secret, for your own good," kind of secret or a, "don't tell your mommy and daddy, this'll be *our* little secret" kind of secret. The Peddler seemed genuine enough, but most monsters do at first. They rarely show their true colors at first encounter. That's how they lure you in. I'd learned that lesson well enough with Oblivion.

Lost in thought, I nearly collided with a bundled-up little girl wobbling nearby.

"Eyes ahead!" Mel teased as my legs nearly split beneath me in my attempt to avoid the girl. "I'd think it had been a lifetime since you skated last."

My tightened chest relaxed. "It's been at least that long. Not the sort of activity that attracts a lot of vampires."

Mel laughed, flashing her pearly whites. "Vampires on Ice! You know, like Disney on Ice, but with fangs. I could totally be the next Disney princess, you know."

I raised an eyebrow. "A vampire as a Disney Princess? Are you serious?"

Mel nodded matter-of-factly. "You're a queen! And since I'm your progeny, that means I'm a princess already. Think Disney would go for it? Every brooding vampire tween needs a role model with bite."

I laughed and shrugged. "You never know. Representation matters. Maybe you'll inspire the next generation of bloodsuckers to aim higher."

"I know, right? I mean, they already did *Zombies*. Across two sequels, they added werewolves and even aliens to the musical series. Why *not* vampires?"

We shared a grin, coasting on, even though I didn't know what the hell Mel was talking about. Did Disney seriously do a zombie-themed musical? I shuddered thinking about it. What ever happened to the good old days when vampires and zombies were monsters... and Disney characters were *genuinely* terrifying?

What? You don't know what I'm talking about? Let me explain.

Disney might not be a mill for horror flicks. But there are undercurrents in their films that will scare the shit out of you if you're paying attention.

Take Pinocchio, for example.

If you're a vampire and find yourself standing in front of Pinocchio, you'd better hope he sticks to the truth. Especially if the little hormone-crazed marionette is staring at your chest. Don't ask him about it. Don't let him say a word. If he lies, it'll be a wooden nose to the heart for you. He's like a walking vampire killer. Until he becomes a 'real boy.'

Don't get me started on the anti-witch stereotyping in even the most beloved classics. Maleficent, the "Mad" Madam Mim, and Ursula, to name a few. None of them have happy endings, either. Look it up.

How are young witches supposed to grow up with a wholesome worldview when the only characters they relate to end up dead or diseased at the end of the story?

At least Broadway got it right with *Wicked*. Except for the fact that the actress is in green-face through the entire show. I mean, come on! Most witches aren't *really* green.

Another damn stereotype perpetuated by the system.

But at least the musical gave us a witch we could cheer for.

For a moment, as my mind wandered, considering the absurdity of Mel's Disney princess dreams, I forgot the chaos swirling around us and lost myself in the crisp night air. All I really had to worry about was avoiding a collision with humans.

A legitimate concern. I'd hate to sever someone's limbs with my skates. Dismemberment has a way of ruining someone's holiday season. And triggering my thirst.

Beyond such worries—which I tried to keep tucked away in the back of my mind—it wasn't as horrible an experience as I'd expected. While I'd never admit it to Mel or anyone else, I was having a shockingly good time. It was peaceful; almost relaxing. I couldn't recall the last time I did something so mundane as *skating*.

I barely realized Mel was still chatting away beside me. Rambling on about the same convoluted topic.

"I think it's bullshit," Mel added. "Sure, I mean, vampire romances cast us in a more desirable light. But we're more than sex dolls that bite. Sure, there are a few vampire heroes in major movies, but there's *nothing* for young vampires to look up to. Nothing so aspirational as a *princess*!"

I laughed out loud. When Mel turned on "chatterbox" mode it was hard to shut her down. "You're really stuck on this, aren't you?"

"Think about it," Mel added. "Maybe if Jinx had a Disney princess vampire she could model her existence after, she wouldn't be such a bitch. If I didn't have you as a role model, I'd probably be just like her."

I shook my head, growing more serious. "I'm not so sure Jinx is just another youngling vampire girl gone wild. She's too strong, too calculating. The way she commands those orphaned vamps... it reminds me of someone far older."

Mel tilted her head. "But you said vampires rarely gain extra abilities until at least their first century, right? Takes that long to cycle the energy of enough souls from feeds to develop new powers."

I nodded. "Usually that's true."

Mel bit her lip and tilted her head. "What if a youngling bit a lot of people? Went on some kind of major binge and devoured hundreds of souls. As many in a few weeks that most vampires do over the course of a century. Could she develop abilities, then?"

"It's possible, but unlikely. I'm not sure how our metabolism works, exactly, but when we get a taste of a soul, the part that lingers in someone's blood, we have to savor it to benefit from it. More like tasting wine in the Alps than drinking beer from a funnel at a frat party."

"But it's not *impossible*. We can't really rule anything out at this point."

I took a deep breath, the cold winter air filling and chilling my lungs. "Jinx didn't reveal any unique abilities. That's what I'd expect if she'd extracted a new power from human souls. It was more like she had the heightened speed and strength that *only* comes with age."

"What about all those piercings?" Mel asked. "I mean, that's not the kind of style you'd expect from an *ancient* vampire. Not unless you consider the punk rock era ancient. Besides, we heal. She either doesn't take those piercings out or she has to re-pierce herself every time she puts one in!"

I mulled over Mel's theory as we glided across the ice. "With time, we become resilient to pain," I explained. "The piercings may sting at first, but if she's a century old or more, she'd be numb to it by now."

Mel was quiet for a moment. "What if she's like Jector?"

I shuddered. Flashes of my vampire brother—who was known by the human world as Jack the Ripper—blinked through my mind. He was the strongest vampire I'd ever faced. With so many vampires rallied behind his cause for the crown, his challenge to *my* throne, it was a wonder he didn't slaughter all of us before we figured out a way to send him back to hell.

"It's possible," I admitted. "When a wraith escapes vampire hell, they can attack humans and use their blood to reforge a body. If Jinx siphoned enough blood after clawing her way back to our world through a convergence, it could explain her abilities."

Mel nodded slowly. "And if she has a hellhound like Jector did, that would explain her strength."

I rubbed my brow even as I did my best to keep my eyes straight ahead while we skated around and around. "There's no evidence of a hellhound, but that doesn't mean we won't find one somewhere. I can get Goliath on it and see if he can track one down. My gut says something else is going on. She has ancient strength, no doubt, but her behavior is more befitting a youngling. I just can't imagine an ancient vampire who has stayed under the radar for centuries would suddenly behave so recklessly."

Mel shrugged. "Well, it's hard to say why people, or vampires, do what they do. I wouldn't judge her age based on her style, though. Sure, she *looks* like a bit of a punk rocker, but she still could be ancient, staked in the last couple decades, and come back with a more modern vibe than someone like Jector."

I pressed my lips together. Mel had a fair point. "Anything is possible. Perhaps she's been off the grid for a long time. Maybe she turned before the Council started keeping better records. There are rogue bloodlines out there that have never reported to the Council. When Nico discovered them, he forced them to register. But the world is a big place. It would be absurd to think we've accounted for all of them."

Mel did a little spin right in front of me on her skates. What a little show off. "All possible. Though, you know, a loner doesn't just decide on a whim to start raising hell. If she's from a bloodline that's kept to itself for centuries, why risk it all to join up with a bunch of reckless younglings? There has to be some kind of motive behind it all."

"No, you're right," I agreed. "It doesn't add up. Let's just hope Ladinas hasn't eliminated all the vamps we staked tonight. He agreed to keep a couple, at least, for questioning."

Mel winced. "More interrogations. You realize, usually when we take someone hostage and start interrogating them, the shit hits the fan."

I shrugged. "Not *always*. But maybe that's why Ladinas was so skeptical. We'd hate to see a Jector situation repeat itself. I'm pretty sure, though, that the vampires we actually staked were genuine younglings. They went down easy enough. It's Jinx I don't know about."

My words hung in the air for a while. Then Mel started humming. I didn't recognize the tune. Most likely one of those damn pop ditties that work their way in your ear like a worm and don't leave until they eat away all your intelligence.

No matter, she'd moved on in her mind. I decided to follow her lead for once. Everything was on thin ice, and not just my feet in my skates. My position in the Underground, my relationship with Ladinas and Alice. It was already cracked and it wouldn't take much more before I'd find myself in frigid water.

I glided along the ice, momentarily distracted by the feel of the blades slicing smoothly beneath my feet. It had been decades since I last went skating. I never imagined I'd find myself back on the ice after all this time.

A laugh escaped my lips. "Would you look at me, upright and mobile on these things? Who knew I still had it in me?"

Mel smiled. "Hey, once you learn, you never really forget. It's like riding a bike."

She spun gracefully, the picture of ease and fluidity. I envied her natural talent, though I was enjoying myself too, despite the wobbliness. After the chaos of recent weeks, it felt good to let loose and relax, if only for a little while.

Chapter 4

My head was clearer than before—mostly. The last thing I really wanted to do was deal with Ladinas, but Mel was right. If we were going to figure out who Jinx really was, I needed his input. Before, he was about four hundred years older than me. Now that he'd spent a century in a pocket dimension with Alice, while I was on earth for only a few days, I suppose he *technically* gained another century on me. Not like there was anything he'd seen in the pocket dimension that would help, but if he could wrack his mind, try to imagine Jinx without the pink hair and piercings, maybe he'd be able to identify her.

Chances were, though, even if he'd met her before, she wasn't on his radar. Vampire societies are even more hierarchical than human ones. If Jinx was some kind of small-time vampire, why would a high-and-mighty onetime *prince* know who she was? Not to mention, in the olden days it wasn't like vampires on opposite sides of the world were in regular communication.

The fragrance of blood and frankincense hit me like a sledgehammer as we stepped out of the elevators and into the Underground. Ladinas and the team must've fed when they returned. "Smells like dinner," Mel remarked. "Almost like coming home to the smell of chocolate chip cookies in the oven."

Mel wasn't wrong. The frankincense aside, the smell of blood triggered a subtle growl in my gut.

Muggs cocked his head, tilting his ear down the hall. "I can hear Ladinas and Alice across the compound."

I waved a hand dismissively, nose wrinkling. "I don't need the play-by-play of whatever weird foreplay they've got going on."

Muggs furrowed his brow. "That's not what I mean. They're arguing about the younglings, how to go about questioning them before killing them."

I bit my lip and raised an eyebrow. "Arguing, huh?" Not like I was rooting for their relationship to fail. At this point, I didn't *want* Ladinas back. Not like that. But after what I'd been through, I'd be lying if I wasn't a little bit delighted to imagine that Ladinas and Alice might be having relationship problems. Petty of me? Of course, but you know—never mind. I was going to say, "I'm only human," but that would be a lie.

Mel cracked her knuckles, the sound sharp in the concrete hallway. "I'd better get to the infirmary. Got a lot of bullets to dig out of cold, dead flesh tonight."

"Careful. Make sure Antoine restrains them with silver, just in case they wake up angry and murderous." I met Mel's gaze steadily. She had proven herself loyal time and again. She was always eager to step up.

Mel nodded, eyes glinting with determination, and strode down the hall towards the infirmary. Muggs trailed after her, his staff rhythmically tapping the floor ahead of him as he muttered something about keeping the volatile baby vamps in line.

I watched them go, lips pressed into a thin line. The Underground was meant to be a sanctuary, yet more and more, it felt like a prison. After a night fighting younglings and ice skating, I needed a change. Not to mention, a minute to gather my emotions before dealing with Ladinas' bullshit.

I stalked to my room, my fingers still hooked around the handle of the strange gift bag the disappearing Peddler gave me earlier in the evening. Despite holding the damn thing, I'd almost forgotten I had it, not to mention my encounter with the old man. Under other circumstances, I'd have given it to Muggs and asked his opinion. But something was *different*. It was like every time I'd thought about the gift bag, its contents, or my encounter with the Peddler, it faded from my memory like a passing dream. But at the same time, I had to keep the bag close. It called to me, like the ring enthralled Gollum in the *Lord of the Rings*.

Something about his sly grin, his strange words and too-knowing eyes made me want to keep the contents of the bag a secret. A strange urge I couldn't quite explain.

When I tossed the bag onto my bed, the lamp tumbled out and landed beside it. I reached for the lamp, intending to shove it back into the bag, but a surge of energy rushed up my arm.

I dropped the lamp in surprise as smoke billowed out, filling the room. When it cleared, the Peddler stood before me.

I shrieked, then immediately felt embarrassed. Not just because I was half-dressed. I was a 131-year-old vampire, dammit. I wasn't supposed to get scared like that. People were supposed to be frightened of me!

But there was something inhuman about him. An aura of power that raised the hairs on my neck like static electricity.

"What the hell are you doing here?" I clenched my fists and placed them on my hips. I wasn't going to let this damn Peddler, or *whatever* he was, get the satisfaction of seeing me unsettled.

The Peddler smiled, his eyes glinting. "I'm not who I appear to be. I'm bound to that lamp you so carelessly tossed on your bed."

I snorted. "So what, you're some kind of peeping genie?"

"No, I'm a djinn," he replied.

"Djinn? Genie? What's the difference?" I crossed my arms.

"Hollywood," the djinn shook his head. "Our kind are no better represented in film than yours."

"Right." I scratched the back of my head. "So, do I get wishes and shit?"

"Not exactly," he said. "I can make real three of your deepest desires. I don't grant wishes, but I can alter past events of your life. Anything you wish went differently. Any fork in the road you've faced, I can place you on the path you didn't take."

I laughed harshly. "Yeah right. I've dealt with time travel and alternate timelines before. That butterfly effect crap isn't worth the risk."

The djinn's smile turned sly. "Are you so certain, Mercy Brown? This is a rare opportunity. I can unlock your deepest regrets, rewrite your most painful memories, offer you the life you've always wished for..."

"Thanks, but no thanks," I cut him off. "I don't need any damn wishes, so take a hike."

The djinn's face darkened, his eyes flashing dangerously. "I cannot. My power builds within me and must be released. Until you make three appeals to alter your past, I can use my magic for nothing else. Why not allow me to show you what *might* be possible?"

He took a step closer. I stood my ground. "I'll pass. Go find some other sucker."

"Blood sucker?" The djinn cocked an eyebrow.

"Sure. But maybe not. If you change something for someone else would it alter my reality?"

"Of course!" the djinn clapped his hands. "But you wouldn't know it. For you, it would be as though the new reality is your only reality. Only the benefactor of a djinn's gift can remember how things have changed. For the one who holds the lamp also retains her memories."

I narrowed my eyes. "In that case, maybe I'll just string you along. I'm not making your wishes. I won't change my history. But I won't let you go, either. You can hang out in your dusty little lamp and play with yourself for all eternity for what I care."

"If I do not change three things for you, the swelling of my unused power could prove... catastrophic. Who are you to reject the opportunity to make a change? Surely there's something, no matter how small, you'd have done differently if you had a chance to do it all over again. Everyone has regrets. Just imagine how different your present *and* your future might be if you'd only made a few different choices along the way!"

I rolled my eyes. "Yeah, yeah, I get it. Past, present, and future. I don't need any visit from Christmas ghosts. Tell Chuck Dickens to kiss my ass. I'm not interested."

"This is not a wish I can fulfill! I can only alter events of *your* past. Since you never met Mr. Dickens, I cannot give you a life in which he once smooched your behind. But if there's anyone else you've met who you'd like me to make kiss your—"

I raised my hand to cut him off. "It was an expression. How long have you been in that little lamp, anyway?"

"It's not as it seems. I don't live within the lamp. It's more like a talisman, it's connected to me. If I give you my lamp, it means I've chosen you."

I snorted. "Lucky me. Why would you choose me, anyway? What kind of crap have you been up to before now? How many times have you altered the course of history by dipping into people's pasts?"

"Our kind is mostly harmless, though infinitely powerful. We stick to ourselves, and we use our power in moderation. But we cannot use our power to serve ourselves in large enough quantities to keep up with the power that swells within. Once or twice a century, we must choose someone with great need, significant regret, and grant three of their deepest seeded desires. When we act in this way for another, it allows us a great release, after which, we can return to our modest lives. As for how many times I've changed history, well, it's hard to say. Any time someone's past is changed, it is to everyone else as it has always been. But it is necessary. If my power swells much more, it will pour from me like a fountain, unfettered, and there's no telling how much damage it might do to your world."

I jabbed a finger at the djinn. "Well, you chose poorly. I don't want your wishes. No release for you. You're just going to have to stay... blue-lamped or whatever."

The djinn opened his mouth to interject, but I cut him off.

"Save it. I know how these stories go. The moral is always to be grateful for the shit you have now instead of chasing ghosts from the past or daydreaming about the future."

"I told you, that's not what this is about! If I do not get my release--"

I crossed my arms. "Yeah, it would be *catastrophic.* Spare me. You don't think making a wish would be just as bad? Changing the past never turns out well. So you can take your three wishes and shove them right up your smoky ass."

The djinn glowered, wisps of smoke curling from his sleeves. "I do not need you to articulate your wishes, Mercy Brown. I need only look into your heart to discern your deepest desires."

I snorted. "Good luck with that. My heart is a dark and dreary place. You won't find much."

"We shall see," the djinn remarked before raising his hands and snapping his fingers. He vanished in a puff of vapor. Probably went back into his lamp or whatever. I let out a breath. Crisis averted, for now anyway. I'd have to keep an eye on that damned lamp.

With the djinn gone, I finished changing and headed out to check on the young vampire prisoners. Time to see if Mel had revived any, or if Ladinas and Alice had any prepared for interrogation. I'd deal with the damn djinn later. For now, the greater shroud of mystery surrounded Jinx.

My boots echoed on the concrete floor as I strode from my room down the dim hallway. The Underground wasn't much to look at, just a maze of windowless rooms and corridors beneath an abandoned warehouse. But it was home, for better or worse.

As I approached the end of the hallway, I could hear muffled voices coming from one of the interrogation rooms. I quickened my pace, curious to hear what progress Ladinas and Alice had made. As I entered the dimly lit room, I saw

Ladinas hunched over a silver-bound and gagged vampire, the vampire prince's fingers tapping against his chin in contemplation.

"Ah, Mercy, good timing," Ladinas said without looking up. "We were just getting ready to take a break and gather our thoughts."

I nodded, my eyes scanning the room. There were three other vampires strapped to chairs, their eyes wide with fear, sweat glistening on their foreheads. I could almost smell the fear on them—or maybe that was just the usual vampiric B.O. Talk about nauseating.

"Any luck?" I asked, crossing my arms.

Alice shook her head, her eyes dark with frustration. "Not much. They're stubborn, and they know how to keep their mouths shut."

I sighed and reached for my wand. Sometimes, if conventional interrogation tactics don't work, a few spells will do the trick. It wasn't necessarily the spells I *knew* that could make someone talk. All I needed to do was offer enough of a display of magic that they'd believe I *might* be able to do anything at all. The only limit to what these younglings might believe I *could* do was my imagination.

For just a second—a *half second*—a thought crossed my mind. My imagination. What if anything really was possible, if I could alter something from my past? What if I could change my past? What would I change? Would I go back and live a normal life? Would I live out my life? What if my case of consumption wasn't so bad it would have killed me; if Nico didn't turn me into a vampire...

It wasn't a serious thought. But when confronted with a chance to actually change the past who wouldn't wonder what things might be like otherwise?

I pushed the thought out of my mind. I had younglings to interrogate. Prisoners to *intimidate.*

But as I raised my wand, I felt a sudden coldness in the air. A shiver ran down my spine, and the hairs on the back of my neck stood up. Something was wrong.

Suddenly, a voice spoke in my mind, chilling me to the bone. It was the djinn, his power seeping into my thoughts.

"Mercy Brown," he hissed. "You will regret your decision to deny my gift. I will make you see the error of your ways, even if I have to drag you kicking and screaming through time and space."

I stumbled back, clutching my head as the djinn's power coursed through me. I could hear Ladinas and Alice shouting my name, but it was distant, as if coming from another world. The world around me grew dark, and then suddenly everything went black.

When I opened my eyes again, I was no longer in the Underground. I was standing in a vast, open field, the sun beating down on my skin. And it didn't burn... not even a little.

I looked around, disoriented and confused. This wasn't where I had just been. How had the djinn transported me here?

Then I heard a voice, a voice I hadn't heard in years. It was my mother's voice. She was talking to someone, but I couldn't see who.

"Mercy, sweetie, come here," she called out, beckoning me over to where she stood. I took a few hesitant steps forward, and then I saw her. She was standing with my father, who I hadn't seen since he and I reconciled after he'd come back from the dead. Long story there, but he looked kinder now, less disheveled. Like he didn't have the burden of hatred against our kind, of dying and coming back again, weighing on his shoulders. They were both smiling at me, and it was like a punch to the gut.

"What the hell is going on?" I muttered, taking another step forward until I was standing in front of them.

"Mercy, honey," my mother said, taking my hand. "We're here because we want to show you something. Something that we think you need to see."

My heart raced as she led me over to a nearby tree, where a young girl was sitting with her nose buried in a book. It was me, at maybe ten or eleven years old. I watched as my younger self turned the page, her eyes lighting up with wonder as she read the words.

"Look at her," my mother said, squeezing my hand. "Look at how happy she is. That's the girl you used to be, before everything happened. Before I got sick..."

"Before consumption. Before I turned to witchcraft..."

"Before you became a vampire," my father added.

I snorted. "What the hell? Do I even see myself? And why do you two look like you used to when I was a little girl but not... me?"

"This is only one place, one fork in the road, to where you might return," my father intoned. Then I realized he wasn't my father at all. He was the damn djinn. "Wish it so, and I will take you back. I'll make you forget."

I shook my head. "If I forgot, what good would that do? All the shit that happened would still happen. Mom would still get sick and die. My dad would get lost in his religious zeal again. I'd rebel and become a witch until I got sick and became a vampire all over again."

"Not necessarily," the djinn said, my father's face falling away, my mother disappearing entirely. "How many things each day occur by *random* chance? There's no telling what might be different a second time around. Your mother might *not get sick.* Besides, you'll have a soul again. A soul that's learned from your life before, even if you won't remember it all. You might make different choices."

I felt tears prick at the corners of my eyes as I watched my younger self giggling at something in the book. It had been so long since I'd felt that kind of pure joy.

"You can have that again, Mercy," the djinn said, appearing again as my father and resting a hand on my shoulder. "You don't have to live in the past, or in fear of the future. You can find a way back to that happiness."

I blinked, feeling like I was seeing the world in a different light. Maybe there was a way to change my past, to make things right. But at what cost? Was it worth it to forget everything that had led me to where I was now, even if it meant a chance at happiness?

"I... I don't know," I stammered, my mind racing with conflicting thoughts and emotions.

The djinn's grip on my shoulder tightened. "Decide, Mercy. Time is running out."

I closed my eyes, taking a deep breath. When I opened them again, I knew what I had to do.

"I can't," I said firmly, meeting the djinn's gaze. "I can't forget everything that's happened. I can't pretend that my past didn't lead me to where I am now. I may not be happy, but I'm me. And I'd rather face my future head-on, with all its uncertainty, than try to start over. Besides, what would happen to the future if I accepted this life, if I wasn't there to stop Moll, to dismantle the Order of the Morning Dawn, to fight against all the assholes I've defeated through the years?"

"Have you considered that if you'd never become a vampire, Moll might not have succeeded to begin with in her scheme to gain power? That the Order of the Morning Dawn might not have a single, notorious vampire to hunt across the centuries? That if you didn't become a vampire, *Alice* wouldn't, either? Perhaps there'd be *no* Order of the Morning Dawn at all if you simply lived out your human life."

I snorted. "That's a lot of 'ifs' and 'mights.' You said it yourself. Too many events happen by random chance. There's no way to know how things would play out, even if nothing changed at all and someone hit the reset button on history."

"The choice is yours," the djinn said. "But I can show you what might be in store for you if you return to your first life."

I rolled my eyes. "How about you just send me back? I have vampires to interrogate, damn it."

The djinn laughed. "If you make the right choice, Mercy, nothing you're facing now in your present, or will face in the future, will be an issue at all. Allow me to show you what could become of you if your life turns out just a *little* differently."

I clenched my fists. "I really don't want to know, but I have a feeling you won't let me out of this goddamned vision until you're done."

"Very astute of you!"

I grunted. "Fine. Get it over with. Show me whatever you want. It won't change my mind, though."

The djinn—the bastard now appearing as my *mother* again—took my hand. He leaned in toward my ear, but his voice was soft, like my mother's. As much as I could remember it, anyway. "We'll see, sweetie. We'll see."

Chapter 5

THAT DAMN DJINN LOOKED just like her. After so long I'd thought I forgotten what she looked like. He must've drawn her appearance from somewhere deep in the recesses of my mind, something beyond conscious recollection. My mother's warm smile cut through me like a knife as she extended a hand. "Come, my child. Let me show you what might have been."

I hesitated, knowing it wasn't *really* my mother, but the djinn's pull was irresistible. The world melted away, reforming into the familiar surroundings of my childhood home. I was staring at *myself*. Technically, I was nineteen. The same age at which I was turned, but I seemed younger. I was thin and pale, which I suppose wasn't much of a change. But as a vampire I was a vivacious thin, and my paleness wasn't so sickly. The old me I was witnessing was recovering from my bout of consumption, but she was very much alive. My parents enfolded me in their arms, joyful tears streaming down their faces. Even Edwin, my pipsqueak of a brother, managed a smile.

"Welcome back home," my mother said. "We were so afraid we'd lost you."

"Praise the Lord!" my father said, grinning from ear to ear with a happiness I'd never seen grace his stuffy countenance.

The scene shifted with a blur that clouded my vision before new figures formed again in front of me. Apparently the djinn was taking me on a tour through time, what *could* be if the wish I'd nearly articulated in my mind became real.

I was older now. Pretty, but lacking my vampiric allure. It was funny seeing myself *look* older even though in this vision I wasn't nearly as old as I truly was as a vampire.

I watched myself stroll through a sunny meadow, humming a hymn I must've learned at church. Even though I looked a little older, seeing the *sun* on my face was startling. I looked so *alive*.

I heard a voice from a distance. I turned—and so did the *other* me in the field.

"Beautiful day, isn't it?" A handsome young stranger said as he approached me.

"Indeed, good sir!" I said. I chuckled to myself. I was so *damn polite*. Who was I, really?

The young gentleman fed me some line about how he could swear he'd seen an angel in the fields and had to come and see for himself. I watched myself blush—something I couldn't do as a vampire. The man had kind eyes, dark wavy hair, and a lopsided grin.

"The name's Henry," the man said, his eyes locked on the version of me who populated this farce of a vision. "And you are?"

I groaned as I watched my slightly older looking, but younger self melt under Henry's flirtations. It was the start of *something*. That's why the djinn showed it to me.

A chance at romance. An opportunity for love. What a bastard. The djinn was reading my mind, showing me only what he thought I'd missed, what I'd never found as a vampire.

More visions flickered by—picnics, dances, stolen kisses. Henry proposed on a moonlit beach and I said yes without hesitation. Our wedding was simple, but beautiful. I could see the happiness on my face as the ceremony ended with a kiss. I had never felt such happiness and hope for the future.

But it wasn't real.

"Enough," I said through gritted teeth. "I've seen what you want me to see. A perfect little human life, free of darkness and full of love. But it's a fantasy. My true path led me to vampirism and, despite the difficulties, I don't regret the choices that brought me here."

The Djinn's facade flickered, showing the cruel intelligence lurking beneath the false-face of my mother. "I never said life would be easy. But things that matter rarely are. Behold."

The vision sped forward once more, blurring past me in a rush of color and light. When it settled, I found myself in a cozy bedroom, propped up against pillows in an enormous bed. My swollen belly protruded beneath the blankets. I looked maybe a decade older, laughter lines creasing the corners of my eyes. Henry sat beside me, his hand wrapped around mine. My husband's hair was thinner than when we'd first met, and his belly larger—though not so large as mine.

"It's time," he said, eyes crinkling as he smiled. "I'm here. Squeeze my hand as hard as you must. I can take it"

Yeah right, I thought to myself. If I'd squeezed his hand as hard as I could as a vampire, I'd break every bone. But this wasn't vampire Mercy. This was a human Mercy who *might* have been if I hadn't become a vampire. If I'd somehow survived.

Waves of pain rippled through my pregnant body, revealed in a clenched face and a scream. A woman appeared at the door carrying a bag of supplies. The midwife. Hospital births weren't really a thing in those days. The midwife was an older woman with a kind face, her long hair pulled into a bun. She knew what she was doing and moved with purpose. She placed herself at the end of the bed, her calm voice guiding me through the contractions. My husband held me close, whispering words of encouragement.

With a final push, my baby entered the world. His loud wails filled the room. For a moment, I thought I actually *felt* my heart flutter.

My son? I had a *son?*

My husband cut the cord with tears in his eyes before placing the swaddled newborn in my arms.

"He's perfect," the Mercy of the vision murmured, overcome with emotion. I sensed it, too. Tiny fingers grasped at mine. The love I felt in that moment was unlike anything I'd ever experienced. For the first time, the vision didn't feel like a fantasy. It felt real—full of messy, imperfect joy and new life.

The scene changed again. I saw myself standing outside, watching three young children play tag in the grass. Their bright laughter carried on the breeze. From the age of my oldest in the vision a good decade had passed since the last vision.

I saw Henry sneak up behind me—the other me. Arms encircled my waist from behind.

"Look at them," my husband said proudly. "We did good."

The smooth skin and raven hair of my vampire form were gone. A few wrinkles betrayed my age and my hair was thinner, the darkness invaded by a few strands of gray. But my eyes were full of light, blue like the sea, not red like blood; not haunted like those of my true immortal self.

I had lived an entire human life in these visions, filled with love and family. It was everything I could never have as a vampire. Everything the Djinn wanted me to regret.

The vision blurred again, years passing in an instant. Now I stood beside a grave, my husband's name carved into the stone. My children, grown into adults, gathered around to comfort me.

"He loved you so much, Mom," my daughter said, squeezing my hand. Though grief hung heavy in the air, I also felt profound gratitude. We'd built a good life together. I could see it in the compassion on my children's faces, the wisdom in their eyes that came from being nurtured and loved.

The Djinn appeared beside me, gloating. "You could have had this, Mercy. You could have it still, if only you allow me to change your past. Does your immortal life compare?"

I wiped away a tear, gazing at the family who surrounded me. "It's beautiful. But it's not real."

The vision jumped ahead once more. I lay frail in bed, my remaining years dwindling. Grandchildren and great-grandchildren filled the room. Their tears and whispered goodbyes overflowed with love.

The Djinn smiled, victorious. "I've shown you true happiness. A life lived to the fullest, with family always beside you, even to the very end. Can you really walk away from this?"

The elderly me reached out and pulled a young girl close, hugging her tightly. Then I met the Djinn's gaze.

"My life is no less full for the lack of this fantasy you've invented. My loyalty and love for those I call family now is just as real. I won't regret what might have been. Take me back."

The vision faded.

The Djinn's smug expression soured, but he inclined his head. "As you wish."

The comforting scene dissolved, replaced by the icy darkness of some kind of crypt.

"Where the hell are we?"

"In the darkness of your mind. This mind. The mind of a vampire. This is the loneliness your life has borne. Would you not prefer the life I offered you?"

"I won't play your games," I told the Djinn firmly. "You can't manipulate me with some make-believe life."

The Djinn's eyes narrowed. "You are certain? I could show you so much more."

I crossed my arms. "Yeah? You just showed me a life when my mother survived. But that's not what happened."

"There's no guarantee that she'd die again if I took you back far enough. There are enough random possibilities at play she *could* survive. Anything is possible. Do not forget I'd send you back with your memories as a vampire still intact."

I nodded, the whole thought of going back in time while knowing so much about a future that wouldn't come to pass was too much to consider. "You make it sound so wonderful. But you don't know how things would play out. My mother might die again. Show me a world where my mother died, where I got sick as before. What would it look like if I didn't become a vampire in that sanatorium? Change nothing else. Nothing before that. Nothing after. Allow those events to play out as they must."

"As you wish." With a wave of his hand, the Djinn conjured another vision. I saw myself, a young woman again, recovering from consumption in the sanatorium. Alice was in the bed beside me—as she had been on that fateful night. She was reading her bible, lecturing me on the significance of Jesus' Sermon on the Mount.

"Boring," I yawned. "Skip ahead."

The Djinn complied. Now I was home, reunited with my father and brother. But my father's embrace felt more confining than comforting. Edwin stood stiffly apart, his youthful face pinched and judgmental.

I sighed. "Typical. Skip ahead. A few more weeks."

Another wave, and there I was—but not much older, with bruises on my arms. My father loomed over me, spouting scripture in a harsh tone before backhanding me across the face. What the hell had I done? Edwin watched wide-eyed, making no move to intervene.

"It's your sin, you foolish girl! You think I don't know what you've been doing in the woods? You're a witch! You brought this evil upon us! Your mother was taken from all of us as *your* punishment!"

I clenched my fists. I wanted to tear my father apart, but this was *just* a vision. Felt real, though. Truth was, I'd only turned to witchcraft *after* my mother died. Because my father had become so distant. So neglectful and abusive. He'd become so absorbed in his zealous little boy's club—which I later found out was connected to the Order of the Morning Dawn—that dabbling in witchcraft was my way of passively giving him the middle finger.

Clearly, though, he didn't understand why I'd done what I did. He thought I'd been a witch even longer than I was—and it was my *fault* apparently that my mother contracted consumption.

I glared at the Djinn. "You showed me a fairy tale before. This is what my life will become if I go back."

"You don't know that."

I huffed. "You told me before. You can change one decision. What decision created the vision before? What decision changed this time?"

The djinn shook his head. "A choice of little direct consequence. Nothing you'd ever think *could* change, but I can make it happen. I can still give you the life I showed you before. You need only wish it!"

I stared at the djinn with a blank stare. "You don't know that. You're the one who said that random events never repeat the same way twice. You're not offering me a better life. You're tempting me with versions of life that might never pan out."

"But you forget, Mercy, you'd still have two more wishes, two more changes, even after your new life begins. If things do not go as you hope, simply use another wish! I can show you once again the possibilities, give you a preview of what might happen."

I laughed and shook my head. "And fuck up things even more? Like you said, buddy. There are no guarantees. I'm fine with the life I have. Thank you very much."

"That's not true," the djinn said. "You have regrets."

I shrugged. "Who the hell doesn't? It's one thing to realize I've made poor choices in the past, or even made good choices that didn't pan out as I'd hoped. That's just life."

"I'll return you home if you wish. But it's only a matter of time before another regret stirs in your heart. I'll be there to show you what might be."

I sighed. "And my answer will remain the same. Hell-fucking-no."

Chapter 6

I BLINKED, THE DJINN'S vision fading as the interrogation room swam back into focus. The youngling was still chained to the chair, glaring at me defiantly. I could feel Mel's hand on my arm, her voice laced with concern as she asked if I was alright.

"Of course. What do you mean?" I brushed her off, not wanting to explain what I'd seen.

Ladinas's brow furrowed, his crimson eyes piercing mine. "You went into some kind of daze. Your eyes rolled back in your head."

Shit. I didn't need them worrying about me right now. I glanced at Ladinas, then Alice, and finally Mel, forcing a sly wink. Hopefully, they'd think it was just a clever trick to throw off the youngling. But Mel's eyes were still wide, her grip tightening on my arm. Damn it, she wasn't convinced.

I shook Mel off and strode towards the prisoner, whipping out my wand and pressing it to his throat. His beady eyes narrowed as I demanded, "Tell me who Jinx is."

He spat at me. "I ain't afraid of your stupid little stick. Jinx would kill me if I talked."

"Would she now?" I smirked, tightening my grip on my wand. If he was really scared of Jinx, that gave us an opportunity. I'd make this bloodsucker piss himself yet—and my spell would show us his greatest fear. "*Somnum exterreri!*"

A bolt of dark energy burst from the tip of my wand. The youngling's eyes snapped wide as the spell flooded his mind, searching, probing his deepest seated fears.

Stepping back, I met Ladinas's questioning gaze. "It'll make his worst fears seem real. We'll be able to see everything, like a projection." I glanced at the youngling, whose eyes were already glazing over. "If he's really so scared of Jinx, we're about to find out why."

Ladinas chuckled, crossing his arms. "Brilliant. Let's see what this little shit is made of."

A ripple in the air around the youngling heralded the arrival of his nightmare. At first, it was only a flicker—a flash of pink hair and pale skin. Then she solidified, sauntering into the room as if she owned the place.

Jinx.

She circled the youngling, trailing sharp nails across his shoulders. "Did you think you could escape me, pet?" Her voice was like velvet and venom. "You belong to me now. No one will save you."

The youngling whimpered, cowering under her predatory gaze. My spell had crafted every detail perfectly, from the piercings lining her lips to the predatory gleam in her pale eyes.

"Please, I didn't tell them anything!" He grasped at Jinx's hands, trembling. "I swear, mistress, I've been good!"

Jinx grabbed a fistful of his hair, yanking his head back to expose his throat. "Liar. You've always been worthless." A fang slid from her lips, descending towards his neck.

"That's enough." I snapped my fingers, banishing the illusion. The youngling slumped in his chair, chest heaving.

Mel stepped forward, brow creased with concern. "A vampire biting another vampire?"

"You should have let that play out," Alice added. "We were seeing what he feared about Jinx. What if she *feeds* on other vampires? That could explain--"

I shook my head. "Maybe. Or Jinx is the one who turned him and he's reliving the most terrifying moment of his life. I wouldn't read too much into it."

Alice crossed her arms. "He's *already* a vampire. How can his greatest fear be something he's already been through?"

I cocked an eyebrow before stepping up to Alice, my face only inches from hers. "Who is in charge here, bitch?"

"Stop it, both of you!" Ladinas shouted, his eyes focused more on me than Alice. "The spell frightened him enough. We can use that."

The youngling's eyes flew open as Ladinas loomed over him, panic etched into every line of his face.

I leaned against the wall, content to let Ladinas take the lead. No need to rub it in that my spell had been more effective than Alice's suggestion of sending in a burly prisoner.

Ladinas grabbed the youngling's chin, forcing him to meet his gaze. The youngling whimpered, shrinking in his seat.

"You have two options," Ladinas said softly. "You can tell us everything you know about Jinx's operations, or you can suffer the same fate your 'mistress' intended for you." His nails dug into the youngling's skin, puncturing the flesh. A bead of black vampiric blood welled up, trailing down his captive's neck.

The youngling squeaked. "I'll tell you anything, just please don't kill me!"

"Smart boy." Ladinas released him, the hint of a smile on his lips. "Now. Where is Jinx headquartered?"

"I don't know!" The youngling tugged at his restraints. "I don't think she has a place of her own. She comes and goes as she pleases, but she stays with us most of the time."

Ladinas's eyes narrowed. "I don't believe you."

Before I could stop him, he lashed out, backhanding the youngling across the face. The crack of bone on bone echoed in the small room.

"Ladinas!" I snapped. He froze, startled, and turned to face me. "He's talking, damn it! Let him talk!"

Ladinas's jaw tightened, annoyance flickering in his eyes. But he nodded, stepping back to give me space.

I turned my attention to the youngling, who was whimpering through his swollen jaw. "Relax. You're a vampire. A few minutes and you'll heal up, good as new. No lasting harm done. Just tell me the truth, and I'll make sure my companion behaves himself."

The youngling looked past me, eyeing Ladinas warily. But he nodded.

"Jinx isn't one of us," he said, the words muffled.

"What do you mean 'not one of us'?" I asked. "She's not a vampire?"

The youngling shook his head. "She's a vampire, sort of. But she's different. I can't explain it."

"How old is she?" I asked.

The youngling sighed. "I don't know."

"Is she your sire?" Alice asked.

The youngling pressed his lips together. "Yeah. I mean, I think. It's all such a blur. I don't remember being turned. All I know is that she's different. She's not like the rest of us."

"Different in what way?" Alice asked, stepping up beside me. "She feeds from *you*, doesn't she? That's why she's so strong..."

"I—I really shouldn't say—"

I twirled my wand in my hand. "I can bring her back again if you'd like. We're going to find out the truth one way or another. But if you help *us* out, we can keep you safe. I can protect you."

Ladinas huffed. "We can end his existence painlessly, at least."

I pressed my lips together. "Don't mind him. He's in a bad mood. I told you I'd protect you. Once I've dealt with Jinx, you won't have anything to be afraid of."

The youngling trembled. "You can't kill her. It's impossible."

"Of course it's possible," I said, steadying my voice. "I know you haven't been a vampire for long, but when you burn out a vampire's heart..."

"You don't understand!" the youngling added. "She doesn't *have* a heart! I told you, she's not one of us. Not exactly, anyway."

My stomach twisted. Didn't have a heart? I endured most of my vampiric existence without a heart. A spell had bound my vampiric life to the soul of my brother—so long as he remained in hell, I endured. I was practically unkillable in those days. I got my heart back later. Long story. But I knew what the youngling was saying wasn't *impossible*. It would certainly explain a lot. Though, in my case, I never had a taste for *vampire* blood.

"Are you sure she doesn't have a heart?" Alice asked. "Or is that just something she told you? Like, she's heartless, or whatever."

"She literally doesn't have a heart!" the youngling insisted. "I don't know why or how. But you aren't the first who've come after us. There've been hunters..."

My heart skipped a beat. Sebastian? He was the only hunter I knew who'd been in the region. But if it was Sebastian, if he'd confronted Jinx. I feared the worst. "What happened to the hunter?"

"I don't know," the youngling admitted. "He staked Jinx, set her on fire, and left. He didn't even know the rest of us were there and saw it all. After he was gone, Jinx rolled out the flames, laughed, and removed the stake from her chest as if it was nothing more than a large splinter."

I didn't know if the hunter *was* Sebastian. Not for sure. But he was the only hunter I'd ever faced who bested me. As strong as Jinx was, I doubted there were too many hunters who'd stand a chance against her. Unless she *allowed* the hunter to think he'd killed her just to get him off their trail.

Whatever the case, at least I knew whoever the hunter was who went after Jinx was still alive. Somewhere. That meant if it *was* Sebastian, he was fine.

Had I made a mistake leaving Sebastian back in Maine, returning to Ladinas and the team? I couldn't go there in my mind. It was just a little crush. Sebastian was focused on saving his wife. He didn't have room in his heart for anyone—much less a vampire like me. There wasn't anything I could change, even with the djinn's help, that would change any of that.

"Why don't you give it another go?" Ladinas asked. "Cast the spell again. See how it plays out."

I shrugged. "I could. But he's talking. I don't think he knows much else."

Ladinas nodded at Alice. "Get rid of him. We'll move on to the next prisoner."

Before I realized what happened, Alice plunged a stake back into the youngling's chest.

"Take it out!" I insisted. "I told him I'd protect him!"

"Burn him," Ladinas said as he pivoted on the ball of his foot to leave the room.

I snapped back at Alice. "Don't you dare."

"He's beyond saving," Alice said. "These younglings have been feeding on innocents. We have no choice."

"There's always a choice!" I insisted. "Pull out that damn stake. He's stuck in hell like that. If you really want to drive him mad to the point he can't be saved, that's the way to do it!"

Alice ignored me and retrieved a small blow torch from a table on the edge of the room. She was going to burn out the boy's heart. That's when I lost it.

I lunged at her, pushing her back with all my strength. Ladinas rushed in to break us apart, but I was too angry to hear anything he said. I could take Ladinas. I could beat Alice. But not both of them at once.

Alice and Ladinas teamed up on me. Mel tried to get between us, but a backhand from Alice sent her flying and crashing against the wall.

"You bitch!" I shouted. "Don't lay a hand on my girl!"

"I didn't mean to—"

I aimed my wand at Alice. I could have done it. *Incendia* could burn her heart out if I focused my power straight at her chest. I was about to end her then and there when two powerful hands grabbed me from behind.

"Mercy!" Ladinas screamed as he spun me around and pinned my shoulders to the wall. "Get it together! We're on the same team!"

"Fuck you and your team!" I screamed as I shook myself free and rushed to Mel's side. I helped her to her feet.

"Mercy," Ladinas begged. "You don't *mean* that. If it makes you feel any better, we can spare this youngling for now. But if he steps out of line…"

"It's too late for compromises," I insisted. "Come on, Mel. We're getting the hell out of here. Let these assholes deal with Jinx on their own."

Chapter 7

I STOMPED DOWN THE hall, fists clenched, fury pulsing through my veins. Mel hurried to catch up, her combat boots thumping against the stone floor.

"Mercy, wait. This is an overreaction."

I whirled on her, eyes flashing. "Overreaction? Did you see what just happened in there?" My nails dug into my palms. "Get your things. We're leaving."

Mel grabbed my arm. "We can't just leave. There are convergences here, and Ladinas said--"

A portal yawned open behind her with a crackle of energy. Muggs stepped through, pale eyes solemn on his angular face. He must've heard everything from his room.

"She's right, Mercy. You must stay. You *are* the guardian of the region."

I bared my fangs at him. "Let Ladinas and his precious Alice handle it. You have half an hour to gather your things before we head out."

Muggs held my gaze, unflinching. "I will not leave unless you compel it. My duty is to you, as your progeny, but there are greater things at stake here."

Rage ignited in my chest like a furnace. How dare they defy me? I was their sire, their leader, their queen—they would obey my command.

I surged forward and seized Muggs by the throat, slamming him against the stone wall. The familiar's eyes widened in surprise before his expression settled into grim determination.

"You will do as I say," I hissed, fingers tightening, "or I will destroy you myself."

Muggs stared back at me, resolute. "If you command it, I cannot resist. But I only follow you under protest. This is a mistake."

The fury bubbled over, a roaring fire in my veins. Why was *everyone* questioning me? I wouldn't command Muggs to follow me. It was his choice. But at the moment I was so goddamn pissed it took everything I had to stop myself from doing something I'd regret—like removing his head from his shoulders.

Mel grabbed my arms, hauling me back with all the strength she could muster. "Mercy, stop!"

I whirled on her, snarling. She met my rage with steely resolve.

"Get a hold of yourself. You're not thinking clearly." Her fingers dug into my arms as I strained against her. "Muggs is right. We can't leave now. There's too much at stake."

I wrested out of her grip, chest heaving. The fury still simmered inside me, urging me to violence, but beneath it was the slow creep of shame. They were right—I knew they were right. I was meant to guard this place, for better or worse. No matter my personal grievances with Ladinas and Alice. But there were others who could do the job now.

I turned away from them with a sharp exhale, pinching the bridge of my nose. When I spoke again, my voice was tight with resentment.

"You have one hour to decide. I won't compel either of you to follow me. I'll come back to deal with the convergence if the situation demands, but for now, between Ramon, Adam, Willie, and everyone else, it's handled."

Mel and Muggs shared another look, this one relieved.

"We're coming with you," Mel said firmly. "Wherever you go, we go too."

"You don't have to--"

Muggs sighed. "I'll come with you, if only because if the convergence here demands attention, I can bring you back a lot faster than you can drive."

I threw up my hands in exasperation, the fight draining out of me. "Fine. Your choice. Meet me in an hour and we're out of here."

They nodded, wisely keeping their thoughts to themselves, and hurried off to gather their things. I sank onto the edge of my bed with a groan, burying my face in my hands. This wasn't how I expected things would go when I came back to the Underground. I'd *accepted* that Ladinas and Alice were together.

That wasn't it.

It wasn't even that they didn't agree with my position. It was the *disrespect.* I wanted to save these younglings. Not just because I was partially responsible for what they became, but because I'd been pulled back from the ledge more than once in my time. If it wasn't for a few vampires who had faith in *me*—if Sebastian didn't have faith in me—I'd be dead, damned, or worse.

They didn't trust my judgment. They thought I was volatile. And I *was*. But they were the *reason*. They could disagree with me any day of the week, but when we didn't see things the same way, we were supposed to talk it through. It was like ever since I'd had my issue with Oblivion, Ladinas thought he could just overrule my decisions.

But I wasn't the one whose mind was warped. At least I was trying to *save* these vampires. It was more like the century Ladinas and Alice spent in the pocket dimension calloused them to the point that they were now two nasty feet, just scurrying around, and stinking up the joint with their corns and fungus.

A familiar tingle ran down my spine. I lifted my head to find the djinn lounging against the wall, regarding me with an infernal smirk.

"What now?" I snapped.

"You're wondering what choices you could have made in the past that would have stopped Alice from ever returning to Rhode Island."

"Am not."

The djinn arched a brow. "Sure you are. I can show you a few possibilities if you'd like to consider your options."

"No, thanks." I didn't need to dwell on the past. Not when the present was complicated enough.

"I insist." He snapped his fingers dramatically. Smoke filled the room, stinging my eyes—but when it cleared, everything looked exactly the same.

But the djinn was gone. I reached into my closet to grab my suitcase and things—only to discover half my wardrobe was *different*.

"What did you do?" I shouted into the air. "You changed some of my shopping choices? Diabolical!"

The stupid djinn didn't respond. What the fuck ever.

I stomped out of my room, suitcase in hand, scanning the hallway for any other surprises. Instead, I found Demeter leaning against the wall, pale arms folded over his chest.

My steps faltered. Demeter was dead. Killed in that whole ordeal with Samuel Parris and the Order of the Morning Dawn. "What the hell?"

Demeter blinked at me with a frown. "Are you ready or not? We only have a brief window to get this done."

"Ready for what?" My heart pounded as I struggled to make sense of the impossible. None of this was right. The djinn was responsible. But what *choice* did I make that killed Demeter? Oh, that bastard. He was tempting me to make a wish that would bring back a part of my old team.

"Seriously, Mercy?" Demeter's frown deepened. "Did you hit your head or something? We need to move. Now."

He strode off toward the security room. I stumbled after him, shouting for Mel and Muggs. No response. By the time I caught up to Demeter, Ladinas was emerging from the security room, concern etched into his face.

"What's going on? Where are Mel and Muggs?" I demanded. My hands curled into fists, nails biting into my palms.

"This isn't funny." Ladinas's tone was grim. "We need to focus if we're going to have a chance at taking out Jector."

"What are you talking about?" Panic rose in my chest like a tide. Jector was *alive*? Nothing about this situation made sense. I struggled to think through the haze of confusion and fear clouding my mind.

"Did you hit your head?" Ladinas asked. "Demeter said you were out of sorts. Jector's army is approaching. We only have a short window of opportunity. We have to take him down before he closes in on us. He's back to finish what he started."

I dragged in a sharp breath and held it. This wasn't like the visions the djinn showed me before. I wasn't watching a potential past that I'd never experienced from afar. I was no spectator. It was as if I was experiencing the *present* after some choice I'd made in the past was altered.

I released my breath in a hiss. "What the hell are you talking about? Jector's dead. We killed him months ago."

Ladinas's eyes narrowed. "Don't joke about this. Jector convinced the lion's share of the vampires all around the world to follow him over you. He only let you live out of respect for Nico, but we've been undermining his efforts ever since. He's returned to Providence to eliminate you once and for all."

"Undermining his efforts?"

"Destroying cities. Enslaving humans—those he doesn't kill or turn—and raising them like cattle. He's destroyed half the world in less than a year. How don't you remember any of this?"

The words hit me like a slap. Jector alive. Cities in ruins. None of it made sense. I stared at Ladinas, searching for any sign this was all some twisted prank. There was nothing but grim determination in his gaze. What choice could I have *possibly* made that led to *this* outcome?

"Mel and Muggs?"

Ladinas clenched his fists. "Murdered. By Jector. This must be a spell. What did you cast? I know you've been experimenting with memory spells, something to remove the pain. I told you, Mercy—"

"It was nothing like that." I shook my head. "I'll be fine. Demeter was right. I hit my head training, but it's all coming back."

Panic morphed into anger, hot and acidic in my veins. Mel and Muggs were gone. Killed by the bastard I'd already destroyed once.

"Where the hell is Alice?" I demanded. She was the last person I wanted to see, apart from the dickwad staring straight at me. Still, I had to ask. If I was going to figure out what that damn djinn did, Alice was a part of it.

Ladinas whipped around, turning his back to me, his hands shaking at his sides. "Demeter's rounding up our fighters now. We have to end this once and for all. Are you with us or not? We can't do this if you're not at a hundred percent."

I gritted my teeth against the surge of rage and grief. Mel. Muggs. They didn't deserve to die like this.

"I'm with you," I said, fists clenching at my sides. "Let's go kill this son of a bitch."

For the first time, a grim smile touched Ladinas's mouth. He nodded at me and hurried back down the hall.

I followed Ladinas down to the armory, my mind racing. None of this made sense. Mel and Muggs were dead, but Demeter was alive and well. Jector was suddenly a vampire emperor. And Alice...

My stomach twisted as I thought of her. Whatever the djinn had done, it was clear he'd messed with my past. I just didn't know how deep the manipulation went. Was this permanent? I still had two wishes left, right? Was this another "preview" of what might be, or had that damn djinn taken it upon himself to change something without my consent?

Consent matters, dick face! I'd make sure he got the message *loud and clear* the next time I saw him.

He'd be back. Eventually. He still owed me *at least* two wishes. And if I could figure out what *exactly* he changed in my past that led to this warped reality, I'd use one of them to fix it.

I had to admit, though, if that was what the djinn did, it was clever. He was trying to convince me to use all three wishes. He said he *needed* me to do it or he'd go "boom." Whatever that meant. What better way to force me to make at least two out of the three wishes than to grant one by sorting out something deep in the recesses of my subconscious mind that he knew would screw up everything and leave me with no choice but to wish he fix it.

In the armory, Demeter tossed me a black duster. I caught it and shrugged it on, the weight of several devices I didn't know how to use settling on my shoulders. I didn't question it. He and Ladinas already thought I was losing my marbles. I'd make do.

"We'll find him just north of here," Demeter said. "Jector's forces have already started fortifying the area, but if we move quickly, we can still flank them before he moves in on our location."

I nodded, slipping a Glock and a few magazines loaded with wood-tipped bullets into my jacket. I also grabbed a few extra stakes for good measure. "Here's to hoping that Jector is craving a good stake. Medium rare."

"There's the jokes," Ladinas chuckled. "Try not to hit your head a second time. Our chances of beating Jector are slim as it is."

My fists tightened around two stakes. I'd already killed the bastard once. This time, I'd make sure he stayed dead.

We piled into a few SUVs and sped off into the night, the three of us silent. My mind raced as fast as the tires on the road, trying to piece together what choice the djinn must've altered. I had to figure it out if I had any chance of fixing this shit show. Provided the djinn didn't just tell me what he changed. But I wasn't banking on that.

Somehow, Alice was at the center of it all. And when this was over, the djinn and I were going to have words.

Demeter sat beside me in the back. I wasn't sure if I should ask him any more questions, but figured I should. If I could fix this, it wouldn't matter much how crazy he thought I was. Then again, the thought struck me. If I *fixed* this, I might save Mel and Muggs, but I'd kill Demeter—again.

Ugh.

"Do you know what happened to Alice?" I asked, keeping my voice down lest Ladinas pick up on the conversation. He could hear me, most likely, if he was trying to. But I was hoping the rumble of the engine would keep him distracted enough that he wouldn't notice.

"How *don't* you know?" Demeter shook his head. "Mercy, you better get it together."

"I'm sorry. Things are coming back. I'm good for the fight, I swear. I just need a little help patching up my memories."

Demeter nodded. "It's not your fault, you know. He doesn't blame you."

"Blame me for what?" I asked.

"You thought she was an angel, some agent of the Order of the Morning Dawn. You thought about trying to recruit her but ultimately decided she was too great a liability."

I snorted. "I *killed* her?"

Demeter nodded. "You remember, right?"

I winced. "I think so."

I didn't remember. I wasn't sure *how* I'd killed her, but I clearly found a way. At least now I knew what had happened. That was the choice that was changed. If I'd gone after Alice and killed her somehow *before* she'd struck Muggs with celestial magic, before he helped change Goliath's spirit and sent the hellhound to imprint on *me,* then we wouldn't stop Jector.

Killing Alice... ended the world.

Fuck me. Didn't see *that* coming. But that's exactly why I told the djinn I didn't want to change a damn thing. You never know what dominoes are going to fall. And this time, it seemed, attacking that angel rather than looking for a way to use her to help kill Jector was my fatal mistake.

Alice was gone, sure. I'd secretly wondered how things might be different if she'd never come back to Rhode Island. But I didn't want her *dead.* And now the world was paying the price.

I cleared my throat. "Demeter. Can I ask you something?"

Demeter nodded and smiled at me. I'd forgotten how kind he was. For a vampire. "Anything."

"If you had to die to save other people's lives, would you do it?"

Demeter tilted his head. "You're not thinking about sacrificing yourself to stop Jector, are you?"

I shook my head. "Just answer the question."

Demeter pressed his lips together. "How could I save *my* life and continue to live with myself if I knew someone else had to pay the price?"

"So if you could give your life to bring back Alice, Muggs, and Mel. You'd do it?"

Demeter pinched his chin. "Sure. But it doesn't work that way, Mercy. If you let Jector kill you, it won't bring them back in your place."

I sighed. "I know. That wasn't what I was thinking. But it helped to hear you say it."

Little did he know I was asking *him* what he'd do. Because I knew if I asked the djinn—whenever I saw him next—to fix this situation, he'd die instead. I don't think if Demeter answered differently, I wouldn't make the djinn reset reality. But at least, this way, I could feel a little *less* guilty about it.

Because the longer I had to deal with this new reality, the more I was realizing it was no dream, no vision cast by the Ghost of Christmas Present. The djinn changed something that had screwed over the world—and I had to set it right.

Until then. I had to survive. Long enough to use my next wish, at least.

Chapter 8

THE RUINED CITY STRETCHED endlessly outside the SUV's tinted windows, a post-apocalyptic wasteland of charred rubble and empty streets. None of the usual city traffic. Not a single soul in sight.

My knuckles turned white around my wand. "Where the hell is that bastard hiding?"

"About half a mile ahead. Abandoned mansion." Demeter didn't look up from his laptop, fingers flying over the keys. The tapping grated on my nerves.

"You sure your intel is solid? Place looks deserted."

"Best I can sort out," Demeter added. "The more old human infrastructure fails, the harder it is to get information on this damn thing. It's a wonder I can still connect to the internet via satellite. I'm sure we'll lose that sooner or later."

I shook my head. "Unbelievable."

Demeter's gaze flicked to Ladinas. "Take a left up ahead. Look for an over-grown drive about a quarter mile down the road on your right."

Ladinas nodded curtly, eyes fixed on the road. His hands tightened around the steering wheel.

I peered out the window again at the ruins of familiar shops and restaurants, now just piles of rubble and ash. "Christ, it's the freaking apocalypse out here."

"Just about." Demeter's tone was grim. "But we're still kicking, right?"

I forced a weak chuckle. "Yeah, sure. Kicking and screaming."

If it hadn't been for that stupid djinn and his meddling, Demeter would still be dead. Pushing up daisies, not kicking anything. Didn't have the heart to tell him that, though.

Not like he'd understand.

The streets were lined with wreckage and destruction, buildings collapsed and cars overturned. The smoke and ash in the air made it difficult to see, but I could make out flashes of fire and glimpses of movement. It was like a scene from a war movie, except we were right in the middle of it.

My mind was a maze of tangled thoughts, scattered like the debris that littered the surrounding landscape.

BANG!

The sound was so loud, so offensive, that I didn't know how to react. With the sound came a violent force that ripped through the SUV, sending us into a chaotic spiral. The world outside became a blur of destruction and chaos, the ringing in my ears drowning out everything.

The impact of the collision sent a shockwave through my body, my seatbelt digging into my chest and my head snapping back. As the SUV rolled over and over, I could feel the pressure on my body constantly shifting and changing. My hands fumbled around for something to hold on to, anything to brace myself against the chaos.

All I had was my wand in one hand and a fist full of seatbelt in the other. I didn't always wear a seatbelt. Most vampires don't. But with Ladinas driving, it was usually a good idea. Just to prevent too much jostling. He had a bad habit of barely braking at all before turning. I was glad I had it on.

When the SUV finally skidded to a stop on its side, I shook off the daze and fumbled for the door handle, kicking the door open. I half-crawled, half-tumbled out, covered in cuts and bruises.

The others spilled out after me. "Ambush!" Ladinas growled, clutching a nasty gash on his forehead.

I spat a gob of blood and peered into the gloom. A dark shape bounded away into the ruins, too fast to make out. "Jector," I hissed. That bastard had known we were coming and was waiting for us.

Ladinas helped Demeter to his feet, laptop in pieces. "We need to go. Now."

I shook my head and gripped my wand tighter, knuckles protesting. "No. That son of a bitch isn't getting away this time."

"We're outmatched," Ladinas argued. "We need to regroup."

"I don't care." I strode toward the ruins, anger burning hot in my veins. "I'm going to kill that bastard if it's the last thing I do."

After all, I'd killed him once. What if I never saw the djinn again? This might be the only chance I had to stop Jector. The world might stay mired in this apocalyptic nightmare forever if I didn't end this here and now.

Ladinas caught up to me, eyes blazing. "I won't let you face him alone."

Demeter hobbled after us. "We're a team. We stand together."

I wanted to argue, to order them away to safety. But they were right. We *were* a team. Once upon a time. In this world, though, we still were. I nodded, throat tight, and we ventured into the ruins together.

The city was eerily silent. Not even the chirp of crickets broke the quiet. My senses strained for any sign of Jector, but it was like he'd vanished into thin air.

"There," Demeter whispered, pointing. A flicker of movement in an old factory ahead.

We crept forward, wands and stakes at the ready. The factory was cavernous, shadows lurking in every corner. Metal walkways crisscrossed overhead, cobwebs clinging to the rails.

"Careful," Ladinas warned. "That son of a bitch already ambushed us once. I have no doubt that's his plan *again.*"

I shrugged. "Not very original. We'll deal with him. Killed him once. I'll kill him again."

Demeter tilted his head. "Say what?"

I grunted. "I mean, Nico killed him once. It falls to me to do it again. This bastard used to be Jack the Ripper, and as is usually the case, the sequel is worse than the original. Time to put him out of his goddamn misery."

We moved through the wreckage. Jector was there, somewhere, lurking and waiting. It was a wonder he wasn't flanked by an army of bloodsuckers. But killing me? Well, that was personal. A *family* affair. At least he had the gonads to face us himself.

A dark shape detached from the shadows and hurled itself at us. Ladinas fired his crossbow, but Jector dodged the bolt easily. He slammed into Ladinas, sending him flying into a stack of crates. They collapsed with a crash.

"Ladinas!" I shouted. Rage boiled up inside me and I extended my wand and shouted. *"Enerva! Incendia! Anima Ardentis!"*

The last spell did nothing. Of course not. In this reality, I hadn't learned it yet. Didn't matter. Jector was moving too damn fast. He dodged every spell I lobbed his way.

Jector bared his fangs in a snarling grin and launched himself at me. I braced myself, ready to meet his attack—

Only to have Demeter fling himself between us. Jector's fist plunged through Demeter's chest, crushing flesh and muscle.

Demeter gasped, eyes wide with shock and pain. Then his knees buckled, and he collapsed.

"No!" I screamed. I flung myself at Jector, wooden stake in hand. I went for his heart, but the bastard was fast. Just as fast as I remembered. I wasn't a match for him back then, not alone, and I wasn't now, either. But I had to try.

Jector slammed into me and I tumbled to the ground, wand skittering away. He loomed over me, eyes glowing with triumph. "You've lost, sister. Now pledge your loyalty to me and I'll spare your existence. Do it for daddy. He'd want to see us working together."

I grunted. "You know what, you son of a bitch? Nico never even talked about you. All the years we were together. He was so goddamn ashamed of you he couldn't even bring himself to mention your name!"

Jector's face contorted into a mix of fury and disgust as he grabbed my neck and lifted me, squeezing until black spots danced in my vision. As darkness crept in at the edges, I glimpsed Ladinas struggling to rise, blood dripping down his face, and Demeter lying motionless on the ground.

A sharp pain struck my chest. The bastard staked me. Before I could even curse at the bastard, my vision went dark.

Great, I thought. *Just what I wanted. Another trip to vampire fucking hell!*

And that's where I was. Not like there was a lot of scenery in vampire hell to recognize the place. It was the *lack* of anything at all—aside from a few screeching wraiths overhead—that gave it away.

I scrambled back as Goliath emerged from the shadows, hellfire glowing in his eyes. In my reality, he was loyal. He imprinted on me but with little more than a lick. He protected me. This wasn't the same Goliath.

"Easy boy," I said softly. Goliath growled, the sound vibrating against my chest. No luck. This mutt wasn't here to play fetch.

I dove to the side as Goliath lunged, his jaws snapping shut where I'd just been. Rolling to my feet, I sprinted into the darkness. Goliath bounded after me, his pounding footsteps shaking the ground.

"Djinn!" I screamed. "Get me the fuck out of here!" No response. The bastard djinn had gotten me into this mess, but he wasn't coming to pull me out.

Goliath slammed into my back, his weight crushing me to the ground. I struggled beneath him, claws and teeth snapping inches from my face. Hot, fetid breath washed over me as Goliath strained against my trembling arms. It was all that prevented him from ripping out my throat.

Then a flash of light.

With a gasp, I jerked awake.

What a relief. Good timing, but I knew I wasn't waking up in paradise. Talk about out of the fire and into the frying pan.

No longer in hell, I found myself chained in a stone chamber, moonlight filtering through a high window. My limbs were bound by silver, preventing me from moving.

A robed figure stood over me, pale hands tracing the length of my body. Cold, sharp nails left stinging trails along my skin. Icy fear flooded my veins. Whoever this was, they had me at a disadvantage. Never a good position for a vampire to be in.

"Who the fuck are you?" I demanded, trying to sound braver than I felt.

The figure pulled back her hood, revealing a cascade of pink hair and facial piercings. My heart sank. Of course. The one person who hated me enough to go through all this trouble.

"Jinx," I said flatly.

She smiled, showing pointed fangs. "Hello, Mercy. I'm surprised you know who I am."

There was no sense explaining it. Like she'd believe I'd met her in another reality. My first thought? This was bad. Very bad. Jinx might look like a punk kid, but she was older and stronger than she appeared. If she was working with Jector, I was well and truly screwed. My second thought? Now that she had me in a vulnerable position, it might incline her to tell me a little about herself. Villain types like her can't resist the chance to talk about themselves. To boast a little. Comes with the territory.

If I ever got out of this mess and back to my world, I could use whatever I learned now.

I licked my lips, stalling as I tried to figure a way out of this mess. "I've heard of you. Nice to finally meet."

Jinx laughed. "No it isn't. But I appreciate you saying so."

"Any time," I grunted. "Now, how about you cut me loose? It's girls' night! We can go out on the town, you and me. What do you say?"

Jinx traced a nail down my cheek, the sensation like a razor blade. "Maybe I'll do that, if you cooperate. Jector wants you to join us. Says a powerful witch would be useful to have around. Not to mention, you're his sister. You could be a valuable ally."

I rolled my eyes. Of course, he wanted me to *join* him. Just like before. "And if I don't join?"

"Then I get to play with you." Her eyes gleamed with malicious glee. "Rumor has it you're a real bitch to kill. Many people have tried—vampire and human alike. I really hope you don't disappoint. I could use a challenge."

I forced a sneer. "Good luck with that."

Jinx laughed, the sound echoing oddly in the stone chamber. "We have all the time in the world, Mercy. You'll find my Jector is a patient lord."

I cocked an eyebrow. "*Your* Jector?"

Jinx's eyes flashed. "Always has been. Always will be." She traced a nail down my cheek again, slowly, deliberately. "We shared many nights together, Jector and I. Sowed chaos through the streets of London, painted them red under cover of darkness. We were... inseparable."

Her gaze grew distant, nostalgic. I frowned, doing the math in my head. Jector was Jack the Ripper. If Jector had turned Jinx a century and a half ago, and she'd been with him through those early nights in London...

"He's your sire?" I asked, realization dawning.

Jinx's eyes refocused on me, hard and cold. "And my lover. After Nico killed him... can you imagine being killed by your *own* sire? Don't answer that. You were Nico's favorite pet. Whatever. The point is, after that, I had no choice but to hide. I'm tough, but I couldn't stand up to Nico. But when my sweet Jector escaped hell, when his wraith siphoned enough blood to forge a new body, I sensed his resurrection and came to find him. We have a second chance, Jector and I. And we've nearly conquered the entire world! Just a few rogue nations left, and a few places stuck in perpetual sunlight this time of the year. But we'll get there, eventually."

I snorted. "You're insane. My brother is a psychopath, and you're just as bad!"

Jinx backhanded me, the force of the blow nearly breaking my jaw. Blood filled my mouth as I spit a tooth onto the stone floor. It would grow back. Eventually.

"Watch your tongue," she hissed, "or I'll rip it from your mouth."

I glared up at her, vision swimming. Best I resist the urge to speak my mind. I had to survive this. Just long enough to find that damn djinn again. And now I knew who I was dealing with.

It all made sense. Too much sense. In my timeline, Jinx was pissed that I'd killed Jector. She'd found him, just as she had in this reality. But after I killed him, she went into hiding *again*. She waited, bided her time, until she found a chance for revenge. Abandoned vampire younglings looking for an older, stronger vampire to guide them? That was the opportunity she was looking for.

She tried to kill me once. That's why she went straight after me and let the others distract my team. For Jinx, this was personal. I knew we'd fight again. If not in this reality, then in mine. Once I got home. If I got home. Either way, Jinx and I would throw down.

But in *this* reality? She didn't hold a grudge against me. Not yet. Perhaps I could use that to my advantage. If I played along, if I let her and Jector believe I was considering joining them, maybe I'd exist long enough to find the djinn.

Not the best move. Demeter was dead. Again. Ladinas was out there somewhere. But none of that would matter if I found the djinn. The big question was why hadn't he shown himself since he sent me here? What the hell was he waiting for?

And there was still more to learn about Jinx. I knew her motive now. But what of all the things that youngling said about her? Did she really drink *vampire* blood? Was she really a vampire, or was she something else? Had she become what she is before, or after I killed Jector? All questions I had to learn the answers to. All things I could only find out if I sucked it up—terrible pun for a vampire, I know—and pretended to join their side.

Not like I could just up and agree. They wouldn't believe me if I turned to their side too easily. I'd have to resist a little. Play along, but give them enough hope that I was considering their proposal that they didn't kill me outright. It was a balancing act, but one way or another, I had to see it through.

This world was already fucked. But if I got back to my world, well, I still had a chance to save it from whatever Jinx was planning.

I doubted this was what the djinn intended. But I finally had a way to learn what I could about Jinx. If I made it back to my reality, I'd be able to use it. If not, well, it would come in handy here, too. I had to know who I was dealing with. A fortuitous coincidence, perhaps, that I encountered Jinx *here* and now. Merry Christmas to me. Not what I asked for, but maybe, just maybe, it was what I needed.

Chapter 9

I DIDN'T ALWAYS KNOW the etymology of brown nosing. Not until a few years ago when I put two and two together. I knew it was like ass kissing. I just didn't realize the connection between the two phrases. That you get a little brown on your nose when you have your lips buried in someone's backside. Gross, right? Who even comes up with phrases like that? And why is ass kissing, or brown nosing, supposed to earn someone's favor?

It's not like if you put your lips on my ass or your nose in my anus, I'll suddenly think more highly of you. Quite the opposite, in fact. Language is weird. Just like people who literally kiss butts.

I say all that to make it clear than when I say I had to do a lot of brown nosing in the weeks that followed, I'm speaking *metaphorically*.

I didn't see Jector much. He didn't have time to pay me many visits. Come to find out, world domination and inaugurating the apocalypse really fills your night planner.

Because vampires don't have day planners—for obvious reasons. Most days involve a lot of ass sitting and television. Sometimes, we read books. Things like that. But Jector was occupied even when the sun was up. I suspected he'd left town, was rallying vampires who'd bought what he was selling, and taking over small nations.

That left me with Jinx. I wasn't sure how much time had passed. It was weeks or months. Less than a year. Long enough, though, I was starting to fear that I'd never see the djinn again.

If I didn't see him, I'd never see Mel or Muggs, either. In this world, they were dead.

Thanks to Jector. The nerve for him to think I'd ever bend my knee to his rule *after he killed my progenies.* Jector's ego was as big as his aquiline nose. It obstructed his eyes to the point he was blind to what should have been obvious. I'd *never* be on his side. Not really.

But I'd play along as long as I had to. What other choice did I have? This world was shit already. My only real hope was that if I ever got back to my reality, I'd come back with gifts. Just in time for the holidays. Presents, in the form of knowledge about Jinx, that we could use to take her down.

Ho, ho, ho. That's what I'd say when I got home. No, not to wish anyone a Merry Christmas. That's just what I'd call Alice when I saw her again.

But damn it if I didn't even miss her, the bible-thumping, man-stealing bitch and my former nemesis. She was dead in this world—and as much as I hated to admit it, the world was a better place with Alice in it. Even if it was a slightly more annoying and infuriating place. It was better, nonetheless.

Jinx didn't trust me with my wand. But they didn't keep me in silver anymore, so there was that. And from time to time, she brought me a handsome fellow for a bite. Blood tasted just as great in every reality. Even if my company was ass.

But I learned a few things. Jinx never drank from the humans she brought. Was it true? Did she *really* drink vampire blood? If so, why? What had happened to her that changed her essential dietary requirements?

I also learned that Jinx wasn't her real name. I know. Shocker of the century. Jector called her Juliet. Coughs and gags.

But she didn't change her name because she didn't like it, or because she didn't really fit the Shakespearean trope of a desirable but unattainable woman. She assumed the "Jinx" persona to hide away for fear that someone would recognize her as the onetime companion of Jack the Ripper.

That also explained the pink hair and piercings.

All fascinating shit. It still didn't get to the core of what I needed to learn. What *was* she? If Jinx was still a vampire, but fed solely on other vampires, what had changed? Why didn't she bite me once? Probably because I was Jector's sister, he probably forbade it. They were trying to earn my trust so they could use my gifts to their advantage. But when it came to the crucial information I needed if I was ever going to defeat her—in this reality or mine—Jinx remained a mystery.

Jinx stormed into my cell, pink hair swaying and combat boots thumping. Her piercing scowl betrayed an annoyance I hadn't seen since we first met.

I leaned against the wall, feigning nonchalance. "Trouble in paradise?"

She growled, clenching her fists. "That bastard's too busy for me again. After years of waiting, thinking he was gone forever, he finally returns just to ignore me."

I shrugged, suppressing a smirk. "Can't say I'm surprised. You really think a power-hungry megalomaniac like Jector has room in his undead heart for anything but world domination?"

"You shut your mouth!" She lunged at me, pinning me to the wall. Her fangs glinted as she hissed in my face, rancid breath assaulting my senses. "You know nothing about our love!"

I snorted. "Please. The only thing Jector loves is chaos and corpses."

She slammed me into the wall, cracking the stone. My skull reverberated with the impact as I struggled against her grip.

Finally, I gasped, "Alright, alright. I'll stop."

She released me with a snarl, chest heaving. I rubbed the back of my head, glaring at her.

After a long moment, she sighed, features softening. "I'm sorry. It's just... we had plans. A future together, you know?" She slumped against the opposite wall. "How did it come to this?"

I hesitated, then sat beside her. "Jector was always cruel, Jinx. You just didn't want to see it." I sighed, memories flickering through my mind. "Love makes fools of us all."

She glanced at me, eyes glimmering. "Even you?"

I stiffened, looking away. Some wounds cut too deep. "Especially me."

Jinx rested her head on my shoulder. A fragile moment of intimacy between sworn enemies.

"You're the only one who understands," she whispered.

I tensed but didn't pull away. A *moment* of vulnerability. If I wasn't her prisoner, I might have even felt bad about taking advantage of her in that moment. But I needed answers.

I cleared my throat. "You never told me how you two met."

She smiled, gaze distant. "It was a dark and stormy night." She chuckled at the cliche. "I was working the streets, desperate to make enough coin for a hot meal and a bed at the inn. The rain was pouring down in icy sheets, chasing away even the most dedicated of customers."

She shivered, wrapping her arms around herself. "And then I saw him. Tall, pale, otherworldly. Like a prince from a fairytale. I called out to him, offered a discount, a package deal on a suck and a fuck on account of the weather, but he just... looked at me. His eyes were crimson, as you know. They reflected the glare of the street lamps."

"He grabbed me then, fingers like steel around my arm. I screamed, but no one came. The streets were deserted." Her voice dropped to a whisper. "He sank his teeth into my neck. The pain was... exquisite. I'd never felt so alive as in that moment, balanced between life and death, agony and ecstasy."

A blush stained her cheeks as she glanced at me. "And then I woke up. The hunger was unbearable, a gnawing pit inside me that nothing could satisfy. All I could think about was finding him again."

"You revived? Someone healed you and completed your turn?"

Jinx nodded. "Not sure who or how. It remains a mystery to me still to this day. Not even Jector knew who did it."

I shook my head. "A witch, perhaps."

"Or it was fate. Divine chance. It's not unheard of. Maybe one in a thousand vampire victims will turn without some kind of medical or magical intervention. But whatever the case, when I woke, I needed him. I was his, and he was mine."

I swallowed the urge to vomit. I mean, what kind of screwed up love story was this? But Jinx clearly believed in it. "So you tracked him down? You used your connection to him as your progeny to draw you to him?"

She smiled softly. "It took weeks. I didn't know how to do any of that. Instead, I followed the trail of corpses left in his wake. I smelled the blood and came running, but he was always gone before I arrived. I finished his leftovers. But finally, I tracked him down to a dilapidated townhouse, feasting on the remains of his latest victim." Her eyes glowed with remembered delight. "Our eyes met across the bloody ruin of that room, and I knew we were meant to be."

I grimaced. "How sweet."

Jinx glared at me. "You don't understand. What we have, it transcends petty romance. We are eternal, bound together by blood and death for as long as we both shall live." Her eyes flashed silver. "Which will be forever. Especially now that he's back. Not even the true vampire death could keep us apart!"

A chill ran down my spine at the fanatic gleam in her eyes. There's nothing quite so *dangerous* as blind love. If you could call it that. It was more like an obsession and infatuation, a serious case of Stockholm syndrome. Though, with vampires and their progenies, it was more common than you'd think.

I schooled my expression into one of rapt interest. "Fascinating. But you still haven't told me why you don't drink human blood."

Jinx looked away, a hint of color in her pale cheeks. "Jector and I used to feed together. Then, over time, he tempted me to feed secondhand, to allow him to feed first, then I'd feed from his veins. It was intoxicating!"

I snorted. "I bet. You aren't the first vampire to experience that."

She nodded. "I've developed a taste for secondhand blood. The blood of other vampires, filled with the power and vitality of their recent kills. It's like nothing you could imagine. I just can't stomach human blood straight from the source anymore." Her eyes gleamed. "The strength, the energy thrumming in my veins. For a few moments, I can match even the most ancient ones in power."

"I see." An idea was forming in my mind, dangerous but with the potential for escape. I licked my lips and gazed at Jinx through half-lidded eyes. "Have you ever considered branching out on your own? You're clearly not getting what you need from Jector anymore."

Jinx bristled. "How dare you! Jector is my sire, my mate, the love of my eternal life. I will never leave him."

"I don't mean leave him," I said hastily. "Just... supplement your diet. You said it yourself, other vampires' blood gives you strength and power. Don't you want more of that? Maybe if you were stronger in his absence, if you did something he'd notice that he *had* to notice, he'd stick around a little more."

If I could lure her, I knew a spell. It wasn't one I'd often practiced, but I'd learned it from Hailey, who dabbled more in blood witchery than I was keen to. If my blood was *in* her, I could use it to control her, to manipulate her, even for just a time. I didn't have my wand, but if I focused my mind enough, if I reached out from blood to blood, my blood within my flesh to that in hers, I could influence her in ways she might not even realize.

I'd never tried the spell myself, but I knew the mechanics of it. It was the best chance I had given my predicament. And Jinx had given me an opportunity.

She hesitated, gaze turning inward as she considered it. I pressed my advantage. "You could overpower me easily, force me to give you my blood. But how much more satisfying would it be if I gave it willingly?" I tilted my head to the side in offering, exposing the vulnerable curve of my neck.

Jinx stared at me, eyes like flames fixed on my flesh. "I can't. He forbids it!"

"Because I'm his sister?" I tilted my head. "I think Jector only fears that if you bite me against my will it will poison his attempt to win me over to his cause. But I'm not objecting. You *have* my consent, Juliet."

Jinx shook her head, but I could see the hunger burning in her gaze. "No. It's not right."

I leaned forward, reaching out to brush her cheek with my fingertips. She didn't pull away. "You deserve this, Juliet. You deserve to take what you want for once, instead of always waiting for Jector's permission."

Her breath hitched at my touch, eyes fluttering half-closed. I felt the connection between us strengthen, like a thread pulled taut from my mind to hers. She wanted this. She wanted to feed from me, to take my strength into herself. I could feel that desire like an ache.

"Jector doesn't control you," I whispered. "You're so much more than just his consort, Juliet. You have your own desires, your own needs. It's alright to indulge them."

She surged forward, pinning me to the wall behind us as her fangs sank into my neck. A sharp cry escaped me at the pain, but I didn't fight her. I let the connection between us guide her, pouring all the desire and hunger I could muster through that thread into her mind.

The pain lessened quickly, morphing into something like pleasure as she fed in earnest, her own satisfaction and the rush of power from my blood feeding back to me through our connection. I felt some of my strength fading, being drawn into her, but less than I might have expected. The magic didn't require an incantation, just focus. I had to reach beyond the confines of myself, to draw on the power of my own blood, regardless of its vessel—mine or hers.

Juliet moaned against my throat, hands clenching on my arms. I stroked her hair, murmuring encouragement and endearments as she fed. We were bonded now, in a way, and I meant to use that to my advantage. She would be mine, just as I needed her to be.

She drew back finally, licking the wound on my neck to close it as she gazed at me through half-lidded eyes. I could feel the thrum of power in her, my strength added to hers. It was intoxicating in its own way, and I struggled not to get lost in the feedback loop of sensation and emotion between us.

"You see?" she purred, tracing a finger down my cheek. "You're mine now, little witch. And I'll keep you as long as you continue to please me."

I forced a smile, inclining my head in acquiescence. "As you say, my lady." The honorific was bitter on my tongue, but necessary. I couldn't afford to anger her now, not when I was so close.

She laughed, the sound rich and throaty, and pressed closer against me. I endured the unwanted intimacy, hiding my revulsion behind a mask of devotion. I had her now, but I couldn't reveal that just yet. Patience, I counseled myself. The fruits of victory would be all the sweeter for waiting to pluck them.

"You're learning," she purred. "Perhaps Jector was wrong about you after all. Stay clever, little witch, and I'll keep you as my pet."

"As you command," I said softly.

She laughed again and released me, smoothing her hands down the front of my shirt. "Until next time, then." With a wink, she sashayed out of my cell, the door clanging shut behind her.

I sagged back against the wall, pressing a hand to my neck. The wound was already closed, but I could still feel the echo of her fangs in my flesh. Revulsion and anger warred with grim satisfaction in my gut. The trap was set. Now all I needed was the right bait to spring it.

Chapter 10

THE CELL DOOR CREAKED open and a disheveled man stumbled in, collapsing to his knees. His wrists were slashed, blood dripping onto the stone floor.

My fangs throbbed at the scent, a primal hunger awakening in my gut. I hadn't fed in days. Before I could stop myself, I seized the man and sank my teeth into his flesh. The hot, metallic taste of blood flooded my mouth as I drank deeply.

When the last drops were drained, I cast the corpse aside. My veins thrummed with renewed vitality, but a bitter aftertaste lingered. Using humans as cattle went against my moral code.

The door creaked again. Jinx sauntered through, a wicked grin splitting her pale face. Her fiery gaze raked over me and a surge of heat coursed through my body. What the hell was wrong with me? I wasn't into women. Not like that. But since she bit me, with my blood in her system, there was something *different* about both of us. Something we couldn't resist. Animalistic. Primal. Reptilian.

She *wanted* me. I couldn't tell her no.

Jinx pressed me against the wall, her lithe body molded to mine, and nuzzled my neck. A jolt of pleasure shot straight to my core. My breaths came fast and shallow as she trailed kisses up to my ear.

"I've been waiting for this," she purred, nipping at my earlobe. "Fresh off a feed. It'll be even more intense than before!"

Revulsion and desire warred within me. I didn't want this. Did I?

Sharp teeth pierced my skin. Ecstasy and agony blurred as more of my blood flooded her mouth, our life forces merging. It was depraved, obscene, but I craved more.

I clutched at her, fingers tangling in her pink hair. When she pulled back with a gasp, crimson stained her lips. Our gaze locked and understanding passed between us. This was bigger than either of us. We were bound now, connected in a way I never could've imagined.

"Take me to bed," I rasped.

A slow, wicked smile spread across her face. "My pleasure. And yours."

We stumbled through her ostentatious mansion, kissing and clawing at each other's clothes. By the time we tumbled onto her bed, we wore only tattered remnants.

Jinx straddled me, pinning my wrists above my head. The ache between my legs bordered on painful. I needed her, as much as I hated to admit it.

"Beg for it," she purred, rolling her hips against mine.

I gritted my teeth, refusing to give her the satisfaction. She nipped at my throat, each bite harder than the last, and I shuddered with pleasure and pain.

"Please," I gasped. She pulled back, eyebrows raised in challenge, and I growled in frustration. "Dammit, Jinx. Take me!"

Triumph lit her eyes as she leaned down to kiss me, hard and hungry. I kissed her back with equal fervor, desire burning away any thoughts of resistance. Our tongues danced and dueled, tasting of blood and lust.

She exposed her neck to me. "Bite me! Drink of me as I drank of you!"

I didn't protest. My fangs pierced her skin, one more set of piercings to accompany dozens, and her blood filled my waiting mouth. The connection between us swelled even more, to where resisting it was pointless. I didn't want to resist, anyway. I only wanted one thing: more!

She slid down my body, leaving a trail of bites in her wake, before settling between my thighs. A cry escaped my lips as she tasted me for the first time, and I fisted my hands in her hair, torn between pushing her away and pulling her closer.

I was at her mercy now, in more ways than one, and we both knew it.

She lavished attention on my most sensitive flesh until I was writhing and pleading incoherently. Only then did she slide back up my body and position herself at my entrance.

"Look at me," she commanded, eyes glowing crimson with hunger and desire. I obeyed, trapped in her gaze. "You're mine now, Mercy."

She thrust her fingers into me then, hard and deep, and I cried out at the mix of pain and ecstasy. Our blood bond surged between us, amplifying every sensation until I couldn't tell where I ended and she began.

We moved together as if we'd been lovers for centuries rather than mere hours. Every touch, every kiss, every bite was familiar yet new, a contradiction that made no sense and perfect sense all at once.

The coil of pleasure in my core wound tighter and tighter until I thought I might shatter from the intensity. Jinx's movements grew erratic as she neared her peak as well, but she kept her eyes on mine.

"Come for me," she rasped, reaching between us to stroke my throbbing flesh. Her touch sent me tumbling over the edge into an abyss of ecstasy. My vision went white as I came undone around her, crying out her name.

She followed soon after, burying her face against my neck as she found her release. We held each other for long moments, panting harshly, still joined in the most intimate of ways.

A flicker of movement caught my eye, and my gaze landed on the lamp sitting innocently on the nightstand. In that instant, clarity returned in a rush of horror and dismay.

I shoved Jinx off me with a snarl, ignoring her startled protest. "How did you get that lamp?"

She pouted, reaching for me again. "Don't worry about it, baby. It's just an old lamp."

I slapped her hands away and bared my fangs. "Answer the damn question!"

Her eyes narrowed, and for a second I glimpsed the predator lurking beneath her punk rock exterior. Then she sighed and ran a hand through her pink hair. "I've had it for a while. Before you, even."

"That's impossible," I spat. "How could you possibly know about that lamp? Or anything about me, for that matter?"

A sly smile curved her lips as she traced a finger down my chest. "You really haven't figured it out yet? This is my wish, Mercy. The world I've always wanted, crafted from a single wish to give you the power to make it happen."

I stared at her, stunned speechless. She couldn't possibly know—but she did. She knew everything.

Jinx brushed her knuckles over my cheek, her touch gentle and almost reverent. "The djinn showed me thousands of possibilities and the choices that could lead to each one. In only one did I find what I thought I wanted. Jector back with me!

You were the only one whose choices could change to make it so." Her eyes shone with fervent belief. "You were the key to my heart's desire, so I gave you the rest of my wishes. The djinn insisted you wouldn't disappoint, and you didn't! All you had to do was think it once, that you'd wished you'd killed Alice when you had the chance. When we fought at that club, and you fought with Ladinas and Alice after, I knew we could do it. The djinn and I! So I wished him to you. A fleeting thought on your part was all it took for our djinn to act!"

The full scope of her madness and manipulation crashed over me in a wave of horror and fury. This twisted reality, the lives destroyed, all of it resulted from her selfish wish.

Rage ignited in my veins, hot and primal. I bared my fangs again and threw myself at her with a roar.

She darted away, grabbing the lamp off the nightstand and holding it aloft. "Ah ah ah! Not so fast."

I skidded to a stop, trembling with the effort to restrain myself. One wrong move and she might smash the lamp to pieces.

Jinx tilted her head, regarding me with a sly smile. "Going to be a good little vampire for me? We have such fun games left to play."

"There will be no more games," I growled. "Give me the lamp or I swear I'll rip your throat out."

Her eyes narrowed. "You don't mean that. You love me! You want me! And even if you don't, I have what you want now. If I break this lamp, the djinn's power will be released and there won't be any wishes left to set things right." She shook her head, pink hair swaying. "We have something special, you and I. This is better than I ever imagined! You were right before. I deserve better than Jector. I deserve this! I deserve you! And you want it, too. You can't deny it. Give yourself over to what we felt together before. We can kill Jector, both of us, and be together. Two queens, the world at our service!"

Panic and rage warred inside me as she raised the lamp higher, poised to dash it against the wall. I reached out with the blood connection between us and seized control of her limbs through sheer force of will.

"Don't," I whispered. "You have no idea what you're about to unleash. The djinn said if his last wish isn't used, if his power is released unfettered, it could be devastating. It might even destroy the world!"

Jinx struggled against my control, her eyes flashing with fury. "Give yourself to me. We share blood now. Trust me, it cannot be undone now that we've *both* fed from each other! When two vampires feed as we have from one another, the bond is forever. Your blood in me, and mine in you. We will feel what we felt for eternity!"

I shook my head. "Juliet... I..."

"If you reset the world, we might forget each other, but we'll sense the loss! We can't risk that! I know this isn't your ideal world, but at least we know we can be together here. We'll kill your damn brother! We can make this world whatever we want."

"I won't forget you," I said. "We're bound by blood and the lamp's power. That's how it works. Those who hold the lamp, who make the wishes. They don't forget when the djinn changes the past. They remember it all. We won't forget each other. And if you truly don't need Jector, let me set it right. We can enjoy a better world. A place without all of this devastation. We can enjoy it together."

I wasn't sure she bought it. It's hard to be convincing when you don't believe your own words. I was no longer overwhelmed by my passions, nurtured by my blood in her veins. The stark shock of the *truth* snapped me out of it. But if she believed it, for even a second, I could fix this. I could call the djinn and set things right.

And she saw the deceit in her tear-filled eyes. She raised the lamp overhead, preparing to drop it. "For never was a story of more woe. Than this of Juliet and her deceitful, vampire hoe!"

Far be it from me to disregard a bastardized Shakespeare reference. But I didn't have time to appreciate it. I focused my will. Whatever control I had over her because of my blood in her veins. I had to use it. "You won't drop it. You can't drop it. I won't let you!"

Jinx screamed in agony. "You bit me too. This shit goes both ways! If you can control me, I can control you too!"

I resisted the urge to make a going "both ways" joke, which would have been fitting given our recent encounter. Never thought I'd go there but, you know, you live forever, you experiment eventually. It was kind of fun, but it wasn't like I was of sound mind.

Even as I fought against Jinx, I couldn't deny that there was a pull between us, an attraction that I could easily succumb to if I allowed it. But at the moment, the thought of everyone I'd lost—of Mel and Muggs especially, and even goddamn Alice—overpowered the lust elicited by our shared blood.

Jinx wasn't a witch, but with her blood in me and mine in hers, it was hard to tell where my volition began and hers ended. And vice versa. Trying to force Jinx to hold on to that lamp took more concentration than I had.

The lamp fell from her hands. It was like I saw it happen in slow motion. My entire world falling to the ground, everything I ever knew, the people I cared about, broken into a hundred pieces as the lamp struck porcelain tile and shards scattered across the floor.

An inky magic exploded out from what used to be the djinn's lamp. It blasted past us in a breath-stealing surge.

I seized Jinx by the shoulders and shook her, rage boiling inside me. "What have you done?"

The ground started to tremble and buck beneath our feet, tremors rippling out from the shattered lamp.

Jinx just smiled, eyes glazed and pupils blown wide. "We'll always be together now," she purred. "We are vampires. The world can burn, but we will survive. Nothing else matters."

I wanted to slap that serene expression right off her face. "You stupid girl! We're not invincible. And where are we going to find blood if everyone else in this godforsaken reality dies?"

Her smile faltered for a moment, a flash of confusion passing over her features. Then her expression settled back into blissful madness. "The end of everything will be our eternity. You and me, just the way it was always meant to be."

"You're out of your mind," I hissed, shaking her again. Rage and terror warred inside me as the tremors grew stronger, rattling the walls of the mansion. Whatever the djinn's power was, he was right. It was too much. It was destructive.

Jinx wrapped her arms around my neck, pulling me close. "You know you wanted this," she whispered against my lips. "Admit you feel it too. Our souls were made to burn together."

I wrenched myself out of her grasp, stumbling away from her toxic touch. She was wrong—so utterly wrong. We were not meant to be together. I felt the twisted connection between us too, but there was a difference between us. I could be a little crazy. Jinx was a straight-up sociopath. Just like my brother, her *boyfriend*.

Of course, I'd once been with Ramon. Maybe I had a type. Jinx certainly did. What did that say about me?

Jinx's expression hardened at my rejection, lips peeling back from her fangs in a snarl. "After everything I did for you, you ungrateful bitch. I gave you the world, and this is how you repay me?" Her hands curled into claws, and for a moment I thought she might attack me.

Then a tremendous cracking sound rent the air, and a fissure split the floor between us. Jinx shrieked, arms pinwheeling for balance, but the ground gave way beneath her. With a despairing wail, she tumbled into the yawning chasm and vanished from sight.

The earth continued to shake and break apart; the mansion crumbling around me. But I could only stand in place, stunned by how swiftly everything had fallen apart. The end of the world was here, brought on by one girl's madness and misguided obsession.

Because of Jinx, we were all doomed. Even now, I could feel the djinn's power rising, an unstoppable tide of chaos and destruction. She had gotten her wish after all, in a way—we would be together forever, locked in the ruins of this world she had built.

And as the ground opened up to swallow me as well, one last thought echoed in my mind. What a crazy bitch.

Chapter 11

DARKNESS ENGULFED ME AS I plummeted down the endless chasm. The crack in the earth had swallowed me whole when the djinn's magic exploded. I'd been falling for what seemed like an eternity, resigned to my fate, when suddenly I spotted my wand tumbling through the void alongside me. I lurched and grasped desperately, finally securing the wand in my grip. I knew no spell could likely save me now, but having something, anything, was better than the emptiness.

A blinding light burst from the wand, forcing me to shut my eyes. When I was able to open them again, I found myself nestled in a plush bed, soft blankets cocooning me. The sweet scents of gingerbread and holly filled the air, though no source was visible. "What the fuck?" I muttered, sitting up in bewilderment. I looked down to see I was dressed in obnoxious candy cane striped pajamas. "You've got to be kidding me." At least I still had my wand.

I threw off the covers and climbed out of the monstrosity of a bed. Beside it sat a pair of horrendous elf shoes, complete with jingling bells on the tips. "Yeah, that's a hard pass," I scoffed, leaving them where they lay. I moved cautiously across the room and stepped out into a hall decked from floor to ceiling in Christmas decor. Trees, obnoxious trains chugging around the room on tracks, toot, toot, toot. Not to mention the twinkling lights and garland. Cheery holiday music blared from somewhere.

"What in the absolute hell is happening?"

I crept down the hallway, keeping my wand at the ready. The further I went, the more over-the-top the decor became. It was like someone had bought every single Christmas decoration at a hundred Wal-Marts and tossed it all over the place.

As I entered what appeared to be a living area, a fire roared in the hearth. Above it hung an ornate portrait that made me stop dead in my tracks. It was an image of me in a tuxedo, arm in arm with a blood-spattered Jinx in a wedding dress.

"Going to say it again—what the fuck?" I muttered. Before I could study the portrait further, a singsong voice rang out behind me.

"Hey baby. You're home!"

I whirled around to see Jinx sauntering toward me, clad in nothing but a skimpy red bikini with white trim. Her hair was now fire-engine red to match, her piercings gone, sky-high red stilettos on her feet. She looked like some kind of demented Mrs. Claus. I was momentarily speechless. Both because of how bizarre the situation was and because... well, she was hot as hell. Whatever happened, the blood bond we shared was still screwing with my passions.

"Like what you see?" Jinx purred, sidling up close. I felt the pull of her, that intrinsic attraction, but my confusion outweighed any desire.

"What is going on here?" I demanded, taking a step back. "How did we end up... wherever here is?"

Jinx pouted prettily. The way she stuck out that bottom lip. It took everything I had to resist pressing my lips to hers. "Does it matter? We're together now, just like you wished."

I shook my head. "No, this isn't right. The world was being torn apart, remember? People were dying. How did we get from that to this Christmas explosion?"

Jinx shrugged, still attempting to seduce me with her body language. "Come to find out, when you kill a djinn, you become one. And all those overdue wishes get passed down too. Since we shared blood, I could make your wish for you. And this..." She gestured around her. "...is what I created! For us!"

I looked around at the chaotic holiday mess surrounding us. "It looks like Father Christmas ate too many cookies and puked everywhere," I said flatly.

Jinx pretended to pout. "You don't like it? But I made it just for you, baby!"

I pinched the bridge of my nose, exasperated. "Okay, Djinn Jinx. Tell me the truth. What exists outside these tacky walls? Is the real world still intact?"

Jinx winced slightly. "Well, yes and no..."

"What do you mean 'yes and no'?" I demanded. "Is the world out there back to normal or not?"

Jinx bit her lip. "I wanted to give you back the world you loved. And since I...care for you now, I did that. But I'm a djinn. And I love you. Our blood is mingled forever. I can't exist without you."

She stepped closer, trailing one finger down my arm. I suppressed a shiver at her touch.

"So I brought back everything as it was," she continued. "Your friends are alive."

I tilted my head. "Mel and Muggs? Even Alice?"

Jinx smiled widely, proud of herself. "Everything is the way it was before. Just after our little fight in that club."

I exhaled in relief. "Thank the gods. I could kiss you for that."

Jinx grinned slyly. "I wouldn't stop you."

I rolled my eyes. "Down girl. I need to see them first; make sure everyone's okay. After that, well, whatever happens with us... happens."

I headed for the door, but Jinx grabbed my arm. "Yeah, about that. We can't actually leave."

I whirled around. "Why the hell not?"

"Because I'm a djinn now, bound to my lamp. This place." She gestured around us. "We're trapped here until someone finds the lamp and releases me. But don't worry!"

She clasped my hands eagerly. "My powers will grow until I can break free. Until I have to find someone to... release my power... to grant them wishes. But you..." Her face fell. "...you'll have to stay."

I yanked my hands away. "Are you kidding me?"

Jinx smiled hopefully. "It's okay! I can give you anything you want here. Fulfill your every dream!"

I raked a hand through my hair in frustration. Trapped in this Christmas nightmare with Jinx? What fresh hell was this?

I paced the room, my mind racing. This was insane. One minute I was falling through a void, the next I'm the Christmas prisoner of a love-struck vampire-djinn?

You couldn't make this shit up.

"How did this even happen?" I muttered. "The lamp, the wishing...you said we were bound in blood?"

Jinx nodded eagerly, her bells jingling. "When you drank from me to save me. Our blood mixed. So when I became a djinn, I could make a wish for you."

"And this is what you wished for?" I gestured at the tacky Christmas decorations incredulously.

Jinx pouted. "I just wanted to make you happy. Give you everything you ever wanted."

I pinched the bridge of my nose. "Not like this. My friends, my life—it's out there. I don't need all this..." I waved my hand "...stuff."

Jinx looked hurt. I sighed. "Look, I appreciate what you were trying to do. But we need to find a way out of this mess."

Jinx perked up. "We will! Once my power grows, we can do anything. We'll have all the time in the world."

She sauntered over, running her hands up my arms. I shivered at her touch despite myself.

"Just you and me," she purred. "Think of the fun we'll have."

I gently removed her hands. "Let's just take this one day at a time, okay?" I said. "It's gonna be a long eternity if we don't work together to get out of here."

Jinx smiled and squeezed my hand. "As long as we're together."

I shuddered, but at the moment, my only chance was to do exactly what I'd said. I needed Jinx. It wasn't a total lie. I desired her as much as I despised her. I mean, apparently we were married in this makeshift magic lamp of reality. If the portrait was accurate. Not like I remembered ever proposing or saying any vows, or whatever. But the combination of love and loathing was pretty typical of a lot of marriages. We had a lot to figure out if we were going to survive this magical mishap. But for now, I didn't have a choice.

A candy cane vampire and a scantily clad djinn. We either did this together or we'd be stuck in this magical winter wonderland forever.

Chapter 12

Jinx nestled into my side, her cold skin pressing against mine. I sighed, running a hand through her Christmas red hair. There was no point in fighting her here. This was her realm. She was stronger than I was. She had djinn magic now, too. There was only one way forward. We had to make this work. I had to convince her that this life in a lamp was no life at all—that whether it be together, or if we go our separate ways, we needed to find a way back to the land of the living.

"Why don't you want to stay like this forever?" she asked. "No more responsibility, no more fighting... no more Ladinas and Alice."

I laughed a little. "Well, that's a selling point."

"I know, right? Just the two of us."

I took a deep breath. "You know, it's not that simple. We can't hide from the world forever. And as much as I think I desire you right now, we barely know each other. A lot of what we're feeling is the blood."

Jinx frowned. "I don't believe that. What we have is real."

I sighed, brushing my fingers along her cheek. She leaned into my touch, a soft purr vibrating in her throat. It would be so easy to give in, to stay wrapped up in this dream world. But I couldn't ignore the gnawing feeling in my gut, the voice in the back of my mind telling me this was wrong. My feelings were just as fake as this winter wonderland Jinx created inside her lamp. Or were they? Was I feeling something real for this crazy, semi-demented girl? I mean, I understood her better than I cared to admit.

We both had serial killer sociopathic exes. I had Oblivion... and Ramon. She had Jector. We both became vampires in the same era. We'd seen the same changes in the world over the same period of time. While I wasn't a djinn, I was a witch. We both had magic *and* vampirism. And we both secretly wanted someone to love.

I just hadn't ever considered a woman before. It wasn't my thing. Maybe sharing blood manipulated my passions. Or maybe they just opened me up to an experience I hadn't considered in the past. Damn it if I wasn't half-way convinced that what I was feeling was more than what it was. It all happened so fast, though. How could it possibly be *real*? We barely knew each other. Did that even matter? I didn't know what to believe. This whole thing was just so damn messy. There was no way to know for sure.

"Maybe you're right," I said. "But we owe it to ourselves to find out. And we have people depending on us, a city full of vampires and humans alike that need our help."

"Your help, maybe. No one really needs me."

"Not true." I shook my head. "What about all those younglings? Look, I tried to help them. Ladinas and Alice want to eliminate them. But if you could guide them, if you got your shit together and led them the right way..."

"I don't know," Jinx sighed. "I've been hiding for so long, living in secret. Leading a brood of younglings? I mean, the only reason I tried it was because the djinn told me that if I did, I'd get to meet you. If I met you, I could give *him* to you and he'd do what he could to use your past to bring Jector back."

I shook my head. "Motives be damned, right? I mean, I didn't expect shit when I met you. I didn't think when I allowed you to seduce me in that damn prison cell that I'd feel anything at all. I was just trying to get the hell out of there."

Jinx laughed. "I know you were. I didn't expect this either. Even with the bite, with our blood mixed, there's something different. Not like when I fed from other vampires in the past. If that was what this was, I'd feel this way about *every* vampire I bit. I don't, though. I thought I loved Jector, but this is... better."

I took her hands in mine. My thumbs traced her knuckles. "Look, I don't know what the future holds for us. Maybe you're right. I can't deny that I *want* this to be real. None of that matters though if we don't get out of here and give ourselves a chance to find out for sure."

Jinx was silent. I could see the indecision in her eyes, torn between what she wanted and what was right.

"I don't want to lose you," she whispered. "Say we try to get out of here. When I fed from you my feelings for Jector went away. What if we feed again and our feelings disappear?"

I squeezed her hand. "If this is meant to be, if we're truly destined for each other, if this is more than the blood, then the feelings will last. You deserve something real. We both do. If that's us together, so be it. But if this is genuine love, we have to believe it can survive real life."

Jinx took a deep breath. "I don't know. It already *feels* real to me! I'm fine with that. I don't need to know if this is anything else."

"I understand," I said. "I'm honestly not much more experienced in matters of genuine love than you are. But I've been through enough to know that I'm not going to settle for something if it's less than real."

"What if the blood bond never fades?" Jinx asked. "It might not, you know. Maybe my feelings for you replaced my feelings for Jector precisely because we're meant to be! Think about it!"

"If that's the case, we'll stay together." It wasn't a lie. If I found a way to break this blood bond and I still desired Jinx, how could I deny it? But I also would not give in to these passions—more than I already had—just to entertain an illusion, a fantasy.

She stared at our joined hands, pale flesh intertwined, and let out a shuddering breath. "You promise?"

"I promise." I leaned in, pressing my lips to her cheek. It was the most I could allow myself without giving myself over to desire. But Jinx tilted her head and let her lips graze mine. So soft. Delicious. I allowed a single kiss.

When we broke apart, Jinx nodded. "Okay. I trust you. Do what you need to do."

I took a deep breath to steady myself. The lingering taste of Jinx's lips made it difficult to focus, but I had to try. There were people out there depending on me - young, reckless vampires who needed guidance and purpose. I couldn't abandon them for a fantasy world, no matter how sweet.

"Let's think this through," I said, pacing the room. "You're a djinn, which means you have power over reality here in this lamp. Can you... I don't know... weaken the blood bond between us?"

Jinx wrinkled her brow. "I don't think so. My abilities don't really work that way. At least not yet. A djinn's power grows over *time*. Our blood bond existed before we came here. All I can really change here is what we see."

I bit my lip. "Illusions, then."

"Not really," Jinx said. "This isn't an illusion. It's more like a small, different, but still viable plane of limited existence. What I make here is real. It's just bound to this little lamp world."

I pinched my chin. "Alright. So we can't weaken your magic, or the magic that holds us here, but what if we could do the opposite? What if we could make your power stronger?"

"How do we do that?" Jinx asked.

"We feed. More blood. It doesn't just make us move faster or give us more physical strength. I think if we do it right, it'll give us more power. If my magic grows, and our bond cycles our growing power, you'll get stronger. Strong enough to leave the lamp and find someone who can wish us free."

Jinx cocked her head. "Wish us free? Who could possibly change a past decision that might do that? What change could someone make that would free us while also protecting our feelings?"

"Use the convergence. When you leave the lamp, you can jump between realms. You'll be connected to my power. I think. So long as you keep the lamp with you. You can jump back and forth between worlds. It'll make you skip through time and space. You can find someone, somewhere, at some point in history who can change things."

"Is that wise? I mean, if I go back far enough, it could change literally *every-thing*. I just saved the world for you. I won't destroy it again just to get us out of here."

I took Jinx's hands in mine. "Maybe I'm a fool to do it, but I trust you. Remember how the djinn worked before? He showed us visions. Possibilities. Things we couldn't predict. If you have that power, you'll see things neither of us can possibly imagine. If there's a way. You'll find it."

"But changing the past... there's no way to do that, even in a slight way, without altering important things in the future."

I rested a hand on Juliet's cheek. "But you'll still have me, Juliet. I'm a witch. That means I can channel my power through our blood bond. You don't need to grant anyone a wish. Just look into the vast knowledge you'll have at full strength by examining the past. Find an answer."

"What if there is no answer?" Jinx asked.

"Then we have this," I said with a nod. "We'll make the best of it. But we can't resign ourselves to this little world until we've tried everything."

Chapter 13

Jɪɴx sɴᴀᴘᴘᴇᴅ ʜᴇʀ ғɪɴɢᴇʀs. The djinn magic she had gained—courtesy of killing the previous one by destroying his lamp—was pretty damn impressive. Within the confines of the lamp, she could do just about anything. If I focused, since we were connected, I suspected my abilities were greater in the lamp, too. If only by proxy.

The magic that accompanied Jinx's snap was momentarily blinding.

I blinked.

Then I opened my eyes to a sea of chiseled abs and bare skin. Jinx had conjured up what looked like an army of shirtless male models, all wearing just Santa hats and barely-there briefs.

"Well, someone's been naughty this year," I smirked.

Jinx grinned, her colored hair bouncing as she surveyed her handiwork. "Only the highest quality meats. Kiss the chef?"

I pecked her cheek. Leave it to Jinx to turn a feeding frenzy into a Chippendales show.

We moved through the crowd of conjured men, trailing our fingers along their firm chests and stomachs. I felt that familiar ache in my fangs, begging for freedom. Jinx caught my eye, her own fangs on full display, and giggled.

"This one's my favorite," she said, stopping in front of a mountain of a man wearing nothing but a Santa hat and a strategically placed knit stocking.

I snorted. "Subtle." Still, I couldn't deny he was an impressive specimen. Jinx and I shared a look, then sunk our fangs into either side of his neck. The rich, metallic taste of blood flooded my senses. Power thrummed through my veins with each draw. Judging by Jinx's delighted moans, she felt the same rush.

When we finally pulled back, lips stained red, I turned to Jinx. "How did you do it? How can you create men with souls we can feed from?"

She gave a nonchalant shrug. "Beats me. But in my lamp, I'm basically a goddess of my own realm. I can make whatever I want in here." She snapped her fingers, and "Jingle Bell Rock" started blaring from invisible speakers. Except it was a modified rendition. As the men moved around, I realized they had bells for testicles. And the lyrics of the song sounded mostly the same until the chorus.

Jingle bell, jingle bell, jingle bell cock...

I just shook my head, amazed and entertained at her power. We were trapped, but at least we could enjoy the ride.

Jinx grabbed my hands and pulled me into an impromptu dance among our bare-chested men. I couldn't help but laugh as we spun and gyrated wildly. The heavy beat of the music synced with the heady thrum of blood through my veins.

I drew Jinx in close and sank my fangs into her offered neck. Her blood was just as potent, sweeter than honey, flooding me with even more power. She returned the favor, her bite sending delicious shivers down my spine. We continued like that, feeding from each other, from our conjured men, the magic cycling between us.

With each exchange, I could feel my own magical abilities growing, my witch-craft strengthening. Jinx seemed to sense it too, her red eyes illuminated like cinders.

"I'm almost there," she said, wiping away a trickle of blood from her chin. "I can feel it. I nearly have enough magic now to get out of this blasted lamp."

I took her hands in mine. Conjured blood covered our skin, warm and slick. But I didn't mind. With a snap of her fingers, we'd be squeaky clean.

"You'll have to find someone out there," I told her. "Someone to take your lamp and grant your three wishes. Just choose wisely, Jinx. If you can see their pasts, you need to see it through. What change might result in our freedom?"

She smiled, cupping my cheek. "Have a little faith, babe. I'll save us both."

With that promise lingering between us, we returned to our feast, ready to push her magic to its limits. Freedom awaited, if we dared reach for it. It wasn't the most fool-proof plan I'd ever conjured. Changing people's past decisions, altering their memories, it always had unintended consequences. But if Jinx was careful, she could use her abilities to examine dozens, if not hundreds or thousands or even millions, of possible futures. Statistically speaking, there had to be *something* that would work.

If she gave the lamp to the right person... or vampire... or whatever.

It was the best plan—the only plan—we had. If it *didn't* work? Well, we'd be stuck in that damn lamp for god knows how long.

Still, hope blossomed in my undead heart. We had a chance, however slim.

I drew Jinx in for a soft kiss, savoring the lingering tang of blood on her lips. "I'll be here waiting," I murmured. "Make a wise choice, Jinx. There has to be someone out there whose decisions could save us."

She smirked, trailing one black-painted nail down my throat. "Oh, I'll find some hapless schlep who I can manipulate, who will jump at the opportunity to make his wishes. Worst-case scenario, if he's hot, maybe we can promise him a three-way. What guy would turn *that* down?"

I chuckled. "I don't know. The pope?"

"Nah," Jinx shook her head. "I don't think even he could turn *us* down."

Her grin turned wicked, flashing the points of her fangs. "Have a little faith in me, darling."

Despite the bravado in her words, I sensed Jinx's own apprehension. We were both trapped by our natures, unable to break free alone. But together, perhaps we could find the loophole that would unravel our cages.

I pulled Jinx close once more, savoring the press of her body against mine. No matter what happened when she left this place, I would be here, waiting for her return.

"Come back to me," I whispered fiercely.

She shook her head. "I'll do you better than that. I'll bring *you* to *me*. We're doing this."

Her smile softened, pink eyes meeting my gaze. In them I saw centuries of pain and hope, all the things that bound kindred spirits like us.

I didn't like this. I was usually the one taking all the risks, jumping into the fray, making the careless but necessary choices. I didn't like it when others made choices on my behalf. Maybe that's why I had so many issues with Ladinas lately. But this was different. Maybe it was the blood talking. But I trusted Jinx. "Promise me I'll see you soon."

She pressed one last kiss to my lips. "Always."

Chapter 14

THE MAKESHIFT WORLD WITHIN the lamp enveloped me like a suffocating shroud. Sure, it was festive, and it was practically snowing half-naked men all around me, but without Jinx there it felt cold and depressing. Jinx's voice echoed strangely from beyond its confines. She was out there, somewhere, searching for a way to free us from this cursed prison.

I focused my mind, visualizing the connection between us. This was her lamp, her reality. If I could somehow use our connection to make *this* reality reflect what she was seeing *out there,* then maybe I'd be able to help out. It took a little effort, a lot of focus, but the bond we shared was in our blood. It was strong. It was like tuning a couple of frequencies, the ebb and flow of the wavelengths jarring until they matched in sync. When I tuned her lamp to her sight, the tacky Christmas decorations faded away, replaced by Jinx's vision. A kaleidoscope of images flooded my mind as she flitted from place to place. The city streets. An old warehouse. The pier. She was moving too fast, her thoughts a chaotic jumble.

"Slow down," I said. "Can you hear me?"

Jinx paused for a moment. "Mercy! Yeah, I hear you. I'm just not sure where to start."

I sighed. "Try Muggs first. He knows magic. As one of my progeny, he'll want to help. Just one problem, though."

"What's that?" Jinx asked.

"He's most likely back at the Underground. I can help you get in if you'd like. But the vampires there *will* remember you from our fight in the club. If they see you, it could get nasty."

"Just point me the right way," Jinx said. "Your security systems won't keep me out and no one who I don't want to see me will. I'm a badass djinn, remember?"

I laughed a little. "That's right."

It's harder to give someone directions than you realize when all you can see is what they see. But I knew how to get her close enough to the underground that if she located it, she could probably zap herself in. If "zapping" is the right word for the spells a djinn casts.

I saw Muggs sitting in his parlor, blind eyes blinking the moment she appeared. He must've sensed her magic and entered his spirit-gaze. That was the only way he could see anything at all—by perceiving the magic around him.

"Well, well," he said. "I know who you are. What is this magic within you? We've been wondering about you and your strength."

Jinx tilted her head. "You're not afraid of me? I pop into your room like that and you're just... curious?"

Muggs laughed and folded his hands in his lap. "You don't get to be my age—my recently gained immortality aside—by jumping to conclusions. However, you also don't advance to old age if you're too trusting and reckless. I'll just say I've mastered the *balance* between action and inaction, haste, and naivety."

Jinx sighed. "Look, a lot has happened since the club. I'm not here to fight or cause trouble. Mercy's in trouble."

Muggs raised an eyebrow. "Mercy? What kind of trouble?"

"She's trapped inside a djinn lamp," Jinx explained. "We both got sucked in, but I got out. After I became a djinn myself. I'm trying to free her."

Muggs leaned forward, intrigued. "A djinn lamp? Is this what she purchased when we were out and about the other night?"

"Well, she didn't exactly buy it," Jinx said. "But yes, it's a genuine djinn lamp. We killed the djinn inside, but in doing so I got bound to the lamp in his place. Mercy got trapped with me."

"Hmm," Muggs chuckled. "Sounds like Mercy to rush headlong into a problem like this *alone*. Especially recently."

"Recently?" Jinx asked. I winced a little. Here came the tirade. What Muggs really thought about me. Everything I didn't really want to hear. "Mercy's greatest flaws are also her greatest strengths. She's prone to mothering. She just cares so much about her people—even though she doesn't admit it—that she'd place herself in danger a thousand times before risking any of us. It gets her into trouble from time to time."

"She has a good heart," Jinx said. "Better than mine. But no matter. What's done is done. Can you help?"

Muggs pinched his chin. "Trapped in a djinn lamp. That is quite the predicament. I suppose you're searching for a magical solution? Some way to undo the binding?"

"Yes and no," Jinx said. "I don't know how much you know about djinn, but we don't just grant whatever wishes someone wants. If that was the case, all I'd have to do is ask you to wish her free and, poof, she'd be free. All I can do is look at someone's history and give them the chance to take roads untraveled, to make different choices than they did before."

Muggs' eyes widened. "That's an awfully dangerous skill!"

Jinx nodded. "Tell me about it. But I have to fix things. Mercy thought you might have a few regrets, something that we might change that could fix all this."

Muggs furrowed his brow. "Well, you're free to peruse my mind if you'd like, but you won't find many regrets. Any I have are buried so far in my past that I imagine the consequences in the future would be quite profound given the number of events that might be altered if I were to do things differently."

"Is there anything else you can do? Any strange magic you know about that might work?"

Muggs considered this carefully. "Mercy is like a daughter to me. And a mother." Muggs waved his hand through the air. "Vampire family trees are like phone poles."

"So you'll help?" Jinx asked.

"If I can help free her, I will." He held out his hand. "Let me examine this lamp."

Jinx placed the lamp in his palm delicately. I watched through her eyes as Muggs turned it over, inspecting the intricate patterns on the ceramic. It was the first time I'd seen *this* lamp. I imagined it was made, somehow, when Jinx became a djinn. Forged from her magic, most likely. The djinn before said a lamp wasn't really a prison, more like a totem that bridged the realm of the djinn to earth. Still felt like a prison, though. And was there really one djinn realm, or was each lamp a djinn realm unto itself?

"Be careful," Jinx cautioned. "If you break it, the power it releases could destroy everything. Seen it happen."

Muggs nodded solemnly and closed his eyes, running his fingers along the lamp's surface. I felt a strange tingling sensation, like static electricity passing through my body. The lamp glowed faintly.

"What's happening?" I asked Jinx.

"He's studying the magic," she explained. "Trying to figure out a way to get you out of there."

The glow intensified until it blinded me completely. I shut my eyes, but the light burned through my eyelids. A kaleidoscope of images flashed before me—places and people I didn't recognize. Muggs' memories, centuries of history, passing in seconds. When he connected to the lamp, it was like I was the djinn, exploring the contents of his mind.

When it finally ended, I blinked away the dancing spots in my vision. "Did you see all that?"

Jinx was holding the lamp again. "I saw it."

Muggs cleared his throat. "I'm sorry. This magic is beyond me. But what did you see, exactly?"

"Your history," Jinx said. "You were right. You have no regrets that if changed would lead to the result we're seeking."

"I'm afraid there's nothing else I can do," Muggs said regretfully. "Though perhaps you should consult the one who has been closest to Mercy through every-thing. If Mercy's decisions brought her to this point, Mel also had an influence on many of those decisions. If you can accurately predict the consequences of a minor change at some point in the recent past with little collateral damage, she will give you the best chance at success."

I agreed with Muggs and told Jinx as much. I was a bit surprised Muggs allowed her to leave without following. I mean, I was *inside* her lamp and I doubted Muggs even realized I'd left my room. There was no way to know for sure exactly how much time had passed in the Underground since I was first raptured into the djinn's vision and these events started playing out.

"She's most likely in the security room looking at the feeds, or wandering around the facility with her tablet, doing the same," I told Jinx. "Be careful though, because even if you can't see her, she's probably watching you. If you're visible in the halls, anyway. She'll think you're a threat and rally the team against you. All she'd have to do is sound an alarm."

The vision cast into the lamp-world around me moved rapidly up and down. Jinx had nodded.

Then she moved swiftly through the underground, using her power to hide herself from the cameras. She was basically invisible—which could be a pretty handy trick to master. If I ever got out of this, I'd have to see if I could figure out a cloaking spell of some sort.

We arrived outside the security center. Jinx materialized, and I spotted her reflection on one of Mel's monitors. Her pink hair, piercings, and punk rock get up were back. Being a djinn had its perks. She could alter her appearance on a whim, it seemed. Before Mel could react, Jinx placed a hand on her shoulder.

"Don't be alarmed, I'm here to help Mercy," she said.

Mel jumped up, reaching for her sidearm. "You! I remember you from the club. What are you doing here?"

Jinx raised her hands. "Things have changed since then. Mercy's in trouble, trapped inside my lamp. I need your help to get her out."

Mel's eyes narrowed. "What do you mean, she's trapped? Where is this lamp?"

"It's… complicated," Jinx sighed. "We killed the djinn that was bound to it, and I took his place. But Mercy got sucked in too."

"Got sucked in?" Mel tilted her head.

"Well, in a manner of speaking. We sucked each other in, is more like it. We did a lot of sucking."

Mel gulped. "I'm not sure I want to know more."

"I'd say it's not what you're thinking," Jinx snickered. "But it's probably exactly that. And more. But she thinks you might be the best chance of getting her out of the lamp."

"What do I need to do?" Mel asked.

"Let me search your memories and choices. If I can find the right point to change events, I may be able to free Mercy."

Mel hesitated, then slowly nodded. "Do what you must."

Jinx placed her hands on either side of Mel's head. As she sifted through the possibilities, my vision went black. Too many visions flashed in front of me and it was more like watching nothing at all than anything in particular. I hoped Jinx had better luck making sense of it all.

Mel's mind was a tad more *chaotic* than Muggs'.

"Allow me to confer with Mercy," Jinx said, her voice shaking. "There's one option, but it has… consequences."

"Consequences?" Mel asked. "What consequences?"

"Like I said. I'll be back."

The next thing I knew, Jinx was standing in front of me. It was a little weird. The lamp was still tuned to her vision, so all I saw beyond her frame was my giant face staring at the two of us. I shuddered. "Can you change the channel, please? I give myself the heebie jeebies."

Jinx laughed and snapped her fingers. We found ourselves in a lavish room in turn-of-the-century decor. The *twentieth* century, that is. Not the twenty-first. I plopped down on a velvet couch—not unlike the one in my throne room back in the Underground. "So, what did you find out?"

Jinx sighed. "Here's the thing. If Mel doesn't go sit on Santa's lap and stays with you instead—which she'd considered doing anyway since she was worried about you—it changes several things."

I snorted. "Some people never grow up. I told her an old man like that with a young thing like her on his lap might end up with a heart attack. But she didn't listen."

Jinx faked a smile. "Well, here's what would happen. The Peddler would approach both of you. While he'd give *you* the lamp, Mel touches it first. The djinn binds itself to her instead, which screws up all our plans. Sort of. The djinn sees in her memories a few choices she could make that would keep Jector alive, which is what I'd originally wanted him to do. So, he just sort of rolls with it."

I cleared my throat. "Get to the point, Jinx."

"Alright. Well, things end up *very* similar to how they worked with you. Except, instead of you, Mel gets trapped in the lamp. She and I don't fall in love, though. Mel said something about how she doesn't have a taste for fish. Not sure what that meant. Then she refused to bite me after I bit her. We didn't form the connection."

I tilted my head. "Then how did *she* end up in the lamp?"

"She's the one who broke it in that alternate reality," Jinx said. "The world still gets destroyed, but she saves it all, and ends up in exactly my position. But not being a witch, or having another vampire with her like me, she's stuck there for a couple of centuries before she gets enough power to get out and find someone to grant wishes to. Nothing too exciting happens after that. I stopped watching once I realized you probably wouldn't go for it. Here's the thing, though. You and I go free. We meet back in this world. You find me, and we have a moment.

Things move a lot more slowly. We remember everything from here, but it's like a dream. Thing is, Mercy... the love *is* real. In this version of reality, anyway."

I grunted. "Well, I'm not sacrificing Mel for us. Sorry, Jinx. There has to be another way."

"I expected you'd say that," Jinx admitted. "I don't blame you. But it's still good news. It means if things don't pan out exactly like we expect, at least we know there's more to this with us than the blood."

I shrugged. "Maybe. I don't know how to say this, Jinx. But I'm really not one to believe in destiny, soul-mates, or any of that shit. We make choices. We'll have our memories of this moment now, no matter what happens. We won't forget what we've been through. If we *want* to be together after this is over, if both of us want it, we will be. If we don't, we won't really care much that we lost it. Whatever happens, it's what needs to happen. But we can't use Mel."

"I know. I mean, should I try Ladinas and Alice?"

"That's a hard no." I shook my head with more vigor than was probably necessary. "They won't go along with this like Muggs and Mel did. They'll probably try to kill you somehow, or break the lamp, and fuck everything up. Bringing them into this is a last resort."

"Then the only decision that can change that will keep you out of this, that will keep both of us free, is if I don't break the lamp."

I grunted. "Look, Jinx. I know I tried to stop you from doing that, but afterwards, you fixed the world. You set things right. I don't know if we can jeopardize that. Besides, can a djinn grant her own wishes?"

"Not exactly." Jinx shook her head. "First, I only used the wish the former djinn whose place I took owed you. I revised your past choice the way you wished you hadn't. That's what fixed things. And I think we can do it if you do the magic for me."

"I'm not the djinn. How will that work?"

"Through our bond. You use my magic, but you are the one to cast it."

I tilted my head. "Sounds like a loop-hole. How do we know it will work?"

"Look, I didn't write the laws that govern djinn magic. But I suspect whoever did wasn't thinking about a couple vampires who'd fed on each other getting sucked into a lamp with one of them inheriting the djinn's position. I mean, who would think up fuckery like that?"

I smirked. "Sounds like something straight out of one of those weird Theophilus Monroe novels."

Jinx cocked an eyebrow. "Who? Never heard of him."

I chuckled. "Never mind. He's just one of those strange authors who thinks up all kinds of crazy shit and writes stories about it. Some people actually read it. Vampires, too. Great way to pass the time when the sun's up."

"I'll have to check him out. But do you think we could try it? It might just work. If I can undo the choice to break the lamp, you'll still have that last wish. All we'll have to do is convince the Peddler to grant it."

Chapter 15

I focused on Jinx, my hands clasped in hers, and reached for that well of power within me. It surged, nearly overwhelming, and I gritted my teeth against the force of it.

"It's no use," I growled. "I can't grant your wishes. I'm not the damned djinn."

Jinx shook her head. "I don't think that's the issue. The problem is that *I'm* the djinn. I can't own the lamp and my power can't be used to grant my own wishes. Even if you're the one using the power. I thought we might exploit a loophole in the process, but it seems that the issue is less about who's casting the magic and more about who is making the wish."

I sighed, pinching the bridge of my nose. "Who the hell are we gonna give the lamp to, then? It was a shot in the dark before, and neither Muggs nor Mel could do anything that would fix our situation.."

"Ladinas." Jinx shrugged. "Or Alice, perhaps. What if we convinced Ladinas *not* to oppose you when you tried to argue that the younglings should be saved?"

I grunted. "He's as dense as a board. He will not listen to reason."

Jinx shrugged. "If he knows what's at stake, he might. If he knows the consequences that followed. I can show him *all* of that. You know well enough. A djinn can be quite convincing."

I rolled my eyes. "Yeah, well, he's going to be more than a little skeptical when *you're* the djinn who shows."

"I could alter my appearance," Jinx suggested. "Or not. I mean, he'd have to be a little curious about how I became a djinn or why I'd risk approaching him at all."

I sighed again, even more dramatically this time. "Fine. I guess it's worth a shot. But even if Ladinas agrees, have we really considered the ramifications of everything? Ladinas doesn't oppose me. I don't get all pissy and stomp out of there. Muggs and Mel don't follow me and I never meet the Peddler. No Peddler, no lamp. None of this happens."

"The Peddler would have found you eventually," she said with a shrug. "When I had the lamp, I sent him after you. It was your argument with Ladinas and Alice that *primed* you to make the wish I needed you to make. Even though you only made it subconsciously. If you remember *everything*, though, which I think you should, you can manipulate things differently this time."

I rubbed my brow. All this timeline bullshit made my head hurt. This was exactly what I wanted to avoid when I told the Peddler to go suck it in the beginning. When I refused to make a wish at all. "What if we forget everything, though? What we're talking about could cause... what is it that the Doc called it in *Back to the Future?* A paradox! That's right. When the event changed in the past from people in the future erases the events from the future that influenced that action to begin with. Something like that. I think."

"I don't know," Jinx admitted. "But I trust our bond. It held up through my undoing your first wish, right? We shouldn't have remembered anything if that was the case. We shouldn't have been trapped together in the lamp. But we were. It seems our blood-bond connects us in a way that supersedes all of that."

I nodded slowly. "Sure. But then, if that's the case, this won't do shit. I'll still be stuck here with you."

Jinx's lip trembled. She looked genuinely hurt. "Stuck *with* me? I thought you wanted to be with me..."

I sighed. "That's not what I meant. Damn it. I meant stuck here. You aren't my prison. This lamp is the prison. I want to be free from this place *together.*"

Jinx licked her lips. I wasn't sure if I'd convinced her or not. Hell, I wasn't sure if I'd convinced myself. I didn't know what was real anymore. What actions would change things for the better? What would the unintended consequences be of everything we tried? "Look, Mercy. I can see the consequences of any wish I encourage someone to make. That's why we didn't act on Mel's wish, right? Because it would have trapped her here instead of you."

I shook my head. "You don't know Ladinas. If he thinks we're fucking with things we shouldn't be, he won't give up the lamp so we can go look for someone else to make wishes instead. He's a stubborn son of a bitch like that."

"Maybe, maybe not," Jinx said. "But we're running short on ideas and I can feel my power swelling now by the second. Mercy, if we don't do this, the lamp will explode right in Mel's hands killing both of us, not to mention your progeny, and will probably end the world... *again.*"

I grunted and diverted my eyes. "I just *hate* the idea of putting this in Ladinas' hands."

Jinx took both my hands in hers. "Look at me, Mercy."

Reluctantly, I met her eyes with mine. "Yeah, I'm looking at you."

"Is Ladinas really an awful guy? Or are you just harboring resentment because of your past with him? Like, has he ever hurt you on purpose? I get that the whole thing with Alice was painful, but the guy was trapped in another dimension with her. Sort of like we're trapped together now. I mean, I know it's different, but what would you do if you thought you were stuck somewhere and could never go back to the world you knew? What *will* you do if none of this works and you and I have to make the best of a life together in the lamp?"

"Exactly that," I admitted. "Make the best of it. Figure out a way to move on. Try to find happiness. Together."

"Which is what Ladinas and Alice did. You can't expect to go back to how things were before, after what we've been through together here. Suppose we get free. This experience changed us. It changed *both of us...*"

I allowed Jinx's words to linger in the air for a while, considering what they meant. She was right, of course. This was a totally different kind of trans-dimensional experience than Ladinas and Alice went through. They didn't have any way to contact the outside world. But maybe that was better. I mean, so long as we thought we could find a way out of this mess, the less likely we were—well, the less likely I was—to just accept it.

"Tell me, Juliet. If I didn't insist we fight against this, fight to get free, what would *you* do?"

"I'd stay here. But I can't ask you to accept that. Things are different for me. I spent the last century and a half pining away for a sociopath who I thought I loved and I'd never get back. I spent my existence in hiding. You've made something of yourself out there. I can't ask you to leave all of that behind *for me.* That would be selfish."

I took a deep breath. "And I can't let you settle for what your existence has been so far. There's still a lot of good you can do, Juliet. I could use your help. Who cares who you *used* to think you loved, or what mistakes you made? We can do good out there now, together..."

Jinx leaned over and kissed me on the forehead. "That's why I'm willing to try anything I can to get us out of here. Whatever it takes. I might be resigned to a life of insignificance. But you give me hope that *more* is possible."

I chuckled. "And you helped me see that it's not always the big things, the actions that change the world, that make someone happy. It's the little moments, like this one, that really matter. Sometimes there's so much pressure on me to fix shit, to fight the bad guy, to be the goddamn bloody queen, that I think my happiness doesn't matter. You've shown me that I don't have to sacrifice what I want for who everyone else thinks I'm supposed to be."

Jinx almost blushed a little. Vampires rarely do that. Must've been the djinn magic that rouged her complexion. "Was that the blood talking? Influencing your feelings?"

I squeezed her hands in mine. "It was real. I mean, that's not passion talking. It came from the heart. It had to be real. Right?"

Chapter 16

My dead heart pounded against my chest as I watched Jinx's vision projected on the walls of the lamp. She materialized in Mel's bedroom, the lamp I was trapped in sitting innocently on the nightstand. I shuddered, unnerved at the sight of my prison so close, yet so far away.

Jinx gestured to the lamp, her pink hair swirling around her shoulders. "Will you release your claim on this?" she asked Mel, her voice echoing around me. "We wish to give it to Ladinas. He's the key to freeing Mercy."

Mel nodded, her expression solemn. She lifted the lamp gingerly, as if it were a bomb that could detonate at any moment. "About Mercy, is she…"

"She's well," Jinx said, brushing the back of her hand against Mel's cheek. "She cares about you very much. We're doing everything we can to bring her back to you."

Mel nodded quickly. "Please. Thank you, I mean. Just do what you have to do. And let me know if I can help!"

As Jinx left, the projection of her vision turning away from Mel and to the corridors of the Underground, I sagged against the curved walls. Doubts swirled through my mind. This could go wrong in so many ways. Time travel was tricky business, and even if Ladinas agreed to help, who knew what unintended consequences could unfold?

Maybe I was being selfish, trying to escape. The world was safe. The destruction I'd thought I'd unleashed on the world was averted when Jinx undid the wish I'd never meant to make. But if Jinx didn't release her djinn power somehow, it would be apocalypse part deux. She couldn't hold on to that much power forever. Someone had to make a fucking wish or three.

The most I could hope for was that Ladinas was smart enough to realize that whatever wishes he made—apart from the one that we thought might save me—would be minor enough that they wouldn't matter. Maybe he'd wish that he hadn't cut his toenails too short. Yes, even vampires have to clip their nails once every decade. If he hadn't cut them so short back in 2020, maybe his big toenail wouldn't be ingrown. Or maybe he'd regret a wardrobe choice, turning the heat up too high in the underground, or forgetting to set the mouse traps. Things like that. Things that couldn't possibly have world-ending consequences if he'd made different choices.

Who was I kidding, though? People don't dwell on regrets like that. All I could hope was that Ladinas would agree with the plan. It would save me, and I could convince him to use his remaining two wishes innocuously. If he still had them to make. Would Jinx still be a djinn? Probably. But maybe not. Would there be a way we could use those wishes to free her? Would my freedom free her by proxy, just like when she got bound to the lamp, it imprisoned me at the same time?

I usually had plans with semi-predictable outcomes. Sure, shit usually got screwed up somewhere along the way. But it was usually shit that was within the realm of predictability. The ways this could go wrong were too many to count.

Step on a butterfly. Start World War Three.

I watched through Jinx's eyes as she made her way to Ladinas' quarters. He was pacing back and forth, muttering to himself. When Jinx appeared, he practically jumped out of his skin.

"What are you doing here?" he demanded, dropping into a fighting stance.

Jinx held up her hands. "I'm not here to fight. I need your help."

Ladinas narrowed his eyes. "My help? With what?"

"It's about Mercy," Jinx said. "She's in trouble, and you're the only one who can save her."

At the mention of my name, Ladinas' entire demeanor changed. His shoulders tensed and his voice dropped to a menacing growl. "What did you do to her? If you've hurt her, I'll stake you dead."

"I didn't hurt her!" Jinx insisted. "I would never. I... I love her."

Ladinas looked utterly bewildered. "You what? That's impossible. You two tried to kill each other the last time you met. You don't even know one another."

Jinx sighed. "It's complicated. Things have changed between us. I promise, I only want to help her. Will you?"

Ladinas studied her for a long moment. "You swear this isn't some kind of trick? If you are here to deceive us in any way, if you've done something to Mercy..."

"I swear it!" Jinx insisted. "I know only a short amount of time has passed for you. But for Mercy, it's been a lot longer. She found something out on the streets. Something powerful. She's in trouble."

Ladinas held his gaze on Jinx for a moment before his countenance softened. "You'd be a fool to come here alone. I don't even know how you got past our security measures. All I can assume is that you speak the truth."

"I do," Jinx nodded. "I swear it."

Ladinas sighed and ran a hand through his hair. "Very well. Tell me everything."

Jinx launched into the tale, explaining how Mercy had found an ancient lamp containing a djinn, how they'd worked together to defeat it, and how in the process Jinx had absorbed some of its power. By the time she finished, Ladinas was pacing the room, cursing under his breath.

"You're a fool! I've dealt with djinn before! You can't kill a djinn, Jinx."

"What do you mean?" Jinx asked. "I was there. I smashed his lamp. The release of his power unmade the world, but when I realized I'd become the djinn I used Mercy's last wish, a regret she'd already articulated, to fix things! The problem was that she and I were bound... because we..."

"Because you what?" Ladinas asked.

"We shared each other's blood," Jinx admitted.

"Christ's sake!" Ladinas huffed. "No wonder you think you're in love."

"I don't think!" Jinx insisted. "It's real. You don't know what you're talking about. Maybe it started that way, but..."

Ladinas just shook his head. "You two are in over your heads. You cannot kill a djinn, Jinx. He's still alive. The punishment for attempting to kill a djinn, for breaking one's lamp, is that you assume the djinn's place in the lamp until your power swells. Then, the djinn returns to reclaim his lamp, and you get what's coming to you."

I gulped. "Jinx! Ask him how he knows all this. If it's true, we need to get those wishes cast before the old Djinn returns!"

I could only hope she heard me. But a high-pitched cackle and a slow clap interrupted my attempt to listen in on her conversation with Ladinas.

I turned to see the Peddler standing in the middle of the room, more youthful in appearance, but with the same shit-eating grin he'd flashed when he first gave me his blasted lamp. I scowled at him. *"It's you."*

His slow clap continued. "Bravo, Mercy. Of course I'm me! Would you expect me to be anyone else? I mean, I wouldn't be me, if I wasn't me. Not the brightest vampire in the coffin, are you?"

I sneered. "Your metaphors suck. Vampires don't like the bright. But don't worry, I'm the darkest bitch you've ever screwed with."

The Peddler cracked his knuckles. "Oh, goodie! You realize, mi casa es mi casa! I'm a god in here. You can't possibly defeat me inside my lamp!"

I cracked my neck. Because cracking knuckles was for pussies. What the Peddler didn't understand was that I had access to Jinx's power. We were more evenly matched than he knew, and I was about to give that bastard everything he deserved.

Chapter 17

THE STENCH OF CIGAR smoke filled my nostrils as I stared up at the massive silverback gorilla barreling towards me. The Peddler was too much of a coward to face me head-on. He had to make monsters, creatures, whatever, to fight against me. All the while, he sat back, feet kicked up on a hammock he'd made out of nothing, puffing on a stogie.

I braced myself, fangs bared. The beast slammed into me with the force of a freight train, but I managed to grab hold and dig my heels in. My muscles strained against coarse black fur as I wrestled the snarling primate. With a guttural roar, I heaved the gorilla overhead and slammed it onto the stone floor, leaving it dazed.

I whirled on the Peddler, eyes blazing. "Enough games," I snarled. "Face me yourself, coward."

The Peddler merely smirked, exhaling a plume of acrid smoke. With a wave of his hand, a dense swarm of locusts manifested and dove at me. I recoiled as their razor wings cut into my skin like shrapnel.

"Incendia!" I shouted, slashing my wand through the air. A wall of flame incinerated the locusts instantly. I stalked through the smoldering husks towards the Peddler, murder in my eyes. The smug bastard just sat there, regarding me with amusement.

"Give it up, Mercy," he purred. "You're out of your depth here."

I bared my fangs in a snarl. "I don't give up that easily. Why don't you come down here and fight me like a man?"

The Peddler arched a brow. "And why don't you use that bitch of yours against me? I'm sure your little girlfriend would be happy to lend you her power."

My eyes flicked to the surrounding walls, still projecting Jinx's view on earth. Ladinas, Jinx and Mel were huddled together, deep in discussion. I caught Muggs out of the corner of my eye, adding his dollar and a half to the conversation. He never just added two cents. It gave me a little hope seeing them all together that they'd come up with *something*. What were they planning? I didn't have time to ponder it further before another attack came.

A cyclone whipped around me, spinning faster and faster until I lost all sense of direction. My body felt as though it might tear apart at the seams. I cried out, grasping for anything to anchor myself, but there was nothing.

The Peddler's obnoxious laughter echoed through the vortex. "Ring around the vampire, pocket full of... well, nothing rhymes with vampire, does it?"

I squeezed my eyes shut, focusing my mind. I reached out and tapped into Jinx's djinn magic, visualizing a massive weight to crush the insufferable bastard. I hurled it at him with all my might—only to have it vanish just before impact.

The Peddler patted his stomach with a satisfied sigh. "Ah yes, my power returns. You'll have to do better than that, Mercy. Give me everything you've got!" His eyes gleamed with greed and something else... triumph?

My chest tightened as the truth dawned on me. This was a trap. The only way to defeat the Peddler was to use Jinx's magic against him. But when I called it back into the lamp, he stole it back straight away. The only power strong enough to contend with him was the one thing I couldn't use against him. I was well and truly screwed.

The Peddler smirked, reading the realization on my face. "My, my, what a predicament you've found yourself in! Give me everything! See if you can beat me before I take my power back. If you're clever enough with it, you just might pull it off!"

I grunted. "Do you *ever* shut up?"

The Peddler pinched his chin. "Good question. Let me think about that. Um... No! But you can make me. Call forth whatever you desire. A ball gag might just do the trick! Could be fun, too!"

I gritted my teeth, wand trembling in my grip. "You think I'm stupid enough to fall for that? I'd need Jinx's power to do it."

The Peddler shrugged. "Worth a shot. Very well, have it your way." He waved a hand and vanished in a puff of smoke, the walls of the lamp folding in on themselves until everything went black.

I blinked, finding myself back in Providence, on Federal Hill. Christmas lights all around. Carolers singing as they passed by with rouged cheeks and hot chocolate.

The worst part of it was that I couldn't see through Jinx's eyes anymore. I had no idea what she and my friends were up to. I was afraid if I tried to connect to Jinx through our blood, I'd only give the Peddler more access to the magic she needed to grant Ladinas' wishes. So instead, I sat on a bench. If I couldn't fight him, maybe I could distract him. Take a page out of his book and talk his ear off until Jinx, Ladinas, and anyone else they'd recruited to their brain trust among my friends figured something out. "Enough games! Show yourself, you son of a bitch!"

Laughter echoed through the room as the Peddler materialized before me. He stomped his foot and pouted. "You're such a grinch! Where's that holiday spirit? You could really use a little more jolly!"

I bared my fangs and hissed at him. "How about my boot up your ass? Sounds jolly to me!"

The Peddler sighed and did a little spin. When he returned, he was fat, had a long white beard, and was dressed in red. Just like freaking Santa. "Looks like someone's been a naughty girl. Better add you to my list!"

I stared at him blankly. "What the hell do you think you're accomplishing by this? I'm not giving you more power. I'm not seven. Threatening me with the naughty list doesn't work anymore."

"But that's no fun at all!" Peddler Claus pouted. "The naughty list is where it's at! Why don't you sit on my lap and tell me what you'd like me to stick up your chimney shoot this Christmas?"

I tilted my head. "You're a fucked up genie, you know that?"

"It's Djinn!" The Peddler clenched his fists. "I'm not a Disney character. I'm not even blue!"

I grimaced. "Yeah. Sorry about that. Sore spot, much? I mean, c'mon dude. Do you know how many times I've gotten the whole 'I vant to suck your blood' schtick from assholes over the years? It's just fiction. Don't take it so personal."

While we were talking, something in the air shifted. The energy changed. I couldn't tell if it was a *surge* of djinn magic or if someone—Jinx most likely—had somehow siphoned power out of the lamp. Whatever it was, *something* was happening.

The Peddler's wide and shifty eyes told me everything I needed to know.

Whatever was happening wasn't good—for him. Which meant more likely than not, it was great for me.

I raised my wand again and aimed it at him. "*Incendia* motherfucker!"

This time my spell struck true, engulfing Peddler's Santa suit in flames. He quickly stopped, dropped, and rolled. Damn fire safety courses.

Then the Peddler formed a cloud overhead and drenched himself in rain that in the December air he'd made, quickly turned to snow. But it put out the fire.

And the world flickered around us. "What's happening?"

I shrugged. "I don't know. Looks like my friends figured something out."

The Peddler sneered. "They don't know what they're messing with. That prince of yours! You really think he's going to save you? He'll fuck it up, just like he fucked Alice!"

I tilted my head. That did it. I charged after the Peddler with fury. If he was weaker now, he was going to get a full dose of my fury. But as I dove at him, my fangs bared and aiming for his neck, a wooden stake materialized in his hand—and struck me directly in my heart.

The last thing I heard was a yawn. "Did I do that?"

All I could think was *that was the shittiest Steve Urkel impression ever...*

What happens to a vampire if she's staked *inside* a djinn's lamp? Would I end up in vampire hell? Or some place else? I was about to find out.

At least, I thought I was.

Until a half-second later. When a stake is yanked out of your chest, it's the strangest sensation ever. I can't really explain it. It's sort of like when a man who is way too big pulls out of you. Except this came from the chest. When my vision cleared, I was still in the damn lamp. Still in the fake Federal Hill decorated for Christmas. But a dark figure blocked out some of the lights.

I rubbed my eyes. Ready to spring back to my feet to teach the Peddler a lesson. But it wasn't the Peddler.

"Hey, Mercy. Weather in here is shit."

I tilted my head. "Ladinas? What are you doing here?"

A slight grin curled on his lips. "Well, that's a long story. And I think I'm going to have a century to tell it. But I won't make you sit around and listen that long. You're free to go if you'd like."

Chapter 18

THE CHRISTMAS LIGHTS TWINKLED in the crisp night air as I sat beside Ladinas on the park bench. Carolers strolled by, their off-key rendition of "God Rest Ye Merry Gentlemen" grating on my nerves.

I turned to Ladinas. "You know, you could change all this." I gestured broadly at the holiday cheer. "Now that you're the new Jinx. The temporary djinn for the next century and all. You can make this place whatever you want."

Ladinas chuckled, the sound low and smooth like dark chocolate. "I don't know. I'm starting to like it this way." He leaned back casually, though his eyes scanned our surroundings with practiced vigilance. "Might keep it like this until after New Year's. Then all the Christmas crap's gotta go."

I barked out a laugh. "Amen to that." Then I furrowed my brow, perplexed. "But I still don't get how you did it. Or why."

Ladinas regarded me solemnly. "I didn't make a wish. But the power inside Jinx was too immense. We knew if she relinquished it back to the old djinn..." He trailed off, jaw tightening.

I didn't need him to finish. That wily bastard would've slaughtered me in an instant.

"There was only one solution," Ladinas continued gravely. "We had to destroy the lamp."

I tilted my head, mind racing to comprehend the implications. "But wouldn't that, you know, annihilate the world or something?"

"Muggs teleported us to Ramon's place. Adam helped construct a pocket dimension." Ladinas' voice turned distant, as though reliving the memory. "We shattered the lamp inside it. That's where you'll wake up when you leave."

He refocused on me, ruby-red eyes piercing in their intensity. "With Jinx no longer a djinn, even temporarily, you're free. You can go whenever you want."

I sat silent, stunned by this revelation. By the sacrifice Ladinas had made, all for me. Once again, that damn vampire had saved my ass.

When I found my voice, only two words came out—the truest ones I could offer.

"Thank you."

Ladinas waved a hand dismissively. "Don't thank me yet. We still have a problem."

I arched a brow. "What now?"

"In a century, the djinn will regenerate and come for his power again." Ladinas leaned forward, gaze unwavering. "Since we're vampires, I figure you and Alice will still be kicking around—unless you do something suicidally stupid like let a hunter stake you."

I snorted. As if.

"When the time comes, you can make three harmless wishes. Regret throwing your favorite red coat in with your unmentionables and ruining it, or whatever." A wry smile touched his lips. "Then the djinn goes back in his lamp to recharge for another hundred years. We'll be free of the bastard again."

"And you're sure this pocket dimension prison will hold him?" I asked dubiously. The djinn had slipped free of far more elaborate traps.

"Adam designed it," Ladinas replied. "If anyone can contain that menace, it's him. When the time comes, the djinn might panic if he can't find his way back. You'll need to send him here so he can hop back in the lamp and I can go. Then, of course, you can take me home again. With Adam's help, of course."

His jaw tightened again, a shadow dimming his gaze. I suspected what troubled him—the same worry needling at me.

"Alice is going to be furious about this, isn't she?" My voice came out small. Guilt twisted my barely beating heart at the thought of Ladinas torn between us again.

"Alice and I have said our goodbyes." Ladinas took my hand, his skin cool against mine. "Because we're vampires, a century isn't forever. But you..." His fingers tightened around mine. "You were never meant to be in that lamp. When

I broke the lamp, I took over and Jinx was free. But the djinn wasn't letting you go."

I shook my head. "Because he's a sadistic bastard. He wanted to use me to draw back the power from Jinx. He just didn't foresee *you* breaking the lamp. He probably figured you'd make a wish. I thought that's what you were doing, too. No wonder it took some time to pull off the plan. I'll tell you what, that djinn really put me through a rigamarole."

Ladinas nodded. "Yeah, well, we knew you'd handle yourself. You always do."

"I take it nothing you could wish was going to work, huh?"

His eyes gleamed oddly. "When Jinx asked what I regretted most, I had only one answer."

I stared at him, frozen by the raw emotion in his tone and touch. By the love and sorrow etched into the lines of his ageless face.

"Hurting you," Ladinas whispered. "I never meant to. I just didn't know if we'd escape that place. When Alice and I were trapped. But I never stopped loving you, Mercy. Even if it's different from what I feel for Alice. "

A lump formed in my throat, and for a moment I couldn't speak. Then I swallowed hard and squeezed his hand back.

"I know," I said softly. "And I don't blame you. I'm sorry for being such a bitch about it."

Ladinas barked out a laugh, some of the tension easing from his shoulders. "You certainly were!"

"You weren't supposed to agree" I mock-scowled at him and swatted his arm.

Ladinas grinned, a flash of fang glinting in the multicolored Christmas lights. "I couldn't resist."

His mirth faded, expression turning solemn once more. "You can go whenever you wish. I'll be fine here. I have all the power I could want to amuse myself." He shrugged. "Might as well enjoy a much-needed vacation with no responsibility for once."

I studied him, considering. "I could stay with you, you know. You and Alice had your century. This could be ours..."

Ladinas squeezed my hand. "That would be selfish of me. There are others who need you more than me. Mel and Muggs especially. The entire team. Hell, the world needs their bloody queen back."

My cheeks heated as I added, "And Juliet."

Ladinas tilted his head. "Jinx?"

I nodded. "That's just a nickname."

Ladinas regarded me knowingly. "Does she make you happy?"

I bit my lip. "Honestly, it's too soon to know. I feel something with her. But it's all so new. So much of what I feel is clouded by the blood bond it's hard to know."

"It doesn't matter how it started. Every relationship starts with a *chemical* reaction of some kind. You think a blood bond is all that different from hormones? Just as powerful. But a lot of lifelong human marriages began with hormones."

I chuckled. "I suppose you have a point."

"Who cares if she isn't what you always imagined for yourself? You deserve to be happy. If Juliet makes you happy, be with her. You deserve something good for yourself for once in your existence."

"Thank you," I said again, throat tight. "For everything."

Ladinas smiled, though sadness lingered in his eyes. He lifted my hand and brushed his lips against my knuckles.

I didn't trust myself to speak, so I simply leaned over and kissed his cheek. He tensed, then relaxed into the fleeting touch.

And before either of us could speak again, he snapped his fingers. In a flash, I was gone.

Chapter 19

THE HALLS OF THE Underground were a blur as I raced through them, Mel's words echoing in my head. A strange creature on the loose, zapping people with magic and driving them insane with lust. Just another day in the life of a vampire witch trying to keep the city from imploding.

I rounded the corner and nearly collided with Alice, her katanas at the ready.

"Whoa, easy there," I said. "Have you seen Juliet?"

Alice nodded her head, ponytail swishing. "She's getting her team of baby vamps suited up. We're just about ready to move out."

I nodded, scanning the chaotic hallway. My team was coming together, prepared to face yet another threat. The weight of responsibility pressed down on me, but I shoved it aside. This was the first *real* mission we'd had that demanded the entire team since Ladinas left. But there was no time for doubt. At least none that I could show.

I took a deep breath and shouted, knowing my voice would carry through the stone halls. "Hey Muggs! Get your old ass up to the armory. It's time to move out!"

I hurried towards the elevator, Mel falling in step beside me. The sooner we got topside, the better chance we had of containing this thing. Whatever the hell it was.

We'd just stepped into the elevator when Muggs appeared in his trademarked swirl of green druidic energy. I jumped back, cursing.

"Dammit Muggs! How many times have I told you not to do that?"

He gave me a toothless grin. "At least a hundred. Never seems to stick, though."

I rolled my eyes. "Right. So what do we know about this thing?"

Mel piped up. "People are reporting strange attractions. Love at first sight turned to pandemic status. Everyone's statuses on social media are changing to 'In a Relationship' with random strangers. But then people who love some people, get loved by other people. Everyone loves everyone, pretty much, so as you can imagine, the love turns to jealousy, rage, and murder. 'Its complicated' follows shortly thereafter."

Muggs tugged at his beard. "Sounds like the work of a Cupid."

"So we had to deal with a Djinn for Christmas, and now a Cupid for fucking Valentine's Day?" I threw my hands up in frustration. "You really can't make this shit up."

Mel gave me a sympathetic look. "The good news is, the problem seems pretty localized right now. If we can neutralize this thing quickly, we might be able to contain the spread."

She paused, lips quirking into a grin. "Though at the rate this love bug is moving, it may end up spreading faster than gonorrhea in a college dorm."

I barked out a laugh at that. But Muggs just shook his head, face grim.

"This is nothing to joke about," he rumbled. "Cupids aren't the cute little baby angels you see on Valentine's cards. They're dark creatures. Dangerous. And a hell of a lot uglier than you can imagine."

I raised an eyebrow at him. "How do you know what they look like? No offense, but you're blind."

Muggs nodded solemnly. "Exactly. They're *that* ugly."

The elevator dinged as we reached the armory at the warehouse level.

The doors slid open, and I stepped out into a flurry of activity. Weapons were being loaded, last-minute gear adjustments made. My gaze landed on a flash of pink in the crowd, and I smiled as Juliet hurried over to greet me.

She pressed a quick kiss to my cheek, eyes bright with excitement. "My team's all ready to move out. Antoine and the rest of the original team are already waiting on the street in the SUVs."

I slung an arm around her shoulders, giving her a quick squeeze. "Perfect. You ready to go kick some Cupid ass?"

Her nose crinkled. "We're fighting Cupid?"

"Not the cute little cherub you're probably picturing," I said grimly. "According to Muggs, Cupids are more like a monster species. They use love and desire to sow chaos and destruction." I glanced over at Muggs, who nodded in confirmation. "Ugly bastards, and dangerous as hell. So watch yourself out there."

Juliet's lips curved into a wicked grin. "The bigger they are..."

"The harder they fall," I finished with a smirk. I gave her another quick peck on the lips before releasing her and heading over to join Mel and Muggs.

I slid into the passenger seat of the SUV as Mel hopped into the driver's seat. Muggs materialized in the backseat in a swirl of green magic.

"Seriously, Muggs? You can't just climb in the back like a regular person?"

Muggs waved his hand through the air. "These SUVs are tall. Teleportation is easier on my back! I'm old, you know."

"And you're a *vampire!* You don't have back issues. That's just an excuse."

Muggs grinned widely. "Pish posh!"

All I could do was roll my eyes.

"Everyone in position and ready to move out," Mel reported, fingers tapping away at her tablet. "All signs point to the Cupid being holed up around the old Ridley Hotel downtown."

"Lovely," I said dryly. I looked over my shoulder at Muggs. "I don't suppose you've got any useful intel on these things? Weaknesses? How to kill them?"

"Never tried to kill one," Muggs admitted. "Cupids are rare, and usually they wreak their havoc for a night or two, then disappear. So that's the good news."

"And if this one wants to stick around a little longer?" I asked.

Muggs licked his lips. "They can be weakened by certain herbs like rosemary and vervain, and iron seems to disrupt their magic. But the only sure way to kill one is to pierce its heart."

"Is that all? So this is basically like hunting an out-of-control vampire..."

"With its own arrow," Muggs added. "A stake or bullet won't work."

I sighed. "Naturally. Shit can't ever be easy, can it?"

The End of Book 6
To Be Continued in *Bloody Hearts*
Valentine's Day, 2024

Also By Theophilus Monroe

Bloody Mad
Bloody Wicked
Bloody Devils
Bloody Gods

The Legend of Nyx
Scared Shiftless
Bat Shift Crazy
No Shift, Sherlock
Shift for Brains
Shift Happens
Shift on a Shingle

The Vilokan Asylum of the Magically and Mentally Deranged
The Curse of Cain
The Mark of Cain
Cain and the Cauldron
Cain's Cobras
Crazy Cain
The Wrath of Cain

The Blood Witch Saga
Voodoo and Vampires
Witches and Wolves
Devils and Dragons
Ghouls and Grimoires
Faeries and Fangs
Monsters and Mambos
Wraiths and Warlocks
Shifters and Shenanigans

The Fury of a Vampire Witch
Bloody Queen
Bloody Underground
Bloody Retribution
Bloody Bastards

Bloody Brilliance
Bloody Merry
More to come!

The Druid Detective Agency
Merlin's Mantle
Roundtable Nights
Grail of Power
Midsummer Monsters
More to come!

Sebastian Winter
Death to All Monsters
More to come!

Other Theophilus Monroe Series

Nanoverse

The Elven Prophecy

Chronicles of Zoey Grimm

The Daywalker Chronicles

Go Ask Your Mother
The Hedge Witch Diaries

AS T.R. MAGNUS

Kataklysm
Blightmage
Ember

Radiant
Dreadlord
Deluge

About the Author

Theophilus Monroe is a fantasy author with a knack for real-life characters whose supernatural experiences speak to the pangs of ordinary life. After earning his Ph.D. in Theology, he decided that academic treatises that no one will read (beyond other academics) was a dull way to spend his life. So, he began using his background in religious studies to create new worlds and forms of magic–informed by religious myths, ancient and modern–that would intrigue readers, inspire imaginations, and speak to real-world problems in fantastical ways.

When Theophilus isn't exploring one of his fantasy lands, he is probably playing with one of his three sons, or pumping iron in his home gym, which is currently located in a 40-foot shipping container.

He makes his online home at www.theophilusmonroe.com. He loves answering reader questions—feel free to e-mail him at theophilus@theophilusmonroe.com if the mood strikes you!

WS - #0221 - 290724 - C0 - 229/152/24 - PB - 9781804674857 - Gloss Lamination